Three Men

A Novel

by

Maxim Gorky

Three Men
A Novel
by Maxim Gorky

Copyright © 2024

All Rights reserved.

ISBN: 978-93-69076-62-8

Published by

DOUBLE 9 BOOKS
2/13-B, Ansari Road
Daryaganj, New Delhi – 110002
info@double9books.com
www.double9books.com
Tel. 011-40042856

This book is under public domain

ABOUT THE AUTHOR

Alexei Maximovich Peshkov, better known as Maxim Gorky, was a renowned Russian and Soviet writer and a strong advocate for socialism. Born on March 28, 1868, in Nizhny Novgorod, Russia, he became one of the most prominent figures in Russian literature during the late 19th and early 20th centuries. Gorky's works often reflected his deep concern for the oppressed and his belief in social justice, which made him a leading figure in the socialist movement. His literary contributions include novels, plays, and short stories that critiqued social inequality and the human condition. Gorky was nominated five times for the Nobel Prize in Literature, a testament to his influence and the impact of his writing. His personal life included a marriage to Yekaterina Peshkova, from 1896 to 1903, though he later separated from her. Maxim Gorky spent his later years in Gorki-10, Russia, where he died on June 18, 1936, at the age of 68. His legacy as a writer and a proponent of socialist ideals continues to be a significant part of Russian literary history.

CONTENTS

CHAPTER I

There are many solitary graves amid the woods of Kerschentz; within them moulder the bones of old men, men of an ancient piety, and of one of these old men, Antipa, this tale is told in the villages of Kerschentz.

Antipa Lunev, a rich peasant of austere disposition, lived to his fiftieth year, sunken in worldly sins, then was moved to profound self-examination, and seized with agony of soul, forsook his family and buried himself in the loneliness of the forest. There on the edge of a ravine he built his hermit's cell, and lived for eight years, summer and winter. He let no one approach him, neither acquaintances nor kindred. Sometimes people who had lost their way in the woods came by chance on his hut and saw Antipa kneeling on the threshold, praying. He was terrible to see—worn with fasting and prayer, and covered with hair like a wild beast. If he caught sight of any one, he rose up and bowed himself to the ground before him. If he were asked the way out of the forest, he indicated the path with his hand without speaking, bowed to the ground again, went into his cell and shut himself in. He was seen many times during the eight years, but no man ever heard his voice. His wife and children used to visit him, he took food and clothing from them, bowed himself before them as before others, but, during the time of his anchorite life, spoke no word with them any more than with strangers.

He died the same year that the hermitages of the wood were swept away, and his death came in this fashion.

The Chief of Police came through the forest with a detachment of soldiers, and saw Antipa kneeling, silently praying in his cell.

"You there!" shouted the officer. "Clear out of this, we're going to smash up this den of yours!"

But Antipa heard nothing, and however loudly the captain shouted, the pious hermit answered him never a word. Then the officer ordered his men to drag Antipa out of his cell. But the soldiers were troubled before the gaze of the old man, who continued in prayer so steadfastly and earnestly, and paid no heed to them, and, shaken by such strength of soul, they hesitated to carry out the command. Then the captain ordered them to break up the hut, and they began to remove the roof silently and very carefully, to avoid hurting the worshipper within.

The axes rang over Antipa's head, the boards split and fell to the ground, the dull echo of the blows sounded through the wood, the birds terrified by the noise fluttered uneasily round the cell, and the leaves trembled on the trees. But the old man prayed on as though he neither saw nor heard. They began to break up the flooring of the hut, and still its owner knelt undisturbed, and only when the last timbers were thrown aside and the captain himself went up to Antipa and caught him by the hair, only then did he speak, his eyes lifted to heaven, quietly, to God, "Merciful Father, forgive them."

Then he fell back and died.

When this happened, Jakov, the eldest son of Antipa, was twenty-three years old, and Terenti, the youngest, eighteen. Jakov, handsome and strong, gained the name of "scatter-brain," while still a youngster, and by the time his father died, was already the chief loafer and bully in the country-side. All complained of him—his mother, the Starost, the neighbours: he was imprisoned, he was whipped, with and without legal condemnation, but nothing tamed his wild disposition, and day by day he felt more stifled and constrained in the village among the pious people, busy and hard working as moles, scorners of every new thing, holding fast to the precepts of their ancient faith. Jakov smoked tobacco, drank brandy, wore clothes of German cut, and went to no prayers or religious services, and if decent folk admonished him and reminded him of his father, he would say scornfully, "Wait a bit, good people, all in good time. When I have sinned enough, I will think of repentance. It's too early yet; you need not hold up my father as an example to me—he sinned for fifty years, and repented only for eight after all. My sins now are nothing but as the down on the young bird, but when my full feathers are grown, then I may think of repentance."

"An evil heretic," was Jakov Lunev's name in the village, where they hated and feared him.

Some two years after his father's death, he married. The farm that his father established by thirty years strenuous labour, he had thoroughly ruined by his spendthrift life, and no one in the village would give him a daughter in marriage. But somewhere in a distant village he found a pretty orphan-girl, and he sold a pair of horses and his father's bee-farm, to raise the money to celebrate his wedding. His brother Terenti, a timid, silent, humpbacked youth, with unusually long arms, was no hindrance to his mode of life; his mother lay sick on the stove, and from there only called to him with hoarse foreboding voice, "Accursed one! Take heed to your soul. Come to your senses."

"Don't worry yourself, my dear mother," answered Jakov. "Father will put in a word for me with the Almighty."

At first, for close on a year, Jakov lived in peace and content with his wife, and even took to working, but then began to loaf again, disappeared from the house for a month at a time, and came back to his wife, worn out, bruised and hungry.

Jakov's mother died; at the funeral, in a drunken fit he assaulted the Starost, his old enemy, and was arrested in consequence, and imprisoned. His term of imprisonment at an end, he reappeared in the village, gloomy and ill-tempered. The village people hated him still more and extended their hatred to his family, especially to the silent, hump-backed Terenti who had been the sport of the boys and girls from his childhood. They called Jakov jail-bird and thief, but Terenti, monster and wizard. Terenti endured insult and mockery silently, but Jakov broke out in open threats, "All right, just wait a bit, I'll teach you."

He was close on forty years of age when a conflagration broke out in the village; he was accused of incendiarism and sent, a prisoner, to Siberia.

Jakov's wife, who lost her reason at the time of the fire, was left in the care of Terenti, and with her, her son Ilya, a boy of ten, sturdy, black-eyed, and serious beyond his years. Whenever the lad appeared in the village streets, the other children ran after him, throwing stones at him, and the bigger ones would shout, "Ah! the young devil the prison brat, bad luck to you!"

Terenti, unfitted for laborious work, dealt up to the time of the fire in tar, needles and thread, and such small wares, but the catastrophe which destroyed half the village made an end both of the Lunevs' house and Terenti's whole stock-in-trade, so that all the Lunevs then possessed in the world amounted to one horse and thirty-three roubles in money.

As soon as Terenti found that his native village would offer him no way whatever to earn a living, he entrusted his sister-in-law to the care of an old peasant woman at fifty kopecks a month, bought a ricketty old cart, and placed his nephew in it, determined to make for the chief town of the district, where he hoped for some assistance from a distant relative, Petrusha Filimonov, a servant in a small tavern.

Secretly and like a thief in the night, Terenti left his home. He guided his horse silently, often looking back with his large dark eyes. The horse trotted on, the cart jolted from side to side and Ilya nestled into the hay, and soon slept the deep sleep of childhood.

In the middle of the night the boy was awakened by a strange terrifying sound, like the howl of a wolf. It was a clear night, the cart was standing at the outskirts of a wood, and the horse moved round it cropping the dewy grass. A great pine tree, its highest branches scorched, stood far apart in the plain, as though driven out from the forest. The boy's eager eyes looked anxiously for his uncle; but through the quiet night from time to time the only distant sound was the dull thud of the horse's hoofs, or the noise of its breathing like heavy sighs, and the same mysterious terrifying sound filled the air, and frightened the lad.

"Uncle?" he called softly.

"What is it?" answered Terenti, at once, and the doleful sound ceased suddenly.

"Where are you?"

"Here. Go to sleep again."

Then Ilya saw his uncle, sitting on a mound at the edge of the wood, like a black tree-stump rising out of the earth.

"I'm frightened," said the boy.

"What then—frightened? Why? there's nothing here."

"Some one was crying."

"You've been dreaming," said the hunchback softly.

"No! truly, he *was* crying."

"A wolf perhaps, far away. Go to sleep again."

But Ilya could sleep no more. He was frightened at the clear stillness, and in his ears the mournful sound still rang. He looked cautiously at the country round, and then saw that his uncle was gazing in the direction where, over the mountain, far in the midst of the wood, stood a white church with five towers, the large round moon shining brightly above it. Ilya knew that this was the church of Romodanov, and that two versts from it nearer to them, in the wood above the valley, lay their village Kitschnaja.

"We haven't come far," he said, thoughtfully.

"What?" asked his uncle.

"We must get on further, I said, some one might come."

Ilya nodded in the direction of the village with a look of hate.

"We'll get on presently," replied his uncle.

And again all was quiet round about. Ilya squatted with his knees up to his chin, supported himself against the front of the cart and began to gaze in the same direction as his uncle. The village was not visible in the dense black shadow of the forest, but it seemed to him that he saw clearly every house and all its people, and the old white willow by the well in the middle of the street. Against the willow's roots lay his father bound with a rope, his shirt torn to rags, his hands tied behind his back, his naked breast thrust forward, and his head as though it had grown to the willow stem. He lay motionless as a dead man, and looked with terrible eyes at the peasants, crowding before the house of the Starost, There were very many, all angry, they shouted, cursed him——. The memory troubled the boy, and a lump came in his throat. He felt he must soon cry for sorrow and the coldness of the night, but he did not wish to disturb his uncle, and mastering himself he huddled his little body closer together.

Suddenly a low wail sounded again. First a deep sigh, then sobs, then loud, unspeakable lamentation.

"Oh—oh! oh—oh—oh!"

The boy shivered with terror and stared round him. But the sound quivered again through the air and grew in volume.

"Uncle! Is it you crying?" called Ilya.

Terenti neither spoke nor moved.

Then the boy sprang from the cart, ran to his uncle, fell in front of him, clasped his knees, and burst into tears. He heard his uncle's voice broken by sobs.

"They've driven us out—driven us out. Oh! God! Where shall we go? Where? oh!"

But the boy said, swallowing down his tears:

"Wait—when I grow up—I'll show them—just wait."

He cried his sorrow out and then fell asleep. His uncle lifted him in his arms and laid him in the cart, but he himself went apart again and cried aloud once more, lamenting in bitter agony.

CHAPTER II

Ilya remembered quite clearly in after life his arrival at the town. He awoke early one morning and saw before him a broad, muddy river, and on the further side on a lofty hill a heap of houses, with red and green roofs and tall trees with dark foliage between them. The houses crowded picturesquely up the slopes of the hill, and above on the summit stretched out in a straight line and looked proudly down and away across the river. The golden crosses and domes of the churches stood out above the roofs up into the sky. The sun was newly risen; its slanting rays glanced back from the windows of the houses, and the whole town blazed in bright colour and glittered in shining gold.

"Ah! how beautiful it is. Look, look," said the boy, half aloud, staring with wide eyes at the wonderful picture, and gazed in silent delight for a long time.

Then the anxious thought arose in his mind, where he should live in that heap of houses—he, the little, black-haired, touzled youngster, in worn breeches of hemp-linen, and his clumsy humpbacked uncle. Would they even be admitted into this clean, rich, golden city? He thought that the little cart must be standing still on the river's bank just because no such poor, ragged, wretched folk might enter the town, and his uncle, no doubt, had gone on to beg permission to come in.

Ilya looked for his uncle with troubled eyes. In front of their cart and behind it stood many waggons; on one, wooden tubs full of milk, on another great baskets of poultry, cucumbers, or onions, bark baskets full of berries, sacks of potatoes. On the waggons and round about them sat or stood peasants and peasant women, and they were people of a strange kind. They spoke loudly with clear intonations and were not dressed in blue linen, but in clothes of gay-coloured calico and bright red cotton. Nearly all of them wore boots, and when a man with a sword at his side, a police officer or sergeant, went up and down past them, they were not in the least disturbed, and did not once salute him, and that seemed very strange to Ilya; he sat on the cart, staring at the lively scene, steeped in bright sunshine, and dreamed of the time when he too should wear boots and a shirt of red cotton. Far off, in the midst of the peasants, uncle Terenti came, as it were, to the surface.

He advanced across the deep sand with big, confident strides, and held his head high; his face wore an expression of gaiety, and he smiled at Ilya from a long way off, and stretched out his hand to show him something.

"The Lord is good to us, Ilya! Don't be frightened any more! I've found uncle Petrusha straight off. There—catch—get your teeth into that!" and he held out a cake to Ilya.

The boy took it almost reverently, put it inside his shirt, and asked anxiously:

"Won't they let us into the town?"

"They'll let us in this very minute.... The ferry-boats will come and then we'll get over the river."

"They'll take us too?"

"Of course, we can't stay here."

"Oh! and I thought they'd never let us in—and where shall we live over there?"

"I don't know yet. The Lord will show us the way."

"Perhaps we'll live in the big house there with the red——"

"Oh! you silly boy; that's the barracks where the soldiers live."

"In that one then—there—that one?"

"Hardly, it's a bit too high up for us."

"That doesn't matter," said Ilya, in a tone of conviction. "We'll manage to crawl up to it."

"Oh you——!" sighed uncle Terenti, and disappeared again somewhere.

They found shelter, quite at the end of the town, near the market-place, in a big grey house; all round its walls leant outbuildings of every kind, some comparatively recent, others as old as the house itself, and of the same dirty grey colour. The doors and windows were warped, and everything in the house creaked and cracked. The outbuildings, the fence, the gates, everything was falling to pieces together, and the whole formed a mass of half-rotten wood overgrown with greenish moss. The window panes were dim with age; a couple of beams in the front wall bulged right out, and altogether the house was an image of its owner, who used it as a tavern. He, too, was old and grey; the eyes in his worn face were like the glass panes in the windows; as he walked, he leant heavily on a thick staff—evidently it was not easy for him to carry his big paunch—and he, too, creaked and cracked all the time.

Uncle Terenti established himself in one of the countless corners of the building—in a cellar, on a bench by a window opening on a corner of the courtyard. In this corner lay a great rubbish heap, and an old sweet-scented lime tree stood there between two elder bushes. It was three days after their arrival before the proprietor of the house noticed Ilya for the first time, as he tried to hide behind the rubbish heap and stared with terrified eyes.

"Where do you belong, youngster? Hey!" he asked in his creaking voice, pointing at Ilya with his stick. "How did you come here? Hey!"

Ilya blinked and said nothing.

"Hullo, where does this youngster belong here? Send him off! out with you, you rascal! Wait a bit, I'll show you!—Hey!—Oh, you scamp! What—you belong to the man who does the washing up, do you? Are you his son? Not? Oh! a relation are you? The humpbacked rascal might have said he had a relation with him! Now then, Peter, what are you looking at? The humpback has a relation with him! What's the meaning of that? That won't do!"

The potman Petrusha put his red face out of the bar window opening on the courtyard and shouted, shaking his curly head:

"He's only got the youngster for a little while. Take, care Vassily Dorimendontytch—he's a poor orphan—I know about it—but if you don't like it, he shall clear out at once."

When Ilya heard that he was to go away, he began to scream with all his might, then darted across like an arrow and slipped through the window into the cellar like a mouse into its hole. There he threw himself on the bench, buried his head in his uncle's coat and began to cry, quivering from head to foot. But his uncle came and soothed him:

"No! No! don't be frightened! He only shouts like that to make pretence. He's going silly with age; he isn't the chief person here—it's Petrusha. Petrusha settles everything here. Just be friendly with him, be very polite to him! And as for the landlord—he doesn't count for anything!"

In the early days that Ilya lived in the house, he crept everywhere and examined everything. The place pleased him and astonished him with its extraordinary roominess. It was crammed so full that Ilya truly believed more people lived there than in the whole village of Kiteshnaja, and it was as noisy inside as in a market place.

Both storeys of the house were used for the tavern, which was visited by a constant stream of customers—whilst in the attics lodged sundry women apparently always drunk, one of whom, Matiza, big and dark, with a deep bass voice, drove fear into the heart of the lad with her wild, staring black eyes. In the cellar lived the cobbler Perfishka, with his crippled, ailing wife and his seven-year-old daughter; also an old rag picker, "grandfather" Jeremy; a lean old beggar-woman, called in the courtyard by no name but "Screamer," because of her habit of shrieking out loud at all times and seasons, and the tavern cab driver, Makar Stepanitsh, a grave, silent man, advanced in years. In one corner of the courtyard was a smithy; here from morning to night the fire flamed, wheel tires were welded, horses shod, while the hammers clinked and the tall sinewy smith, Savel Gratschev, for ever sang long-drawn songs in a deep, sorrowful voice. Sometimes Savel's wife appeared in the smithy, a little round, fair-haired woman, with blue eyes. She always wore a white kerchief round her head, and by this white head stood out often quite strangely against the dark hollow of the smithy. She laughed almost all the time a little silvery laugh, while Savel chimed in at times loudly as though with a hammer stroke. But more often his answer to her laughter was a kind of growl. Men said that he loved his wife passionately, while she led a wanton life.

In every cranny of the house there was some one, and from early morning to late at night the whole place quivered with noise and outcry as though it were an old rusty kettle in which something seethed and boiled. In the evening all these people crept from their holes into the courtyard, to the bench that stood by the house door; the cobbler Perfishka played on his harmonica, Savel hummed his songs and Matiza, if she were drunk, sang something very strange, very mournful with words that no one understood, sang and wept bitterly at the same time.

In one corner of the courtyard all the children of the house crowded in a circle round grandfather Jeremy, and begged him:

"Grandfather dear! Tell us a story!"

The old rag picker looked at them with his bleared red eyes, from which tears constantly ran down over his wrinkled cheeks, and then pulling his foxy old cap further over his forehead, began in a thin, quavering voice.

"Once in a land, I don't know where, a heretic child was born of unknown parents, who were punished for their sins by Almighty God with this child...."

Grandfather Jeremy's long, grey beard shook when he opened his black, toothless mouth, his head nodded to and fro and one tear after another rolled over the wrinkles on his cheeks.

"And this heretic child was altogether wicked; he did not believe in Christ the Lord, did not love the mother of God, always went past the church without lifting his cap, would not obey his father and mother."

The children listened to the thin, quavering voice of the old man and looked silently into his face.

The fair-haired Jashka, son of the potman Petrusha, listened and looked more attentively than all the rest. He was a lean, sharp-nosed boy, with a big head on a thin neck. When he ran, his head always rolled from one side to the other as though it would shake loose from his body. His eyes were big and strangely restless. They shifted anxiously over everything as if they were afraid to rest anywhere, and when at last they rested on anything they rolled oddly in their sockets, and gave the lad a sheepish expression. He stood out from the rest also by his delicate bloodless face, and his clean, respectable clothes. Ilya quickly made friends with him, and the very first day of their acquaintance Jashka asked his new playmate with a mysterious air:

"Are there many wizards in your village?"

"Of course," answered Ilya, "several, and witches too—our neighbour could work magic."

"Had he red hair?" asked Jakov, in a trembling voice.

"No, grey. They always have grey hair."

"The grey ones are not wicked, they are good-hearted. But the red-haired ones—ah, I tell you, they drink blood."

They were sitting in the prettiest, pleasantest corner of the courtyard behind the rubbish heap under the lime tree and the elder bushes. It was reached through a narrow crack between the sheds and the house; it was always quiet there, and nothing could be seen but the sky over their heads and the house wall with three windows, two of them boarded up. It became the favourite corner of the two friends. The sparrows hopped twittering about the lime-tree branches, and the boys sat on the ground at its root and chattered of everything that interested them.

All day long before Ilya's eyes whirled a great, gay something, noisy and shouting, that blinded and deafened him. At first he was quite confused by the wild pell-mell of this life. In the bar Ilya would often stand by the table where uncle Terenti, dripping with sweat, and wet with water, rinsed the dishes and glasses and saw how people came, and ate, and drank, shouted and sang, kissed and fought. They were covered with sweat, dirty and tired; clouds of tobacco smoke enwrapped them, and in this fog they rioted like madmen.

"Hullo!" his uncle would say to him, while his humpback shook, and he bustled unceasingly with the glasses. "What do you want here? Get along into the yard, else the landlord will see you and pitch into you."

Deafened with the noise of the bar, Ilya betook himself to the courtyard. Here Savel was striking great blows on the anvil with his hammer and quarrelling with his mates. Out of the cellar the jolly song of the cobbler Perfishka rang out into the open, and from above came the scolding and shrieking of the drunken women. Savel's son Pashka, called "the rowdy," was riding round the yard on a stick shouting angrily to his steed: "Get on you devil." His round, pert face was covered with dirt and soot; there was a boil on his forehead; his strong healthy body shone through the countless holes in his shirt. Pashka was the leading bully and brawler in the courtyard; twice already he had thrashed Ilya soundly, and when Ilya complained tearfully, his uncle shrugged his shoulders and said:

"What can I do? You must bear it. It'll pass off."

"I'll give it to him next time though, see if I don't," threatened Ilya through his tears.

"No, don't do that," said his uncle decidedly. "You mustn't do that, anyway."

"Then he may do it and I'm not to?"

"He!—he belongs here, d'you see, and you're a stranger."

Ilya went on pouring out threats against Pashka, but his uncle became angry all at once, and stormed at him, a thing that very rarely happened. So the consciousness dawned in Ilya, that he was not the equal of the children who belonged to the place, and while from that time he hid his enmity to Pashka, he clung all the closer to Jakov.

Jakov always behaved himself very well; he never fought the other boys and seldom so much as shouted at them. Even in the games, he hardly ever joined the others though he loved to speak of the games the children of the rich played in the town park. Jakov's only friend among the other children of the house, excepting Ilya, was Mashka, the seven-year-old daughter of the cobbler Perfishka. Mashka was a dirty, delicate, sickly child. Her little head of black curls flitted about the court from morning to night. Her mother sat almost all the time in the doorway leading to the cellar. She was tall, with a long plait of hair down her back, and sewed incessantly, bent double over her work. Whenever she raised her head to look after her daughter, Ilya could see her face. It was a purplish, expressionless, bloated face—like the face of a corpse. Even her pleasant black eyes had about them something fixed, immovable. She spoke to no one, even to her daughter she used to beckon if she wanted her. Only very rarely she would cry in a hoarse, half-choked voice:

"Mashka!"

At first, something about this woman took Ilya's fancy. But later, when he learnt that she had been a cripple for three years and would soon die, he grew afraid of her.

Once, as Ilya passed close to her, she stretched out an arm, caught him by the sleeve and drew him, terrified, up to her.

"Please, please, my son," she said, "be good to our Mashka! Be good to her." Speech came from her with difficulty, she struggled for breath after it. "Be—very good to her, my dear."

She looked with imploring eyes in his face and let him go. Ilya from that time took charge of the cobbler's daughter with Jakov, and looked after her carefully. He liked to fulfil the request of a grown-up person the more, as most of them only spoke to him to order him about. The men and women were always very harsh to the children. Makar, the coachman, kicked at them, or struck them in the face with wet cloths if they wanted to look on at the cleaning of the carriages. Savel raged at every one who looked with curiosity into his smithy and threw coal-grit at the children. The cobbler flung the first thing that came handy at the head of any one who stood in front of his cellar window and blocked out the light. Sometimes they would strike the children for want of any other occupation or by way of playing with them. Only grandfather Jeremy never struck them.

Ilya was soon convinced that life in the village was far pleasanter than life in town. In the village he could go where he liked, but here his uncle forbade him to leave the courtyard. In the village there were cucumbers and peas, or anything you liked, to eat on the sly. But here there was no garden, and nothing to be had without paying for it. There it was spacious and still, and every one did just the same work; here every one quarrels and fights; every one does what he likes, and all are poor and eat strange bread and are half starved. Day after day Ilya drifted on, round about in the courtyard, and it became dreary to him to live in this hateful grey house with the dim windows.

One morning at the midday meal, Terenti said to his nephew with a deep sigh, "The autumn's drawing on, Ilyusha. Oh dear! that's when the pinch will come for us, come with a vengeance. My God!"

He was silent for a long time, lost in thought, looking sadly into his dish of cabbage soup. The boy, too, was thoughtful. They both took their meals at the table where the hunchback washed the dishes. A wild tumult filled the bar room.

"Petrusha thinks you ought to go to school with your friend Jashka. Ah—yes—it's very important. I see that in this place being without education is like being without eyes. You're fairly lost! But you'll need new shoes and new clothes if you go to school, and where are they to come from out of my five roubles a month ... Oh God! in Thee I set my trust."

His uncle's sighs and sad countenance made Ilya's heart sink, and he said gently, "Come, uncle! We'll get out of this place!"

"But where," asked the hunchback gloomily, "where can we go?"

"Why not into the wood?" said Ilya, gleefully excited at his idea in a moment, "grandfather lived ever so many years in the wood you used to tell me. And there are two of us. We could strip bark from the trees, and catch foxes and squirrels. You'll get a gun, and I'll catch birds in traps. Yes, and there are berries there and mushrooms. Shall we go there uncle?"

His uncle looked on him kindly and said with a smile:

"And what about wolves? and bears?"

"But we'd have a gun," cried Ilya boldly. "I won't be afraid of wild beasts when I'm grown up! I'll strangle them with my hands! I'm not afraid now—not of anything. Life is no joke here. If I am little I can see that, and they knock you about here worse than in the village. Yes! I can feel it, I'm not made of wood. When the smith gives me a whack on the head, it sings for the whole day. All the people here look as if they'd been beaten, even if they do put on airs."

"Ah! poor laddie!" said Terenti feebly, then put down his spoon and went away—went very quickly.

In the evening of this same day, Ilya sat on the floor beside his uncle's table tired out with his voyages of discovery in the courtyard, where there was never anything new. Half asleep, he heard a conversation between Terenti and grandfather Jeremy, who came to drink a glass of tea at the bar. The old rag-picker had struck up a friendship with the hunchback, and always when he came from work settled himself near Terenti to drink his tea.

"It don't matter," Ilya heard Jeremy's creaking voice, "only trust in God! See! Think only one thing, God! You're just His slave, for it says in the Bible a servant! So make sure of that! God's servant, that's what you are, and everything you have belongs to God; good or bad, everything is God's. He will know how to decide for you. He sees your life. He, our Father, sees—everything.... And a glorious day will come for you when He says to His angel, 'Go down, my servant in Heaven and lighten the burden of my servant Terenti!' And then your good fortune will come to you—believe it—it will come!"

"I do trust in the Lord, grandfather. What else have I left?" said Terenti gently. "I believe in Him. He will help."

"He? He will never leave a man in the lurch on this earth, I promise you. The earth is given to us by God, to try us, to see if we fulfil His commands. He looks down from above and gives heed. 'Children of men, do you love one another, even as I bade you?' and when He sees that life weighs heavy on Terenti, He sends a good message to old Jeremy. 'Jeremy, help my true servant!'" Then suddenly the voice of the old man altered, till it was almost like the voice of Petrusha the potman when he was angry, and he said to Terenti:

"I will give you some money, so that Ilyusha can have clothes for school. I'll give you five roubles. I'll scrape it together somehow. I'll borrow it for you. But if you are ever rich, you'll give it me back."

"Grandfather," cried Terenti.

"Sh! Don't say anything! Besides you can let me have the boy, he hasn't anything to do here anyhow. He can help me, instead of interest on the money; he can pick me up a bone or a bit of rag. I shan't need to double up my old back so often."

"Ah! God bless you," cried the hunchback with a shaking voice.

"The Lord gives to me, I to you; you to the lad and the lad to the Lord again. So it goes round the circle, and no one of us owes anything to the others. Hey! Isn't that good? Eh? Ah! my brother. I have lived and lived and seen—seen, and have seen nothing but God. Everything is His, everything belongs to Him, everything comes from Him and is for Him!"

Ilya went to sleep while they talked. But next morning early, old Jeremy waked him with the joyful summons:

"Now then, up with you, Ilyusha, you're to come with me. So cheerily! cheerily! rub the sleep out of your peepers!"

CHAPTER III

Ilya's daily work arranged itself fairly comfortably under the friendly hand of old Jeremy. Every morning he roused the boy early, and from then till late at night both tramped round the town and collected rags, bones, old paper, old iron, scraps of leather, and anything else of a similar kind. The town was large and there were many remarkable things to be seen in it, so that at first Ilya only half helped the old man, while he gazed constantly at the people and the houses, marvelled at everything, and questioned the grandfather unceasingly.

Jeremy was glad to chatter. With head bent forward and eyes searching the ground he passed from courtyard to courtyard, tapped the pavement with the iron ferule of his stick, wiped the tears from his eyes with his torn sleeve or the point of the dirty rag bag, and told all kinds of histories to his small companion, without ceasing, in a sing-song monotonous voice.

"This house belongs to the merchant Sava Petrovitch Ptschelin—a rich man is the merchant Ptschelin ... his house is full of silver and crystal."

"Grandfather, dear," asked Ilya, "tell me, how does a man get rich?"

"He must work for it, toil for it, that's the way. They work day and night and pile gold on gold, and when they have piled up enough, then they build themselves houses and get themselves horses, and all kinds of belongings, and everything the heart can wish, bright, new things. And then they hire clerks, and servants, and people who work for them, and they rest and enjoy the day. When any one has managed like that, men say of him, he has become rich by honest work. Ah! But there are some who grow rich through sin. People say of the merchant Ptschelin, that he destroyed his soul while he was quite young. Perhaps it is only envy that makes them say it, perhaps it is true. He is a wicked man, this Ptschelin, and his eyes look so frightened, they are always wandering here and there as if they wanted to hide. But perhaps it is all lies, as I said, that they tell of Ptschelin. It happens lots of times that a man becomes rich all at once quite easily, if he just is lucky, if fortune smiles on him. Ah! only God lives in the Truth, and we men know nothing! We are only men, and men are the seed God sows—grains of corn, my dear boy! God has sown them on the earth. 'Grow! and I will see what kind of bread you will make!' That's how it is! And that house there belongs to a certain Mitri Pavlovitch Sabaneyev. He is even richer than Ptschelin, and he is really a downright swindler. I know it! I don't judge him, for judgment is for God, but I know it right enough—as a matter of fact, he was overseer in our village, and robbed us all, cheated us!—God had patience with him for a long time, but in time He began to make up His account. First Mitri Pavlov became deaf, then his son was killed by a horse, and just lately I heard that his daughter had run away."

The old man knew everything and everybody in the town and spoke of them all quite simply without malice. Everything he told seemed to have been purified, as if all his histories were cleansed in his never ceasing tears.

Ilya listened attentively while at the same time he looked at the big houses, and said now and then:

"If I could only have half a look inside!"

"You'll soon see inside, wait a bit! Learn diligently and work! Wait till you grow up, then you'll soon see what is inside there. Perhaps some day you'll be rich too. Learn first to live and to see. Yes—yes—I have lived and lived and seen and seen. That's how I have ruined my eyes. Now the tears keep flowing, and so I have grown so thin and feeble. My strength has flowed away, I think, with my tears, my blood is all dried up."

It was pleasant to Ilya to hear the old man speak of God with such conviction and love. Through hearing him speak, there grew up in his heart a strong, invigorating feeling of hope for something good and joyful awaiting him somewhere in the future. He was gayer and more of a child at this time than when first he found a resting-place in the town.

He helped the old man zealously to rummage in the dust heaps. He found it most exciting to burrow into these heaps of every kind of rubbish with a stick, and specially pleasant to see the old man's joy when he made an unusual find among the rubbish. One day, Ilya found a big silver spoon in a drain, and the old man bought him half a pound of ginger bread for it. Then once he dug out a little purse covered with green mould, with more than a rouble in money inside it. More often he found knives, forks, metal rings, broken brasswork, pretty tin boxes—formerly full of blacking or pickled fish—and once, in the valley where the refuse of the whole town was unloaded, he grubbed out a heavy brass candlestick quite uninjured. For every valuable find of this sort Ilya received some dainty or other from the old man as a reward.

Whenever Ilya found anything out of the common, he would cry out gleefully: "Grandfather! Look! See here! this is something like!"

Then the old man would look anxiously all round him and say in a warning whisper:

"But don't shout so—don't shout for any sake!"

He was always anxious if they made any unusual discovery, and would take it quickly out of Ilya's hands and conceal it in the big sack.

"Ha! Ha! I've hooked another big fish!" Ilya would cry, delighted with his success.

"Be quiet, youngster! Quiet, my boy," the old man would say in a friendly tone, while the tears ran and ran from his red swollen eyes.

"But look grandfather," Ilya would break out again, "what a tremendous big bone!"

Bones and rags did not excite the old man. He took them from the bag, wiped off the dirt with wood shavings and stuffed them quietly into the sack. He had sewed for Ilya a little sack and given him a stick with an iron point, and the youngster was not a little proud of this equipment. In his sack he collected all kinds of small boxes, broken toys, pretty potsherds, and it filled him with joy to feel all these things in the bag on his back, and to hear how they rattled and rustled. Old Jeremy made it the lad's business to collect all these trifles.

"Do you collect just these pretty things and carry them home. You can share them with the children and make them happy. God is pleased when a man makes his brothers happy. Ah! my son, all men long for happiness, and yet there is so little. So very little in all the world. So little that many a man never meets happiness all his life, never."

Ilya preferred rummaging in the town refuse heaps to pottering about courtyards. There in the open space, there was nobody except two or three old people like Jeremy who searched the rubbish as he did. In the courtyard, on the contrary, there was need of constant anxious attention, lest a house servant should come out, broom in hand, and chase them away with angry words, or even with blows. Every day Jeremy said to his companion when they had searched for about two hours:

"That's enough just now, Ilya, that's enough, laddie! We'll sit down a while and rest, and have a bit to eat."

He took a piece of bread out of his pocket, made the sign of the cross over it, and divided it. They both made a meal, and after eating, rested full half an hour, camped on the edge of the valley. The valley opened on to the river, and they could see the stream quite plainly. It swept slowly past the valley in broad, silver-shining streaks, and when Ilya followed the

flow of the water, he felt in his heart a keen desire to glide away with it—
somewhere, anywhere. On the further side of the river, the green, newly-
mown meadows stretched away and away, haystacks rising up among them
like grey towers, and far on the horizon the dark jagged line of the forest
stood out against the blue sky. A sense of rest and kindliness brooded over
the meadow lands, inspiring the thought that a pure, transparent, sweet-
smelling air drifted over them, while here it was so suffocating with the reek
of the rotting refuse; the stench of it gripped the lungs and irritated the nose,
and tears ran from Ilya's eyes as well as from the old man's.

"See, Ilya, how great and wide the world is!" said Jeremy; "and
everywhere in it there are men living—living and tormenting themselves—
and the Lord looks down out of Heaven and He sees everything and knows
everything. All that a man so much as thinks, is known to Him, wherefore
He is also called by the Holy Name, Lord God of Sabaoth, Jesus Christ. He
knows everything, counts everything, thinks of everything. The spots of sin
upon your soul you may conceal from men, but never from Him. He sees
all. He thinks of you. 'Ah! thou sinner, thou miserable sinner! Wait, I must
chastise thee.' And when the time comes, then He punishes—punishes you
grievously! He gave command to men, 'Love ye one another,' and He has
so ordered it that he who does not love his fellow-men is loved by no one.
Such men live lonely in the world and their lot is heavy, and they have no
gladness."

Ilya lay on his back, and looked up into the blue sky, whose limits he
could not determine. Melancholy and sleepiness fell on him, vague, confused
pictures drifted before his soul. It seemed to him as if far above in the sky,
there hovered a mighty being, transparently clear, gentle and comforting,
at once good and powerful, and that he, the little boy, might raise himself,
with the old grandfather Jeremy and the whole earth, up into the boundless
space, the blue ocean of light and shining purity, and his heart was full of
peaceful, quiet joy. In the evening, when they returned home, Ilya trod the
courtyard with the important self-assured gait of a man who has completed
a good day's work. In the well-earned desire for rest, he retained not the
least pleasure in such foolish things as other little boys and girls delight in.
By his serious demeanour and the sack on his back, stuffed full of rare and
fascinating things, he inspired a decided respect in all the children.

The grandfather smiled in a friendly way at the youngsters and chaffed
them:

"Here children, see! the Lazaruses have come home again. They have
hunted through the whole town and shoved their noses in everywhere. Run
along Ilya, wash your face and come into the bar for tea."

Ilya went to his corner in the cellar with important strides, and a crowd of children followed him, keenly curious as to the contents of the sack. Only Pashka stood in his path and asked him pertly:

"Hullo! Rag-picker! Show us what you've brought."

"You'll have to wait," answered Ilya with decision. "Let me have my tea, then I'll show you."

In the bar, uncle Terenti met him with a friendly smile.

"Ha! Ha! little workman, back again? Tramped yourself tired, eh, young'un?"

Ilya liked to be called a little workman, and he received the title from others besides his uncle. Once when Pashka had played some pranks, his father Savel took his head between his knees and thrashed him soundly.

"I'll teach you, you rascal! You'll play your tricks again, will you? Take that then—and that—and one more! Other children no older than you earn their own bread, and you can do nothing—nothing but stuff yourself and tear your clothes!"

Pashka screamed till the whole house rang, and kicked hard while the rope's end whistled about his back. At first Ilya heard his enemy's cries of pain with a certain sense of satisfaction, and at the same time the words of the smith, which he took to himself, filled him with a consciousness of his superiority to Pashka. Then the thought roused compassion in him for the victim.

"Uncle Savel, please stop!" he called out suddenly. "Uncle Savel!"

The smith gave his son one cut more, then looked at Ilya and said crossly:

"Shut up! You! Speak up for him, will you? Look out for yourself!"

Then he swung his son on to one side and went into the smithy. Pashka got on to his feet and tottered with wavering steps into a dark corner of the courtyard. Ilya followed him pityingly. Pashka knelt down in the corner, pressed his head against the fence and began to scream more loudly than ever, rubbing his back with his hands. Ilya felt a wish to say something friendly to his humbled enemy; presently he asked:

"Does it hurt much?"

"Get away! Get out!" screamed Pashka.

The ill-tempered tone angered Ilya, and he said in a prim way:

"You used to be always knocking the others about, and now——"

Before he could finish Pashka flung himself upon him and dragged him to the ground. Ilya was immediately filled with rage, gripped fast hold of his antagonist and both rolled on the earth in a knot. Pashka bit and scratched while Ilya, with his hand twisted firmly in his adversary's hair, bumped his head vigorously against the ground till Pashka cried:

"Let go!"

"There! you see!" said Ilya, proud of his victory, as he got on to his feet, "you see, I'm stronger than you. So don't try that game on me again, unless you want another licking!"

He walked off wiping the blood from his scratched face with his sleeve. The smith was standing in the middle of the yard with lowering brows. When Ilya saw him, he shivered and stood still, convinced that the smith would take vengeance on him for Pashka's defeat. But the smith only shrugged his shoulders and said: "Now then, what are you glowering at? Never seen me before? Get along with you!"

But the same evening as Ilya stepped through the door, he met Savel again; the smith flipped him lightly on the head with his finger and said smiling:

"Hullo! young dust-grubber, how goes business? Eh?"

Ilya giggled happily; he was delighted. The gloomy smith, the strongest man in the yard, who inspired every one with fear and respect had joked with him. The smith gripped the lad's shoulder with his iron hand, and increased his delight still further by saying:

"Eh, you're a sturdy youngster! It's not so easy to bowl you over. When you grow a bit I'll take you on in the smithy."

Ilya caught the smith round his huge thigh and pressed against him. The giant must have felt the tumultuous beating of that little heart, that his clumsy kindness had set going. He laid a heavy hand on Ilya's head, and after a moment's silence said in his deep voice:

"Ah! poor motherless lad. There! there!"

Beaming with happiness, Ilya set to at his usual evening's task, the distribution of the treasures he had collected in the day. The children had been waiting for him for ever so long. They sat in a circle on the ground about him and gazed with greedy eyes at the dirty sack. Ilya fetched out of the bag a couple of strips of calico, a wooden soldier, bleached by wind and weather, a blacking pot, a pomade box, and a teacup with a broken rim and no handle:

"That is for me!—for me—for me!" came the children's voices, and from all sides little dirty hands caught at the rare treasures.

"Wait! Wait! No grabbing!" commanded Ilya. "Do you call that playing fair if you all snatch at once? Now then, I'll open the shop. First, I'll sell this piece of calico, quite wonderful calico, the price is half a rouble. Mashka, buy it!"

"It's bought," shouted Jakov instead of the cobbler's daughter, and drew out of his pocket a potsherd he had held in readiness and pressed it into the merchant's hand. But Ilya would not take it. "What sort of a game's that? You must bargain—my goodness! You never bargain. In the market you must bargain!"

"I forgot," Jakov excused himself, and now began an obstinate haggling. Seller and buyers grew wildly excited, and while they chaffered, Pashka quickly snatched what he wanted out of the heap, and ran off, dancing and shouting in mockery:

"Ha! ha! I've got it! I've got it! You sleepyheads, you silly duffers!"

At first Pashka's thievish ways enraged all the children. The little ones cried and howled, while Jakov and Ilya chased the robber, but usually without success. By degrees they became accustomed to his knavery, looked for nothing better from him and paid him out by refusing angrily to play with him. Pashka lived for himself, and thought of nothing but how to play his evil tricks. The big-headed Jakov, on the other hand, was a kind of nursemaid for the curly-haired daughter of the cobbler. She took his care for her interest as something quite natural, and if she called him always coaxingly "Jashetschka," she also scratched and struck him fairly often. Jakov's friendship with Ilya grew from day to day and he was always telling his friend his most wonderful dreams.

"I dreamed last night that I had a heap of money—bright roubles, a whole sackful, and I carried the sack into the wood on my back. Then all at once some robbers came at me with knives—horrible! I ran away, of course, and then in a minute the sack seemed alive. I threw it away and—you'll never guess—all sorts of birds flew out of it. Whirr! Whirr! Siskins and tits and finches, oh such a tremendous lot! They lifted me up and carried me through the air—high, ever so high."

He broke off and looked at Ilya with his prominent eyes, while a sheepish look came into his face.

"Well, what next?" Ilya prompted him, eager to hear the end.

"Oh! I flew right away," Jakov ended his tale thoughtfully.

"But where?"

"Where? Oh—just—just right away."

"Oh you!" said Ilya disappointed and contemptuous. "You never remember anything."

Grandfather Jeremy came out from the bar and called, shading his eyes with his hand:

"Ilyusha! Where are you? Come to bed it's getting late."

Ilya followed the old man obediently and went to his bed, made of a sack full of hay. He slept soundly on his sack, and lived happily with the old rag-picker, but all too fast this pleasant easy life slipped away.

CHAPTER IV

Grandfather Jeremy kept his word; he bought Ilya a pair of boots, a thick heavy coat and a cap, and thus equipped, the youngster was sent to school. Full at once of curiosity and anxiety he went, and gloomy and sick, with tears in his eyes he came home. The boys had recognised him as old Jeremy's companion and had jeered at him in chorus:

"Rag-picker! Stinking rag-picker!"

Some pinched him, others put their tongues out at him, and one specially impudent boy went up to him, sniffed the air, and shouted, turning away with a grimace of disgust:

"Ah! how beastly the lout smells!"

"Why do they laugh at me?" Ilya asked his uncle, full of wrath and doubt. "Is there any shame in being a rag-picker?"

"No! No!" answered Terenti, stroking his nephew's hair, and trying to hide his face from the boy's inquiring eyes. "They only do it—oh just—because they're ill-mannered. Don't worry! Try to bear it! They'll soon have enough of it, and you'll get used to it."

"But they laugh at my boots, too, and my overcoat; they said they were odds and ends dug out of a rubbish heap!"

Grandfather Jeremy comforted him, blinking in a friendly way.

"Bear it, dear lad! There's One will soon make it up to you: He! There's no one else that matters."

The old man spoke of God with such joy, such confidence in his justice, as though he knew well all the mind of God, and was initiated into all His intentions. And Jeremy's words relieved a little the boy's feeling of heart-sickness. But the next day the feeling rose up in him stronger than ever. Ilya had become accustomed to regard himself as a person of importance, a real workman. Why, Savel the smith spoke in a friendly way with him, and these school-boys laughed and mocked at him. He could get no peace, no respite. Every day the bitter insulting expressions of the school became more marked, and drove deeper into his soul. The school hours were for him a heavy, burdensome duty. He kept himself apart, held no intercourse with the others. Through his quickness of comprehension he attracted the attention of the teacher, and being held up as an example to the others, his relations with his schoolfellows became, if possible, more strained than before. He sat on the front bench, and never lost the sense of his enemies at his back. They had him constantly before their eyes, and readily discovered anything about him that might appear ridiculous. And they laughed at him all the time. Jakov attended the same school and was at once tarred with the same brush as his comrade. They usually called him "Muttonhead." He was absent-minded, learnt with difficulty, and was punished almost every day, but remained absolutely indifferent to all punishments. Mostly he seemed hardly to notice what went on round about him, and lived in a world of his own, at school as at home. He had his own thoughts, and by his odd questions moved Ilya to astonishment nearly every day. For instance, he would say, casually, gazing meditatively before him, "Tell me, Ilya, how is it that such little eyes as men have can see everything? One can see the whole street, the whole town; how can anything so big get into our little eyes?"

Or he would stare up into the sky and say suddenly:

"Ah! the sun."

"Well—what?" asked Ilya.

"How it blazes away!"

"Well, what then?"

"Oh nothing. D'you know what I was thinking? The sun and moon must be parents and the stars are their children."

At first Ilya pondered deeply over his odd sayings, but by degrees these fancies began to worry him, because they took his mind off the things that were happening close to him. And there were many things happening, and the boy had soon learnt to take good heed of them.

One day he came home from school and said with scorn to old Jeremy:

"Our teacher—ah!—he's a good one! Yesterday the son of Malafyeyev the merchant, smashed a window, and he let him off very easy, and to-day he's had the window mended and paid for it out of his own pocket."

"But see then, how good he is!" answered Jeremy.

"Good? Oh yes—very good! A little time ago Vanika Klutscharev broke a window, and he made him go without his dinner, and then he sent for Vanika's father and said: Here, pay me forty kopecks; and so Vanika got a licking from his father—that's how good he is!"

"You mustn't trouble over things like that, Ilyusha," said the old man, blinking nervously. "Try and think that it doesn't concern you. It's for God to decide what is wrong and not for us. We don't understand, we can only find out the bad things, and we're not quick to see the good. But He can weigh everything. He knows the measure and the value of everything. Look at me, I have lived so long and seen so much and no one could count how much wrong-doing I've seen. But I have never seen the truth. Eighty years have gone over my head, and it cannot be in all that long time that the truth has not come near me. But I have never seen it, I don't know it."

"Ah!" said Ilya doubtfully, "What's there to know in this? If this one must pay forty kopecks so ought the other, that's the truth."

But the old man would not agree. He said many things about himself, about the blindness of men, and how they are not fit to judge one another rightly, and how only the judgment of God is just.

Ilya listened attentively, but his face grew darker and his eyes more gloomy.

"When will God come and judge us?" he asked suddenly.

"No man knows; when the hour strikes, then He will come down from the clouds to judge the living and the dead: but no man knows when it will come to pass. But on Saturday we will both go to the holy service."

"Yes, let's go."

"All right."

On Saturday Ilya stood with the old man on the church steps between the two doors, with the beggars. Whenever the outer door was opened, Ilya felt the cold air blowing in from the street, his feet were numbed, and he moved gently with short steps up and down on the pavement. But he saw through the glass panes of the church door how the candle flames made beautiful patterns of quivering points of gold, and lit up the glimmering metal on the priest's garments, the dark heads of the reverent multitude, the faces in the sacred pictures and the splendid carving of the holy shrines.

People seemed better and kinder in the church than in the street. They looked more beautiful too in the golden candlelight that illuminated their dark forms, standing in reverent silence. Whenever the inner door opened there streamed out on the steps the solemn, deep-toned waves of song, warm, heavy with incense; gently they wrapped the lad round, and he breathed in the sweet-scented air, with delight. It was good to him to stand there beside old Jeremy, as he murmured prayers. He heard the glorious, solemn song that flooded the house of God, and waited impatiently for the door to open again and let the loud, joyful sound sweep over him, and the warm balsam-laden air cling round his being. He knew that up there in the church choir Grishka Bubnov was singing, one of the worst of his tormentors in the school, and Fedka Dolganov, too, a strong, quarrelsome lout, who had thrashed him more than once. But now he felt no hate towards them nor desire for revenge, only a little envy. He would have liked to sing in the choir and see the faces of the people. It must be so beautiful to sing there at the middle door by the altar, high above the people, and see their quiet, peaceful faces. When he left the church, he felt as though he had grown better and was ready to be reconciled to Bubnov and Dolganov and all his schoolfellows. But on the following Monday, he came home from school sombre and affronted even as before.

Everywhere, where men are gathered together in any numbers, there will be one who is ill at ease among them, and it is not at all necessary that he should be either worse or better than the rest. The ill-will of a crowd can be aroused by a lack of intelligence or by a ridiculous nose. It simply chooses some one as the object of its sport, inspired by nothing but the wish to amuse itself. In this case the lot had fallen on Ilya Lunev. No doubt in the course of time, he would have ceased to fill the *rôle* that his comrades had allotted to him, but now there came into Ilya's life, events that shook his soul profoundly with their terrible impressions, and so far lessened his interest in the school, that he became indifferent to its small unpleasantnesses.

The beginning came one day when Ilya, returning with Jakov from an excursion, noticed a crowd in the gateway of the house.

"Look!" said Jakov to his friend, "they're fighting again. Come along, let's get in quick!"

They hurried full speed to the house, and as they came into the courtyard, saw that there were strange men gathered there who called out:

"Send for the police! Tie his hands!"

Pressing round the smithy was a dense crowd of men, silent, motionless, with frightened faces. Children who had crept to the front, struggled away terrified. At their feet on the snow lay a woman, with her face to the ground. Her neck and the back of her head were covered with blood, and a pasty mass of something, and the snow round about her was reddened with blood. By her lay a crumpled white kerchief and a pair of big smith's tongs. Savel crouched in the smithy door and stared dumbly at the woman's hands. They were outstretched, buried deep in the snow, and the head lay between them as though she had tried to take refuge from him in the earth and hide there. The smith's brows were drawn gloomily, his face convulsed, his teeth clenched fast, the cheek bones stood out like great swellings. He supported himself with his right hand against the door post, his black fingers moved quiveringly like a cat's claws, and except for his fingers he was motionless. But to Ilya it seemed as though his close-locked lips must open, and his mighty breast cry out with all its strength. The crowd gazed without a sound; their faces were stern and earnest and though noise and tumult filled the courtyard, by the smithy all was still and motionless.

Suddenly old Jeremy crept with heavy steps from the crowd, all torn and covered with sweat, with trembling hand he held out to the smith a cup of water and said: "There! drink!"

"Don't give him water, the murderer! It's a rope round his neck he deserves," said some one, half aloud.

Savel took the cup in his left hand and drank—drank deep, and when all was gone, he looked into the empty vessel and said in a dull voice:

"I warned her. Let be, you harlot," I said, "or I'll strike you dead. I forgave her—how many times I forgave her. But she would not leave it— and so—now—it has come to pass. My Pashka is an orphan now, look to him, grandfather. God loves you, look to my boy!"

"Ah! ah! you— —" lamented the old man bitterly and gripped the smith by the shoulder with his trembling hand, while some one in the crowd called out: "Listen to the villain! *He* talks of God."

The smith cast a terrifying glance on the bystanders and suddenly roared like a wild beast.

"What do you want? Off with you—all!" His cry fell on the crowd like a whip stroke. They recoiled from him with a dull murmur. The smith rose up and made a stride towards his dead wife, but turned at once and made for the smithy, drawn straight up to his full height. All could see how, there in his workshop, he sat down on the anvil, caught his head in his hands as though he suddenly felt an unbearable pain, and slowly rocked his body to and fro. Ilya was filled with compassion for the smith; he walked away as if in a dream, and wandered round the court, from one group to another, without comprehending a word of what was said near him. A great red stain swam before his eyes, and his heart was oppressed within him.

The police appeared on the scene and dispersed the crowd. Then they arrested the smith and led him away.

"Good-bye—good-bye, grandfather," cried Savel as he strode out of the gate.

"Good-bye, Savel Ivanitsch, good-bye, my friend," called out old Jeremy in his thin voice, hastily, as though he would hurry after him.

No one except the old man bade farewell to the smith.

The people stood about the yard in little groups, speaking of the event, and looking furtively at the place where the body of the murdered woman lay under a coarse mat. In the door of the smithy, where Savel had crouched, a policeman now settled himself, pipe in mouth. He smoked, spitting to one side, and listened to old Jeremy and looked at him with dull eyes.

"Was it he, then, who committed murder?" said the old man, slowly and mysteriously. "The power of darkness has done it, and that alone. Man cannot murder man—man in himself is good, and God is in his heart. It is not he who murders—do not believe it!"

Jeremy laid his hands on his breast, as though to ward off something from himself, and went on to make clear to the bystanders the significance of what had happened.

"Long ago the Dark One whispered in his heart, 'Kill her!'" he said, turning to the watchman.

"Ah! Long ago, you say?" said the other importantly.

"Long—long ago! 'She belongs to you,' he said, and that is not true; a horse, that may belong to me, a dog may be mine, but a woman belongs to God. She is one of the children of men. She has received from God in Heaven all her troubles and burdens, and bears them even as we. But the Dark One never ceases to whisper, 'Kill her, she is yours.' He longs that men should strive against God. He himself struggles against God, and he seeks for companions among men."

"But it wasn't the Devil who used the tongs, but the smith," said the policeman, and spat on the ground.

"But who put it into his mind?" cried the old man. "Remember that! who put the thought in his mind?"

"Look here," said the policeman, "what have you to do with the smith? Is he your son?"

"No, No! Indeed."

"But you're related to him, eh?"

"No. I have no relations."

"Well then, what are you so excited about?"

"I—Ah God——!"

"I'll tell you," said the policeman roughly; "you chatter because you're a silly old man. Now then, clear out!"

He blew a thick smoke cloud from the corner of his mouth, and turned his back on the old man. But Jeremy was not to be kept back, and spoke on quickly, tearfully, gesticulating with his hands.

Ilya, pale, with wide eyes, had wandered about the court, and now stood beside a group composed of the coachman, Makar, the cobbler, Perfishka, and Matiza, and a couple of other women from the attics.

"Before she was married even she used to carry on with the others, my dear," said one of the women. "I know well enough. Why, Pashka isn't Savel's son, his father was a teacher, who lived with Malafyeyev the merchant—he was always drunk."

"You mean the one who shot himself?" asked Perfishka.

"Right. She got herself mixed up with him."

"All the same, he had no right to kill her," said Makar judicially; "that is a bit too much. Suppose he kills his wife, and I kill mine, and every one—
—"

"That would be jolly work for the police," said the cobbler. "My old woman's been no good for ever so long, but I put up with it."

"Put up with it, do you? you devil!" snarled Matiza.

Even Perfishka's crippled wife had crept out of the cellar and sat huddled up in rags in her usual place in the doorway. Her hands rested still on her knees; she held her head up and gazed at the sky with her dark eyes. Her lips were firmly pressed together, and the corners of her mouth drawn down. Ilya looked first at her dusky eyes, then, like her, at the sky, and thought to himself that perhaps Perfishka's wife saw the Lord God up there, and was silently praying for something.

By degrees all the children of the house collected by the cellar door. They pulled their clothes closer about them, and sat on the cellar steps pressed close together, listening with fearful curiosity to what Savel's son was telling them of the crime. Pashka's face was troubled, and his eyes, generally so saucy, looked uncertainly and waveringly round about him. But he felt himself the hero of the day; never had people paid him so much attention as to-day. Now for the tenth time he retold the same history, and his tale sounded quite indifferent, quite unmoved.

"When she went away yesterday, father gnashed his teeth, and raged more and more, and growled all the time. He pulled my hair every minute. I soon saw something was up, and then she came back. The house was shut up, we were in the smithy, and I was standing by the bellows. All at once I saw her come nearer, and stand in the door. 'Give me the key,' she said.

But father took the tongs and went at her. He went quite slowly—creeping slowly. I shut my eyes, it was awful. I wanted to cry out 'Run, mother!' but I couldn't. When I looked again, he was still going slowly towards her, and his eyes burned! Then she tried to go—she turned her back—she tried to run — —"

Pashka's face quivered and his thin angular body began to shudder. He drew in a deep breath, then breathed out again, and said:

"Then he hit her on the head with the tongs."

A movement ran through the children, who had not stirred hitherto.

"She stretched out her arms and fell forward, as if she were diving into the water."

He stopped speaking, picked up a shaving, looked at it carefully, and threw it away over the heads of the children. They all sat still, silent and motionless, as if they expected him to speak again. But he said no more, and let his head fall on to his breast.

"Did he kill her quite dead?" asked Masha in her thin, trembling voice.

"Silly!" said Pashka, without raising his head.

Jakov put his arms round the little one and drew her close to him, while Ilya moved nearer to Pashka and asked him gently:

"Does it hurt you?"

"What's that to do with you?" answered Pashka, crossly.

All the children looked at him silently.

"She was always idling about," said Mashka's clear voice, but Jakov interrupted her uneasily.

"Idling? But think what the smith was like, always so cross and grumbling, enough to make any one afraid, and she so lively, like Perfishka—it was dull for her with the smith."

Pashka looked at him and spoke solemnly and gloomily like a grown-up person.

"I always said to her, 'Mother,' I said, 'look out for yourself, he'll kill you,' but she wouldn't listen. She always told me not to say anything to him. She bought me sweets and things, and the sergeant gave me five kopecks every time—every time I took him a letter from her—I got five kopecks. He's a good fellow, and so strong, and he's got a big moustache."

"Has he a sword?" asked Mashka.

"Rather," said Pashka, and added proudly, "Once I drew it out of the sheath—my word! it was heavy!"

"Now you're an orphan like Ilyushka," said Jakov thoughtfully, after a pause.

"Hardly," answered Pashka angrily. "Do you mean I've got to go and be a rag-picker? I should think not."

"I don't mean that."

"I shall just live as I like," went on Pashka proudly, with his head held up and his eyes sparkling. "I'm not an orphan, I'm only just alone in the world, and I will just live for myself, my father wouldn't send me to school, and now they'll put him in prison, and I shall just go to school and learn more than you."

"Where will you get the clothes?" said Ilya, and looked triumphantly at Pashka, "you can't go there in rags."

"Clothes? I will sell the smithy!"

All looked respectfully at Pashka, and Ilya felt himself beaten. Pashka observed the impression his words produced, and held himself still straighter.

"Yes, and I'll buy a horse, a real live horse, and I'll ride to school."

This idea pleased him so much that he even smiled, only a very, very shy smile that flitted over his mouth and was gone in a moment.

"No one will beat you now," said Mashka suddenly to Pashka, and looked at him enviously.

"He'll soon find some one willing," said Ilya in a tone of conviction.

Pashka looked at him, then spat to one side and said,

"What do you mean by that? Just you try it on with me!"

Jakov joined again in the conversation.-"How strange it is, children! there was some one—walked about and talked—and so on—full of life like all the rest, and one blow on the head with the tongs—and that's the end."

The children looked attentively at Jakov whose eyes stood out oddly under his brows.

"Yes, I thought of that, too," said Ilya.

"People say dead," went on Jakov slowly and mysteriously, "but then what is it to be dead?"

"The soul has flown away," explained Pashka moodily.

"To Heaven," added Masha, and looked up into the sky, while she nestled closer to Jakov. The stars were already flaming; one of them a great bright star that did not twinkle, seemed nearer to the earth than the rest and looked down on them like a cold unmoving eye. The three boys turned their faces upwards like Mashka. Pashka glanced up and at once slipped away. Ilya looked up long and keenly, with an expression of fear, always at the one point, and Jakov's big eyes wandered here and there over the deep blue heavens as if they were seeking something there.

"Jakov!" called out his friend, looking down again.

"What?"

"I was thinking——" Ilya broke off.

"What were you thinking?" asked Jakov, speaking softly too.

"About the people here."

"What then?"

"How they——I can't bear it. Here is some one killed, and they all run about the place and seem so busy and talk all the time; but no one cried, not one."

"Yes, Jeremy did."

"He always has tears in his eyes. But Pashka, how he behaves—as if he were telling a tale."

"It isn't that, really. It pains him, but he's ashamed to cry before us; but now he's gone away, and is crying—as he's reason enough to."

Huddled close together, they sat still for a minute or two. Mashka had fallen asleep on Jakov's knees, her face still turned to the sky.

"Are you afraid?" asked Jakov very softly.

"A little," replied Ilya, in the same tone. "Now her soul is wandering round here. Yes—yes, and Masha is asleep; we must take her into the house, and I'm so afraid to go away from here."

"Let's go together."

Jakov laid the head of the sleeping child against his shoulder, put his arms round her slender body and rose with an effort, while he whispered to Ilya, who stood in the way, "Hold on, let me go in front!"

He stepped down into the cellar, staggering under his burden, while Ilya followed so close that he almost trod on his friend's heels. It seemed to Ilya that an invisible shape glided behind him, that he felt its cold breath on his neck, and he feared every moment to be gripped by it. He touched his friend on the back and called to him in a barely audible voice:

"Go quicker!"

CHAPTER V

Old Jeremy's health began to fail soon after these events. He went out collecting rags more and more seldom, and stayed at home most of the time, moving languidly about the courtyard, or lying in bed in his dark cabin.

The spring came on, and as the sun's rays streamed down from the blue sky with more warmth, the old man would sit in a sunny corner and count something on his fingers in an absorbed way, while his lips moved soundlessly. More and more seldom could he tell the children stories, his tongue moved with more and more difficulty. He had hardly begun to speak before a fit of coughing stopped him. Something rattled hoarsely in his chest, as though it wanted to be free.

"Please go on," Masha would command, who loved stories beyond everything.

"Wait—wait!" the old man would reply, drawing his breath with difficulty. "Wait—in a minute—it'll stop in a minute."

But the cough would not stop, but shook the exhausted frame more and more fiercely.

Sometimes the children would go away without waiting for the end of the story; as they went they would look at the old man with a strange sorrowful expression.

Ilya observed that the rag-picker's illness caused unusual anxiety both to the potman Petrusha and his uncle Terenti. Several times a day, Petrusha would appear on the steps leading from the court to the bar, take a look with his cunning grey eyes at the old man and ask:

"Now then, how goes it, grandfather? Better, eh?"

He would swagger about in his pink cotton shirt, his hands in the pockets of his wide linen trousers, whose ends were tucked into brilliantly polished boots. He was always chinking the money in his pockets. His round head was beginning to go bald already above the forehead, but there was still a good thick tuft of fair, curly hair on it, and he loved to throw it back in a foppish way. Ilya had never taken kindly to him, and now his feeling of aversion grew stronger every day. He knew that Petrusha did not like Jeremy. One day he heard the potman giving Terenti instructions concerning the old man.

"Keep an eye on him, Terenti! He's an old miser. He's got a pretty store of cash sewed up in his pillow somewhere. Keep your eyes open! He isn't long for this world, the old mole; you're a friend of his and he hasn't a living soul left him in the world! Remember that, my boy!"

In the evenings Jeremy came into the bar to Terenti as before; he conversed with the hunchback about God and Truth and the concerns of mankind. Since he had lived in the town the hunchback had become still more deformed; he seemed to have been bleached by his occupation. His eyes had got a dull, shy expression, and his body was as though melted in the hot vapours of the bar. His dirty shirt used to slip up on to his hump and leave his naked loins visible. All the time he was speaking with any one he kept both his hands behind his back, trying constantly to draw his shirt into its place, and this habit gave him the air of trying to stuff away his big hump.

When Jeremy sat outside in the courtyard, Terenti would come out frequently on to the steps and look at him, and his eyes twitched as he shaded them with his hand. The straw-coloured beard quivered on his pointed face as he asked the old man in his weak voice, embarrassed as from a guilty conscience, "Grandfather! do you want anything?"

"Many thanks. No—nothing. I don't need anything," the old man would answer.

The hunchback turned slowly on his withered legs and went back into the bar. But the old man felt himself growing weaker every day.

"It'll soon be all over with me," he said one day to Ilya, who was sitting near him. "It's time for me to die—there's only one thing still——"

He peered round the courtyard mistrustfully and went on in a whisper:

"I'm dying too soon, Ilyushka! My work is not done. I haven't had time. I've stored up money—money. I've pinched and saved for seventeen years; I wanted to build a church with it. I meant to make a temple for the Lord in the village—my home. Ah! there's need of it—such need for men to have a temple to God; our only refuge is with God. It's too little, all I've saved, it won't do it, and what shall I do with what I have? I don't know. O God! show me the way. And the ravens already flutter about me, and croak and smell a fat morsel. Listen, Ilyushka, I've got money; don't say a word to any one, but listen."

Ilya listened; he felt himself uplifted as the sharer of a great important secret, and understood very well whom the old man spoke of as the ravens.

A couple of days later when Ilya came back from school and went to his accustomed corner, he heard strange sounds in the old man's room. It was like some one murmuring—sobbing with a hoarse rattle in his throat, as though he were being strangled. Every now and then a whisper was audible.

"Ksch! Ksch! Go away!"

Full of anxiety the lad went to the door of the room, but it was fast shut. Then he cried out in a trembling voice:

"Grandfather!"

Behind the door the only answer he heard was a painful breathless whisper:

"Tsch! Ksch! O Lord, have mercy—have mercy—have mercy!"

And suddenly all was still. Ilya sprang back from the door, and hesitated a moment what to do; then he went to part of the wooden partition, and, quivering with excitement, looked through a crack in it. It was dark and obscure in the old man's little room. The light could hardly penetrate the little dirty window. The sound of a spring shower was heard, as the rain drops struck the pane and the water ran down into a hollow in the yard outside the window. Ilya looked closely into the room and saw the old man lying in bed stretched out on his back and fighting the air above him with his hands.

"Grandfather!" cried the boy again, full of terror.

The old man started, lifted his head, and murmured aloud:

"Ksch! Petrusha—let it alone, think of God, it belongs to Him! I must build Him a temple with it. Ksch! Go away! Off! you raven. O God! it is Thine—Thine—guard it, take it for Thyself. Have mercy! have mercy!"

Ilya shivered with fear and was unable to stir from the spot. He saw Jeremy's black, withered hands move feebly in the air, and threaten some invisible person with his crooked fingers.

"See! it belongs to God, don't touch it!" and then the old man raised himself up and his hair bristled. Suddenly he sat upright in his bed. His white beard quivered like the wings of a flying dove. He stretched out his arms, as if to thrust some one away from him with a last effort, and fell on the ground.

Ilya shrieked and ran away. In his ears rang the whisper, "Ksch! Ksch!"

He burst into the bar room and cried breathlessly: "Uncle—he's dead!"

Terenti gave an "Ah!" of astonishment, then moved nervously up and down, pulling at his shirt and looking at Petrusha behind the bar.

"Uncle, go to him!—go quick!"

"There, what are you waiting for," said Petrusha, decidedly. "Go along. God have mercy on his soul! He was a sturdy old man. I'll go with you to see him. Ilya, you stay here. If anything is wanted, fetch me, d'you hear? Jakov, look after the bar, I shan't be a minute."

Petrusha left the bar room without undue haste, putting his feet down noisily. The two boys heard him speak again to the hunchback behind the door:

"Get on—get on—you lout!"

Ilya was seized with a great fear, from all he had seen and heard, but it did not prevent him from seeing quite exactly all that went on around him.

"Did you see how he died?" asked Jakov, who had taken his place behind the bar.

Ilya looked at him and answered with another question: "Why have they gone there?"

"To look at him—you called them."

Ilya was silent. Then he closed his eyes and said,

"It was awful. How he pushed them away!"

"Who?" asked Jakov, stretching his head forward with curiosity.

"The Devil," answered Ilya, after a short thoughtful pause.

"Did you see him?"

"What do you say?"

"Did you see the Devil, I say?" cried Jakov, devoured with curiosity, going quickly up to Ilya. But Ilya shut his eyes again and said nothing.

"Are you very frightened?" questioned Jakov further, and plucked Ilya by the sleeve.

"Wait," said Ilya, becoming mysterious all of a sudden, "I'll go after them for a minute, eh? But don't tell your father, will you?"

"I won't say a word. But come back soon."

Spurred by suspicion, Ilya hurried from the bar and in a moment was down again in the cellar. He stole, carefully, noiselessly as a mouse to the chink in the partition and looked through again. The old man was still alive, he could hear the rattle in his throat. But Ilya could not see him; the dying man's body lay on the floor at the feet of two dark figures, that in the darkness seemed grown into one enormous mis-shaped creature. Then Ilya saw how his uncle knelt beside the bed, and held the pillow which he was hurriedly sewing up. He heard the threads drawn through the stuff quite clearly; Petrusha stood behind Terenti and bent over him. He threw back his hair and whispered angrily:

"Get on—get on! you abortion! I always told you—keep needle and thread ready! But no! you haven't even a needle threaded. Oh you! Silly fool! You've made a nice mess of it—there—that'll do. God have mercy on his soul! It'll do. What's that? Pull yourself together, coward!"

The low whispering of Petrusha, the gurgling sighs of the dying man, the sound of the needle, and the monotonous rush of the water that ran into the hole in front of the window, all combined into a dull noise beneath which Ilya felt his senses wavering. He left the wall, where he had listened, and crept out of the cellar. A great black patch whirled before his eyes like a wheel, making him sick and giddy. He had to cling to the railing as he climbed the stairs to the bar room, and felt his limbs drag heavily. When at last he reached the tap-room door, he stood still and began to weep. Jakov hurried to him and spoke cheerily to him. Then he felt a slap on the back and heard Perfishka's voice, "Hullo! What's up? Speak up man! Is he dead? Ah!"

And pushing Ilya aside, he ran down the steps again so fast that they shook beneath his feet. But at the bottom he stood on the last step and cried out loudly and complainingly:

"Ah! these sharpers!"

Then Ilya heard his uncle and Petrusha come up the stairs; he did not want to cry before them, but he could not hold back the tears.

"Jakov," called Petrusha, "run down to the police station; say the old rag-picker has gone to his God—make haste!"

"Oh you," cried Perfishka, who had come up again with them, "So you've been there already, eh?"

Terenti passed by his nephew and could not look him in the face; but Petrusha laid his hand on Ilya's shoulder and said:

"Crying, lad? Cry away! that's right, it shows you have a grateful heart, and understood what the old fellow did for you. He was very, very good to you."

After a while he took Ilya by the hand and led him aside saying:

"But you needn't stand right in the doorway, all the same."

Ilya wiped away the tears with his shirt sleeve and let his glance stray over the bystanders. Petrusha had gone behind the bar again and was throwing back his curls. In front of him stood Perfishka, looking at him with a mocking grin. His face had an expression as though he had just lost his last five-kopeck piece at pitch and toss.

"Well, what's the matter, Perfishka?" asked Petrusha as he drew the drink.

"Matter? Oh! Aren't you going to give me a fee?" he answered suddenly.

"How d'you mean? For what?" asked the potman, indifferently.

"Oh you scoundrel!" cried the cobbler crossly, and stamped on the ground. "My mouth's wide open, but the roast pigeon is not for me. Well, well, that's done, anyhow. Here's luck, Peter Sakinytsch."

"What's the matter? What are you jawing about?" asked Petrusha and smiled as unconcernedly as he could.

"I only mean—I'm speaking quite simply——"

"Ah! you want a drink, that's it, eh?"

"Ha! Ha!" the cobbler's gay laugh sounded loudly.

Ilya tossed his head as though to shake off something and went outside.

That night he lay down to sleep very late, and not in his corner of the cellar but in the tap room under the table where his uncle washed the glasses. The hunchback made a bed there for his nephew, then began to wash down the tables. A lamp burned on the bar, lighting up the bulging teapots and the bottles in the cupboards against the wall. In the room it was dark. The black night came close up to the window; a fine rain pattered on the panes and the wind rustled softly.

Like a great hedgehog, Terenti crept about between the tables, sighing frequently. Whenever he came near the lamp his figure threw a great black shadow on the floor. It seemed to Ilya that the soul of old Jeremy glided behind his uncle and whispered in his ear:

"Ksh—Kshsh."

The boy was frightened and shivered. The damp atmosphere of the bar oppressed him. It was Saturday. The floor was newly washed, and smelt mouldy. Ilya wanted to beg his uncle to lie down beside him as soon as possible, yet a painful, perverse feeling held him back from speaking. In his mind he saw the bent figure of old Jeremy with his white beard, and his friendly words rang in his ears all the time.

"Mind my son—God knows the measure of all things—mark that!"

"Oh, come and lie down!" Ilya burst out at last.

The hunchback started and looked up terrified.

Then he said, softly, fearfully:

"What? Who is there?"

"It is I. Come and lie down, I say."

"Soon—soon—soon," cried the hunchback quickly, and began to twist about the tables like a top. Ilya perceived that his uncle was afraid of him and thought in the stillness with a feeling of pleasure:

"Right—that's right."

The rain drummed on the window panes and from all round came dull sounds. The lamp flame flickered up. Ilya covered his head with his uncle's fur jacket and lay there holding his breath. Suddenly something moved near him. A paroxysm of terror seized him; trembling, he put his head out and saw Terenti kneeling on the ground, his head bent, so that his chin touched his breast. And Ilya heard him praying in a whisper:

"O Lord, our Father in Heaven, O Lord——!"

The whisper reminded him of the death rattle of the old man. The darkness in the room began to move, the floor seemed to go round and round, and the wind howled in the chimney: "Hu—u—u——!"

"Stop that praying!" called Ilya's clear voice.

"What? What is it?" said the hunchback half aloud. "Go to sleep, for Christ's sake."

"Stop praying," repeated the boy, commandingly.

"Yes—yes. I'll stop."

The dampness and the darkness in the room weighed more and more heavily on Ilya, his breathing was oppressed and his soul was filled with fear and sorrow for the dead old man, and with a deep ill-will against his uncle. At last he sat up and groaned aloud.

"What is the matter? What is it?" called out his uncle frightened, and put an arm round him. But Ilya pushed him back, and spoke in a voice choked with tears, but ringing with bitter pain and horror.

"O God! If only I could go away and hide from it all. O God!"

He could not speak for tears. His breathing was laboured in the heavy air of the tap room, and, sobbing, he hid his face on the floor.

CHAPTER VI

Ilya's character underwent a great change as a result of these experiences. Formerly it was only from his school fellows that he had held aloof, as he had never become accustomed to their behaviour towards him or felt the smallest inclination to yield to it. In the house, on the contrary, he had always been frank and trustful, and had felt a singular joy, if any one of the grown-up people took any notice of him. Now, however, he kept away from every one, and grew serious beyond his years. His face wore an unfriendly expression, his lips were compressed, he observed his elders with attention and listened to their conversations with a searching look in his eyes. The memory of all he saw on the day that old Jeremy died weighed heavy on him, and it seemed to him that not only Petrusha and his uncle, but also he himself was guilty before the old man. Perhaps Jeremy had thought as he lay there dying and saw his store rifled, that he, Ilya, had betrayed the treasure. This fear had arisen in Ilya quite suddenly, but had grown in strength and filled his soul with doubt and torturing pain. He locked his thoughts in his heart and thereby there grew in him a mistrust of all the world, and as often as he noticed anything wicked in any one, his heart was a little easier, as though his own guilt towards the dead were lessened thereby. And he found so much evil among men and women. Every one called Petrusha a hypocrite and a liar, but all flattered him to his face, bowed respectfully to him, and addressed him with humility as Peter Akimytsch. Every one called big Matiza of the attics by a hateful name; when she was drunk they all pushed or struck her, and once as she sat below the kitchen window, the cook poured a pail of dirty water right over her, and yet they all took from her endless small kindnesses and services, and gave her no thanks but foul names and blows. Perfishka would call her to watch his ailing wife, Petrusha would get her to wash down the bar room before holidays for nothing, and she was always mending shirts for Terenti. She went everywhere and did everything without a complaint and very handily, tended the sick devotedly and loved to play with the children.

Ilya saw that the most hard-working man in the whole house, the cobbler Perfishka, was looked upon universally as a ridiculous figure, and that no notice was taken of him except when he sat on the bench in the bar room with his harmonica, half drunk, or reeled about the courtyard singing his jolly little songs.

No one could see how carefully he carried his crippled wife up the stairs, how he put his little daughter to bed, tucked her in, and made all sorts of droll faces to entertain her. No one noticed him when he taught Masha, with laughter and fun, to cook the dinner and clean the room, then settled to his work, sitting far into the night bent over a dirty shapeless boot.

When the smith was taken off to prison, no one but the cobbler troubled about his boy. But he took Pashka at once, and the unruly lad waxed the thread, swept the room, fetched water, and went to the shop for bread, kvass and onions. Every one had seen the cobbler drunk on holidays, but no one heard him next day, when, sober once more, he excused himself to his wife:

"Forgive me, Dunya, I'm not really a drunkard, I only took a mouthful to cheer me up. I work all the week—it's very weary, and then I just go and have a drink, and——"

"But do I complain of you? My God, I'm only so sorry for you," answered his wife in her hoarse voice, that sounded like a sob in her throat. "D'you think I don't see how you slave? The Lord has put me like a heavy stone round your neck. If only I could die! then you'd be free of me!"

"Don't talk like that! I won't have you say such things. It's I who trouble you, and not you, me, but I don't do it out of wickedness, only I'm so weak. See now, we'll move into another street. Everything shall be different, door and windows and everything. The windows shall look out on the street, and we'll cut out a boot in paper and stick it on them. That'll be our sign. Everybody will come to us in a crowd, and the business will flourish. Ah! then! work—work—that's the way to fill the cupboard!"

Ilya knew every detail of Perfishka's life. He saw how he toiled like a fish that tries to break the ice closing round it, and respected him the more because he jested all the time with every one and had a smile for all occasions, and played so beautifully on the harmonica.

Meanwhile Petrusha sat behind the bar, played cards with an acquaintance now and again, drank tea from morning to night, and scolded the lads who waited on the customers. Soon after Jeremy's death he installed Terenti as barman, while he amused himself by strolling about the court whistling, observing the house from all sides and tapping the walls with his fists.

Ilya observed many other things, and everything was hateful and depressing, and repelled him from his fellows more and more. Sometimes all the thoughts and impressions that accumulated in him roused a strong desire to pour out his soul to some one. But he had no desire to talk to his uncle. After the death of Jeremy, there grew up as it were an invisible wall between them, which prevented the boy from approaching Terenti as often and as frankly as before. Even Jakov could throw little, if any, light for him on the experiences of his soul; for he lived apart from every one in his own special way. The death of old Jeremy troubled him, he often thought sadly.

"How dull everything is—if only grandfather Jeremy was alive, he used to tell us stories; there's nothing so nice as stories, and he could tell them so well."

"He could do everything well," answered Ilya gloomily.

One day Jakov said to his friend, mysteriously:

"Shall I show you something? Shall I?"

"Yes—do."

"But promise you'll never say a word."

"I promise."

"Say—may I be damned in Hell, if I do."

Ilya repeated the formula, whereupon Jakov led him to the old lime-tree in the furthest corner of the courtyard. There he lifted from the stem a strip of bark, cunningly fastened, and behind it Ilya saw a big hollow in the tree. It was a space cleverly scooped out with a knife, and adorned with gay rags, scraps of paper, and bits of tin foil. In the depth of the hollow stood a small figure, cast in bronze, and a wax candle end was fixed upright before it.

"Did you see it?" asked Jakov, putting the bark again over the opening.

"Yes, I saw. What is it?"

"It's a chapel," explained Jakov. "At night I can always come out very quietly and light the candle and pray. Isn't it beautiful?"

Ilya liked his friend's idea, but at once perceived the danger.

"Suppose any one saw the light. You'd get a fine thrashing!"

"Who's going to see it in the night? They're all asleep, the world is all quiet. I'm very little and God can't hear my prayer at the end of the day, but He'll hear it at night when it's quiet, don't you think?"

"I don't know, perhaps He will," said Ilya thoughtfully, looking into the pale, big-eyed face of his comrade.

"And you? Will you come and pray too?"

"What will you pray for?" asked Ilya. "I should ask God to make me very clever, and after that, to give me everything I want. What will you ask for?"

"I? I should ask for that too," answered Jakov. After a moment he added: "I should just pray without asking for anything special, just pray, that's all, and He can give what He likes, but if you think the other way's better, then I'll do the same as you."

"All right," said Ilya.

They decided to start praying the next night at the lime-tree, and both went to bed firmly determined to wake and meet at the corner. But neither then nor on the following night could they wake, and they overslept on many other occasions; then new impressions came to bear on Ilya and the thought of the chapel fell into the background.

In the twigs of this same lime-tree where Jakov had established his chapel, Pashka set bird snares, to catch finches and siskins. He had grown clumsy and thin, and his eyes looked this way and that like the eyes of a beast of prey. He had now no time to loaf about the court. He was kept busy with Perfishka all day, and the friends only saw him on holidays, when the cobbler was drunk. Pashka used to ask them what they were learning at school, and would look gloomy and envious when they gave accounts coloured with a consciousness of their superiority.

"You needn't be so stuck up, anyhow," he said once. "I'll learn something, too, some day."

"But Perfishka won't let you."

"Then I'll run away," answered Pashka, shortly and decidedly.

And as a matter of fact soon after this speech the cobbler went round the courtyard saying with a laugh:

"My young companion has run away, the young devil! Couldn't get on with my leather science!"

It was a rainy day. Ilya looked at the worried cobbler and then at the dull grey skies, and felt pity for the froward Pashka who might now be wandering God knows where. He stood by Perfishka under a shed, leant against the wall and looked across at the house. It seemed to him that day by day it became lower, as though it were sinking into the earth under the burden of the years. Its old ribs stood out more and more sharply, as though the dirt that had accumulated within them for years could no longer find room, and were pushing them asunder. Saturated with misery, wild riot and mournful drunken songs its only abundance, pounded and bruised by never-ceasing footsteps, the house could no longer endure its life, and slowly crumbled to decay, while its dim windows stared mournfully upon God's world.

"Heigh-ho!" began the cobbler, "the old shop'll soon smash up and strew its spawn over the earth, and we that live in it, we'll scatter to the four winds, we'll seek out new holes somewhere else—we'll soon find 'em, as good as these. Then we'll begin a new life—new windows and new doors, and new bugs to bite us. Well, let's have it soon, I've had enough of this pig-sty—only in the end one gets used to it, devil take it!"

But the shoemaker's dream was not to be fulfilled. The house did not crumble down, but was bought by Petrusha. As soon as the sale was complete, Petrusha spent two days creeping into every hole and corner, and feeling and testing the old box of rubbish. Then came bricks and boards, scaffolding surrounded the whole house, and for three months on end it creaked and quivered under the blows of the workmen's hatchets. All round there was sawing and chopping, nails were driven in, old beams torn out with loud crackings and whirls of dust, and new ones put in the places, till at last the old shanty had received a new clothing of planks, and its façade was widened by a new outbuilding. Broad and thickset, the house rose now from the ground straight and sturdy, as though it had driven new roots far into the earth; along its front just below the roof, Petrusha had a big hanging sign put up, which bore the statement in golden letters on a blue ground:

"The Jolly Companions Tavern, P. S. Filimonov."

"And inside it's rotten through and through," said Perfishka mockingly.

Ilya, to whom he made this comment, smiled in sympathy. To him, too, this house, after its rebuilding, seemed a gigantic fraud. He remembered Pashka, who must now be living in another place, and seeing quite different things.

Ilya dreamed, like the cobbler, of other doors and windows and men. Now life in the house became even more unpleasant than before. The old lime-tree fell a victim to the axe, the intimate little corner in its shadow disappeared, and a new outbuilding occupied its place, and all the other favourite places where the children used to sit together and chatter, existed no longer. Only where once the smithy stood, there was one quiet little corner left, behind a heap of old chips and rotten wood. But to sit there was to court uncanny feelings, as though beneath the pile of wood lay Savel's wife with a shattered skull.

Petrusha set aside a new place for Terenti—a tiny little room next the big bar room. Through the thin partition with green paper penetrated all the noise, the smell of brandy and the reek of tobacco. It was clean and dry in Terenti's new room, and yet it was more uncomfortable there than in the cellar. The window looked on the grey wall of the shed, which concealed the sky with the sun and stars, whereas, from the old cellar window, any one kneeling down could see them all quite easily.

Terenti henceforth wore a lilac-coloured shirt, and over it a coat that hung on him as it might have done over a box. From early morning till late at night he took his place behind the bar. He spoke distantly now to every one and held few conversations, and these in a dull, snappy way, as though he were barking, and looked at his acquaintances across the counter with the eyes of a faithful dog that guards his master's property. He bought Ilya a grey cloth jacket, boots, an overcoat, and a cap. When the lad put them on for the first time, the memory of the old rag-picker came vividly before him. He hardly ever spoke to his uncle and his life passed by, monotonous and still; and although the unusual unchildlike feelings and thoughts which had grown in him kept his mind busy, he was burdened with the weight of a suffocating dreariness. More and more often his thoughts turned back to the village. Now it seemed to him quite clear and definite, how much better it had been to live there. Everything there was quieter, simpler, more intelligible. He remembered the dense woods of Kerschenez, and his uncle's tales of the hermit Antipa, and the thought of Antipa aroused the memory of another lonely soul—of Pashka. Where was he now? Perhaps he, too, had fled to the woods, and there dug out a cave to live in. The storm-wind rages through the forest, the wolves howl; it is so terrifying, and yet so good to listen. And in the winter everything shines in the sun like silver, and all is so still, so quiet, that nothing can be heard but the crunch of the snow under foot, and if you stand a moment motionless, you hear only the beating of your own heart. But in the town, it is always wild and noisy, and even the night is filled with clamour. Men sing songs, shout for the police, groan aloud, the carriages pass to and fro, and shake the window-panes with their rattling. Even in school there is much the same confusion; the boys cry out and do all sorts of mischief, and the grown-up people in the streets roar and insult one another and fight and get drunk. And all this not only causes unrest, at times it is absolutely horrible. Mankind here is mad, some are liars, like Petrusha, some evil-tempered and passionate like Savel, others miserably wretched like Perfishka or Uncle Terenti or Matiza. Ilya was specially surprised and provoked at the hateful conduct which the cobbler had lately displayed.

One morning, as Ilya was getting ready for school, Perfishka came into the bar, all dishevelled and heavy with want of sleep. He stood silently at the counter and looked at Terenti. His left eyelid quivered and blinked constantly and his underlip hung down in a strange manner. Terenti looked at him, smiled, and poured him out a small glass, three kopecks worth, Perfishka's usual morning allowance.

Perfishka took it with a shaking hand and tossed it off, but neither smacked his lips after it as usual, nor showed his approval by an oath, and forgot entirely to take his accustomed morsel of food. With his blinking left eye he looked once more at the new barman searchingly, while his right eye remained dull and motionless and seemed to see nothing.

"What's wrong with your eye?" asked Terenti.

Perfishka rubbed his eye with his hand, then looked at his hand and said loudly and emphatically:

"My wife, Avdotya Petrovna is dead."

"What? Truly?" asked Terenti, crossing himself with a glance at the sacred image. "The Lord have mercy on her soul!"

"Eh?" said Perfishka sharply, still gazing into Terenti's face.

"I said, 'The Lord have mercy on her soul!'"

"Oh!—yes—yes! She is dead," said the cobbler. Then he turned suddenly on his heel and went out.

"A strange man," muttered Terenti, shaking his head. Ilya, too, found the cobbler's behaviour very strange. On his way to school he went for a moment into the cellar to see the dead woman. It was all dark and stuffy; the women had come from the attics and were talking half aloud in a group round the death-bed. Matiza was dressing the little Masha and asked her:

"Does it catch you under the arm?"

And Masha, standing with her arms stretched out sideways said crossly:

"Yes—ye—es!"

The cobbler sat bent forward at the table and looked at his daughter, his eye blinking all the time. Ilya gave a glance at the pale, swollen face of the dead; he remembered her dark eyes, now closed for ever, and went out with a painful gnawing feeling at his heart.

When he returned from school and went into the bar room, he heard Perfishka playing the harmonica and singing in a merry tone:

"Ah, my bride, my only dear,
My heart is gone, I sadly fear,
Why have you stolen it away,
And where on earth is it to-day?"

"Oh yes! the women have turned me out!—get out, you villain, they screamed—old tippler, they called me. But I don't mind a bit. I'm a patient lamb. Blackguard me as much as you like, hit me if you like. Only let me live a little—just a little if you please. Aha! my brothers, every man likes to enjoy his life, eh? Call it Vaska, call it Jakov, the soul's the same all the time."

"Tell me who is weeping there?
What does he want, in this affair?
Be still my friend and don't complain,
But stuff your mouth with bread again."

Perfishka's face wore an expression of idiotic happiness. Ilya looked at him and felt disgust and fear. He thought in his heart that without a doubt God would punish the cobbler heavily for such behaviour on the day of his wife's death. But Perfishka was drunk the next day too, even behind his wife's coffin he reeled as he walked and winked and laughed. All held his conduct blameworthy, he was even struck in the face.

"Do you know," said Ilya to Jakov the day of the funeral, "Perfishka is a downright unbeliever!"

"Oh! bother him!" answered Jakov indifferently.

Ilya had noticed already that Jakov had altered considerably. He hardly ever appeared in the courtyard, but sat indoors all the time and seemed to take pains to avoid Ilya. At first Ilya thought that Jakov envied him his success at school and was sitting indoors over his school work. But he soon showed that he learned with even more difficulty than before; constantly his teacher had to reprove him for his inattention and his failure to understand the simplest things. Ilya did not wonder at Jakov's indifference over Perfishka, for Jakov took no special interest in the affairs of the house, but he did wish to understand what was passing in his friend's mind and he asked him:

"Why are you so down on me now? Don't you want to be friends?"

"I? Not be your friend? What on earth are you saying?" said Jakov taken aback, and then called quickly with an eager expression:

"See now, go into the house. I'm coming in a moment—I'll show you."

He jumped up and ran off, while Ilya went to his room in great perplexity.

Jakov soon appeared. He closed the door behind him, went to the window, and took a red book from his coat pocket.

"Come here!" he said, softly, with an important air, sitting down on Terenti's bed and making room for Ilya beside him. Then he opened the book, laid it on his knee, bent over it and began to read aloud, following the words along the grey paper with his finger:

"And sudden—suddenly the bold knight saw a mountain a long way off, so high that it reached to heaven, and midway up its slope was an iron tower. There the fire of his courage flamed up in his brave heart. He put his lance in rest and charged forward with a mighty shout, and sp—spurring his horse, he rushed with all his-gi—gigantic strength against the door. There was a—fearful clap of thunder—the iron tower flew into fragments, and at the same time there streamed out of the mountain fire and v—va—vapour, and a voice of thunder was heard, at which the earth trembled and the stones rolled from the mountain down to the horse's feet. 'Ha! Ha! Is it thou, bold madcap. Death and I have long awaited thee.' The knight was blinded with the fire and smoke."

"But who—who is this?" asked Ilya, amazed at the excitement that quivered in his friend's voice.

"What?" said Jakov, lifting his pale face from the book.

"Who is this—this knight?"

"He's a man, that rides a horse, with a spear, his name is Raoul the Fearless—a dragon has carried off his bride, the beautiful Louise—but listen," Jakov broke off impatiently.

"Hold on a minute—tell me, what's a dragon?"

"Oh! it's a snake with wings and feet with iron claws, and it has three heads, and breathes fire, and—d'you see?"

"My word!" cried Ilya, opening his eyes wide, "that'll be a handful to tackle!"

"Yes, just listen."

Sitting close together, trembling with curiosity and a strange delightful excitement, the two boys made their entry into a new wonder-world where huge evil monsters met their death beneath the mighty strokes of brave knights, where all was glorious and lovely and wonderful, and nothing resembled the dull monotony of daily life. There were no drunken, stupid, dwarfed little men, and instead of half-rotten wooden barracks, were gold-gleaming palaces and impregnable mountains of iron soaring to heaven, and while in thought they wandered through this wondrous fantasy realm of romance, at their backs the mad cobbler played his harmonica and sang his rhyming couplets:

"I'll serve the devil only
While my life is whole,
So when I am done for,
He cannot catch my soul."

"That's the way, my brothers," he went on, "keep it up every day. God loves the happy men."

The harmonica began to whimper again as though it taxed it to overtake the hurrying voice of the cobbler, then he sang a jolly dance tune, his voice as it were running a race with the accompaniment:

"Never mind if in your youth
Your lot be cold and rough,
Once you make your way to Hell,
You'll find it hot enough."

Every verse gained laughter and applause from the audience. The sounds of the harmonica mingled with the clatter of glasses, the heavy tread of the drinkers, and the noise of the benches dragged here and there, and the whole blended into a wild tumult, not unlike the howling of the winter storm through the forest.

But in the little cabin, shut off from this chaos of noise only by a thin partition of wood, the two boys sat bent over the book, and one read aloud softly,

"The knight caught the monster in his iron embrace, and it bellowed like thunder with wrath and pain."

CHAPTER VII

After the book of the Knight and the dragon came other wonderful works of the same kind—"Guak, or Invincible Loyalty," then "The History of the Brave Prince Franzil of Venice and the Young Queen Renzivena," and all impressions of reality in Ilya's mind gave way before the knights and ladies. The comrades in turn stole twenty kopeck pieces out of the bar till, and so had no lack of books. They became acquainted with the adventurous journeys of "Jashka Sinentensky," they delighted in "Japantsha the Tartar Robber-chief," and more and more they deserted the harsh pitiless realities of life for a realm where man at all times could tear asunder the bonds of Fate and make a prize of happiness. They lived long in the thrall of these fairy tales. Ilya retained the memory of only one event of his daily life during this time. One day Perfishka was summoned to the police station. He went in fear and trembling, but came joyfully back, and with him, Pashka Gratshev, whom he held fast by the hand lest he should run away again. Pashka's eyes looked as quick and bright as ever, but he had become terribly thin and yellow, and his face had no longer its former froward expression. The cobbler brought him into the bar, and began to relate, his left eye twitching rapidly.

"Behold, my friends, here we have Mr. Pavlusha Gratshev back again as large as life—just back from the town of Pensa conveyed by favour of the police. Ah! what people there are in the world! No staying happily at home for them! When they're hardly able to stand upright they're off into the wide world to seek their fortune."

Pashka stood by, one hand in the pocket of his tattered trousers, while he strove to detach the other from the cobbler's hold, looking at him sideways, darkly.

Some one advised Perfishka to give him a good sound thrashing, but the cobbler answered seriously, letting the boy go:

"What for? let him wander a bit, perhaps he'll find his happiness."

"He'll get jolly hungry, anyway," threw in Terenti, then added in a friendly tone, giving Pashka a bit of bread.

"Here, eat it, Pashka."

Pashka took the bread quietly and went towards the tap-room door.

"Whew!" the cobbler whistled after him, "going off again? Good-bye then, my friend."

Ilya, who had witnessed this scene from the door of his room, called Pashka back.

The lad stayed a moment before answering, then went up to Ilya and asked, looking suspiciously round the little room:

"What do you want?"

"Only to say how d'ye do."

"All right, good day to you."

"Sit down a minute."

"Why?"

"Oh, we'll have a chat."

The short sulky questions, and the hoarse, harsh voice made a painful impression on Ilya. He wanted to ask Pashka where he had been all the summer and what he had seen. But Pashka, who had found a chair and begun to gnaw his bread, started questioning on his own account.

"Finished school?"

"Early next year I'm done."

"Well, I've done my learning too!"

"Why—how?" said Ilya, incredulously.

"I've been pretty quick, eh?"

"Where did you learn?"

"In prison, with the prisoners."

Ilya approached him and asked, looking respectfully into the thin face, "How long were you in? Was it bad?"

"Oh, not so bad—four months I had of it in several prisons and different towns. I got to know some fine people there, my boy, ladies too—real swells! Spoke different languages and knew everything. I always swept out their cells. Very nice people they were, if they were in gaol."

"Were they thieves?"

"No, regular villains," answered Pashka, proudly.

Ilya blinked and his respect for Pashka increased still more.

"Russians?"

"A couple of Jews too—fine fellows! I tell you, my lad, they knew their way about. Stripped everyone that they got a hand on—properly. Got caught in the end, and now going to Siberia!"

"But how did you learn things there?"

"Oh! I just said 'teach me to read,' and they did."

"Have you learnt to write too?"

"Writing I'm not so good at, but I'll read as much as you like. I've read lots of books already."

Ilya became excited now the conversation turned on books.

"I read with Jakov, too," he said, "and such books!"

Both began to name all the books they had read, in rivalry. Pashka had to admit with a sigh:

"I see, you've read the most, you lucky devil, and your books are nicer too. I've read mostly poetry. They had a lot of books there, but nearly all verses."

Jakov came in at this point, he raised his eyebrows and laughed:

"Now then sheep, what are you laughing at?" Pashka greeted him.

"Hullo! Where have you been?"

"Where you'll never be able to go."

"Just think," put in Ilya, "he's been reading books, too!"

"Really?" said Jakov, and came nearer in a more friendly way.

The three boys sat close together, in lively desultory conversation.

"I've seen such things, I couldn't even tell you!" cried Pashka, proud and excited. "Once I went two days without eating—not a bite! I've spent a night in the forest, alone."

"Was it bad?" asked Ilya.

"You go and try it, then you'll know. And once the dogs nearly killed me. That was in Kazan, where they put up a monument to a man, just because he made verses. A great, big man he was—his legs, I tell you, as thick as that, and his fist as big as your head, Jakov. I'll make you some poetry, boys—I know how, a bit."

He suddenly sat straight up, drew his legs in, and, looking steadily at one point, he said, quickly, with a serious, important air:— —

"Men, well fed and richly dressed
Pass through the streets all day,

But if I beg a bit of bread
They answer—go away!"

He stopped, looked at the other two, and hung his head down. For a minute they all stared in an embarrassed silence, then Ilya asked, hesitatingly:——

"Is that poetry?"

"Can't you hear?" replied Pashka, crossly. "It rhymes—day, away—so of course it's poetry."

"Of course," chimed in Jakov, quickly. "You're always finding fault, Ilya."

"I've made more poetry than that!" Pashka turned to Jakov and went on again:——

"The earth is wet and the clouds are grey,
The autumn draws nearer, day by day,
And I—have no house for the winter's cold
And my clothes are tattered and worn and old."

"Ah!" said Jakov, and looked at Pashka with round eyes.

"That was regular poetry," admitted Ilya.

A fleeting blush passed over Pashka's face and he screwed up his eyes as if the smoke had got into the room.

"I shall make a long poem," he boasted. "It's not so very difficult. You go out and look about you—stream, dream, tree, free—the rhymes come up by themselves."

"And what will you do now?" asked Ilya.

Pashka let his glance wander round; there was a pause, then he said, slowly and vaguely, "oh, something or other," then added decidedly, "If I don't like it, I'll run away again."

For the time being, however, he lived with the cobbler, and every evening the children gathered there. It was quieter and more cosy in the cellar than in Terenti's room. Perfishka was seldom at home. He had sold for drink all that could be sold, and now worked by the day in various workshops, and if there was no work to be got, he sat in the bar-room. He went about half-clothed and barefoot, and his beloved old harmonica was always under his arm. It had come to be almost a part of his body, it had absorbed a portion of his cheerful disposition. The two were very much alike, out at elbows and worn, but full of jolly songs and tunes. In all the workshops of the town, Perfishka was known as a tireless singer of gay rollicking rhymes and dance tunes. Wherever he appeared he was a welcome guest, and all liked him because he could lighten the heavy weary load of existence, with his drolleries tales and anecdotes.

Whenever he earned a couple of kopecks, he gave his daughter the half. His only care now was for her. For the rest, Masha was mistress of her own fate. She had grown tall, her black hair fell below her shoulders, her big dark eyes looked out on the world seriously, and she played the hostess in the underground room most excellently. She collected shavings from the places where new building was in progress, and tried to cook the soup with them, and up to midday went about with her skirts tucked up, quite black, and wet, and busy. But once her meal was prepared, then she cleaned up the room, washed, put on a clean dress, and settled herself at the table before the window to mend her clothes. While she cobbled away with her needle at the rags, she would sing a gay song, and in her liveliness and activity, she was like a titmouse in a cage.

Matiza would often pay her a visit, and bring her rolls of bread, tea, and sugar, and once even gave her a blue dress. Masha received the visit quite like a grown-up person, a proper housewife. She would put the little samovar on the table and serve Matiza with tea, and while they enjoyed the hot stimulating drink, they would chat of the events of the day and Perfishka's conduct. Matiza used to get quite carried away with anger over the cobbler, while Masha, in her clear little voice, would not dispute, out of politeness to her guest, but still would speak of Perfishka without a trace of resentment. In everything that she said of her father, a resolute forbearance was always present.

"Quite true," she would say, in an old-fashioned way, "it is not reasonable for a man to drink so. But he loves gaiety, and only drinks to cheer himself up. While mother was alive, he did not drink much."

"Serve him right, if his liver dries up," grumbled Matiza, in her deep bass, contracting her eyebrows fiercely. "Does the soaker forget he has a child sitting at home? Disgusting brute! He'll die like a dog!"

"He knows that I'm grown up, and can look after myself," answered Masha.

"My God! my God!" Matiza would say, with a big sigh, "the things that go on in this world of God's! What'll happen to the girl? I had a little girl just like you. She stayed at home there, in the town of Chorol, and it is so far to Chorol that if I wanted to go, I couldn't find the way. That's the way with people, they live on the earth, and forget the home where they were born."

Masha liked to hear the deep voice and see the big face and the brown eyes, like those of a cow. And, even if Matiza constantly smelt of brandy, none the less Masha would sit on her lap, nestle against her big, swelling bosom, and kiss the full lips of the well-formed mouth. Matiza used to come in the morning, and in the evening the children gathered in Masha's room. They sometimes played card games of various sorts, but more often sat over a book. Masha listened always with great interest while they read aloud, and would give a little scream at any peculiarly terrifying places.

Jakov was more careful of the child than ever. He brought her from the house bread and meat, tea and sugar, and oil in beer bottles. Sometimes even he gave her any money that was left from the purchases of books. It had become an established thing for him to do all this, and he managed it all so quietly that no one noticed. Masha, for her part, took his labours as a matter of course, and made little to do over them.

"Jakov," she would say, "I've no more coals."

"All right." And presently he would either bring some coal or give her a two-kopeck bit and say, "You'll have to buy some—I couldn't steal any."

He brought Masha a slate and began to teach her in the evenings. They got on slowly, but at the end of two months Masha could read all the letters, and write them on the slate.

Ilya had become accustomed to these relations between the two, and everyone in the house seemed also to overlook them. Many a time Ilya, commissioned by his friend, would himself steal something from the kitchen or the counter and get it secretly down to the cellar. He liked the slender brown girl, who was an orphan, like himself, but he liked her specially because she knew how to face the world alone, and conducted all her affairs like a full-grown woman. He loved to see her laugh, and would always try to amuse her, and if he did not succeed, he grew cross and teased her.

"Dirty blackbird!" he would cry, scornfully.

She would blink her eyes, and reply jeeringly, "Skinny devil!"

One word would lead to another, and soon they would be quarrelling in real earnest. Masha was hot tempered and would fly at Ilya to scratch him, but he readily escaped laughing.

One day, while they were playing cards, he saw her cheat, and in his rage, called at her:

"You—Jashka's darling!" and followed it with an ugly word, whose significance he understood already. Jakov, who was present, laughed at first, then seeing his little friend's face contract with pain at the insult, and her eyes shine with tears, he became pale and dumb. Suddenly he sprang from his chair, flung himself on Ilya, struck him on the nose with his fist, grasped him by the hair and threw him to the ground. It all happened so quickly that Ilya had no time to defend himself, then he picked himself up and rushed headlong at Jakov, blind with wrath and pain. "Wait, my boy, I'll teach you," he shouted furiously. But he saw Jakov with his elbow on the table, crying bitterly, and Masha beside him saying to him with a voice choked with tears:

"Let him alone, the beast—the brute—they're a bad lot, his father's a convict, and his uncle's a hunchback—and a hump'll grow on you too, you beast," she cried, attacking Ilya quite furiously.

"You beastly dirt-grabber—rag-picker! Come here—just you come here, and I'll scratch your face for you—you dare touch me!"

Ilya did not stir. He was much distressed at the sight of Jakov crying, for he had not meant to hurt him, and he was ashamed to scuffle with a girl—though she was ready enough he could see. Without a word he left the cellar and paced the courtyard for a long time, his heart tortured with bitter feelings. At last he went to the window and looked carefully in from above. Jakov was playing cards again with his friend, Masha, the lower part of her face concealed with her cards held fanwise, seemed to be laughing, while Jakov looked at his cards and touched first one then the other. Ilya's heart was heavy. He walked up and down a while longer, then boldly and decidedly went back to the cellar.

"Let me come in again," he said, going up to the table.

His heart thumped, his face burned and his eyes were downcast. Jakov and Masha said nothing.

"I'll never insult you so again, by God, I won't any more," he went on, and looked at them.

"Well, sit down then—you!" said Masha, and Jakov added:

"Silly! You're big enough now to know what you're saying."

"No no, we're all little—just children," Masha put in, and struck the table with her fist, "and that's why we don't need any low words."

"You gave me a jolly good licking, all the same," said Ilya to Jakov reproachfully.

"You deserved it, don't complain!" said Masha, sententiously, and with a darkened face.

"All right—all right I'm not angry, it was my fault," and Ilya smiled at Petrusha's son. "We'll make it up, shall we?"

"All right, take your cards."

"You wild devil!" said Masha.

And with that peace was made. A moment later, Ilya was deep in the game, thoughtfully wrinkling his brow. He always arranged to play next to Masha; he disliked her to lose, and thought of little else all through the game. But the child played quite cleverly, and generally it was Jakov who lost.

"Oh you goggle eyes!" Masha would say, pityingly, "You've lost again."

"Devil take the cards!" answered Jakov, "it's jolly dull, nothing but playing cards. Let's read some more Kamtchadalky."

They got out a torn and dirty book and read the sorrowful history of the amorous and unfortunate Kamtchadalky.

When Pashka saw the three children amuse themselves so pleasantly, he used to say in the tone of a world explorer:

"You lead a pleasant life here, you cunning ones."

Then he would look at Jakov and Masha and smile, then add seriously:

"Go on all the same! and later on you can marry Masha, eh Jakov?"

"Silly," Masha would say, laughing, and then they all four laughed together.

Pashka was generally with them. If they had finished a book or if there was a pause in the reading, he would relate his experiences, and his tales were no less interesting than the books.

"When I found, lads, that I couldn't travel easily without a passport, I had to be very cunning. When I saw a policeman, I used to walk faster, as if some one had sent me on an errand, or I'd get up alongside the nearest grown up person, as if he was my master or my father, or some one; the policeman would look at me and let me go on, he didn't notice anything.

"It was jolly in the villages. They don't have policemen, only old men, and old women and children, peasants that work on the fields. If any one asks me who I am, I say a beggar; whom I do belong to? No one, got no relations. Where do I come from? From the town. That's all. They'd give me things to eat and drink—good things. And then you can go where you like, can run as fast as you like or crawl if you want to. And the fields and the woods are everywhere, the larks sing, you feel as if you could fly up with them. When you're full, then you don't want anything else; feel as if you could go to the end of the world. It's just as if someone was coaxing you on, like a mother with a child. But lots of times I've been jolly hungry. Oho! and my stomach wasted inside, it was so dried up. I could have eaten the dirt, my head was giddy; but then if I got a bit of bread and got my teeth in it—ah—aah—that was good—I could have eaten all day and all night. That was something like! All the same I was glad when I got into prison. At first I was frightened, but soon I was quite pleased.

"I was always so frightened of the police. I thought when they first got hold of me and began to cuff me, they'd kill me. But what d'you think it was like really? He just came softly behind and nipped me by the collar—snap!—I was looking at the watches in a jeweller's window. Oh, such a lot. Gold ones and others. All at once—snap! I began to howl, and he says quite friendly, 'who are you? Where do you come from?' So I just told him—they found it out, they know everything. 'Where do you want to go?' they ask you then. I said 'I'm wandering about'—they laughed. Then I went to gaol. They all laughed there, and then the young gentlemen took me—they were devils if you like—oho!"

Pashka never spoke of the "gentlemen" without interjections—evidently they had made a deep impression on him, though their aspect had become vague in his memory like a big, dark spot. Pashka remained a month with the cobbler, then disappeared again. Later on Perfishka found out that he had entered a printing works as an apprentice and was living in a distant quarter of the town. When Ilya heard it he was filled with envy and said to Jakov with a sigh:

"And we two have got to stay rotting here!"

CHAPTER VIII

At first after Pashka's disappearance Ilya felt as though he missed something, but soon he slipped back into his unreal wonderworld. The book-reading proceeded busily and Ilya's soul fell into a pleasant half-asleep condition.

The awakening was sudden and unexpected. Ilya was just starting for school one day when his uncle said to him:

"You'll soon be done with learning now. You're fourteen years old. You'll have to look out for a place for yourself."

"Of course," added Petrusha, "that won't be difficult among all our acquaintances. There's a place ready for Jashka—another year and he goes behind the counter. And for you, Terenti, I'll open another place close by, you can run it on account, and be your own master. H'm, yes! I may well thank the Lord. He has cared for me."

Ilya heard these speeches as though they came from somewhere a great way off. They bore no relation to anything that he was busied with then, and left him completely cold. But one day his uncle waked him early in the morning and said: — —

"Get up and wash yourself—but be quick."

"Why, what's the matter?" asked Ilya, sleepily.

"It's a place for you. Something has turned up, thank God! You're to go into a fishmonger's."

Ilya's heart sank with unpleasant anticipation. The wish to leave this house, where he knew everything and was used to everything, suddenly disappeared, and Terenti's room, which he had never liked, all at once seemed so clean and bright. With downcast eyes he sat on his bed and had no inclination to dress. Jakov came in, unkempt and grey in the face, his head bent towards his left shoulder. He gave a fleeting glance at his friend, and said:

"Come on! Father's waiting. You'll come here often?"

"Of course, I'll come."

"Now, go and say good-bye to Masha!"

"But I'm not going away for altogether," cried Ilya, crossly.

Masha came in herself at this point. She stood by the door, looked at Ilya, and said sorrowfully:——

"Good-bye, Ilya"

Ilya tugged at his jacket, got into it somehow, and swore. Masha and Jakov both sighed deeply.

"Come and see us soon."

"All right, all right!" answered Ilya, crossly.

"See how he begins to stick it on—mister shopman!" remarked Masha.

"Oh you silly goose!" answered Ilya, softly and reproachfully.

Two minutes later he was going along the street beside Petrusha, who was dressed in his best clothes, with a long overcoat and creaking boots.

"I'm taking you to a most worthy man, that all the town respects," said Petrusha, in an impressive tone, "to Kiril Ivanitch Strogany. He has been decorated and all sorts of things for his goodness and his benevolence; he is on the Town Council, and may be chosen Burgomaster. Serve him well and properly, and he may do something for you. You're a serious lad, and not a spoiled darling, and for him to do anyone a good turn's as easy as spitting."

Ilya listened, and tried to picture the merchant Strogany. He imagined in an odd way that he must be like Jeremy, as withered up and as good-hearted and sociable. But when he reached the fish-shop, he saw behind the desk a tall man with a big belly. There was not a single hair on his head, but from his eyes to his neck, his face was covered with a thick red beard. His eyebrows too, were red and thick, and from underneath them a pair of little greenish eyes looked angrily round about.

"Bow to him," whispered Petrusha to Ilya, indicating the red-bearded man with his eyes. Disillusioned, Ilya let his head sink on his breast.

"What's his name?" a deep bass voice boomed through the shop.

"He's called Ilya," answered Petrusha.

"Well, Ilya, open your eyes and listen to me. From now, there's no one in the world for you but your employer—no relations, no friends, d'you see? I'm your father and mother—and that's all I've got to say to you."

Ilya's eyes wandered furtively about the shop. Huge sturgeons and shad were in baskets with ice, against the walls; on shelves were piled up dried perch and carp, and everywhere gleamed small tin boxes. A penetrating reek of brine filled the air, and all was stuffy and close and damp in the shop. In great tubs on the floor swam the live fish, slowly and noiselessly — sterlet, eel-pout, perch, and tench. In one a little pike dashed angrily and quickly through the water, hustling the other fish, and splashing water on to the ground with great strokes of its tail. Ilya felt sorry for the poor thing. One of the shopmen, a little fat man, with round eyes and a hooked nose, very like an owl, told Ilya to take the dead fish out of the tubs. The lad tucked up his sleeve and plunged his arm carefully into the water.

"Take 'em by the head, stupid," said the shopman, in a low voice. Sometimes by mistake Ilya caught hold of a live fish that was not moving. It would slip through his fingers, dart through the water wildly hither and thither, and strike its head against the sides of the barrel.

"Get on! get on!" commanded the shopman, but Ilya had got a fin bone stuck in his finger, and put his hand to his mouth and began to suck the place.

"Take your finger out of your mouth," resounded the bass voice of his employer. Next a big heavy hatchet was given to the boy, and he was ordered to go to the cellar and smash up ice into even-sized pieces. The ice splinters flew in his face and slipped down his neck; it was cold and dark in the cellar, and if he did not handle the axe carefully it struck the ceiling. At the end of a few minutes, Ilya, wet from head to foot, came up out of the cellar, and said to his employer, "I've broken one of the bowls somehow."

His employer looked at him attentively, then said:

"The first time I forgive you, especially as you came and told me, but next time I'll pull your ears off."

Quite mechanically Ilya adapted himself to his new surroundings, like a little screw fitting into a big noisy machine. He got up at five o'clock every morning, cleaned the boots of his master and the family and the shopman, then went into the shop, cleaned it out, and washed down the tables and the scales. As the customers came, he fetched the goods out, and carried them to the different houses, then returned to the mid-day meal. In the afternoon there was little to do, and unless he were sent anywhere on an errand, he used to stand in the shop door and look at the busy marketing, and marvel what a number of people there were in the world, and what vast quantities of fish and meat and fruit they consumed. One day he asked the shopman, who was so like an owl: — —

"Michael Ignatish!"

"Well — what is it?"

"What will people eat when they've caught all the fish there are, and killed all the cattle?"

"Stupid!" answered the shopman.

Another time he took a sheet of newspaper from the table, and settled himself in the shop door to read. But the shopman tore it out of his hand, tweaked his nose, and said crossly:

"Who said you could do that, fool!"

This shopman did not please Ilya at all. When he spoke to his employer, he said every word through his teeth, with a respectful hissing sound, but behind his back he called him a liar, a hypocrite, and a red-headed devil. Every Saturday and the eve of every saint's day, when his chief had gone to evening service, the shopman had a visit from his wife or his sister, and used to give them a big parcel of fish and caviare and preserves. He thought it a great joke to banter the poor beggars, among whom many an old man would remind Ilya very strongly of Grandfather Jeremy. If such an old man came to the shop door and begged for alms, the shopman would take a little fish by the head and hold it out, and as soon as the beggar took hold of it, the back fin would stick into his palm till the blood came. The beggar would shrink with the pain, but the shopman would laugh scornfully, and cry out:— —

"Don't want it, eh? Not enough? Get out of this!"

Once an old beggar-woman took a dried perch quietly and hid it among her rags. The shopman saw. He seized the old woman by the neck, took away her stolen prize, then, bending her head back, he struck her in the face with his right hand. She made no sound of pain nor said a word, but went out silently with bent head, and Ilya saw how the dark blood ran from her nostrils.

"Had enough?" the shopman called after her, and, turning to Karp, the other shopman, he said:— —

"I hate these beggars, idlers! Beg? Yes, and make a good thing of it! They know how to get along. Christ's brothers they call them. And I, what am I, then? A stranger to Christ, I suppose. I twist and turn all my life, like a worm in the sun, and get no peace and no respect."

Karp, the other shopman, was a silent, pious fellow. He talked of nothing but churches, church music, and church worship, and every Saturday was greatly distressed at the thought that he would be late for evening service. For the rest, he was deeply interested in all sorts of jugglery, and whenever a magician and wonder-worker appeared in the town, off went Karp for certain to see him. He was tall and thin and very agile. When customers thronged the shop, he would wind in and out among them like a snake, with a smile for all and a word for all, and the whole time keeping an eye on the fat face of his employer, as though to show off his quickness before him. He treated Ilya with little consideration, and the boy accordingly was not at all devoted to him. But his employer Ilya liked. From morning till night he stood behind his desk, opening the till and throwing in money. Ilya observed that he did it quite indifferently, without covetousness, and it gave him a pleasant feeling to see it. He liked, too, that his master spoke to him more often and in a more friendly way than to the shopmen. In the quiet times when there were no customers, he would often talk to Ilya as he stood in the shop-door, sunk in thought.

"Now, Ilya. Asleep, eh?"

"No."

"Oh, aren't you? What are you so solemn about, then?"

"I—I don't know."

"Find it dull here, eh?"

"Ye—es."

"Well, never mind, never mind. There was a time when I found life dull, too, from nineteen to thirty-two. I found it very tedious working for strangers, and now ever since then, I see what a bore others find it," and he nodded his head, as much as to say:

"So it is and it can't be helped."

After two or three speeches of this kind the question began to busy Ilya, why this rich and respected man should stay all day in a dirty shop and breathe the sharp, unpleasant reek of salt fish, when he owned such a big, clean house. It was quite a remarkable house; in it all was quiet and austere, and everything was ordered by fixed immutable rules. And yet in its two stories, there lived no one beyond the owner, his wife and his three daughters, except a cook, who was also housemaid, and a manservant, who acted also as coachman, so there was little life in it. All who dwelt there spoke in an undertone, and if they had to cross the big, clean courtyard, they would keep to the sides as if they feared to walk across the wide open space. When Ilya compared this quiet, solid house with Petrusha's, against his expectations he had to admit that the life in the latter was more to be preferred, poor, noisy and dirty though it were. He marvelled at this conviction of his, and could hardly believe in it; but thoughts of this kind filled his brain more and more frequently and distinctly, and the fact that his employer lived so little in his own house, strengthened Ilya still more in his preference. He would have liked to ask the merchant just why he spent the whole day in the unrest, noise and clamour of the market and not in his house, where it was still and peaceful. One day when Karp had gone on some errand, and Michael was in the cellar picking out the dead fish for the almshouse, the master fell again into conversation with Ilya, and in the course of it the boy said with a sudden impulse:

"You might give up your business, sir—you're so rich—it's so lovely in your house and so—so dull here."

Strogany rested his elbows on the desk supporting his head and looked attentively at his apprentice. His red beard twitched oddly.

"Well," he asked, as Ilya stopped, "Said all you want to?"

"Ye—ss, yes," stammered Ilya, a little frightened.

"Come here!"

Ilya went nearer to the desk. His master caught hold of his chin, turned his face up, looked him in the face with screwed-up eyes, then asked:

"Have you heard any one say that or did you think it yourself?"

"I thought of it—really and truly."

"Oh! If you thought it yourself, all right, but I'll just tell you one thing, in future have the goodness not to talk to your employer like that, you understand—your employer. Bear that in mind, and now get to your work!"

And when Karp returned, the merchant began suddenly to speak to him, for no apparent reason, constantly looking sideways at Ilya, so openly, that the boy quickly noticed it:

"A man must follow his business all his life—all—his—life! Whoever does not is an ass. How can a man live without something to do? A man who isn't absorbed in his business, is good for nothing."

"Of course, I quite agree, Kiril Ivanovitch," said the shopman, letting his glance travel round the shop as if he was seeking something more to do. Ilya looked at his employer and fell into deep thought. Life to him among these men became more and more tedious. The days dragged on one after the other like long grey threads, unrolling from some mighty unseen skein. And it seemed to him that these days would never come to an end, but that all his life long he would stand at this shop door and listen to the tumult of the market-place. But his intelligence, already awakened by early experience and by the reading of books, was not hampered by the drowsy influence of this monotonous life, and worked on without a pause, though perhaps more slowly. Every day the lad's soul received new impressions which simmered within him, and filled his head with a cloud of ideas concerning all that passed around him. He had no one to whom he could pour out his thoughts, which were therefore hidden, in his own breast. They were many, very many—they tortured him often, but they were without definite form, they melted one into the other, or contended in opposition and lay on brain and heart like a heavy load. Sometimes it was so painful to this serious silent lad to look on at the concourse of men that he would most gladly have closed his eyes or gone somewhere far, far away—farther than Pashka Gratschev had gone—never to return to this grey dulness and incomprehensible human worthlessness.

On holy days they sent him to church. He came back always with the sense that his heart had been washed clean in the sweet-smelling, warm stream that flowed through the house of God. In half a year he was only able to visit his uncle twice. There, all went on as of old. The hunchback grew thinner and Petrusha whistled louder, and his face once rosy, was now red. Jakov complained that his father treated him harshly: "He's always growling that I must begin to be reasonable, that he can't stand a book-worm: but I can't stand serving at the bar, nothing but noise and quarrels and rows, you can't hear yourself speak. I say, 'put me out as an apprentice, say in a shop where they sell eikons and things, there isn't much to do, and I like eikons.'"

Jakov's eyes blinked mournfully; the skin on his forehead looked very yellow and shone like the bald patch on his father's head.

"Do you still read books?" asked Ilya.

"Rather! It's my only comfort—as long as I can read, I feel as if I were in another place, and when I come to the end I feel as if I had pitched off a church tower."

Ilya looked at him and said:

"How old you look—and where is Mashutka?"

"She's gone to the almshouse for some things. I can't help her much now, father keeps too sharp a look out, and Perfishka is ill all the time, so she has to go to the almshouse. They give away cabbage soup there and that sort of thing. Matiza helps her a bit, but it's hard lines for her, poor Masha!"

"It's dull here—with you—too," said Ilya, thoughtfully.

"Is it dull in business?"

"Frightfully. You've got books at least, and in our whole house there's only one book, the 'Book of Newest Magic and Jugglery,' and the shopman keeps that in his box; and what d'you think, the beast won't let me have it. I hate him. Ah, my lad, it's a beastly life for both of us, isn't it?"

"Looks like it!"

They chatted a while and parted, both very sad and thoughtful.

Another fortnight passed in this same way, when suddenly there came a sharp turning in the course of Ilya's life. One morning, while business was proceeding in a lively manner, the chief suddenly began to look for something in his desk very eagerly. An angry red covered his forehead, and the veins of his neck swelled up.

"Ilya," he shouted, "come and look here on the floor, if you can't find a ten-rouble piece!"

Ilya looked at his master, then glanced quickly over the floor, and said quietly: "No, there's nothing."

"I tell you, look—look properly!" growled his employer, in his harsh bass voice.

"I have looked already."

"Ah, ah! Wait a bit, you impudent rascal!" And as soon as the customers were gone he called Ilya, seized the boy's ear in his strong fat fingers and twisted it, snarling in his harsh voice, "When you're told to look, look! When you're told to look, look!"

Ilya pressed with both hands against his master's body, released his ear from the fingers, and cried loudly and angrily, his whole frame quivering with excitement:

"Why do you bully me? Michael stole the money. Yes, he did. It's in his left waistcoat pocket."

The owl face of the shopman suddenly lengthened; he looked very disturbed, and began to tremble. Then suddenly he let out with his right arm, and struck Ilya on the ear. The boy sprang suddenly up, fell to the ground with a loud groan, and crying, crept on all fours into a corner of the shop. As one in a dream, he heard the threatening voice of his master:— —

"Stay, there, give up that money!"

"It's a lie," squeaked the shopman.

"Come here!"

"I swear—I— —"

"I'll throw the weight at your head!"

"Kiril Ivanitch, it's my own money, may God strike me dead if it isn't."

"Hold your tongue!"

Then silence. The chief went to his room, and from there came at once the loud rattle of the balls on the counting frame. Ilya sat on the floor, holding his head, and looking with hatred at the shopman, who stood in another corner of the shop, and on his side, cast threatening looks at the boy.

"Ah, you vagabond, shall I give you any more?" he asked in a low voice, showing his teeth.

Ilya shrugged his shoulders, and said nothing.

"Wait, my boy. I'll give you something, just in case you forget me."

The shopman strode slowly across to the boy, and looked in his face with round, malignant eyes.

Ilya got up, and with a rapid movement took a long, thin knife from the counter, and said "Come on!"

The shopman stood still, measuring with a fixed glance the strong sturdy figure, with long arms and the knife in one hand, then murmured scornfully: "Pooh, you convict's brat!"

"Just come on, come on!" repeated the boy, and advanced a step. Everything whirled before his eyes, but in his breast he felt a great strength which urged him bravely forward.

"Drop that knife!" said his master's voice.

Ilya shuddered when he saw the red beard and livid face of his master, but did not move.

"Put down that knife, I tell you," repeated the merchant quietly.

Ilya, who felt as though he were moving through a dark cloud, put the knife down on the counter, gave a loud sob, and sat down again on the floor. He felt giddy. His head and his damaged ear pained him. A heavy weight that lay on his breast hindered his breathing, pressed on his heart, and rose up slowly in his throat, choking his speech. He heard his employer's voice as though he were far away.

"Here is your salary due, Mishka."

"But let me — —" the shopman tried to explain.

"Out you go, else I'll call the police."

"All right, I'll go, but keep an eye on that young cub, I advise you. He goes at people with a knife—he, he! His dear father is in Siberia, a convict—he, he!"

"Get out!"

There was stillness again in the shop. Ilya had an unpleasant feeling, as though something were crawling over his face. He wiped off his tears with his hand, looked about him, and saw his master behind his desk, examining him with a sharp searching look. Ilya got up and went towards his place at the door, staggering uncertainly.

"Stop! Hold on a minute," called out his master. "Would you really have put that knife in him?"

"Yes, I would," answered the boy, quietly, but with assurance.

"Oh, oh! What's your father in Siberia for? Murder?"

"No. Setting fire to a house."

"Good enough."

Karp, the other shopman, came back from an errand at this moment. He sat down on a stool near the door, and looked out at the street.

"Listen, Karpushka," began the master, with smile. "I've just sent Mishka packing."

"It's your right, Kiril Ivanovitch."

"Think! He robbed me."

"Impossible!" cried Karp, softly, but evidently frightened, "Is that true? The villain!"

The chief laughed behind his desk till he had to hold his sides and his red beard shook.

"Ho! ho! ho!" he laughed. "Ah, Karpushka, you conjuror, modest soul!"

Then he stopped laughing suddenly, gave a deep sigh, and said, sternly and thoughtfully, "Ah, men, men! All want to live, all want to eat, and every one better than his neighbour."

He shook his head and was silent.

Ilya, standing by the desk, felt hurt that his master paid no further attention to him.

"Well, Ilya," said the merchant finally, after a long, painful silence, "let's have a chat. Tell me, though, have you ever seen Michael steal before?"

"Yes, rather! He stole all the time. Fish and all the rest."

"And why didn't you tell me?"

"I—I——" stammered Ilya, after a short pause.

"Afraid of him, eh?"

"No, I wasn't afraid."

"So—then why didn't you say 'Master, you're being robbed'?"

"I don't know. I didn't want to."

"H'm! You only told me just now out of temper?"

"Yes," said Ilya, defiantly.

"There, see! What a young cub!"

The merchant stroked his red beard for a while, and looked earnestly at Ilya without speaking.

"And you, Ilya, have you ever stolen."

"No."

"I believe you—you have not stolen, but Karp now—this fellow Karp here, does he steal?"

"Yes, he steals," answered Ilya curtly.

Karp looked at him in astonishment, blinked his eyes and turned away as if the matter did not concern him in the least. The master's brows contracted darkly, and again he began to stroke his beard. Ilya felt clearly that something out of the common was impending and awaited the end, strung to the pitch of nervousness. The flies hovered about in the sharp, reeking air of the shop. The water in the tubs of live fishes splashed.

"Karpushka!" the chief addressed the shopman who was standing motionless in the door and looking attentively at the streets.

"What can I do, sir?" answered Karp, and hurried to his employer, looking at his face with submissive, friendly eyes.

"Do you hear what is said of you?"

"Yes, I heard."

"Well, what have you to say?"

"Nothing," said Karp, and shrugged his shoulders.

"Nothing! What d'you mean by that?"

"It's quite simple, Kiril Ivanovitch. I am a man that respects himself and so I don't feel that my character can be hurt by a boy. You see yourself how absolutely stupid he is, and doesn't understand anything. So I can forgive his wicked slander with a light heart."

"Stop, my friend! Let's have none of your juggling, but kindly tell me, has he spoken the truth?"

"What is truth?" answered Karp slowly, shrugging his shoulders and holding his head on one side. "Every one understands the truth in his own way—if you like, you can take his words for truth, but if you don't like, it's just as you wish."

Karp ended with a sigh, bowed to his employer, and made a gesture that indicated how deeply hurt he felt.

"H'm! so you leave it to me—you think the youngster silly?"

"Uncommonly silly," said Karp with brusque conviction.

"No, my lad, that's a lie," said Strogany, and laughed outright. "How he came out with the truth right in your face! Ho! Ho! Does Karp steal? Yes, he steals. Ho! Ho! Ho!"

Ilya had gone from the desk to the door and from there had listened to this conversation, which he felt clearly had in it something insulting to him. When he heard his master laugh, a joyful sense of revenge flooded his heart, he looked triumphantly at Karp and gratefully at his employer. Strogany screwed up his eyes and laughed heartily and Karp hearing his laugh, followed with a dry anxious "He! he! he!"

At the sound of this thin bleating, Strogany ordered sharply:

"Shut up the shop."

On the way to the merchant's house, Karp said to Ilya, shaking his head:

"A fool you are, an utter fool! starting all that rigmarole! d'you suppose that's the way to curry favour? You young ass! d'you think he doesn't know that Mishka and I, both of us, stole from him—he was a young man once— he! he! As he's sent off Mishka, I've that to thank you for to tell the truth, but for telling tales of me—I'll never forgive that, I tell you straight; it's stupid and wrong, too, to say a thing like that—in my presence too. No, I can't forget that; it showed that you don't respect me!"

Ilya listened, not understanding clearly, and said nothing. He had expected Karp to approach him very differently, probably to give him a good thrashing on the way home, and consequently he had been afraid to start. But in Karp's words sounded contempt more than anger, and for his mere threats Ilya cared nothing. It was the evening of that day before the meaning of the speech was clear to Ilya, when his employer sent for him to go upstairs.

"Ah! now you see! go on!" Karp called after him in a voice presaging evil.

Ilya went upstairs and stood at the door of a big room, with a long table under a hanging lamp, and a samovar on the table. His master sat there with his wife and three daughters, all red-haired and freckled.

When Ilya came in they crowded closer together and looked at him timidly out of their blue eyes.

"That's the boy," said his employer.

"You don't say so—such a young rascal," said the wife anxiously and looked at Ilya as if she had never seen him before.

Strogany smiled, stroked his beard, drummed on the table with his fingers, and said impressively:

"I've sent for you, Ilya, to tell you I don't need you any more, so get your things together and start off."

Ilya started and opened his mouth in astonishment, but could not get out a word, then turned and went out of the room.

"Stop!" called the merchant, stretching one arm out after him, and striking the table with his palm, "Stop!"

Then he held up one finger and went on slowly and composedly: "It's not only for that that I sent for you. No. I want to give you a lesson to take away with you. I wish to explain to you why I don't need you any more. You've done all right as far as I am concerned, you're a youngster that has had some education, you're industrious and honest and strong—yes, you've all those trump cards in your hand, and yet you won't suit me any more. I can't do with you in my business. Why? you ask—h'm—yes."

Ilya understood this much, that he seemed at the same time to be praised and dismissed. The contradiction would not come clear in his mind, but roused in him a strange double sensation and brought him to the idea that his employer himself did not know what he was doing. Strogany's face seemed to the lad to confirm this impression; on it there was an expression of tension, as though he were struggling in his mind with a thought for which he could not clearly find words. The boy stepped forward and said quietly and respectfully.

"You dismiss me because I took the knife to him?"

"Heavens!" cried his employer's wife. "Heavens! how insolent!"

"That is it," said the merchant complacently, while he smiled at Ilya, and tapped him with his forefinger, "you are insolent. That is the word—insolent. But a lad that goes out to work must be humble—humble and modest; the Scriptures teach it. He must sink himself in his master. Everything—his intelligence, his honesty, must be used for his master's advantage, and you take a stand of your own, and that won't do at all, you see, and that's why you're insolent; for instance, you tell a man to his face that he's a thief. That isn't good, it is insolent; if you are so honest yourself you might tell me what the man does, but quite privately. I would easily have settled the business, because I am the master. But you say right out—he steals. No, no, that won't do. If there's only one honest out of three that matters nothing; in these cases one must reckon according to circumstances. Suppose there's one honest and nine rascals, that's no good to anyone, generally the one goes to the wall, but if there are seven honest to three rascals, then you're right to speak out, d'you see? right goes with the majority, and one honest, what's the good of him? That's how it stands with honesty, my boy. Don't force your righteousness on people, but find out first if they want it."

Strogany wiped the sweat off his brow with his hand, sighed, and continued with an expression of compassion mingled with self-satisfaction:

"And then you take to the knife."

"O Lord!" cried his wife, and the three girls crowded closer together.

"It is written in the Scriptures, 'He who takes the sword shall perish by the sword.' H'm—yes—for this reason I can't keep you any more, that's the truth. Here take this half rouble and go—go your way, you need have no grudge against me, any more than I have against you. See, I give you half a rouble, take it, and I have spoken to you as one seldom speaks to a boy, quite seriously, that you may take it to heart, and so forth. Perhaps I'm sorry for you, but you're no good to me; if the linch pin does not fit, the wise man throws it away before he starts his journey. So, go your way!"

"Good-bye," said Ilya. He had listened with attention and explained the matter to himself quite simply; he was dismissed because the merchant could not get rid of Karp and leave himself without a shopman.

This thought cheered him and made him content, and his master seemed to him a very unusual man, simple and friendly.

"Take your money!" called Strogany.

"Good-bye," repeated Ilya, and held the little silver coin tight in his hand. "Thank you very much."

"There, he never cried a bit!" Ilya heard his master's wife say reproachfully.

When Ilya, bundle on back, came out of the heavy house door, it seemed to him as though he were leaving a grey, far-off land, that he had read of in some book, where there was nothing, no people, no villages, but only stones, and among these stones lived a good old magician, who showed the way out to wayfarers lost in the desert land.

It was the evening of a clear spring day. The sun was setting and the windows flamed red. Ilya remembered that other day when first he saw the town from the river shore. The bundle, heavy with all his worldly goods, weighed on his back and he slackened his speed. People on the pavements hurried by and struck against his load; carriages rolled noisily past him; the dust danced in the slanting sun rays, and over everything prevailed a sense of noisy, gay, lively activity. All that he had experienced during the year in the town was vivid in his memory. He felt like a grown-up man, his heart beat proudly and free, and in his ears rang the words of his master:

"You are a youngster that has had some education, you're not stupid, you're strong and not lazy; these are the trump cards in your hand."

"Well then, we'll try again," said Ilya to himself while he slackened his pace still more. A stirring feeling of joy possessed him, and involuntarily he smiled at the thought that to-morrow he would not have to go to the fish shop.

CHAPTER IX

When Ilya returned to the house of Petrusha Filimonov, he discovered with pleasure that he had grown considerably during the time he had spent in the shop. Every one made a point of greeting him with flattering curiosity, and Perfishka held out a hand to him. "My respects to my lord the shopman. Well brother, have you served your time? I've heard of your bold strokes. Ha! ha! Ah, brother, men will let you use your tongue to lick their boots, but not to tell them the truth."

When Mashka saw Ilya, she cried joyfully, "Ah, how tall you've grown!"

And Jakov was delighted to see his comrade again.

"This is good," he said, "now we can live together again like we used to. Do you know, I've got a book called 'The Albigenses,' such a story, I tell you! There's a man in it, Simon Montfort, he's a real monster."

And Jakov, in his vague, hurried way, started to tell his friend the contents of the book. Ilya looked at him and thought with a peaceful content, that his big-headed comrade had stayed just as he was before. Jakov saw nothing at all unusual in Ilya's conduct towards the merchant Strogany. He listened to the whole story, then said simply, "That was all right." This unmoved reception of his experience by Jakov was not to Ilya's taste. Even Petrusha, when he had heard Ilya's account of what took place in the shop, had applauded the boy's behaviour and not stinted his approval.

"You gave it him very well, my lad, very cleverly. Of course, Kiril Ivanovitch couldn't send off Karp for you. Karp knows the business, and it wouldn't be easy to replace him. But after such a scene, you couldn't stay on with him. You stuck to the truth, and played with the cards on the table, you must have come off the better."

However, a day or two after, Terenti said to his nephew softly:

"Listen. Don't be too open with Petrusha. Be careful. He doesn't like you. He abuses you behind your back. He says, 'See how the boy loves the truth, but why is it? out of sheer stupidity.' H'm, yes. That's what he says."

Ilya listened and laughed.

"And yesterday, he praised me; said I'd managed cleverly. Men are all like that, they'll praise you to your face, but behind your back they'll say things."

Petrusha's duplicity did not in the least lessen Ilya's heightened self-confidence. He felt exactly like a hero, and was convinced that he had behaved very well with regard to the merchant—better than any other had ever behaved under similar circumstances.

Two months later, when a new place had been sought for Ilya, zealously but in vain, this conversation took place between the uncle and nephew:

"Yes, it's bad," said the hunchback, gloomily, "not a place to be found for you. Everywhere it's the same thing—he's too big! What shall we do, my boy? What I do you think?"

Ilya answered decidedly and with conviction: "I'm fifteen years old. I can read and write. I'm not stupid, and if I'm insolent they'll only send me away from any other place I get. Who can do with an insolent man?"

"But then, what shall we do?" asked Terenti, anxiously, sitting on his bed and supporting himself on it with his hands.

"I'll tell you. Let me have a big box and buy me some goods—soap and scent, needles and books, all sorts of small things, and I'll go round about with them and do business for myself."

"What?—What do you mean, Ilusha? I don't quite understand. In the bar room here, in the noise, it always goes tchk!—tchk! tchk! So that my head's got weak, and then there's something never lets me alone, always the same thing, I can't think of anything else!"

A strange tortured expression showed in the hunchback's eyes, as though he wanted to reckon up something and could not get it right.

"Try it, uncle; let me go once any way."

Ilya entreated, excited by his idea which promised him freedom.

"Well, God help us! we might try."

"Ah! splendid! you'll see how it'll go," cried Ilya delighted.

"Oh dear!" Terenti sighed deeply, and went on sorrowfully: "If only you were quite grown up! Ah! then I could go away, but now you're just an anchor to hold me, it's only for your sake I stay in this beastly hole, and go down, down. I might go to some holy men and say: 'Servants of God! doers of good! interceders! I have sinned, accursed that I am, my heart is heavy, save me, pray for pardon for me to my Father!'"

And the hunchback began to weep quietly.

Ilya knew well what sin oppressed his uncle and remembered it clearly. His heart was uplifted; he pitied, but could find no words of consolation and was silent, till he saw the tears flow from the sunken, introspective eyes of his uncle, then he said: "There—there, don't cry any more! See! Wait till I get on a bit in business, then you can get away from here." After a moment's silence he resumed consolingly, "There—you'll see, you'll be forgiven."

"Do you think so really?" asked Terenti softly, and the lad repeated in a tone of conviction:

"Of course you'll be forgiven, worse things than that have been pardoned, I'm sure of it."

So it came about that Ilya took to the pedlar's trade. From morning to night he traversed the streets, with his box at his breast, while his black eyebrows contracted, and he looked out on the world full of self-confidence with his nose in the air. With his cap drawn down on his forehead, he held up his head and cried with his boyish voice beginning to break:

"Soap! blacking! pomade! hairpins! needles and thread, pins! books—beautiful books!"

Life flowed round him in a gay and tumultuous stream, and he swam with it, free and light-hearted, and felt himself to be a man even as all the others were. He drove a trade round the bazaars, went to the inns, and would order his tea importantly, drink it slowly, and eat a piece of white bread like a man who knows his worth. Life seemed to him simple, easy and pleasant.

His dreams took on clear and simple forms. He imagined how in two or three years he would sit in a clean little shop of his own, somewhere in a good street, not too noisy, and in this shop he would deal in all sorts of clean and pretty wares, that were clean to handle and did not spoil the clothes. He himself would look clean and healthy and handsome. Every one in the street would respect him and the girls would look at him with friendly glances. When his shop was shut he would sit in a clean bright little room near it and drink his tea, and read books. Cleanliness in everything seemed to him the essential determining factor of a well-ordered life. So he dreamed when trade was good and no one hurt him by rough behaviour. But if he had sold nothing and was sitting tired in the bar or somewhere in the street, then all the harshness and hustling of the police, the insulting remarks of customers, the abuse and mockery of his fellows the other pedlars, weighed on his soul and he felt within him a painful sense of unrest. His eyes opened wide and looked deeper into the web of life, and his memory, so rich in impressions, pushed into the wheels of his thought one impression after another. He saw clearly how all men strove for the same goal as he, how all longed for the same quiet, full and clean life on which his desire was set. Yet no one scrupled to thrust aside whomsoever was in his way; all were so greedy, so pitiless, and harmed one another, with no necessity, with no advantage to themselves, out of sheer pleasure in another's pain. They often laughed when they could hurt most deeply and seldom had pity on those whom they made to suffer.

Such images made his work seem hateful. The dream of a clean little shop vanished away, and he felt in his heart an enervating weariness. It seemed to him that he would never save enough money out of his trading to open the shop, and that right on into his old age he must wander about the hot, dusty streets, his box on his breast, and the straps galling his shoulders. But every success in his undertaking awakened new courage and gave new life to his dreams.

One day in a busy street Ilya quite unexpectedly met Pashka Gratschev. The smith's son tramped along the pavement with the assured stride of one free of all care, his hands in the pockets of his torn trousers, wearing a blue blouse, also torn and dirty, which was much too big for him. The heels of his big, well-worn boots clumped on the pavement at every step. His cap with a broken peak rested jauntily over his left ear, leaving half of his close-cropped head exposed to the rays of the summer sun. Face and neck alike were covered with thick greasy black dirt. He recognised Ilya from a distance, and nodded to him in a friendly way, without hastening his easy pace.

"Good luck," said Ilya. "Fancy meeting you!"

Pashka took his hand, pressed it and laughed. His teeth and eyes shone bright and dear for a moment under his black mask.

"How goes it?" asked Ilya.

"It goes as it can. When there's anything to bite at, I bite, and when there's nothing I whine and lie curled up. Ha! ha! I'm jolly glad to meet you anyhow!"

"Why do you never come to see us?" asked Ilya, smiling. It was pleasant to him to see an old comrade glad to meet him in spite of his dirty face. He looked at Pashka's worn boots and then at his own new, shining pair that had cost nine roubles, and smiled complacently.

"How should I know where you live?" said Pashka.

"With Filimonov, just the same."

"Oh! Jashka said you were in some fish shop or other."

Ilya related with pride his experiences in the house of Strogany, and how now he was keeping himself.

"That's the way," cried Gratschev approvingly, "they turned me out of the printing works just the same way, for insolence. Then I was with a painter, mixed the colours and that sort of thing, till one day I sat down on a fresh-painted signboard, and then of course there was a row, they all went for me, master and mistress, and pupils, till their arms were tired out and then sent me to the devil. Now I'm with a well-sinker, six roubles a month. I've just had dinner and I'm going back to work."

"You don't seem in a hurry with your job."

"Oh! devil take it! Whoever knows what work is doesn't get excited over it. I must come and look you up some time."

"Yes! do come."

"Do you still read books?"

"Rather. And you?"

"Yes, when I can."

"And do you still make poetry?"

"Yes, I make poetry."

Pashka laughed again happily.

"You'll come then, won't you? And don't forget the poems."

"I'll come right enough. I'll bring some brandy, too."

"Have you taken to drinking then?"

"Oh, just a little—but now, good-bye."

"Good-bye," said Ilya.

He passed on his way, thinking deeply of Pashka. To him it seemed strange that this ragged fellow had showed no envy of his own shining boots and clean clothes, indeed had hardly appeared to notice them. Again, Pashka had rejoiced openly when Ilya spoke of his independent untrammelled life. His thoughts filled Ilya with an incomprehensible unrest, and he said to himself: "Doesn't this Gratschev, then, want the same things as all the rest. What is there to wish for in life but a clean, peaceful, independent existence?"

Melancholy and unrest of this kind possessed Ilya, especially after he had visited the church. He seldom missed a service, midday or evening. He used not to pray, but would simply stand in some corner and look, without any definite thought, at the worshipping crowd and listen to the singing of the choir. Men stood there, silent and motionless, and there was a certain sense of unanimity in the stillness, as though each were endeavouring to think as all the others thought. Waves of song, blended with waves of incense, swept through the house of God, and often Ilya felt as though he were borne upwards on the stream of sound to float in the warm caressing air above. There was something that comforted the soul in the earnest, solemn voice that filled the church, so different from the hubbub of life and not to be reconciled with it. At first this feeling remained apart from everyday impressions, did not mingle with them and left him undisturbed; but later it came to him to feel as though there was something living in his heart, ceaselessly observing him; shy and anxious it dwelt concealed in a corner of his heart as he went about his accustomed business, but grew in his soul whenever he entered the church and aroused in him a strange, disquieting thought, opposing his dream of a clean, sheltered life. At such times the tales of the hermit Antipa rose in his mind, and the talk of the pious old rag-picker concerning a loving God. "The Lord sees all things, knows all things, beside Him there is nothing."

Ilya would return home full of unrest and perplexity, feeling his dreams of the future fade, and recognising that hidden in him lay something that cared not at all for his little business. But life renewed its claims on him, and this something dived quickly down again to the depths of his soul.

Jakov, with whom Ilya discussed almost everything, knew nothing of this division in his friend's soul. Indeed, Ilya came to the consciousness of it against his will, and never voluntarily let his thoughts run on this incomprehensible sensation.

His evenings were spent pleasantly. As soon as he returned, he went straight to the cellar and said to Masha quite as if he were the master in his own home:

"Now Masha, is the samovar ready?" and the samovar would be already prepared and standing on the table steaming and singing. Ilya always brought some delicacy with him, almond or honey cakes, or gingerbread or syrup, and for this Masha supplied him with tea. Besides, the girl had begun to earn money for herself; Matiza had taught her to make paper flowers, and Masha loved to shape red roses out of the thin rustling sheets. She could earn ten kopecks a day. Her father had contracted typhus, and lay for two months in hospital, returning thin and meagre with beautiful dark curls. His tousled, untrimmed beard was shaved off, and in spite of his yellow sunken cheeks, he looked five years younger. As before he worked in various shops, frequently did not even sleep at home and left all care and management of his home to Masha. She patched his clothes and called her father "Perfishka" like all the rest. The shoemaker made great fun of her demeanour to him, but felt an evident respect for his little curly-headed girl, who could laugh as heartily and cheerfully as himself.

Ilya and Jakov took their tea in the evenings with Masha as a regular custom. The three children sat at table, and drank long and deeply, chattering of everything that interested them. Ilya related all that he had seen in the town, and Jakov, who read all day long, told of his books, the scenes in the tap room, complained of his father and many times poured out a screed, quite confused and unintelligible to the other two. Masha sat all day in her underground room, worked and sang, listened to the conversation of the lads, speaking herself seldom and laughing when she felt inclined. To them all the tea tasted admirable, and the samovar covered with a thick layer of rust grinned at them in a friendly cunning way with its funny old face. Almost every day, just when the children had arranged things to their liking, it would begin to murmur and hum, pretending anger, and it would appear that there was no water in it, Masha must take it out and fill it, and this performance had to be repeated several times every evening. When the moon rode in the heavens, her light would share the festival, falling through the windows into the little room in great, glimmering streaks. This little cave, shut in with a low, heavy ceiling, and half-rotten walls, almost always lacked air and light, water and bread, and sugar and many things, but life went all the more merrily, and every night many generous feelings and many naïve youthful thoughts were born there.

From time to time Perfishka joined the company. Generally he sat on a kind of bench in a dark corner near the sturdy stove, half buried in the ground, or else he climbed on to the stove itself, and his head hung down into the room, so that if he spoke or laughed his little white teeth glimmered in the darkness. His daughter passed him a big mug of tea and a piece of sugar and bread, he would take them, laughing and say: "Many thanks Maria Perfilyevna, I am overwhelmed with your kindness." Many a time he would say with a sigh of envy, "You have a fine life, children—confound you! first rate, just like men and women," and then laughing and sighing he would go on:

"Life gets better and better—it's jollier every year; at your age I got nothing but the strap. It was always on my back, and I howled for pleasure as loud as I could. When it stopped, my back began to hurt and grumble and sulk, because it missed its old friend; but it didn't have to wait long for it—it was a most sympathetic strap. That was all the company I had in my young days. You'll soon be growing up now, and will want to look back at things—the talks, and all the different things that have happened and all this jolly life, and I'm grown big and old—thirty-six—and have nothing I want to remember. Not a spark; nothing has remained in my memory, as if I'd been deaf and blind all my young days, I only remember how my teeth chattered for hunger and cold, and the blue patches on my face; how my bones and my ears and my hair stayed healthy I can't understand. They didn't quite hit me with the stove, but on the stove, bless you, they thrashed me to their hearts' content. That was an education for you; they twisted me about like a bit of thread; but flog me as they liked, and hack me to pieces, and suck my blood as they liked, the Russian in me clung to his life! tough fellows these Russians! Pound them to bits, and they'll come up smiling! See me! they ground me to powder and cut me to ribbons, and here I live happily like the cuckoo in the wood, flutter from one alehouse to another, and am at peace with all the world. God loves me, you know; if he saw me, He'd just say: 'Oh! it's you,' He'd say, and let me go on."

The youngsters listened and laughed. Ilya laughed with the others, though Perfishka's sing-song voice awakened in him a thought which always came back and back obstinately and occupied him greatly. One day he tried to get clear about it and asked the cobbler with an incredulous laugh: "And is there really nothing in all the world that you want, Perfishka?"

"Oh! I don't say that. A mouthful of brandy, for instance, I'm always wanting."

"No, tell me the truth! There must be something in the world that you want," persisted Ilya.

"Want to know the truth, do you? Well then, I should like a new harmonica, a right-down good harmonica, say twenty-five roubles. Ha! ha! *then* I'd play to you!"

He stopped and laughed comfortably. Suddenly a thought pricked him, he became serious and said to Ilya, gravely:

"N—no, brother! I don't want a new one! In the first place, it's dear and I should pawn it for drink, for sure, and secondly, suppose it turned out worse than the one I have, what then? She's a real beauty, the one I've got. Beyond all money. My soul's gone into her, she understands me so well, just my finger on the keys and away she sings! She's a rare treasure—perhaps there's not another like her in the world. A harmonica, she's like a wife. Once I had a wife too, an angel—not a woman, and if I wanted to marry again—how could I? I'd never find another like my dear. Whether you like it or not, you get measuring the new one by the old, and if she isn't enough, it's bad, for me and for her. That's the way of things. Ah! brother, a thing isn't good when it's good, but when it pleases you."

Ilya could readily agree with Perfishka's praise of his instrument. No one who heard it but wondered at its ringing, tender tone. But he could not reconcile himself with the thought that the cobbler had no desire in the world. Clear and sharp, the question met him—can a man live his whole life in dirt, go about in rags, drink brandy, play the harmonica and never long for anything different, better? He had no wish to regard the contented Perfishka as half silly. He observed him constantly with the greatest interest, and was convinced that the cobbler at heart was better than all the other people in the house, tippler and good for nothing though he were.

Sometimes the young people ventured to approach those great and far-reaching questions, which open fathomless abysses before mankind, and draw down by force into their mysterious depths man's eagerly inquiring spirit and his heart. It was always Jakov who began on these questions. He had acquired an odd habit of leaning against everything as though his legs felt insecure. If he were sitting, he either held on to the nearest fixed object with his hands or supported his shoulder against it. If he were walking along the street with his quick, irregular strides, he would grasp the stone posts by the way as though he were counting them, or try the fences with his hand as though to test their stability. At tea in Masha's room, he sat generally at the window, his back against the wall and his long fingers holding fast to the chair or the edge of the table. Holding his big head sideways, with its fine, smooth, tow-coloured hair, he would look at the speaker and the blue eyes in his pale face were either wide open or half closed. He loved, as of old, to relate his dreams, and could never re-tell the story of a book he had been reading without adding something singular and incomprehensible. Ilya reproached him for this habit, but Jakov was undisturbed and said simply:

"It's better as I tell it. One mustn't alter the Holy Scriptures, but any other books, one can do as one likes about. They're written by men and I'm a man too. I can improve them if I want to. But tell me something different. When you're asleep, where is your soul?"

"How should I know?" answered Ilya, who disliked questions that roused a painful disquiet in him.

"I believe they just fly away," Jakov explained.

"Of course they fly away," Masha confirmed him in a tone of conviction.

"How do you know that?" asked Ilya sternly.

"Oh! I just think so."

"Yes, that's it, they fly away," said Jakov thoughtfully, smiling, "They must rest some time, that's how the dreams come."

Ilya did not know how to answer this observation, and said nothing in spite of a keen wish to reply. For a time all were silent. It became darker in the dim cave of a cellar; the lamp smouldered, a strong-smelling vapour came from the charcoal under the samovar. From far away a dull mysterious noise rolled down to them; it came from the bar room in wild riot and confusion above their heads, and again Jakov's voice was heard:

"See, men make a row, and work, all that sort of thing. They call that living, and then all at once—bang! and the man's dead. What does that mean? What do you think, Ilya?"

"It doesn't mean anything, they're old and they've got to die."

"That won't do, young people die, and children—healthy people die too."

"If they die, they're not healthy."

"What do men live for, anyway?"

"That's a clever question!" cried Ilya, mockingly, since he felt able to reply to this. "They live, just to live; they work and try to be happy. Every one wants to live well, and tries to get on; they all look out for chances to get rich and live comfortably."

"Yes, poor people. But rich people, they've got everything to start with, they've nothing to look out for."

"Ain't you clever! Rich. If there weren't any rich, whom would the poor work for?"

Jakov thought a little and then asked:

"You think then that every one lives just to work?"

"Yes, certainly, that is—not quite all. Some work and the rest just live. They worked before, saved money, and now they just enjoy their life."

"And what do people live for, anyhow?"

"Oh! get out with you! Because they want to. Perhaps you don't want to?" cried Ilya out of all patience. He could not have said exactly why he was annoyed, whether that Jakov raised these questions at all, or whether that he asked so stupidly. He felt definite doubts arise in him under the interrogations, and he could find no clear answer.

"Why do you live yourself? tell me that, then, why?" he shouted at Jakov.

"I don't know," answered Jakov resignedly. "I'd just as soon die. It must be beastly; still I'd like to know what it's like."

Then suddenly he began in a tone of friendly reproach:

"There's no reason to get cross. Just think; men live to work, and work comes because of men; it's just like turning a wheel, always in the same place, and you can't see why it goes round. But where does God come in? He's the axle of it all. He said to Adam and Eve, 'Be fruitful and multiply and people the earth,' but why?"

He bent over towards Ilya, and whispered mysteriously with an expression of fear in his blue eyes:

"Do you know, I believe the good God told them why; but then some one came and stole the explanation, stole it and hid it away, and that was Satan; who else could it be? and that's why no man knows why he is alive."

Ilya listened to the disconnected sentences, felt them possess his soul and was silent. But Jakov continued faster and more softly, fear quivered on his pale face, and his speech became more confused:

"What does God want of you? Do you know? Aha!" It sounded like a cry of triumph out of the flood of his trembling words. Then again they poured out of his mouth tumultuously in disconnected whispers. Masha gazed astounded, open-mouthed at her friend and protector. Ilya wrinkled his brows. He was pained that he could not follow Jakov's words. He considered himself the cleverer, but Jakov constantly reduced him to wonder by his wonderful memory and the fluency with which he spoke on all kinds of difficult questions. If he became weary of listening silently, and too straitly caught by the heavy cloud that Jakov's words begot in him, then he used to interrupt the speaker angrily:

"Oh! shut up for any sake! What are you babbling of? You've read too much, that's the truth—do you understand yourself what you say?"

"But that's just what I'm saying, that I don't understand at all," answered Jakov, wounded and obstinate.

"Then say straight out I don't understand anything, instead of chattering like a maniac, while I've got to listen to you!"

"No, wait a minute," Jakov went on. "Everything is beyond our understanding. Take the lamp, for instance—I see there is fire in it, but where does the fire come from? One minute it's there and the next it's gone. You strike a match, it burns—then the fire must be in it all the time—or does it fly about in the air, invisible?"

Ilya let himself be attracted by this new question. His face lost its contemptuous expression, and looking at the lamp, he said:

"If it were in the air, then it would always be warm. But the match burns just the same in the frost, so it can't be in the air."

"But then, where is it?" and Jakov looked expectantly at his friend.

"It's in the match," Masha's voice struck in. But the two friends, absorbed in the weighty argument, let Masha's remark pass unperceived. She was quite used to the treatment and did not resent it.

"Where is it?" cried Jakov again excitedly.

"I don't know, and I don't want to know! I only know you'd better not put your hand in it, and that it is warm when you're near it. That's enough for me."

"Oh! how clever!" cried Jakov with lively displeasure. "I don't want to know. I can say that, any fool can. No, explain to me, where does the fire come from? Bread I can understand, the corn gives the grain, and from the grain comes the flour, and the dough from the flour, and there's the bread. But what is man born for?"

Ilya looked with astonishment and envy at the big head of his friend. Sometimes when Jakov's questions drove him into a corner, he sprang up and uttered harsh, insulting words, more often he drew back to the stove, leant his broad, sturdy figure against it, and said, shaking his curly head and accentuating his words:

"You make my head go round with your topsy-turvy talk. What sort of a life do you live? To stand behind a counter—that's not so very difficult. You want to see the whole of life stand before you like a statue; you ought to wander about the town from morning to night, day after day like I do and earn your own bread, then you wouldn't worry your head over such silly things, you'd think all the time how to manage things so as to get on. Your head's so big that all this trash spreads about in it. Clever thoughts are small, they don't drive your head silly."

Jakov sat silent, bent over his chair, gripping the table. From time to time his lips moved soundlessly, and his eyes blinked. But when Ilya had finished and sat down again, Jakov began to philosophise anew:

"They say there's a book—a science—called 'Black Magic.' Everything is explained in it, how and why and wherefore. I'd like to find that book and read it, wouldn't you? It must be very horrible."

During the conversation, Masha had sat down on her bed and looked with her dark eyes first at one and then at the other. Then she began to yawn, swayed wearily, and finally stretched herself out on her couch.

"Now then, time for bed," said Ilya.

"Wait, I'll just say good-night to Masha and put out the lamp."

Then seeing Ilya stretch out a hand to open the door, he cried pettishly:

"Oh do wait. I'm frightened in the dark alone."

"What a fellow you are!" said Ilya contemptuously. "Sixteen, and like a little child. I'm not afraid of anything, if the devil came in my way, I wouldn't budge an inch. But you——"

He made a scornful gesture. Jakov looked once like an anxious nurse at Masha, and turned the lamp down. The flame flickered and went out and the darkness of night invaded the room silently from all sides, or on the nights when the moon stood high in the heavens, her gentle silver light streamed through the window on to the floor.

CHAPTER X

One day on a holiday, Ilya Lunev returned home, pale, with clenched teeth, and threw himself fully dressed on his bed. Wrath lay on his heart like a cold immovable lump, an aching pain in his neck kept him from moving his head, and he felt as though his whole body suffered from the bitter wrong he had undergone.

That morning a policeman had permitted him, at the price of a piece of soap and a dozen hooks, to take his stand in front of the circus, where a performance was to be given, and Ilya had placed himself conveniently close to the entrance. Then the assistant district superintendent came by, struck him on the neck, overthrew the stand that supported his box, and scattered his wares over the ground. Some things were lost, others fell in the dirt and were spoiled. Ilya picked up what he could and said: "That is not fair, sir."

"Wha—at?" said the other, stroking his red moustache.

"You've no right to strike me."

"Oh! is that it? Migunov, take him off to the station," said the assistant quietly.

And the same policeman who had given Ilya leave to stand there, took him to the station, where he was detained till the evening.

Before this Ilya had had slight conflicts with the police, but this was the first time he had been detained, and his soul was filled with shame and hate. He lay on his bed with his arms locked, and hugged the torturing sensation of pain that weighed on his heart. Behind the wall that separated his room from the bar came a confused noise of bustle and the talking of many voices, like the sound of swift turbid brooks, dashing down from the mountains in autumn.

He heard the rattle of the tin plates, the clink of glasses, the loud calling of the customers for brandy or tea or beer, the waiters' answers. "One minute! coming! coming!" and, piercing the noise like a steel string vibrating, a high, throaty voice sang dismally, "I never thought that I should lose thee." Another voice, a deep bass, that blended with the chaos, sang softly and harmoniously, "Oh, youth that passes quickly by." Then both voices united in a clear stream of melancholy notes that mastered the tumult for a second or two:

"No riches were ever my portion.
And lonely my pathway through life."

Some one cried aloud, with a voice that sounded as though it came from a larynx of dry cracked wood:

"Do not lie! for it is written, 'Be patient and abide, and I will strengthen thee in the hour of trial.'"

"Liar yourself," struck in another voice sharply and briskly, "for it is also written, 'Since thou art neither cold nor hot, I will spue thee out of my mouth.' D'you see? what have you proved?"

Loud laughter followed and then a squeaking voice: "So I gave her one in her silly face, and one on the ear, and one on the teeth, smack! smack! smack!"

"Ha! ha! ha! the devil! and what then?"

The squeaking voice went on, shrilly and rapidly. "She toppled over on to the ground and I hit her again on her pretty mouth—there's one for you, I kissed you once, and now I'll beat you."

"Hullo, you Bible reader!" cried a voice mockingly.

"No. I can't contain myself, I'm so hot-tempered. How can a fellow help it!"

"I love, I accuse, and I punish—have you forgotten? And then again, 'Judge not that ye be not judged,' and the words of King David—have you forgotten?"

Ilya listened to the quarrelling, the song and the laughter for a long time, but all fell alike on his soul and roused no familiar images. Before him in the darkness swam the lean face of the police officer who had so hurt him, with a big hooked nose, greenish, evil, twinkling eyes, and a quivering red moustache. He stared at the face and clenched his teeth harder. But behind the wall the song rose louder as the singers were carried away and let their voices ring out louder and more freely. The warm, melancholy notes found a way to Ilya's heart, and melted the icy lump of rage and bitterness that lay there.

"I wandered on so bravely," sang the high voice, "From mountain land to sea," went on the second, and then joined again:

"Siberia I have traversed
To seek the pathway home."

Ilya sighed and began to attend to the sad words of the song. They stood out against the tumult of the tap room like little stars in a cloudy sky. The clouds hurry on and the stars alternately shine out and vanish.

"My tongue was tortured with hunger,
My limbs were stiffened with frost."

"Sing away, nightingales!" a voice shouted encouragingly.

"They're singing so beautifully," thought Ilya, "that it catches hold of one's heart, and presently they'll get drunk and fight most likely; man never holds on to the good very long."

"Ah! cruel, cruel fate," lamented the tenor, and the bass, deep and powerful, intoned:

"Thou load of iron weight."

Suddenly, before Ilya's mind flashed the vision of old Jeremy. The old man shook his head and spoke while the tears flowed down his cheeks:

"I have seen—I have seen, but have never perceived the truth."

Ilya thought that Jeremy, who loved God from his heart, had saved money in secret; and Terenti feared God, and had stolen it. And all men alike are thus divided in their souls, in their breasts is a balance and the heart inclines like the indicator of the scales, now to one side, now to the other and weighs the good and the bad.

"Aha—a!" some one roared in the bar room, and at once something fell to the ground with a crash that shook Ilya's bed beneath him.

"Stop! for God's sake."

"Hold him! Ah!"

"Help! Police!"

Every moment the noise grew stronger and more vehement, a confused medley of new sounds was added to it, and roared in a wild whirling howl through the air like a pack of evil, hungry, close-chained hounds. Individual voices were lost in the chaos of uproar. Ilya listened with a certain pleasure; it pleased him to find that occur that he had foreseen. It was an exact confirmation of his opinion of mankind. He rolled over on his bed, put his hands under his head and abandoned himself again to his thoughts:

"My grandfather Antipa must have sinned greatly, if he repented in silence for eight whole years, and every one forgave him, spoke of him with respect, and called him righteous; but they drove his children to ruin. One son they sent to Siberia, the other they hunted out of the village.

"Here one must reckon in a special way." The words of the merchant Strogany returned to Ilya's mind. "If there is one honest man to nine rogues, no one is any the better, and the one goes to the wall—it is the majority that is right."

Ilya laughed involuntarily. Through his heart glided a cold, evil feeling of anger against men, like an adder. Well-known pictures rose before him— big, fat Matiza turned in the mud in the midst of the court and groaned:

"A—ah! my dearest mother—my darling mother—if only you would forgive me."

Perfishka, quite drunk, was standing by, swaying to and fro, and said reproachfully:

"How drunk she is! the pig!"

And Petrusha, healthy and red-cheeked, stood on the steps and laughed contemptuously.

Ilya thought of all these things, and his heart contracted, and became even more sober, more hardened.

The disturbance was over in the bar room. Three voices, those of two women and a man, were attempting to sing a song, but without great success. Some one had brought a harmonica; he played a little, very badly, then stopped. By the wall against Ilya's bed, two people conversed half aloud with frequent heavy sighs. Ilya listened with a strange sense of enmity:

"One lives, and works, and toils all one's life; there isn't any sense in it, and all the others live, and our sort goes hungry; we can't stand fast, brother, for all we straddle our legs."

"It's a fact."

"And one can't see how it's ever going to get better. Honest work's no good; builds no stone houses. How long can a man stand such a jolly life? His bit of strength's gone before he knows, then, that means the end."

"Ah! yes—yes—but what's a man to do?"

"And one isn't strong enough or quick enough, for dishonest work. The frog would like to taste the nut, but he's no teeth."

"O God, our Father."

Ilya sighed involuntarily. Suddenly he recognised Perfishka's voice, ringing clearly through the bustle and noise. The cobbler shouted in his quick, sing-song way:

"Fill your cup! fill it up to the brim. 'Tis your master pays, leave it to him. Let us drink, let us love! Through the world let us rove. And who ever says no, to the devil may go."

Cheerful laughter and applause followed. Then again the low voice near the wall:

"I've worked since I was a youngster. I'm near forty. Never once I've earned enough to eat. Sweat comes every day, but not soup, and at home it's all misery and crying. The children whimper, and the wife grumbles; a fellow can't stand it—you just lose your patience and go out and get properly drunk, and when you're sober, all you see is that the trouble's got worse."

"Yes—yes, it's true."

"One prays, 'Father in Heaven, have mercy. Why dost Thou send this misery?' but it looks as if He didn't hear."

"No, He doesn't seem to hear."

Ilya was weary of this mournful lamentation, and the monotonous assenting voice, which sounded even more melancholy than the other that complained. He turned on his bed, and knocked against the wall loudly. The two voices were silent.

He could no longer endure his couch; a torturing restlessness drove him to get up. He stood up, went out into the courtyard and stood on the steps full of a longing to fly somewhere away—where—he did not know.

It was late; Masha was asleep. It was no use to talk to an odd fellow like Jakov, and besides, he, too, was inside the house, in bed. Ilya never cared to go to Jakov's room, for every time Petrusha saw him there he seemed angered and his brows contracted. A cold autumn wind was blowing; a dense, almost black, darkness filled the court and the sky was invisible. All the sheds and outbuildings looked like great masses of darkness solidified by the wind. Strange sounds came through the damp air—a hurrying, a rustling, a low murmuring, like the lament of men over the misery of life. The wind whipped his breast, smote his face, blew a damp, cold breath down his back, a cold shudder ran through him, but he did not move. "I can't go on so," he thought. "I can't. Get out of all this dirt, and restlessness and confusion, live alone somewhere, clean and quiet."

"Who's there?" said a muffled voice suddenly.

"I—Ilya. Who's speaking?"

"I—Matiza."

"Where are you?"

"Here, on the wood pile."

"Why?"

"Only because——"

Both were silent.

"To-day's the day my mother died," after a moment, said Matiza's voice out of the darkness.

"Is it long ago?" asked Ilya, just to say something.

"Oh! ever so long—fifteen years—more. And your mother, is she alive?"

"No. She's dead too. How old are you then?"

"Close on thirty," said Matiza, after a pause. "I'm old already, my foot hurts so, it's swollen as big as a melon and it hurts. I've rubbed it and rubbed it with all sorts of things, but it's no better."

"Why don't you go to the hospital?"

"Too far. I can't go so far."

"Take a cab."

"No money."

Some one opened the bar room door; a torrent of loud sounds poured into the court. The wind caught them up and strewed them hither and thither in the darkness.

"And you, why are you here?" asked Matiza.

"Oh! I was dull."

"Same as I. Up in my room it's like a coffin."

Ilya heard a deep sigh. Then Matiza said, "Shall we go to my room?"

Ilya looked in the direction of the voice and answered indifferently: "All right."

Matiza went first up the stair to her garret. She set always the right foot on each step and dragged the left slowly after with a low moaning. Ilya followed, unthinking, equally slowly, as though his depression of soul hindered his ascent as much as Matiza's foot delayed her.

Matiza's room was long and narrow, and the ceiling was actually the shape of a coffin lid. Near the door stood a Dutch stove, and along the wall, with its head against the stove a wide bed; opposite the bed a table and two chairs; a third chair stood in front of the window that appeared as a dark spot in the grey wall. Up here the howling and rushing of the wind was heard very distinctly. Ilya sat down in the chair by the window, looked round the walls and asked, pointing to a little eikon in one corner:

"What picture is that?"

"Saint Anna," said Matiza softly and devoutly.

"And what's your own name?"

"Anna, too, didn't you know?"

"No."

"Nobody knows!" said Matiza, and sat down heavily on the bed. Ilya looked at her but felt no desire to speak; Matiza also was silent and so they sat for a space, three minutes or so, dumb, with no indication that they noticed one another. Finally Matiza asked: "Well, what shall we do?"

"I don't know," answered Ilya, undecidedly.

"Well, that's good," said the woman, and laughed scornfully.

"What then?"

"First you can treat me; go and get a jug of beer. No—buy me something to eat. Nothing else, just something to eat."

She faltered, coughed, and then added in a shamefaced way:

"You see, since my leg's been bad, I've earned nothing—because I can't go out; all I had is used up; to-day's the fifth day I've sat at home, so it's no wonder. Yesterday it was a near thing, and to-day I've eaten nothing; it's true, by God, it's true."

For the first time Ilya became conscious that Matiza was a prostitute. He looked close into her big face and saw that her eyes smiled a little, and her lips moved as though they were sucking something invisible. He felt a certain awkwardness before her, and yet a strange interest that he could not explain.

"I'll get you something, and beer too." He got up quickly, hurried downstairs and stood a moment before the kitchen door. Suddenly he felt a disinclination to go back to the garret; but it only flickered like a tiny spark in the melancholy darkness of his soul and at once faded out. He went into the kitchen, bought some scraps of meat from the cook for ten kopecks, a couple of slices of bread, and other odds and ends of eatables. The cook put it all in a dirty sieve. Ilya took it in both hands like a dish, went out into the passage and stood a moment, wondering how to get the beer. Terenti would question him if he fetched it himself from the bar. He called the dish-cleaner from the kitchen and bade him get it. The man ran off, was back in a moment and gave him the bottles without a word, and lifted the latch of the kitchen door.

"Hold on," said Ilya, "it isn't for myself; a friend is paying me a visit, it's for him."

"Eh?"

"I'm treating a friend."

"Oh, well, what's the odds?"

Ilya felt that he had no need to lie and was a little uncomfortable. He went upstairs, slowly, listening attentively lest any one should call to him. But there was no sound, save the roar of the storm, no one called him back and he returned to the woman in the garret, with a distinct, though shy, feeling of pleasure.

Matiza set the sieve on her lap, and with her big fingers picked out the grey fragments of meat without a word, stuffed them into her mouth and began to eat noisily. Her teeth were large and sharp, and before she took a bite she looked at the morsel all round as though to select the most tasty side.

Ilya looked at her insolently and tried to imagine how he would embrace her and kiss her, then again feared to conduct himself awkwardly and be laughed at. He turned hot and cold with the thoughts as they came. The wind swept over the house. It forced a way through the window in the roof, and rattled the door, and every time the door shook, Ilya trembled with anxiety lest any one should enter and surprise him.

"Mayn't I bolt the door?" he said.

Matiza nodded silently. Then she put the sieve on the stove, crossed herself before the picture of Saint Anna, and said devoutly:

"Praise to thee, at least my hunger is satisfied. Ah! how little is enough for the children of men!"

Ilya said nothing. She looked at him, sighed, and went on:

"And who desires much, from him also much shall be desired."

"Who will desire it?"

"Why, God! Don't you know that?"

Again Ilya did not reply. The name of God from her lips roused in him a sudden feeling, vague and not to be expressed in words, that resisted the desire of his mind. Matiza supported herself on the bed with her hands, raised up her big body and propped herself against the wall. Then she said in a careless voice:

"Just now, while I was eating, I was thinking of Perfishka's daughter. I've thought about her for a long time. She lives there, with you and Jakov; it won't be good for her, I'm afraid; you will ruin the girl before her time, and then she'll be started on the road I travel, and my road is a foul, a damnable road, and the women and girls that go along it don't go upright as men should, but crawl like worms."

She was silent for a while, looked at her hands as they lay on her knees, then went on again:

"The girl is growing tall. I've asked all my acquaintances, cooks, and other women, to see if I could get a place for the child. No, they say there's no place; they say, 'sell her, it will be better for her,' they say, 'she'll get money and clothes, and somewhere to live'—it seems as though they're right. Many a rich man whose body is failing and his mind filthy, will buy a young girl, when women won't look at him any more, and will ruin her—the beast. Perhaps she has a good time with him, but it's disgusting, all the same, really, and it's better without that. Better for her to live hungry and in honour, than——"

She began to cough, as though a word had stuck in her throat, and then finished her sentence with evident effort, but in the same indifferent voice:

"Than in shame and hungry all the same, like me, for instance."

The wind whistled along the floor and rattled fiercely at the door. A fine rain drummed on the galvanised iron roof, and outside in the darkness in front of the window a soft whistling sound was heard. "E—e—e!"

The indifferent tone, and Matiza's plump, inexpressive face, made a barrier to the feelings surging up in Ilya, and took from him the courage to express his desire. Matiza pushed him away, he thought, and he grew angry with her.

"O God! O God!" she sighed softly. "Holy Mother."

Ilya jerked his chair backwards and forwards crossly, and said:

"You call yourself impure, and all the time you're saying: 'God—God.' Do you think He cares, that His name's always on your lips?"

Matiza looked at him, then after a pause, shaking her head:

"I don't understand," she said.

"There's nothing to understand," Ilya burst out, getting up from his chair. "You're all alike! first you let your sinfulness drive you—then it's 'O God!' If you want God, then leave your sin!"

"What!" cried Matiza, troubled. "What do you mean? Who should call to God if not sinners? Who else?"

"I don't know who else," cried Ilya, feeling an unconquerable desire to wound this woman and the whole human race, deeply and cruelly. "I only know it doesn't belong to you to speak of Him, not you, at any rate. You take Him as a cover for your sins—I see. I'm not a child now. I can use my eyes. Every one laments, every one complains, but why are they all so worthless? Why do they lie, and rob one another? Why are they so greedy for a scrap of bread? Ha! ha! First the sin is committed, then it's 'O Lord, have mercy!' I see through you, you liars, you devils! you lie to yourselves, and you lie to your God."

Matiza said nothing, but looked at him with her mouth open, and her neck outstretched, and an expression of dull-witted astonishment in her eyes. Ilya strode to the door, drew back the bolt with a jerk and went out slamming the door to behind him. He felt that he had insulted Matiza grossly, and he was glad of it; his heart was lighter and his head clearer. He descended the stairs with a firm step and whistled as he went through his teeth; but his wrath still supplied him with hard, contemptuous words. He felt that all these words glowed in him like flames, and illumined the darkness of his soul, and showed the way which led him apart from mankind. The words fitted not only Matiza, but Terenti, too, and Petrusha, and Strogany, and in short, every one.

"That's it," he thought, as he reached the court again. "Just to stand no nonsense from you rabble!"

The wind chased round the court howling and whistling. Somewhere some one was knocking and the air was full of short detached sounds, like horrible, cold-blooded laughter.

Soon after his visit to Matiza, Ilya began to go after women. The first time it happened in this way. He was going home one evening when a girl spoke to him:

"Won't you come with me?"

He looked at her, then walked along beside her silently. He hung his head as he went, and looked round frequently, fearing all the time to meet an acquaintance. After a few paces side by side, the girl said, warningly: "You must give me a rouble."

"All right," said Ilya, "only hurry."

And till they reached the girl's house they exchanged no further word; that was all.

Acquaintance with women led him at once into great expense, and more and more often Ilya came to the conclusion that his pedlar's trade only wasted his time and strength to no purpose and would never help him to the peaceful life he desired to lead. He meditated long, whether to establish lotteries like the other pedlars, and so cheat the public as they did. But further consideration convinced him that these methods were too small and full of anxiety. He would have either to bribe the police or hide from them, and both courses were distasteful to him. He liked to look all men straight in the face and felt it a constant pleasure to be always cleaner and better dressed than the other pedlars, to drink no brandy and practise no deceptions. Self-controlled and self-respecting, he walked the streets, and his clean-cut face with its high cheek-bones had always a serious, sober expression. When he spoke he drew his dark eyebrows together, but he spoke seldom and always deliberately.

Often he dreamed how splendid it would be if he could find a thousand roubles or more. All thieves' tales roused in him a burning interest. He bought newspapers and read attentively all details of robberies and then looked for days to know if the thieves were discovered or no. If they were caught, Ilya would rage and say to Jakov: "Asses! to let themselves be caught, better let it alone, if they don't understand the business. Fools!" One day he was sitting in his room with Jakov when he said:

"The knaves have a better time in the world than the honest people."

A mysterious expression came into Jakov's face. His eyes blinked and he said in the subdued tone that he always had when he spoke of unusual things:

"The day before yesterday, your uncle had tea in the bar with an old man; he must have been a Bible preacher, and this old man said that in the Bible it was written: 'The tabernacles of robbers prosper, and they that provoke God are secure; into whose hand God bringeth abundantly.'"

"You're inventing," said Ilya, and looked attentively at Jakov.

"They're not my words," answered Jakov, and stretched out his hands as though to catch something in the air. "I don't believe that it is in the Bible; perhaps he made it up, the old fox. I asked him once and twice, and each time he said the words the same as before exactly. And there's something in the words sounds right; we must have a look and see if it really is in the Bible." He bent towards Ilya and went on in a low voice: "Take my father, for instance, how peacefully he lives, and yet he does things fit to rouse the anger of God."

"How?" cried Ilya.

"Now they've elected him town councillor."

Jakov let his head fall on his breast, sighed deeply, and said again:

"Everything that concerns man ought to be as clear as spring water to the conscience, and here——Oh! it disgusts me. I don't know any longer what to think. I don't know how to fit myself for this life. I don't want to. Father's always on at me, 'it's time,' he says, 'to stop your child's play, you must be reasonable at last, and make yourself useful.' But how can I make myself useful. I wait behind the counter often when Terenti isn't there, and though I hate it, I do it anyway. But to start something for myself, I don't know how."

"You must learn," said Ilya decidedly.

"Life is so difficult," said Jakov softly.

"Difficult for you? don't talk nonsense," cried Ilya, and sprang from his bed and went over to his friend, who was sitting at the window. "My life is difficult if you like, but yours, what do you want? When your father's old or dead, you'll take over the business, and be your own master, but I—I fag about the streets all day long and see in the shop windows stockings and vests, and watches, and all sorts of things, and I look at myself and think, I can't buy a watch like that. D'you understand? And I should like to ever so much, but what I want most is for people to respect me. Why am I worse than the rest? I'm better, really! Perhaps I'm a rascal, eh? I know people who think no end of themselves and are just rascals, and they get elected town councillors. They've houses and inns; why do such swindlers have all the luck, and I none? I'll get on, too. I'll get hold of my luck."

Jakov looked at his friend and said quietly, but with emphasis:

"God grant that you never get your luck!"

"What! why?" cried Ilya, and stood still in the middle of the room and looked angrily at Jakov.

"You're too greedy, you'll never get enough." Ilya laughed drily and evilly.

"I'll never get enough? Just tell your father to give me half the money he and my uncle stole from old Jeremy, that'll be enough! Yes—I'm greedy am I?—and your father first."

Jakov got up and went quietly with bowed head to the door. Ilya saw his shoulders twitch and his head bend as though he had received a painful blow in the neck.

"Stop," cried Ilya, confused, and grasped his friend's hand. "Where are you going?"

"Let go, brother," half whispered Jakov, then stood still and looked at Ilya. His face was pale, his lips pressed together and his whole figure bowed as though by a heavy load.

"Oh! don't be angry, stay a minute," said Ilya, penitent, and led Jakov from the door back to his chair. "Don't get cross with me—it's true, anyhow."

"I know."

"You know? Who told you?"

"Everybody says it."

"H'm—yes; but those who say it are rascals too." Jakov looked at him mournfully and sighed.

"I didn't believe it; I thought all the time they said it just out of meanness, out of spite. But then, I began to believe, and if you say it, too— then——"

He made a gesture to express his despair, turned away and stood motionless, his hands grasping the chair, and his head sunk on his breast; Ilya sat on his bed in the same mood and said nothing, for he did not know how to comfort his friend. Behind the wall there was outcry and noise, till the glasses rattled and the voice of a drunken woman sang:

"I cannot sleep, I cannot rest,
For slumber will not come to me."

"And this is where one has to live!" said Jakov, half aloud.

"Oh yes!" answered Ilya, in the same tone, "I can easily understand, brother, that you don't like it here. The only consolation is, it's the same everywhere, men are all alike in the long run."

"Do you know that really for a fact; that about my father and Jeremy?" asked Jakov timidly, without looking at his friend.

"I? I saw it myself; do you remember how I ran out? I looked through a chink and saw them sewing up the pillow—the old man was still gasping."

Jakov shrugged his shoulders and said nothing. They sat in silence for a long time, both in the same position, one on the bed, the other on the chair. Then Jakov got up, went to the door, and said to Ilya, "Good-bye."

"Good-bye, brother—take it easy; what can you do after all?"

"I? Nothing, unfortunately," said Jakov, as he opened the door.

Ilya looked after him, then sank heavily on his bed. He was sorry for Jakov, and again hatred welled up in him against his uncle, against Petrusha, against all mankind. He saw that a being as weak as Jakov could not live among them, such a good, quiet, clean-minded fellow. Ilya let his thoughts run freely over men and in his mind different memories rose up showing him mankind as evil, horrible, lying creatures. The times, in truth, were many in which he had seen them so, and it relieved him to let his scorn loose on them; and the blacker they seemed to him, the heavier weighed on him a strange feeling, partly a vague desire, partly a malignant joy at other's suffering, partly a fear at remaining so alone in the midst of this dark wretched existence, that raged round him like a mad whirlpool.

Finally he lost patience at lying alone in the little room, where the noise and reek pressed through the wall, and he got up and went out in the open. Till late that night he roamed the streets, bearing the heavy load of dull torturing thought. He felt as though even behind him in the darkness, some enemy strode and pushed him imperceptibly to all places that were wearisome and melancholy. All that his unseen enemy showed him roused rancour and bitterness in his soul. There is good in the world, good men, and happy events, and cheerfulness; why did he see nothing of this, but come in contact only with what was gloomy and evil? Who guided him constantly to the soiled, the wretched, and the wicked things of life? In the grip of his thoughts he strode through the fields along the stone wall of a cloister outside the town, and looked about him. Heavy and slow the clouds drifted towards him out of a vast dim distance. Here and there above his head the sky glimmered between the dark masses of cloud, and little stars looked shyly down. From time to time the metallic tones of the bell rang through the still night from the tower of the cloister church; it was the only sound in the deathly quiet that enfolded the earth. Even from the dark mass of houses behind Ilya came no sound of noisy bustle, though it was not yet late. It was a cold, frosty night. As he walked Ilya's feet struck the frozen mud. An uneasy sense of isolation and the fear that his brooding evoked, brought him to a standstill. He leaned his back against the stone cloister wall, and thought again who it might be who guided him through life, and full of mischief let loose on him always evil and hateful things. A cold shudder ran through his frame, and almost with a premonition of something awful before him, he started from the wall and hurried back to the town, stumbling more and more often over the frozen mud. His arms pressed close to his sides, he ran forward, and full of fear did not once dare to cast a look behind.

CHAPTER XI

Two days later Ilya met Pashka Gratschev. It was evening, little flakes of snow danced in the air and glimmered in the light of the lamps. In spite of the cold, Pavel wore nothing thicker than a cotton shirt, without a belt. He walked slowly, his head on his breast, his hands in his pockets, and his back bent as though he were looking for something. When Ilya stopped him and spoke to him, Pashka raised his head, looked into Ilya's face, and said indifferently:

"Oh, it's you!"

"How goes it?" asked Ilya, falling into step.

"It's just possible things might be worse. And you?"

"Oh, rubbing along."

"Not very grandly, it seems."

They walked along together silently, their elbows touching.

"Why didn't you come to see us?" asked Ilya. "I'm always inviting you."

"No opportunity, brother. You know people like us don't get much time."

"You could come if you wanted to."

"Don't be cross. You're always saying I ought to come, and for all that, you've never asked me where I live, much less thought of paying me a visit."

"You're right; it's a fact!" said Ilya, laughing. "But tell me now."

Pavel looked at him, laughed too, and went on more cheerfully:

"I live for myself. I've no friends, can't find any who can put up with me. I've been ill—three months in hospital. Not a soul came to see me all the time."

"What was wrong?"

"Caught cold once, when I was drunk. Typhus it was. When I was better, that was the worst. I lay alone all day and all night. You feel dumb and blind, like a puppy they throw into a pond. Thanks to the doctor, I had some books at least, else I should have been bored to death."

"Were they nice books?" asked Ilya.

"Ye-es, they were jolly good, mostly poems—Lermontov, Nekrassov, Pushkin. Lots of times, reading was like drinking milk. Verses, brother! To read verses is like your sweetheart kissing you. A line sometimes goes through your heart and makes the sparks fly—you feel on fire."

"And I've given up reading books," said Ilya, with a sigh.

"Why?"

"Oh, what's the good of them, after all? You read books, and things seem to go one way, and you look at the real thing, and it's all different."

"You're right there! Shall we turn in anywhere? We might have a bit of a talk. There's somewhere I must go, but there's plenty of time. Perhaps you'll come along?"

Ilya agreed and took Pashka's arm. Pavel looked him in the face, and said, smiling:

"We were never really friends, but I'm always very glad to meet you."

"That's your look-out," said Ilya, jokingly. "Don't be glad on my account."

"Ah, brother," Pavel interrupted him, "it's all very well to joke! I had something very different in my mind when you stopped me. But never mind that."

They entered the first public house they came to, sat down in a corner and ordered some beer. Ilya saw in the lamp-light that Pavel's face was thin and sunken. His eyes had a restless look, and his lips, that so often before were half-open in gay mockery, were now pressed close together.

"Where are you working now?" asked Ilya.

"In a printing works again," said Pavel, gloomily.

"Hard work?"

"Oh, no; more play than work."

Ilya felt a vague pleasure to see Pashka, once so gay and assertive, now sad and careworn. He wanted to find out what had changed his friend, and, filling Pashka's glass, began to question him.

"Well, and how does the poetry get on?"

"I let it alone now. But I made a lot of poems a while ago. I showed them to the doctor, he praised them. He got one of them printed in a paper. I got thirty-nine kopecks for it."

"Oho!" cried Ilya. "That's something like! What sort of verses were they? Let's hear them!"

Ilya's eager curiosity and a couple of glasses of beer brought Gratschev into the right mood. His eyes shone and his yellow cheeks reddened. "What shall I say to you?" he said, rubbing his forehead. "I've forgotten it all; by God, I've forgotten it. Wait, perhaps something'll come back to me. I've always a head full of this sort of stuff, like a swarm of bees inside, humming. Often when I sit down to compose, I'm in a fever, something boils away in my soul and tears come into my eyes."

"I say! How does that happen?" asked Ilya, astonished and suspicious.

"Oh! something burns and blazes in you, and you want to express it cleverly and you can't find words, and then it makes you rage." He sighed, shook his head, and went on:

"Before it comes out, it seems tremendous, and when it's written down, it's nothing."

"Say a verse or two now."

The more closely Ilya observed Pavel, the keener grew his curiosity, and following the curiosity another warm, friendly, and at the same time sorrowful feeling.

"Generally I make funny poems, about my own life," said Gratschev, and laughed constrainedly.

"All right, say a funny poem."

Gratschev looked round, coughed, rubbed his chest, and began to declaim hurriedly, in a dull voice, without looking at his friend:

"It is night, and so sad—but piercing the gloom,
The moon throws its beams into my little room.
It beckons and laughs in the friendliest way
And paints a blue pattern so cheerful and gay,
On the dull stone wall, that is damp and so cold,
And over the carpet, all tattered and old.
I sit there, fast bound by the spell of my thought
And sleep never comes, though it's longed for and
sought."

Pavel paused, sighed deeply, then went on more slowly, and in a lower voice:

"Grim fate has close gripped me in shuddering pain,
It tears at my heart, and it strikes at my brain;

Three Men | 109

It robbed me of all, when it caught at my dear,
And leaves me for comfort—this brandy-flask here.
See there, where it stands and gleams through the night,
And beckons and smiles in the moon's faint light.
The brandy shall heal me, my heart shall be well,
It shall cloud o'er my brain with the power of its spell.
Thoughts vanish in vapour, see, sleep is at hand,
Another glass, come! and all trouble is banned.
I drink yet again—who sleeps can endure,
I build against trouble a stronghold sure."

As Gratschev ended, he looked inquiringly at Ilya, then let his head fall lower and said softly:

"That's the kind of thing generally—you see, it's silly enough."

He drummed on the edge of the table with his fingers, and shifted his chair uneasily to and fro. For a moment, Ilya looked at him with a searching glance and his face expressed incredulous astonishment. The bitter, smooth running lines yet rang in his ears, and it seemed to him hardly credible that this thin beardless lad, with restless eyes, in an old cotton shirt and heavy boots, should have composed this poem.

"Well, brother, I shouldn't call that silly," he said slowly and thoughtfully, while he still looked curiously at Pavel. "On the contrary, it's beautiful, it touched my heart—say it again, will you?"

Pavel raised his head, looked delightedly at his listener, and coming closer, asked in a whisper, "No—really—do you like it?"

"Good Lord, what a queer fellow you are. I shouldn't lie to you."

"Well, I'll believe you, you're honest; you're straight, anyhow."

"Say it again!"

Pavel softly declaimed it in melancholy tones, often stammering and sighing deeply when his voice failed him. When he had finished, Ilya's suspicion was strengthened, that Pavel was not really the author of the verses.

"And the others?" he said to Pavel.

"Ah! do you know," said the other, "I'd rather bring my book to you, for most of my poems are long, and I haven't any time now. I can't remember them properly, the beginnings and ends get muddled up; there's one ends like this: I'm going through the wood at night, and I've lost my way and I'm tired—yes, and then I get frightened, it's so quiet all round. I am alone and now I'm looking for some escape from my misery and I lament:

"My feet are heavy,
My heart is weary,
No way is clear;
O Earth my mother,
Guide me and tell me
What course to steer.
Anxious I nestle,
Close to thy bosom;
I listen, I peer—
And out of the dark depths
Comes a soft whisper—
'Hide thy grief here!'"

"Not so bad, eh? That's the way of things. One goes, as it were, through a break in a forest, sees a light all of a sudden, then finds no way that'll lead to it. Listen, Ilya. Will you come with me? Come! I don't want to say good-bye yet." Gratschev got up suddenly, caught Ilya by the sleeve, and looked in his face in a friendly way.

"I'll come," said Ilya. "I'd like some more talk with you. To tell the truth, I hardly know how to believe you made those verses yourself."

"You don't believe? Doesn't matter. You'll see right enough that I did," said Pavel, as they came out into the street.

"If they are your verses, then you're a fine fellow," cried Ilya, in downright bewilderment. "Only stick to it! Show people what life is really like!"

"Right, brother. Once I've learnt properly how, then I'll write. They shall hear it."

"Good! good! Plan it out well! Let 'em know!"

"Often I think, when things are quiet, 'Ah, you people, you're full and warmly clothed, and I— —'"

"It's not fair."

"Am I not a man too?"

"We're all equal."

"He who walks in brave attire
Also eats and drinks his fill,
But he whose only clothes are rags
Has an empty stomach still."

"Ah, the hypocrites!"

"Yes, they are hypocrites, all the lot!"

They strode quickly through the streets, and caught up eagerly the passionate scattered words each threw to the other. The more excited they became the closer together they walked. Each felt a deep pure joy that the other thought as he did, and the joy heightened their mood still further. The snow, falling in great flakes, melted on their glowing faces, settled on their clothes, clung to their boots. They marched on through a thick slush that settled noiselessly on the earth.

"I see the state of things quite clearly," cried Pavel, in a tone of conviction.

"One can't go on living like this," Ilya seconded him.

"If you've ever been to the High School, then you're reckoned a gentleman, even if your father was a water-carrier."

"That's it; and how can I help it that I didn't go there, eh?"

"They're to have all the learning, and I—I'm to have nothing!" cried Gratschev, full of wrath. "Just wait a bit!"

"Oh, curse it!" cried Ilya, who that moment stepped into a mud puddle.

"Keep more to the left."

"Where are we going, anyhow—to the hangman?"

"To Sidorisha."

"Where?"

"To Sidorisha. Don't you know her?"

"N—no," said Ilya, after a moment's pause, and took two or three steps onward. "It's a good long way, we're going."

"Oh!" said Pavel quietly, "I must go, I've something to do."

"Oh! don't mind me! of course, I'll come too."

"I'll tell you Ilya, though it's hard to speak of it."

He spat into the road and was silent for a moment or two.

"What is it?" asked Lunev, pricking up his ears.

"You see," began Pavel, hesitatingly, "it's about a girl. Well, you'll see her. She can search a fellow's heart; she was a servant at the doctor's house, who cured me. I got books from him after I was better. I'd go, and then I'd have to sit in the kitchen and wait, and she was there skipping about like a squirrel and laughing; for me, I was like a wood shaving in the fire. Well, we were alone, things went quickly, without many words. Ah! the happiness! as if heaven had come down to us. I flew to her like a feather into the fire;

we kissed till our lips smarted. Ah! she was as pretty and dainty as a toy. If I caught her in my arms, she seemed to disappear. She was like a little bird that flew into my heart and sang and sang there."

He stopped, and a strange sound like a sob came from his lips.

"And what then?" asked Ilya, carried away by the story.

"The doctor's wife surprised us, devil take her! She was pretty too, and used to speak quite kindly to me before, but now of course, there was a scene. Vyerka was turned out of doors and I with her, and they blackguarded us both horribly, my word! Vyerka stayed with me. I hadn't any work and we starved and sold everything to the last thread. But Vyerka is a girl of spirit. She went off—was away a fortnight and came back dressed like a swell lady—bracelets, money in her pocket." Pashka ground his teeth and said gloomily: "I thrashed her, I tell you."

"Did she run away?" asked Ilya.

"N—No! If she'd left me I'd have thrown myself in the river. 'Kill me if you like,' she said 'but let me alone! I know I'm a burden to you. No one shall have my soul,' she said."

"And what did you do?"

"Do? I struck her once more, then I cried. What could I do; I can't find food for her."

"Why didn't she find a new place?"

"The devil knows. She said, 'it would be better this way.' If children came, what could we do with them, and so——"

Ilya thought for a little, then said: "A sensible girl."

Pashka went on a step or two in silence. Then he wheeled sharp round, stood in front of Ilya, and said in a dull hissing voice:

"When I think that other men kiss her, then it's like molten lead driving through my limbs."

"Why don't you let her go?"

"Let her go?" cried Pavel in the highest astonishment. Ilya understood afterwards when he saw the girl.

They came to a one-storied house on the outskirts of the town. Its six windows were fast shut with thick shutters so that the house had the look of an old straggling granary. The wet, sloppy snow clung to roof and walls, as though it would conceal or smother the house.

Pashka knocked at the door and said:

"This is where they're looked after. Sidorisha gives her girls board and lodging and takes fifty roubles from each of them for it; she has only four altogether. Of course she keeps wine too, and beer, and sweetmeats, and all that you want, for the rest she lets the girls do what they want to, go out if they like, or stop at home if they like, only pay the fifty every month. They are all jolly girls; they make money as easily as——One of them, Olympiada, never takes less than four roubles."

There was a rustling the other side of the door. A yellow streak of light quivered in the air.

"Who is there?"

"I, Vassa Sidorovna—Gratschev."

"Oh! The door opened and a little dried-up old woman, with a big nose in her shrivelled face, held the candle up to Pavel's face, and said in a friendly way:

"Good evening, Pashka. Vyerunka has been waiting for you for a long time, and is quite cross. Who's that with you?"

"A friend."

"Who is it?" came a pleasant voice out of a long, dark corridor.

"A visitor for Vyera," said the old woman.

"Vyera, here's your sweetheart," cried the same clear voice, ringing through the corridor. At once at the end of the passage a door opened and the dainty figure of a girl, dressed in white, appeared in the bright patch of light, with her thick fair hair streaming round her face.

"How late you are!" she said, in a deep alto voice, pouting. Then she stood on the tips of her toes, put her hands on Pavel's shoulders, and looked at Ilya out of her soft brown eyes.

"This is my friend, Ilya Lunev. I met him, and that's how I'm a bit late."

"Welcome," she said, giving Ilya her hand, so that the wide sleeve of her loose white dress fell back almost up to the shoulder. Ilya pressed her hot, dry little hand respectfully, without a word. He looked at Pavel's sweetheart, with that feeling of joyful surprise with which a man greets a slender fragrant birch-tree in a thick wood full of brambles and marshy thickets. As she stood aside to let him enter, he stepped back, bowed, and said politely:

"Please, after you."

"How polite!" she laughed.

Her laughter was pleasant, gay and clear. Pavel laughed too, and said:

"You've turned his head already, Vyerka. See, how he stands there, like a bear in front of the honey jar."

"Is that true?" asked the girl, mischievously.

"Of course," answered Ilya, laughing. "I'm quite bewildered by your beauty."

"Here, you, listen! You just fall in love with her and I'll kill you," Pavel threatened, jokingly. It pleased him that his lady's beauty should make such an impression on his friend, and his eyes shone with pride as he looked at her. She, too, paraded her charms with a naïve coquetry, convinced of their power. She wore nothing but a bodice with sleeves, over a vest and a shining white petticoat; her healthy, sound, snow-white body showed through the bodice-opening. A childish, self-contented smile twitched at the corners of her red lips; it was as though she took pleasure in herself, like a child with a toy it is not yet tired of. Ilya could not take his eyes off her. He saw how gracefully she moved up and down in the room, and how she wrinkled up her little nose, and laughed and chattered, and looked tenderly at Pavel every now and then; his heart was heavy to think he had no such friend. He sat silently and looked about him. A table covered with a white cloth, stood in the middle of the little, tidy, brightly-lighted room; on the table the samovar bubbled cheerily, and everything round about it was fresh and gay; the cups, the wine-bottle, the plate with bread and sausage — everything had a clean new look; it struck Ilya as unusual, and moved him to envy Pavel, who sat there, quite blissful, and began to rhyme extempore:

"The sight of you, like bright sunshine,
Streams over this poor heart of mine.
Forgotten all my grief and pain,
My heart begins to hope again.
To call a beautiful girl one's own
Is the greatest joy that can ever be known."

"Pashka, dear, how nice it is!" cried Vyera, delighted.

"Ah! it's hot! Hullo, you there, Ilya, leave off! Can't you look enough? Get one for yourself!"

"But she must be pretty," said Vyera, with a strange emphasis, looking Ilya in the eyes.

"Prettier than you can't be found," sighed Ilya, and laughed.

"Don't talk of things you don't understand," said Vyera, softly.

"He knows his way about," said Pashka. Then, turning to Ilya, went on, wrinkling his brow: "Here, now, everything is so clean and jolly, and then, all of a sudden—one thinks—It cuts one's heart."

"Don't think then!" cried Vyera, and bent over the table. Ilya looked at her, and saw how her ears grew red.

"You must think—" she went on, softly but firmly—"if I have only a day, still it's mine! It isn't easy for me, either, but I don't mix up the joy and the trouble; I keep it, like the song says: 'The sorrow I alone will bear, the joy together we shall share.'"

Pavel listened, but hardened his heart, in his sulky mood. Ilya longed to say something comforting, encouraging, and, after a pause, began:

"What's to be done when the knots won't be loosened? If I had lots of money, a thousand or ten thousand roubles, I'd give it to you, and say: 'There, take it, take it because of your love,' for I see it and feel it; for you it's a real true heart affair, and that is always pure to the conscience, and all the rest you can spit at."

A warm feeling flamed up and thrilled through him. He stood up when he saw the girl lift her head and look at him gratefully, while Pavel smiled, as though he waited for him to say more.

"It's the first time in my life I've seen such a beautiful thing," Ilya went on. "It's the first time I have seen how people can love one another; and, Pavel, it's the first time I've really got to know you—I've looked into your soul. I sit here and say frankly, I envy you; I'm sad and merry at the same time. God grant that all may be well with you! And—and as for the rest, let me say something. Suppose—I dislike Chuvashai and Mordvij, they're dirty and blear-eyed. But I bathe in the same river and drink the same water as they do. Am I to avoid the river because they are objectionable? Why should I? God cleanses it again."

"That's it, Ilya! You're a good fellow," cried Pavel, excitedly.

"But do you drink out of the river?" said Vyera, softly.

"I must find it first," laughed Ilya. "Pour me out a glass of tea to go on with, Vyera!"

"You're a nice boy!" cried the girl.

"Many thanks," said Ilya, seriously, bowed to her, and sat down again.

His words and the whole scene acted on Pavel like wine. His animated face reddened, his eyes shone with excitement, he sprang from his chair and paced the room joyously. "Ah, devil take it!" he cried, "the world's a jolly place, if men are as simple as children. It was a good thing I did when I brought you along, Ilya! Drink, brother! Fill up, Vyerunka!"

"Now there's no holding him," said the girl, and smiled at him tenderly. Then, turning to Ilya, "he's always like that, either as gay and shining as a rainbow, or dull, and grey, and cross."

"That's not good," said Lunev decidedly. Then all three began to chatter gaily and cheerfully, breaking into careless laughter every now and then.

There was a knock at the door, and a voice asked: "Vyera, may I come in?"

"Come in! come in! Ilya Jakovlevitsch, this is my friend, Lipa."

Ilya rose from his chair, and turned towards the door. A tall, stately woman stood before him, and looked in his face with calm blue eyes. From her dress came a sweet perfume, her cheeks were fresh and red, and her head was adorned with a crown-like mass of hair that made her look even taller.

"I was sitting alone in my room, so bored, and then, all at once I heard you talking and laughing, and so—well, I came here. You don't mind I hope? There's a gentleman without a lady. I will entertain him—shall I?"

With a graceful gesture, she placed her chair near Ilya's, seated herself, and asked: "You're rather bored with them, aren't you? They kiss and hug one another, and you're envious, eh?"

"I'm not bored with them," said Ilya, confused by feeling her so near.

"That's a pity," she said quietly, then turned from Ilya and went over to Vyera.

"Just think, I went to Mass yesterday at the nunnery, and I saw such a pretty nun in the choir, such a dear. I couldn't take my eyes off her, and thought why on earth did she go into the nunnery. I felt quite sorry."

"Why? I shouldn't pity her," said Vyera.

"Oh! Who's going to believe that!"

Ilya breathed in the costly perfume that floated round this woman, he looked sidelong at her and listened to her voice. She spoke with extraordinary calm and self-possession, there was something drowsy in her voice and it seemed as though a powerful, delightful scent streamed from her words also.

"D'you know, Vyera, I'm still considering if I shall go to Poluektov or not."

"I can't advise you."

"Perhaps I will. He's old and rich, and those are two important points. But he's miserly. I want five thousand roubles in my name in the bank, and a hundred and fifty roubles a month, and he only offers three thousand and a hundred."

"Don't talk of it now, Lipotshka!"

"All right, as you like," said Lipa, quietly, and turned again to Ilya. "Now, young man, let us talk a little. I like you, you've a nice face and serious eyes. What will you say to that?"

"I? I shan't say anything," said he, laughing carelessly, but feeling clearly how this woman ensnared him with her magic.

"Nothing? oh! you're bored;—what are you?"

"Pedlar."

"R—really? I thought you were a clerk in a bank, or in some shop. You look very good form."

"I like cleanliness," said Ilya. He felt oppressively hot, and his head was in a whirl with the perfume.

"You like cleanliness?—that's very nice. Are you a good hand at guessing?"

"I don't understand."

"Can't you guess that you're in the way here, eh;" and she looked right through him with her blue eyes.

"Oh! of course. I'll go," said Ilya confused.

"Wait a minute! Vyera, may I take this youngster away?"

"Of course, if he wants to go," answered Vyera, laughing.

"But where?" asked Ilya, in great excitement.

"Oh! go along you silly fellow!" cried Pashka.

Ilya stood there dazed and laughed vaguely, but the beautiful lady took his hand and led him out, saying in her quiet way: "You're not tamed yet, and I'm capricious and obstinate. If I made up my mind to put out the sun, I'd climb on the roof and blow at it till I'd used my last breath. Now you know what I'm like."

Ilya went with her hand in hand, hardly hearing her words and not understanding at all: he only felt she was so warm, and soft and fragrant.

CHAPTER XII

His intimacy with Olympiada, so unexpectedly begun from a woman's whim, rendered Ilya at first quite arrogant. A proud self-confident feeling awakened in him, healing the little wounds that life had dealt his heart.

The thought that a lovely well-dressed lady gave him her precious kisses out of pure affection and demanded nothing in return, raised him more and more in his own eyes, and he felt as though he were floating in a broad stream, borne along by a peaceful flood that caressed his body tenderly and waked strength and courage in his limbs.

"My dear lad," said Olympiada to him, as she played with his hair or passed her finger over the dark down that covered his upper lip. "You're nicer every day, you've such a bold, confident heart, and I can see you're sure to get what you want. I like that. I'm made that way, too. If I were younger, I'd marry you and together we'd have a splendid time."

Ilya treated her with great respect. She seemed so sensible, and he liked her for the way she respected herself in spite of her vicious life. She never drank and used no foul words like the other women that he knew. Her body was as supple and strong as her full deep voice, and as tense as her character. Even her frugality, her love of order and cleanliness, and the readiness with which she could speak on any subject and ward off anything that irritated her pride, delighted him. Sometimes though, if he visited her and found her lying with dishevelled hair and pale, languid face, a bitter feeling of disgust would arise, and then as he looked gloomily into her wearied eyes he could bring no greeting from his lips. She must have understood his feeling readily, for she would wrap the coverlet round her and say:

"Off with you!—go and see Vyera—tell the old woman to bring me some snow-water!"

He would go to the clean little room and Vyera would laugh guiltily at the sight of his gloomy, displeased face. One day she asked him:

"Well, Ilya Jakovlevitsch, how are you getting on? How do you like it here?"

"Ah, Vyerotchka, sin can't stick to you; if you only smile it melts away like snow."

"I'm so sorry for you, both of you, poor fellows."

Ilya liked Vyera very much. He treated her as a little child, was very disturbed if she quarrelled with Pashka, and made the peace between them every time. He liked to sit in her room and watch her comb her golden hair, or sew at something, singing softly. Often he surprised in her eyes a gnawing pain, and sometimes her face twitched with a hopeless weary smile. At such a time he felt even more drawn to her, the misery of this little girl touched him more keenly and he would comfort her as well as he could. But she said:

"No, no, Ilya, we can't go on like this, it's quite impossible; think—I—I must live on in this filth, but Pavel, what place is there for him near me?"

"But he chooses it," said Ilya.

"Chooses?" came like an echo from her lips.

Olympiada interrupted the conversation, entering noiselessly in a wide blue cloak, like a cold moonbeam.

"Come to tea, my lad, and you come in too, presently, Vyerotchka."

Fresh and rosy from the cold water, clean, neat and calm, she took Ilya to her room without many words, and he followed, marvelling that this could be the same Olympiada he had seen before, faded and soiled by lustful hands.

While they drank their tea, she said to him: "It's a pity you're only a peasant lad and have learned so little, that'll make it harder for you in life, but anyhow you must drop your present business and try something else. Wait, I'll look out for a place for you—you must be looked after. As soon as I've fixed things up with Poluektov, I'll manage it."

"Is he going to give you the five thousand?"

"Of course," she answered with conviction.

"Well, if I ever meet him near you, I'll pull his head off," cried Ilya jealously.

"Why? he doesn't get in your way."

"He does, most decidedly, get in my way."

"But he's old and horrid," said Olympiada, laughing.

"Laugh away! I'll never believe that it's anything but a great sin to caress such a dirty beast."

"Wait a little, at least, till I get hold of his money."

The merchant did everything for her that she desired. Soon Ilya was sitting in her new house, seeing the thick carpets and the heavy plush-covered furniture, and listening to his lady's business-like remarks. He found in her no special pleasure in her altered surroundings, she was as calm and self-contained as ever. It was as though only the clothes were changed, nothing else.

"I am now twenty-seven,—when I am thirty, I shall have ten thousand roubles. Then I'll throw over the old man and be free; learn from me, my lad, how to deal with life."

Ilya learnt from her obstinate perseverance to attain a predetermined goal, but often the thought tortured him, that he shared her caresses with another, and a painful sense of degradation and weakness. At such times the vision would rise again of his shop, with the clean room, where he might entertain his lady. He didn't believe that he loved Olympiada, but she seemed quite necessary to him, as a sensible good comrade.

In this way, two months—three months passed away. One day, when he returned home, he betook himself to Perfishka's cellar, and saw with amazement Perfishka at the table with a bottle of brandy, and opposite him, Jakov sat, leaning heavily on the table, his head swaying, and said unsteadily:

"Splendid! If God sees everything and knows everything, then He sees me too. Every one has forsaken me, brother. I'm all alone. My father hates me, he's a scoundrel! He's a robber and a cheat, isn't he, Perfishka?"

"Right, Jakov. It's a pity, but it's true."

"Well, then, how am I to live? What am I to believe in?" asked Jakov, stammering and shaking his dishevelled hair. "I can't believe in my father. Ilya goes his own way. Masha is a child. Where is there a man? Perfishka, I tell you, there's not a man left in the world."

Ilya stood in the doorway, and heard his friend's drunken speech. His heart sank painfully. He saw Jakov's head loll, drooping and weak, on his thin neck, saw Perfishka's thin, yellow face lighted up with a pleased smile, and he would not believe that this could really be Jakov, the quiet, modest Jakov.

"What are you doing here?" he said reproachfully as he entered.

Jakov started, looked with startled eyes into Ilya's face, and said, with a despairing smile: "Ah, Ilya—is that all! I thought—my father——"

"What's all this about, tell me," Ilya interrupted.

"You let him alone, Ilya," cried Perfishka, and rose swaying from his chair. "He can please himself. Thank God that he still likes brandy."

"Ilya," cried Jakov convulsively, "my father thrashed me."

"That's so. I was a witness," explained Perfishka, and smote his breast with his fist. "I saw everything. I can take my oath! He knocked his teeth out, and made his nose bleed."

In fact, Jakov's face was swollen and his upper lip covered with blood. He stood in front of his comrade, and said, smiling mournfully:

"How dare he beat me? I'm nineteen, and I'd done nothing wrong."

"Why did he beat you, then?"

Jakov's lips twitched as though he was about to speak, but he said nothing. His bruised face quivered. He sank heavily on a chair, took his head in his hands, and began to sob aloud, so that his whole body shook. Perfishka, who had supported him as he sank down, poured out a glass of brandy, and said: "Let him cry. It's good when a man can. Mashutka, too, was in a state, quite bathed in tears. 'I'll scratch his eyes out,' she screamed right on, till I took her to Matiza."

"But what happened?"

"I can tell you exactly. It was quite a crazy business. Terenti, that uncle of yours, he began the thing. All at once he said to Petrusha, 'Let me go to Kiev,' he said, 'to the holy men!' Petrusha was delighted; that hump of Terenti's has worried his eyes, and to tell the truth, he's jolly glad to see Terenti's back; it's not nice to have some one about who knows a secret of yours—he! he! 'All right,' he says. 'Go along, and put in a little word for me too with the holy men.' And then Jakov starts in all of a sudden: 'Let me go too,' he says."

Perfishka began to roll his eyes, made a fierce grimace, and cried in a hoarse voice, imitating Petrusha:

"'Wha—a—at do you want to do?'"

"'I want to go with uncle to the holy men.'

"'What do you mean?'

"Jakov says, 'I could pray for you too.' Then Petrusha begins to roar, 'I'll teach you to pray!' Jakov sticks to his point. 'Let me go. God is pleased with the prayers of sons for their fathers' sins.' My word, how Petrusha hit him in the mouth, and again and again."

"I can't live with him," cried Jakov. "I'll go away. I'll hang myself. Why did he beat me—why? All I said came from my heart."

Ilya's heart sank at this outcry, and with a despairing shrug of his shoulders, he left the cellar. He was glad to hear that his uncle was going on a pilgrimage. Once Terenti was gone, he would finally leave this house, take a little room somewhere for himself, and be his own master. As he entered his room, Terenti appeared, following him. His eyes shone, his face wore an expression of joy. He approached Ilya and said: "Well, I'm going. O Lord, how glad I am! To step out of a cave, a cellar, into God's world. Surely He will not despise my prayer, since He lets me get away from this place."

"Do you know what's happened to Jakov?" said Ilya, drily.

"What?"

"He's got drunk."

"What do you say? That is wrong of him! Silly boy! And just now he was begging his father to let him go with me."

"Were you there when his father beat him?"

"Yes, of course. Why?"

"Why, can't you understand? That's why he's got drunk."

"Because of that? It's not possible!"

Ilya saw clearly that Jakov's fate was a matter of indifference to his uncle, and that strengthened his feeling of enmity against the hunchback. He had never seen Terenti so overjoyed, and the sight of this happiness, coming right after Jakov's misery, moved him strangely. He sat down at the window and said:

"Go on into the bar."

"Petrusha is there. I want to talk to you."

"Oh! what about?"

The hunchback came up to him and said mysteriously:

"I'm getting away. You're staying behind and that means—well——"

"Hurry up," said Ilya.

"Yes—yes, I want to; it isn't easy to say," said Terenti, in a subdued way, while his eyes blinked.

"Do you want to talk about me? eh?"

"Yes—yes—about you, too, but presently. I've saved some money."

Ilya looked at him and laughed maliciously.

"What d'you mean? Why d'you laugh?" cried his uncle, frightened.

"Oh, nothing. Well, then, you've *saved* some money, have you?"

Ilya emphasised "saved."

"Yes, that's it," said Terenti, avoiding his look. "I shall give two hundred roubles to the monastery."

"O!"

"And a hundred to you."

"A hundred?" asked Ilya, suddenly, and at once he knew that in his soul for a long time the hope had lived that his uncle would give him not a hundred roubles, but a much bigger sum. He was angered against himself that his heart could entertain so hateful, calculating, an expectation, and against his uncle that the sum was so small. He got up, straightened himself, and said, full of scorn and insolence:

"I'll have none of your stolen money, d'you understand."

The hunchback recoiled in fear and sank on his bed, pale and wretched, his hair bristled, his mouth stood open, and he gazed at Ilya silently with stupid terror in his eyes.

"Well, why do you look like that? I don't want your money."

"Christ!" Terenti groaned hoarsely. "Why not, my dear, why not? Ilusha, you've been like a son to me." Then presently he went on in a whisper. "It was just—for you—for fear of what should happen to you, that I took the sin on my soul; take the money, take it, else the Lord won't forgive me."

"So," cried Ilya, mockingly, "you'll go to your God with an account book! Oh! you! did I ask you to steal old Jeremy's money; think what a good man he was you robbed!"

"Ilusha, you didn't ask to be born, either," said the uncle, and stretched out his hand to Ilya with an odd gesture. "No, take the money, quietly, for Christ's sake, to save my soul; if I come back, then you'll get it all, and meantime take this, my dear boy. God will not forgive my sins, if you don't take the money!"

He was actually begging, his lips quivered, and in his eyes was an expression of fear. Ilya looked at him and could not determine if his uncle really distressed him or no.

"Well, all right, I'll take it," he said at last, and went straight out of the room. He was sorry that he had yielded finally, he felt degraded. What was a hundred roubles to him after all? What big thing could he undertake with that? If his uncle had given him a thousand roubles now instead of a hundred, then he would have been enabled to change his dull uneasy life into a better, that should glide along in peaceful solitude far from mankind.

How would it be to ask his uncle, just how much he had obtained from the rag-picker's hoard? But this thought was too repugnant to him. Ever since Ilya had made Olympiada's acquaintance the house of Filimonov appeared to him dirtier and stuffier than ever. The dirt and the close atmosphere roused in him a physical nausea, as though cold, slimy hands were laid on his body. To-day this feeling was more painful than usual, he could find no spot in the house to suit him, and, without any definite motive, he climbed the stairs to Matiza's garret. As he went, he felt as though this house would somehow, at some time or other, deal him an unexpected terrible injury.

Busy with such thoughts he entered Matiza's room and saw her sitting on a chair beside her bed. She cast a glance at him, warned him with a finger, and whispered in a deep bass voice, like a far-off storm-wind:

"Sh! She's asleep."

Masha lay on the bed, huddled in a heap.

"What kind of a thing d'you call this?" Matiza whispered, and rolled her big eyes angrily. "Thrash children to ribbons, do they, the cursed villains! to lay hands on children! curse them! the scoundrels!"

Ilya stood by the stove and listened, while he gazed at the delicate form of the cobbler's daughter, wrapped in a grey shawl.

"What's to become of the poor things?" rang in his head.

"D'you know that the blackguard struck Masha, too?" went on Matiza. "Tore her hair, the cursed scoundrel, the old bar loafer! Beat his son, and the girl, and he's going to turn them both out of doors, d'you know that? Where are they to go, poor orphans? How— —"

"Perhaps I can find her a place," said Ilya, thoughtfully, remembering that Olympiada needed a housemaid.

"You!" whispered Matiza, reproachfully. "You come in always now as if you were a fine gentleman. You get on and grow for yourself like a young oak-tree, give no shadow and no acorns. You might have done something for her long ago. Aren't you sorry for the child?"

"Wait a bit and don't jaw!" said Ilya, crossly. It was an excuse for him to visit Olympiada at once, and he asked: "How old's Mashutka?"

"Fifteen! Why? What's her age got to do with it? She looks barely twelve, she's so slender and delicate. Heaven knows, she's just a child still.

She's fit for nothing, nothing! What is to become of her? It would be better if she never waked again till the last day."

A vague cloud of ideas filled Ilya's head when he left the garret. An hour later he was standing before the door of Olympiada's house, waiting to be admitted. He waited a long time in the cold, till at last from behind the door a thin, peevish voice asked: "Who is there?"

"I— —" answered Lunev, not very clear who was speaking. Olympiada's servant, a plump, pock-marked person, had a loud harsh voice, and always opened the door without question.

"Whom do you want?" asked the voice again.

"Is Olympiada Danilovna at home?"

The door opened suddenly, and a strong light fell on Ilya's face. The lad fell back a step, half shut his eyes, and looked perplexedly at the door, as though what he saw appeared an illusion. Before him, lamp in hand, stood a little old man, in a wide heavy dressing-gown, the colour of raspberries. His head was all but entirely bald, only a thin crown of grey hair ran from one ear to the other, and on his chin a short thin grey beard quivered uneasily. He looked at Ilya's face, and his keen, piercing eyes blinked evilly, and his upper lip, with its scanty hairs, twitched up and down. The lamp shook and trembled in his thin, swarthy hand.

"Who are you, then? Well, come in. Who are you?"

Ilya understood. He felt the blood mount to his head and an untoward feeling of disgust and wrath filled his heart. This was the rival who shared with him the favours of the stately, beautiful lady!

"I am—a pedlar," he said, in a dull voice, as he crossed the threshhold.

The old man winked at him with his left eye, and smiled. His eyes were red with inflammation, without eyelashes, and instead of teeth, a couple of yellow, pointed pegs showed in his mouth.

"Oh, ho! A pedlar, eh? What sort of a pedlar?" asked the old man, with a cunning smile, and held the lamp up to illumine Ilya's face.

"I deal in all sorts of little things—scent and ribbons, and so on," said Ilya, and hung his head. A giddiness seized him and red spots danced before his eyes.

"Oh, oh! Ribbons and scent. Yes, yes! Ribbons and laces to deck pretty faces. But what do you want here, my young pedlar? Eh?"

"I want to see Olympiada Danilovna."

"Eh, to see her? What do you want of her, now?"

"I have to get some money for things she's had," Ilya brought out, with difficulty.

He felt an incomprehensible fear of this horrible old man and hated him. In his thin, soft voice and in his evil eyes lay something that penetrated within Ilya's heart and took away his courage, and cast him down.

"Money, eh? A little debt. All right, my lad."

Suddenly the old man took the lamp away from Ilya's face, put it down, brought his yellow, withered face close to Ilya's ear, and asked him softly, with another, cunning smile: "Where's the bill? Give me the bill."

"What bill?" said Ilya, recoiling, frightened.

"Why, from your master. The bill for Olympiada Danilovna. You've got it, I suppose? What? Give it here! I'll take it to her. Quick, be quick!"

The old man moved nearer, while Ilya retreated towards the door. His mouth was dry with fear.

"I have no bill," he said loudly in despair, feeling that something terrible must happen the next moment.

The tall, stately figure of Olympiada appeared behind the old man. Calmly, without the trembling of an eyelash, she looked at Ilya over the head of the old man, and said in her measured way: "What is the matter?"

"It's a pedlar, he says you owe him money; you've bought ribbons, eh? and not paid for them? He! He! Well, here he is and wants his money."

He paced with short steps to and fro and blinked suspiciously first at Olympiada, then at Ilya. With a commanding gesture, she waved him to one side, put her hand in the pocket of her cloak, and said to Ilya in a severe tone: "What is it? Could you not come another time?"

"Quite right," squeaked the old man. "Silly fool, isn't he?"

"Coming when he's least wanted—donkey!"

Ilya stood as though turned to stone.

"Don't scream so, Vassili Gavrilovitsch, it doesn't sound well," said Olympiada, and turning to Ilya, "How much? three roubles forty kopecks isn't it? here, take it!"

"And now clear out!" squeaked the old man again. "Allow me. I'll bolt the door myself. I'll do it."

He drew his dressing-gown round him, opened the door, and cried:

"Now then, go along!"

Ilya stood in the frost before the closed door, and stared stupidly at it. He could not yet decide if all that he had just seen were reality, or a hateful dream. In one hand he held his cap, in the other the money Olympiada had given him. He stood there so long that he felt the frost round his head like a ring of ice, and his legs were stiff with cold. Then he put on his cap, put the money in his pocket, tucked his hands into the sleeves of his overcoat, drew in his shoulders, and went slowly down the street with bowed head. His heart seemed ice and in his head a couple of balls rolled here and there and knocked against his temples. Before his eyes swam the dusky face of the old man, the yellow skull illuminated by the cold lamp-light.

And the face of the old man smiled evilly, cunningly, triumphantly.

CHAPTER XIII

On the day following his encounter with Olympiada's aged lover, Ilya walked to and fro along the main street of the town, slowly and silently. He did not call his wares as usual, but looked at his box gloomily, and hidden in his heart there lay immovable, a heavy leaden feeling. He never ceased to see before him the scornful face of the old man, Olympiada's calm blue eyes and the gesture with which she had given him the money. Sharp little snowflakes drove through the dry, frosty air, stinging his face like needles.

He had just passed a little shop, half-concealed in a niche between a church and the big house of a rich merchant. Over the entrance hung an old rusty sign with the inscription:

"Bureau de Change. W. G. Poluektov. Old gold and silver, ornaments for shrines, rarities of every kind, old coins."

As Ilya passed the door, he thought he saw behind the window panes the old man's face, grinning and nodding at him mockingly. He felt an irresistible desire to see the old man closer. He easily found an excuse. Like all pedlars, he collected the old coins that came into his hands, and sold them to the money-changers at an advance of twenty kopecks to the rouble. He had a few at that moment in his wallet. He turned back, opened the shop door boldly, went in with his box, took off his cap and said, "Good-day!"

The old man was sitting behind a small counter, and at the moment removing the metal clasps from an eikon, loosening the little nails with a small chisel. He was deep in his work. He shot a hasty glance at the lad as he came in, then turned again to his work, and said drily without looking up:

"Good day! What can I do for you?"

"Did you recognise me?" asked Ilya.

The old man looked at him again.

"Perhaps. What d'you want?"

"You buy old coins?"

"Show me."

Ilya shifted his box towards his back, and felt for the pocket where he had his purse with the coins—his hand failed to find it; it trembled like his heart, which beat furiously with hate of the old man, fear of him, and a vague impulse to achieve something decisive. Whilst with his hand he felt under the flap of his overcoat, he looked steadily at the little bald head of the money-changer, and a cold shiver ran down his back.

"Well, have you got them?" the old man addressed him crossly.

"One moment," answered Ilya softly.

At last he succeeded in getting out his purse; he went close up to the counter and shook the coins out on to it. The old man gave one look at them.

"That's all, eh?"

He took the silver coins up in his thin yellow fingers, and looked at them one at a time, murmuring to himself:

"Katherine the Second, Anna, Catherine, Paul, another Paul, a cross-rouble, a thirty-two piece. H'm, who's to see what this is? This is no good, it's all worn away."

"But the size shows it's a quarter rouble," said Ilya, harshly.

"Fifteen kopecks you can have for it, no more."

The old man pushed the coins aside, drew out the drawer of his till with a quick movement, and began to feel about in it. A fierce, stabbing rage took possession of Ilya, piercing through him like a frost-cold iron. He struck out with his arm, and his powerful fist caught the old man on the temple. The money-changer fell against the wall and struck his head hard upon it, but braced himself with his breast against the counter, held fast to it with his hands and stretched out his thin neck towards Ilya. Lunev saw the terrified eyes blinking in the dusky little face and the lips quiver, and he heard a penetrating, groaning whisper:

"My darling—my darling."

"Ah! you beast!" cried Ilya in a low voice, and crushed the old man's neck with his hands in disgust. He throttled and pressed him and began to shake him, while the old man's throat rattled, and he tried convulsively to get away. His eyes filled with blood, became bigger and bigger, and gushed with tears. His tongue protruded from his dark mouth and moved to and fro as though mocking the murderer. The warm saliva dropped on Ilya's hand, and a hoarse, whistling, gurgling sound came from the old man's throat. The cold crooked fingers caught at Lunev's neck, but he clenched his teeth, threw back his head, and shook the frail body more fiercely and dragged it over the counter; he would not have loosed his hold on the yielding throat, had any one come behind him and struck him. Filled with rigid fear and glowing hate, he saw Poluektov's dim eyes grow bigger and bigger, and still he gripped him more fiercely, more passionately, and ever as the old man's body grew heavier the weighty load on Ilya's heart was lightened. At last he let go of the body and pushed it away, and the money-changer's corpse sunk slackly to the ground.

Now Lunev looked round him; the shop was deserted and still, behind the door in the street snow was falling thickly. On the floor at his feet lay two pieces of soap, a purse, and a roll of ribbon. He perceived that these objects had fallen from his box, picked them up and replaced them. Then he leant over the counter and looked once more at the old man. He was crumpled in the small space between the counter and the wall. His head hung down on his breast, nothing could be seen but the yellow, bald patch at the back of it. Then Lunev looked at the open till—gold and silver coins shone back at him, packets of paper money met his eyes; he trembled with joy, hastily caught a packet, then a second and a third, stuffed them under his shirt, and looked once more anxiously round.

Carefully, without haste, he stepped back into the street, stopped three paces from the shop, covered his wares with the oil-cloth cover, and then went on in the midst of the thick snow that fell from invisible heights. Round him, even as in him, floated a cold, misty cloud; his eyes strove to pierce it with tense alertness. Suddenly he felt a dull pain in his eyes, he touched them with a finger of his right hand, and stood still, gripped by terror, as though his feet were suddenly frozen fast to the ground. He felt as though his eyes were coming out of their sockets, like those of old Poluektov, and he feared lest they should remain for ever thus protruded, never to be closed, for all men to read in them the crime he had committed. They felt as though they were lifeless. He touched the pupils with a finger, felt a sudden pain in them, and tried for a long time vainly to close the lids. Fear caught the breath in his throat. At last he managed to close them. He rejoiced at the darkness that suddenly enclosed him, and stood motionless, seeing nothing, breathing deep breaths of the cold air. Some one ran against him. He looked quickly round, and saw a tall man, in a short fur coat, passing. Ilya looked after the unknown till he vanished in the thick drifting snow. Then he straightened his cap and strode on, feeling still the pain in his eyes and a weight at his head. His shoulders twitched, his fingers involuntarily clenched, and a daring boldness awakened in his heart and banished his fear.

He went on till the road divided, there saw the grey figure of a policeman, and went, as if by accident, slowly, quite slowly, straight up to him. His heart stopped as he drew near. "Here's weather," said Ilya, going close to the policeman and looking boldly into his face.

"Ye—es! Snowing pretty well! Thank heaven, it'll be warmer now," answered the policeman, with a good-natured expression on his big, red, bearded face.

"What's the time, by the way?" asked Ilya.

"I'll have a look." The policeman knocked the snow from his sleeve, and put his hand under his cloak.

Lunev felt both relieved and again made anxious by the proximity of this man. Suddenly he laughed, in a dry, forced way.

"What are you laughing at?" asked the policeman, opening the front of his watch with his nail.

"If you could see yourself. It's as though some one had tipped a cart of snow over you!"

"No need for that; it's coming down in bucketsful. Just half-past one, all but five minutes. Yes, brother, it's bad for men of my trade this weather. You'll go into the public house, in the warm, and I must stick about here till six. Oh, just see; your box is full of snow!"

The policeman sighed and snapped his watch to.

"Yes, I'm off to the alehouse," said Ilya, with a forced laugh, and added, for no particular reason: "That one, up there, that's where I'm going."

"Don't chaff me!" cried the policeman, sulkily.

In the alehouse Ilya took a seat near the window. From this window, as he knew, the church could be seen next to Poluektov's shop. But now all was covered with a white curtain. Ilya watched attentively how the flakes slowly slid past the window and settled on the ground, covering the footsteps of the wayfarers as with a thick carpet. His heart beat strongly and full of life, but easily. He sat and waited for what should befall, and the time seemed to pass slowly.

When the waiter brought him tea he could not refrain from asking, "Well, how goes the neighbourhood? anything new?"

"It's got warmer, much warmer," answered the other quickly and hurried away.

Ilya waited and waited, he felt as though he were weary and fell into a doze. He poured out a glass of tea, but did not drink it, sat still, and thought of nothing. Suddenly he felt hot; he unbuttoned the collar of his overcoat, and shuddered as his hands touched his chin. It felt as though these were not his hands but the strange cold hands of an enemy that had touched him. He held them up and observed his fingers attentively—his hands were clean, but the thought came to him that he must wash them very carefully with soap.

"Poluektov has been murdered!" cried some one suddenly in the bar. Ilya sprang up from his chair as though the cry had been addressed to him. But all the other customers also were in commotion and rushed to the door, pulling on their caps.

Ilya threw a ten-kopeck piece on the counter, slung his box over his shoulder, and followed in the same haste as the others.

Already a big crowd had collected before the shop of the money-changer. Policemen moved up and down, and full of officious zeal shouted at the people; the bearded one with whom Ilya had spoken was there too. He stood in the doorway, keeping back the crowd that pressed towards it, regarded every one with troubled eyes, and passed his hand constantly over his left cheek that seemed redder than the right.

Ilya found a place near him and listened to the remarks of the crowd. Next him stood a tall, black-bearded merchant with a stern face, who listened with knitted brows to an old man in a fox-skin coat, who was relating in a lively way:

"The errand boy comes to the house and thinks his master has fainted. He runs to Peter Stepanovitch. 'Ah!' he says, 'come quick to our house, the master is ill.' Naturally Peter hurries off, and when he comes in he sees the old man is dead. A pretty business! and think of the audacity, in broad day, in such a busy street, it's past belief!"

The black-bearded merchant gave a low cough, and said severely:

"It is the finger of God! Evidently the Lord would not receive his repentance."

Lunev pressed forward to look again at the face of the merchant and struck him with his box. The merchant called out, pushing him away with his elbow and regarding him angrily:

"Where are you coming with that box of yours?" Then he turned again to the old man: "It is written, 'not a hair falls from the head of a man except by the will of God.'"

"What's one to say?" said the old man, and nodded in agreement: then he added, half aloud, his eyes twinkling, "It is well known that God marks the wicked. The Lord forgive me, it's wrong to speak of it, but it's difficult also to be silent."

"And you'll see," went on the stern merchant, "they'll never find the guilty one; mark my words."

Lunev laughed right out. The sound of this conversation seemed to send new strength and courage streaming through him. If any one at this moment had asked him: "Did you murder him?" he would have answered "yes" boldly and fearlessly. With this feeling in his breast he pushed through the crowd, close up to the policeman.

The man looked at him, gave him a push on the shoulder, and said loudly: "Now then, what are you doing here? Be off!"

Ilya backed away and struck against a bystander. He received another push and a voice cried: "Give him one over the head!"

Then he left the crowd, sat on the church steps and laughed in his heart at all these men. He heard the snow scrunch under their feet and the muttered conversation, fragments of which reached his ears.

"Why must the rascal do his dirty work just when I'm on duty?"

"In all the town he took the biggest discount, he always was a thief."

"It'll never stop snowing to-day, you can't see the shop at all."

"He used to fleece his debtors properly."

"He was a man after all—one can't help pitying him."

"They're all greedy—think of nothing but their profits."

"Look! there's his wife."

"Ah! poor thing!" sighed a ragged peasant.

Lunev stood up and saw a stout, elderly woman in a loosely-fitting dress and a black veil, getting heavily out of a wide sledge covered with a bear's skin. The police officer and a man with a red moustache helped her.

"Ah! my dear, my husband." As her trembling, frightened voice was heard, silence fell on all the bystanders.

Ilya looked at her and thought of Olympiada.

"Where's the son?" said some one, softly.

"He's in Moscow, they say."

"He'll get the bad news soon enough."

"That's true."

Lunev heard, and his heart sank. He preferred to hear that no one lamented Poluektov; although at the same time, he thought all these men stupid and unreasoning, except the black-bearded merchant. This man had an air of strength and of firm faith, but the others stood like trees in a wood, and chattered in their silly way, pleased at the suffering of others.

He waited until the frail body of the money-changer was carried from the shop, and then went home, cold, tired, but calm. Reaching home, he bolted himself in his room, and began to count his money: in two thick packets there were five hundred roubles in small notes, in the third packet, eight hundred and fifty roubles. There was also a little bundle of coupons which he did not count. He wrapped all the money up in paper, and considered where to hide it. As he thought, he felt that his head was heavy and that he was sleepy. He determined to hide the money in the attic, and started out there, holding the parcel in his hand. In the passage he met Jakov.

"Ah, you're back," said Jakov.

"Yes, I'm back."

"How pale you are. Are you ill?"

"I'm not feeling up to much."

"What have you got there?"

"What have——" Ilya began; then suddenly he shivered in fear lest he should babble away his secret, and said hurriedly, swinging his parcel to and fro:

"It's ribbon, that's all, out of my box."

"Coming to tea?" said Jakov.

"I? Oh, yes, in a minute."

He went quickly through the passage. He trod unsteadily, and his head was dizzy, as though he were drunk. As he mounted the attic stairs, he went carefully, in constant fear lest he should make a noise or meet some one. While he buried the money under the flooring, near the chimney, he thought all of a sudden that some one was hidden in the darkness in the corner, watching him; he felt a wish to throw a stone in that direction, but mastered his feelings, and came slowly downstairs again. Now he had no fears. It was as though he had left them with the money; but a fresh doubt waked in his heart: "Why did I kill him?"

Masha greeted him joyfully in the cellar, where she was busy at the stove with the samovar.

"Ah, how early you are to-day!"

"That's the snow," he said; then added, crossly: "What d'you call early? I've come, as usual, when it's time. Can't you see how dark it is, you little goose?"

"It's dark here in the morning; and what are you shouting at?"

"I'm shouting, as you call it, because you talk like the police. 'You're very early—Where are you going?—What have you got there?' What business is it of yours?"

Masha looked searchingly at him, and said, reproachfully:

"How high and mighty you've grown!"

"Oh, go to the devil!" snarled Lunev, and sat down at the table.

Masha felt insulted, and turned away. Looking small and delicate, she shook back her dark hair from time to time, coughing and blinking when the smoke from the samovar she was tending irritated her eyes. Her face was thin, and the eyes shone all the more brightly for the dark circles round them. She was like the flowers that spring up amid grass and weeds in an overgrown garden.

Ilya looked at her and thought how the child lived all alone in this underground cave, working like a full-grown woman, how there was not, and perhaps never would be, any joy in life for her, condemned always to live in this straitened, dirty place. But he might live now as he had always desired, in peace and cleanliness. The thought filled him with happiness. Then at once he felt his unkindness to Masha.

"Masha!" he cried.

"Well, what now, cross-patch?"

"D'you know, I'm a bad lot," said Lunev, and his voice shook, while he wondered in his heart if he should tell her or no.

Masha turned towards him with a smile:

"Pity there's no one to give you a beating, that's what you want, you bad fellow!"

"Oh! have a little patience."

"No—no—you don't deserve any," said Masha, then approaching him quickly, she said in a tone of entreaty: "Ilya dear, ask your uncle to take me with him, will you? Ask him! I'll go on my knees and thank you."

"Where do you want to go?" asked Lunev, tired and too busy with his own thoughts to attend.

"To the holy places. Dear Ilya, ask him."

With hands clasped and eyes streaming, she stood in front of him, as though before a shrine.

"It would be so lovely, in spring, through the fields and woods. I'd go on and on, ever so far. I think of it every day—I dream that I'm going there, how good it would be; speak to your uncle, tell him to take me! He listens to you—I won't be a trouble to him. I'll beg for myself. I'm so little, they'll give to me. Will you, Ilusha? I'll kiss your hand."

Suddenly she seized his hand and bent over it. He sprang up, pushing her back.

"Silly girl," he cried, "what are you doing? I've strangled a man!"

His own words terrified him and he added at once: "Perhaps—perhaps for all you know, I've done something terrible with these hands, and you'll kiss them."

"No, let me," said Masha, pressing closer to him. "What does it matter? I'll kiss them! Petrusha is worse than you, and I kiss his hand for every bit of bread. I hate it, but he wants it, so I do it, and then he pinches me and touches me, the beast!"

Ilya's heart sprang up joyfully in a moment, perhaps because he had said the terrible thing, perhaps because he had not said everything.

He smiled and spoke gently to the child. "All right, I'll fix it up with uncle, I'll manage it, you shall go on your pilgrimage. I'll give you some money for the journey."

"You dear!" cried Masha, and fell on his neck.

"Here let go! Stop it," said Lunev, seriously. "I promise you shall go. Will you pray for me, Mashutka?"

"Pray for you! My God!"

Jakov appeared in the door, and said wonderingly:

"What on earth are you screaming at? Can hear you in the courtyard."

"Jakov!" cried the girl joyfully, eager to tell him. "I'm going away, on the pilgrimage. Ilya's promised to speak to the hunchback, he'll take me with him," and she laughed delightedly.

"Will he do it?" Jakov asked thoughtfully.

"Why not? She won't get in the way, and it's a good thing for her. Look at her, her eyes are shining, hardly like a live person."

"Yes—yes," said Jakov. After a moment's pause, he began to whistle softly.

"What's up," asked Ilya.

"Now I'm done for, all alone here, like the moon in the sky."

"Oh, hire a nurse," said Ilya laughing.

"I'll take to drink," said Jakov, shaking his head.

Masha looked at him, hung her head, and went towards the door; from there she spoke in a reproachful, sad voice:

"How weak you are, Jakov!"

"And you're very strong, aren't you? leaving a friend in the lurch. Nice way you treat me—how shall I endure it without you?"

He sat down at the table opposite Ilya with a gloomy face, and said:

"Suppose I just go with Terenti, too, eh! on the quiet?"

"Do it! I would," advised Ilya.

"Yes, but my father'll put the police on me!"

All were silent. Jakov began with forced gaiety:

"It's jolly to get drunk! You think of nothing, you understand nothing, and it's jolly."

Masha put the samovar on the table, and said, shaking her head:

"Oh, you Aren't you ashamed to talk like that?"

"You can't talk," cried Jakov, crossly. "Your father doesn't worry you— let's you do as you like. You live as you please."

"A nice sort of life!" answered Masha. "I'd run away to get rid of it."

"It's bad for us all," said Ilya softly, and fell to brooding again.

Jakov began looking thoughtfully out of the window.

"If one could get away, anywhere, out of all this, sit in a wood, by a river, and think about things."

"That would be silly, to run away from life," said Ilya, peevishly. Jakov looked at him inquiringly, and said shyly:

"D'you know, I've found a book."

"What sort of book?"

"Very old. It's bound in leather. It looks like a psalter, and it's really a heretic book. I bought it of a Tartar for seventy kopecks."

"What's it called?" asked Ilya. He had no wish for conversation, but felt that silence might be perilous for him, and compelled himself to keep talking.

"The title's torn out," answered Jakov, sinking his voice, "but it's all about the very beginning of things. It's difficult, and so horrible. It says that Thales, of Miletus, first of all said: 'All life proceeds from the water, and

God dwells in matter as the power of life.' And then there was a wicked man called Diagoras, who taught that there were more gods than one, and he didn't believe in God properly. And Epicurus is talked about, and he said that there is a God, but He troubles about no one, and cares for no one. That's to say that if there is a God, men have nothing to do with Him; at least, that's how I understand it. Live just as you please, there's no one who takes any heed what you do."

Ilya got up out of his chair with wrinkled brow, and interrupted his friend's discourse.

"It'd be a good thing to take that book and thump you on the head with it."

"Whatever for?" cried Jakov, hurt at Ilya's comment.

"So's you won't read any more, stupid! And the man who wrote that book's a stupid too." He went round the table, bent over his friend, full of anger, shouting at Jakov, as though hammering his big head with the words.

"There is a God! He sees everything. He knows everything. There's no one beside Him. Life is given to you to try you, and sin to prove you. Can you stand firm or no? If you can't then comes the punishment, be sure of it. Not from men; from Him, d'you see? It'll come; it won't fail."

"Stop!" cried Jakov. "Did I say anything about that?"

"I don't care. Your punishment'll come. How can you judge me, eh?" cried Ilya, pale with excitement, mastered by a quite incomprehensible passion that had caught him all of a sudden. "Not a hair falls from your head, except by His will, d'you hear? And if I have fallen into sin, it was by His will, you fool!"

"Are you crazy or what is it?" cried Jakov, terrified, and leaning against the wall. "What sin have you fallen into?"

Ilya heard the question through the buzzing and roaring in his ears, and it was like a cold breath blowing upon him. He looked suspiciously at Jakov and at Masha, who was also disturbed by his excitement and outcry.

"I was only speaking by way of example," he said, in a dull way, and sat down again.

"You don't seem well," remarked Masha shyly.

"Your eyes are so heavy," added Jakov, and examined him attentively.

Ilya passed his hand involuntarily over his eyes and said, quietly:

"It's nothing; it'll pass off."

A few minutes later he felt he could not endure this painful, distressing association with his friends, and went to his own room without waiting for tea. He had scarcely lain down on his bed before Terenti appeared. Ever since the hunchback had decided to go to the Holy Cities to seek forgiveness for his sins, his face wore a clearer, happier expression, as though he experienced already a foretaste of the joy that release from his weight of guilt would achieve for him. Gently he approached his nephew's bed, and said, smiling and friendly, stroking his beard:

"I saw you come in, and I thought, I'll go and have a chat. We shan't be here together much longer."

"You're really going?" asked Ilya, drily.

"As soon as it's warmer, off I go. I want to be in Kiev for Easter."

"Look here! Couldn't you take little Masha with you?"

"What? No; that's impossible," cried the hunchback, with a gesture of refusal.

"Listen," Ilya went on, obstinately. "She's nothing to do here; and now she's just the age—Jakov, Petrusha, and all the rest, you understand? This house is like a gulf of destruction for every one, a damnable place! Let her go. Perhaps she'll never come back."

"But how can I take her with me?"

"Take her—just take her!" said Ilya, persisting. "You can spend for her the hundred roubles you were going to give me. I don't need your money. And she will pray for you. Her prayers will be worth a good deal."

The hunchback came nearer, and said, after a pause: "A good deal— That's true—You're right. But I can't take the money from you. We'll leave it as we settled. And for Masha, I'll see to it." His eyes shone with joy, and he whispered: "Do you know whom I got to know yesterday? A famous man, Peter Vassilitsch. Have you never heard of the Bible preacher, a man of wisdom! God must have sent him to me, to free my soul from doubt concerning the Lord's forgiveness of a sinner like me."

Ilya said nothing. He only wished that his uncle would leave him alone. With half-shut eyes he looked out of the window.

"We talked of sin and the salvation of the soul," whispered Terenti. "He said to me: 'As the chisel needs the stone to gain its sharpness, so man heeds sin, to wear away his soul, and bring it to the dust at the feet of all-merciful God.'"

Ilya looked at his uncle, and said, with a mocking laugh:

"Tell me, is this preacher like Satan, by any chance?"

"How can you talk like that?" and Terenti recoiled a step. "He's a God-fearing man, he's more famous than Antipa, your grandfather—yes."

"Oh! all right, what else did he say?"

Suddenly Ilya laughed, a dry, unpleasant laugh; his uncle turned away surprised and asked: "What's the matter with you?"

"Nothing. He was quite right, that preacher. Yes—the devil! I think so too, word for word."

"He said, too," Terenti began with relish, "that sin gives the soul wings—wings of repentance to fly to the throne of the Almighty."

"Do you know," interrupted Ilya, "you're rather like Satan, too!"

The hunchback stretched out his arms like a great bird spreading its wings, and stood paralysed with fear and anger.

Ilya sat up on his bed, pushed his uncle aside, and said, gloomily:

"Get away!"

Terenti stood in the middle of the room; he looked darkly at his nephew who sat on the bed, his head on his breast, and his shoulders up to his ears.

"Suppose I won't repent," said Ilya boldly. "Suppose I think I didn't want to sin—everything happened of itself, everything is by God's will, why should I trouble? He knows all, and guides all; if He hadn't willed it, He would have held me back. So I was right in all I did. All men live in unrighteousness and sin, but how many repent?—Well, what do you say to that?"

"I don't understand; God help you!" said Terenti sadly and sighed.

"You don't understand? Then let me alone!"

He stretched himself again on his bed; after a pause, he added:

"Really, I believe I'm ill."

"It looks like it."

"I must get to sleep; go, let me alone. I want to sleep."

When he was alone, Ilya felt a whirlpool raging in his head. All the extraordinary experiences he had lived through in a few short hours, grew to a dense hot mist, and weighed on his brain. He felt as though he had endured the torture for ever so long, as though he had killed the old man not to-day, but many days ago.

He shut his eyes and did not move. In his ears rang the old man's squeaking voice: "Now then, your coins, quick!" and again came that hoarse cry of anguish: "My darling! My darling." The harsh voice of the black-bearded merchant, Masha's entreaty, the words of the heretic book, the pious talk of the preacher, all blended into one wild confused sound. Everything reeled around him, and in swift, ungoverned movement, swept him down. Fear left him, he needed only rest, sleep, forgetfulness. He slept.

In the morning when he waked, he saw by the light on the wall opposite the window that it was a clear, frosty day. His head was dull and confused, but his heart was peaceful. He recalled the events of yesterday, watched the course of his own thought and felt convinced that he would know how to conduct himself. Half an hour later he went down the sunny street, his box against his breast, blinking his eyes before the dazzle of the snow, and calmly contemplating the folk he met. If he passed a church he took off his cap and crossed himself. Even before the church near the closed shop of Poluektov he crossed himself and went on without a trace of fear or remorse or any disturbing feeling. At his mid-day meal in an ale-house, he read in a paper the account of the daring murder of the money-changer. At the end of the article was written: "The police are taking active steps to arrest the criminal." As he read these words he shook his head with an incredulous smile, he was firmly convinced that the murderer would never be arrested, unless he himself desired to be taken.

CHAPTER XIV

In the evening of this day Olympiada sent a letter to Ilya by her servant:

"Be at the corner of Kusnezkaya Street, by the Public Baths, at nine o'clock."

As Ilya read the words, he felt his body contract internally, and he shivered as if with cold. Once more he saw the contemptuous expression on the face of his mistress, and in his ears rang her rough, insulting words: "Couldn't you come some other time?"

He looked the letter all over, and could not determine why Olympiada had appointed this particular meeting place. Then all at once, he feared to understand, and his heart beat fiercely. He was punctual. The sight of Olympiada's tall figure among the many women who were walking, singly or in couples, near the public baths, increased his anxiety and restlessness. She wore an old fur jacket and a veil. He could only see her eyes. He stood before her in silence.

"Come!" she said, and added, softly: "Turn up your coat-collar!"

They walked through the passage of the building, keeping their faces turned aside, and disappeared quickly into a private room. Olympiada quickly threw aside her veil, and Ilya took new courage at the sight of her calm face, its colour heightened by the cold. Almost immediately he felt, however, that he disliked to see her so unmoved. She sat down on the divan, and said, looking in his face in a friendly way:

"Well, my lad! We'll soon appear together before the police?"

"Why?" asked Ilya, and wiped the hoar frost from his moustache.

"How stupid you can seem! As if you didn't know!" cried Olympiada quietly, with a tinge of mockery. Then her brows contracted, and she said, seriously, in a low tone:

"D'you know the police agent was at my house to-day. What d'you say to that?"

Ilya looked at her, and said, drily:

"What's that to me? Don't trouble me with your police, or anything else. Tell me simply why you've brought me here, with all this precaution."

Olympiada looked at him searchingly, then said, with a mocking laugh: "Oh, you'll still play the innocent—but there's no time for that. Listen. When the police officer examines you and asks you when you got to know me, and whether you visited me often, say just the plain truth—exactly—do you hear?"

"I hear," said Ilya, and smiled.

"And if he asks you about the old man, say you never saw him, never; that you know nothing of him, that you never heard that any one was keeping me—d'you understand?"

She looked Ilya through and through with an air of command. He felt an evil thought push up in him, that yet gave him pleasure. He thought that Olympiada feared him, and he found in himself a desire to torture her. He knit his brows and looked in her face with a furtive smile, but said nothing. A spasm of fear twitched her features, and she stepped back a pace, pale, whispering softly: "What is the matter? Why do you look like that? Ilya, Ilya!"

"Tell me, why should I lie?" he asked, showing his teeth scornfully. "I have seen the old man at your house."

Then, resting his elbows on the marble-topped table, he went on slowly and quietly, with a sudden access of bitter anger:

"I did see him once, and I thought: 'This is the man who stands in my way and has spoilt my life;' and if I did not strangle him then and there——"

"Don't tell lies!" cried Olympiada, loudly, and struck the table. "It is a lie! He was not in your way."

"How was he not?"

"He did nothing to you. You had only to wish it, and I'd have given him the go-by. Didn't I tell you I'd show him the door right away, if you wanted it? You smile there and you don't say anything. You never really loved me. It was your own choice to share with him. You worthless——"

"Stop! Be quiet!" cried Ilya. He sprang up, but at once sat down again, as though the woman had crushed him by her accusation.

"I will not be quiet!" she cried aloud. "I loved you because you were good-looking and wholesome; and you, what have you done to me? Did you ever say: 'Choose—him or me!' Did you ever say it? No! You were nothing but a love-sick tom-cat, like all the others."

Ilya started at this insulting reproach. There was a darkness before his eyes, and with clenched fist he sprang up again.

"Stop! How dare you?"

"You'll strike me, will you? Well, then, do it!" and her eyes flashed threateningly and she ground her teeth. "Strike me, and I'll tear the door open and cry out that you killed him and planned it with me. Well, do it!"

For a moment Ilya was paralysed with fear, but the feeling only touched his heart and vanished at once. Only he breathed with difficulty, as though unseen hands had him by the throat.

Again he sank back on the divan, was silent for a while, then gave a forced laugh. He saw Olympiada bite her lips and look as if seeking something round the dirty room, full of a damp, soapy vapour. Then she sat down on the divan close to the door, let her head fall, and said:

"Laugh away, you devil!"

"I will, certainly."

"When I saw you, I said 'that's the man for me, he'll help me, save me.'"

"Lipa," said Ilya gently.

She sat motionless and did not answer.

"Lipa," he repeated, and then with a sense as of hurling himself into an abyss, he said slowly, clearly:

"I did strangle the old man, by God!"

She shuddered, lifted her head and looked at him with wide eyes. Her lips began to tremble and she stammered:

"Silly boy, how frightened you are!"

Ilya understood that it was she who felt the fear, and did not want to believe his words. He got up, moved nearer, and sat down beside her, smiling vaguely. She caught his head to her breast, and whispered in her deep voice, as she kissed his hair: "Ilushka! Ilushka! Why do you hurt me so? I was so glad you killed him, the old sneak."

"Yes, I did it," he said, and nodded his head.

"Sh!" said the woman, anxiously. "I'm glad he's out of the way. That's what should happen to them all—all who ever touched me. You are the only man I ever met. You are the first, my dear one."

Her words drew him closer to her. He nestled with his face against her breast, till he could hardly breathe, but would not loosen his embrace, for he felt she was the only human being that was really near to him, and that more than ever now he needed her.

"When you stand there fresh and healthy, and look at me angrily, then I feel the degradation of my life, and I love you even for that, because of your pride."

Great tears fell on Ilya's face, and as their falling moved him, over his own cheeks flowed a stream that freed his soul. She took his head in her hands, kissed eyes and cheeks, and lips, and said:

"I know it's only my beauty holds you—your heart doesn't love me, and it condemns me. You can't forgive me my life, and that old man."

"Don't speak of him," said Ilya. He dried his face with her kerchief and rose up calm.

"Let come what may," he said slowly and firmly. "If God means to punish, He finds the way. I thank you, Lipa, for your words, what you say is right. I am guilty towards you. I thought you were—only such a one as— — and you are— —forgive me dear!"

He stammered with dry lips and dim eyes. Slowly, he smoothed his disordered hair with a trembling hand, and said in a dull, hopeless way:

"I am guilty of everything. Why? Why? Oh! Satan!"

"Olympiada caught his hand; he sank on the divan beside her and said, not heeding her whispered words:

"Do you understand? I strangled him; do you believe it?"

"Sh!" cried Olympiada, in an anxious muffled voice. "What are you saying?"

She embraced him closely, and looked into his face with troubled eyes.

"Let me go! it—it happened all of a sudden—God knows I didn't mean to do it. I only wanted to see his hateful face again, that's why I went into the shop. I had no intention,—and then it came in a moment, the devil urged me and God did not hold me back. I shouldn't have taken the money, that was silly, ah!"

He sighed deeply, and the hard rind of his heart seemed to loosen. Olympiada was quivering at his story, she held him even closer and whispered brokenly, disconnectedly. Presently she said: "It was a good thing you took the money, they'll think now it was for robbery, and not for jealousy; that would be worse for us."

"I don't feel sorry," said Ilya thoughtfully. "I won't repent. God may punish me! Men are not my judges; what sort of judges would they be! I know no men without sin, not one. I'll wait."

"O God," stammered Olympiada. "What is it? What will happen? Dear, I'm quite stupid. I can't think clearly—but let's go away from here—it's time."

She stood up and swayed like a drunken woman. But when she had fastened her veil, she said of a sudden, quite calmly:

"What's going to happen, Ilya? Will it go hard— —?"

Ilya shook his head.

"Tell the magistrate everything, just as it was; that is, not everything, but— —"

"I'll say it. Do you think I won't stand up for myself, or that I want to go to Siberia for this old wretch and a matter of two thousand roubles? No? I've something else to do with my life!"

His face was red with excitement, and his eyes shone. She came close to him and said in a whisper:

"Did you really only take two thousand roubles?"

"Two thousand and a little more."

"Poor boy; no luck even there!" and the tears shone in her eyes.

Ilya, smiled and said bitterly:

"Ah! d'you think I did it for the money? you know better—wait!—let me go first."

"Come and see me soon; there's no need for us to hide; come soon."

They parted with a long passionate kiss. As soon as Ilya reached the street he hailed a droshky. As he went he kept looking back to see if he were followed. His heart was lighter and a warm, tender feeling for Olympiada awaked in it. By no word or look had she wounded him, when he made his confession, she had rather taken on herself a part of the guilt than thrust him away. One minute before, when she did not know, she was ready to destroy him; he had read it in her face; then suddenly she had changed; he smiled gently as he thought of it.

Next day Ilya felt like the quarry that finds the huntsman on its track. Petrusha met him in the bar room early; he answered Ilya's greeting with a nod, and looked at him strangely, searchingly. Terenti looked hard at him, sighed and said nothing, Jakov met him in Masha's room, and said with a terrified face:

"Last night the Ward Superintendent was here; he asked father all about you. Why did he do that?"

"What did he ask about?" said Ilya quietly.

"Everything—how you live, if you drink brandy, if you go with women,—he mentioned some Olympiada; didn't you know her, he asked. Why did he want to know all this?"

"Heaven knows;" answered Ilya, and left him.

That evening came another letter from Olympiada.

"They've questioned me about you. I have said everything exactly; there's nothing in all that, and it isn't risky. Don't be anxious. I kiss you dearest."

He threw the letter at once in the fire. In Filimonov's house as well as in the bar, the talk was all of the murder. Ilya listened with a distinct sense of pleasure. He liked to pass near men who were discussing his deed, asking for details, which were invented freely, and thought with pleasure what profound amazement he could bring on them if he said:

"I did it—I!"

Some praised the cleverness of the criminal, some pointed out that he had failed to get all the money, some seemed to fear, lest he should yet be arrested, but not one single voice was heard to lament the victim, no one uttered on his account so much as a friendly word. Ilya despised them that they had no pity for the merchant, though he himself had none. He thought no more of Poluektov, only realising that he had taken a burden of guilt on himself and would be punished at some future time. This thought, in the present, disturbed him not at all; he bound it into his conscience and it became a part of his soul. It was like a bruise from a blow, it did not hurt if it were not disturbed.

He was deeply convinced that the hour must come when the vengeance of God would overtake him. God knows everything, and would not forgive the transgressor of His law: but this calm steady readiness to meet the punishment, any day, any hour, enabled Ilya to feel and behave as he did before the murder. Only he watched men more closely, and traced their weaknesses more zealously. This pleased him, though he realised that he was in no way exonerated thereby.

He was gloomier, more reserved, but from morning to night, as usual, he carried his wares about the town, visited alehouses, observed men, and listened to their talk. One day he thought of the money he had hidden and wondered if he would conceal it elsewhere. But at once he said to himself: "It's no good. Let it be. If they look and find it, I'll confess."

There was as yet no search after the money, and it was the sixth day before Ilya was summoned before the magistrate. Before he went, he changed his linen, put on his best jacket, and brushed his boots till they shone. He went in a sleigh. It jolted over the uneven streets till he had difficulty in holding himself upright and motionless. He felt his body so tensely strung that he feared to break something in him by a sudden movement. He mounted the steps of the Court House slowly and carefully, as though he were wearing clothes of glass.

The magistrate was a young man, with curly hair and a hooked nose, wearing gold-rimmed spectacles. When he saw Ilya, he first rubbed his thin white hands, then removed his spectacles and polished the lenses with his handkerchief, looking the while at Ilya with his big dark eyes. Ilya bowed silently.

"Good-day! Sit down there."

He indicated a chair at a big table covered with a dull red cloth. Ilya sat down, carefully pushing away with his elbow a pile of legal documents lying at the edge of the table. The magistrate noticed the movement, politely moved the papers, and sat down opposite Ilya. Without speaking, he began to turn the leaves of a book, and measured Ilya with sidelong glances. Ilya disliked the silence. He turned away and looked round the room. It was the first time he had seen a place so orderly and so richly furnished. All round the walls hung framed portraits and pictures. In one Christ was represented, walking, lost in thought, His head bowed, alone and sad, among ruins. Corpses of men and scattered weapons lay at his feet, and in the background, a dense black smoke rose up into the sky. Something was burning. Ilya looked long at this picture, and tried to understand what it represented. So much so that he was on the point of asking when suddenly the magistrate shut his book with a bang. Ilya started and looked at him. The magistrate's face wore a weary, dull expression, his lips were depressed oddly at the corners, as though some one had hurt his feelings.

"Well," he said, and tapped the table with his finger, "you are Ilya Jakovlevitch Lunev, aren't you?"

"Yes."

"You can guess why I have summoned you?"

"No," answered Ilya, and took another fleeting look at the picture. Then his eyes travelled over the solid, fine furniture, and he was conscious of the perfume the magistrate had been using. It distracted his thoughts and calmed him to observe his surroundings, and envy rose in his heart.

"This is how distinguished people live." The thought went through his head. "It must be very profitable to catch thieves and murderers. I wonder what he gets."

"You can't guess?" repeated the magistrate. "Has Olympiada said nothing to you?"

"No. It's some time since I saw her."

The magistrate threw himself back in his chair, and the corners of his lips went down.

"How long?" he asked.

"I don't know, eight or nine days perhaps."

"Ah! is that so? tell me, did you often meet old Poluektov at her house?"

"The old man who was murdered a little while ago?" asked Ilya, and looked his questioner in the eyes.

"Yes, that's the man."

"I never met him."

"Never?"

"Never."

The magistrate fired off his questions quickly with a certain nonchalance, and when Ilya, who answered very cautiously, was slow to reply, he drummed impatiently on the table with his fingers.

"You knew that Olympiada Petrovna was kept by Poluektov?" he asked suddenly, and looked sharply through his spectacles.

Ilya reddened at the glance, which seemed in some way to wound him.

"No," he said in a dull tone.

"Oh! yes, she was kept by him," repeated the magistrate, angrily, — "to my thinking that is not good," he added, as he saw Ilya about to answer.

"How should there be anything good in it?" said Ilya softly, at length.

"True."

But Ilya said no more.

"And you—you've known her a long time?"

"More than a year."

"You were intimate with her before her acquaintance with Poluektov?"

"You're a cunning fox," thought Ilya, and said quietly:

"How can I say, when I didn't know that she lived with the man that's dead."

The magistrate drew his lips together and whistled, and began to finger the pile of documents. Ilya looked again at the picture; he felt that his interest in it helped him to keep calm. From somewhere, the clear, gay laugh of a child came to his ear. Then a happy, gentle, woman's voice sang tenderly: "My Annie, my little one, my darling, my dear."

"That picture appears to interest you greatly."

"Where is Christ supposed to be going?" asked Ilya.

The magistrate looked in his face with a weary, disillusioned expression, and said after a pause:

"You can see. He's come down to earth to see how men fulfil His commands. He's going over a battle-field—round about are dead men, houses destroyed, fire plundering."

"Can't He see that from Heaven?"

"H'm, it's rather an allegory, it's represented like that, so as to be plainer, to show how little real life agrees with the teaching of Christ, that is——But come, I must ask you a question or two yet."

Ilya turned from the picture and looked in the magistrate's face; a number of little unimportant questions followed, annoying Ilya like autumn flies. He grew tired and felt his attention growing slack and his carefulness wither under the monotonous dull sound. He grew angry with the magistrate, who set these questions, as he well understood, on purpose to weary him.

"Can you tell me perhaps," said the magistrate quickly, apparently without any particular intent, "where you were on Thursday between two o'clock and three."

"In the ale-house; I was having tea."

"Ah! in which inn then? Where?"

"In the Plevna."

"How is it you are so certain that you were there just at that time?"

The magistrate's face looked tense, he leaned over the table and stared into Ilya's face with flaming eyes. Ilya did not reply at once. After a second or two he sighed and said with composure:

"Just before I went in, I asked the time of a policeman."

The magistrate leaned back again, and began to tap his finger-nails with a blue pencil.

"The policeman told me it was twenty minutes to two, or something like that."

"He knows you?"

"Yes."

"Have you no watch?"

"No."

"Have you ever before asked him the time?"

"Yes, it has happened."

"The town hall is near, there's a clock."

"One forgets to look, and then it was snowing."

"Were you long in the Plevna?"

"Till the news came of the murder."

"Where did you go then?"

"I went to look."

"Did any one see you there, in front of the shop?"

"That policeman saw me, he sent me off—pushed me."

"Very good, very important for you," said the magistrate approvingly, then asked at once without looking at Ilya:

"Did you ask the time before the murder or after?"

Ilya saw the drift of the question. He turned sharp round in his chair full of rage against this man with the shining white linen, the thin fingers, well-tended nails, and gold spectacles in front of piercing dark eyes.

Instead of answering, he asked:

"How can I tell?"

The magistrate coughed drily, and rubbed his hands till the fingers cracked.

"Well done," he said in a tone of displeasure. "Splendid!—yes."

And he shifted his chair as though tired.

"Very good; one or two questions now and I'll let you go. Do you know, by any chance, that policeman's name?"

"Jeremin, Matvey Ivanovitch."

The magistrate's tone was bored and indifferent; obviously he did not expect now to hear anything interesting.

Ilya answered, always on the look out for another question like the one as to the time of the murder. Every word echoed in his breast again as though it plucked a tense string in an empty space. But no more cunning questions came.

"As you went down the street that day, did you not meet a tall man in a short fur jacket and black lambs-wool cap? Do you remember?"

"No," said Ilya harshly.

"Now, listen. I'll read over your statement to you, and you will sign it."

He held a sheet of paper covered with writing before his face, and began to read quickly and monotonously. When he had finished, he put a pen in Ilya's hand. Ilya bent down, signed, rose slowly from his chair, and said in a loud, assured voice, looking at the magistrate: "Good-day!"

A short, condescending nod was his answer, and the magistrate bent over his desk, and began to write. Ilya stood thinking. He would gladly have said something more to this man who had held him so long on the rack. In the quiet, only the scratch of the pen was heard, then the woman's voice, singing, "Dance away, dance away, dolly."

"What do you want now?" asked the magistrate, and raised his head.

"Nothing," said Ilya gloomily.

"I told you, you can go."

"I'm going."

"All right, then."

They looked angrily at one another, and Ilya felt something heavy, terrifying, grow in his breast. He turned sharp round and went out into the street. A cold wind greeted him, and for the first time he noticed that he was sweating profusely. Half-an-hour later he was sitting with Olympiada. She opened the door to him herself, having seen him from the window. She met him with almost a mother's joy. Her face was pale, and she gazed restlessly about with wide-open eyes.

"My clever boy!" she cried, when Ilya told her that he had just come from the magistrate. "Tell me, tell me, how did you get on?"

"The brute," said Ilya, in wrath. "He set traps for me."

"He can't help it," remarked Olympiada, in a tone of common sense. "Let him be; it's his infernal duty."

"Why didn't he say straight out—'So-and-so, this is what people think of you.'"

"Did you tell him everything straight out?" she asked, smiling.

"I!" cried Ilya in astonishment. "Why, yes—as a matter of fact—ah, devil take him!"

He seemed quite abashed and said after a while:

"And as I sat there, I thought, by God, I was right!"

"Now, thank heaven, it's all passed over all right."

Ilya looked at her with a smile. "I didn't need to lie much. I'm lucky, after all, Lipa!"

He laughed again in a strange way.

"The secret police are always at my heels," said Olympiada, in a low voice, "and after you too."

"Of course," said Ilya, full of scorn and anger. "They go sniffing around, and want to hem me in, like the beaters do to the wolf in the forest. But they won't do it; they're not the men for that; and I'm not a wolf, but an unlucky man. I didn't mean to strangle any one. Fate strangles me—as Pashka says in his poem—and it strangles Pashka too, and Jakov, and all of us."

"Never mind, Ilushka. Everything will go right now."

Ilya got up, walked to the window, and said, with a despairing voice, as he looked at the street:

"All my life I've had to wallow in the mud. I've always been pushed into things I disliked—hated. I've never met a soul I could look at really happily. Is there nothing pure in life, nothing noble? Now, I've strangled this—this man of yours,—why? I've only smirched myself, and damned myself. I took money. I ought not."

"Don't be sorry!" She tried to console him. "He isn't worth it."

"I'm not sorry for him; only I want to get myself straight. Every one tries, else he can't live. That magistrate, he lives like a sugar-plum in its box. No one will strangle him. He can be good and upright in his pretty nest."

"Never mind, we'll go away together from this place."

"No. I'll go nowhere," cried Ilya fiercely, and wheeled round to her, and added, seeming to threaten some unknown person.

"No—no—patience! I'll wait and see what will come; I'll fight it out still," and he strode up and down the room, and shook his head defiantly.

"Oh!" said Olympiada, in an injured tone. "You won't go with me, because you're afraid of me; you think I should always have a hold on you, you think I should use what I know—you're wrong, my dear. I'll never drag you with me by force."

She spoke quietly, but her lips twitched as though she were in pain.

"What did you say?" asked Ilya, quite surprised.

"I won't compel you, don't be frightened; go where you will!"

"Wait a moment," said Ilya, as he sat down near her, and took her hand.

"I didn't understand what you said."

"Don't pretend!" she cried, and drew away her hand. "I know you're proud, and passionate; you can't forgive the old man; you hate my life—you think that it's all come about through me."

"You're talking foolishly," said Ilya, quietly. "I don't blame you in the very least, I know that for men like me there are no women who are pretty and fine and pure as well. Such women are dear, they are only for the rich, and we must love the soiled and those who are spat upon and abused."

"Then leave me, the spat upon and abused!" cried Olympiada, springing up from her chair. "Go away—go away!"

But suddenly tears shone in her eyes and she covered Ilya with a flood of burning words, like hot coals.

"I myself, of my own will crept into this pit, because there's money in it. I meant to climb up the ladder again with the money, begin a decent life— and you helped me, I know, and I love you, and will love you though you strangle twenty men; it isn't your goodness I love, but your pride, and your youth, your curly head and your strong arms and your dark eyes, and your reproaches that pierce my heart. I shall be grateful for all this till I die.—I'll kiss your feet."

She threw herself at his feet, and embraced his knees.

"God is my witness, I sinned to save my soul. I must be dearer to Him if I don't end my life in this filth, but struggle through it and lead a clean life. Then I will entreat His forgiveness. I will not endure this torment all my life; they have soiled me with mud and filth; all my tears will never wash me clean."

At first Ilya tried to free himself and raise her from the ground, but she clung close to him, pressed her head against his knees and laid her cheek at his feet. And she spoke on with a low, passionate, gasping voice. Presently he caressed her with a trembling hand, raised her, embraced her, and laid her head on his shoulder, her hot cheek pressed close to his, and as she lay supported by his arms on her knees before him, she whispered:

"Does it do any one any good if a woman who has sinned once spends almost her whole life in humiliation? When I was a girl and my stepfather came near me to make me impure, I stuck a knife in him. I did it without a thought. Then they made me drunk with wine and ruined me. I was a girl, so tidy, so pretty and red-cheeked as an apple. I cried for myself. I hurt myself. I cried for my beauty. I didn't want it! I didn't want it! And then I said to myself: 'It's all the same now. There's no going back. Good,' I thought, 'at least I'll sell my shame as dear as I can.' I never kissed from my heart till I kissed you. I always just lived in filth and rioting."

Her words were lost in a soft whisper. Suddenly she tore herself from Ilya's embrace. "Let me go!" she cried, and thrust him away.

But he held her closer, and began to kiss her face, passionately, despairingly.

"Let me go! You hurt me!" she said.

"I can say nothing," said Ilya, feverishly. "Only one thing—no one has had pity on us, and we need have pity on no one. You spoke so beautifully! Come, let me kiss you. How else can I make it up to you? My dear! My dearest! I love you! Ah, I don't know how I love you. I've no words to tell you."

Her lamentation had really roused in him a burning feeling of affection for this woman. Her sorrow and his misfortune were molten together, and their hearts came nearer and nearer. They held one another in a close embrace, and softly told one another all the long sufferings they had endured from life. A courageous, fierce feeling rose in Ilya's heart.

"We were not born for fortune, we two," said the woman, and shook her head hopelessly.

"Good! Then we will celebrate out misfortune! Shall we go to the mines, to Siberia, together? Eh? Ah, there's time for that. As yet we will enjoy our pain and our love. Now they might burn me with red-hot irons, my heart is so light. I repent nothing!"

Outside the window, the sky was a monotonous grey. A cold mist enwrapped the earth and settled in white rime on the trees. In the little garden, a young birch-tree swayed its thin branches gently, and shook the snow away. The winter evening came on.

CHAPTER XV

Two days later Ilya learnt that a tall man in a lambs-wool cap was being sought for as the probable murderer of Poluektov. During the investigations made in the shop, two silver clasps from an eikon were found and it appeared that these were stolen goods. The errand boy who had been employed in the business, stated that these mounts had been bought from a tall man in a short fur jacket, called Andrei, that this Andrei had several times before sold gold and silver ornaments to Poluektov, and that the money-changer had advanced him money. Further it was known that on the evening before the murder and on the same day, a man corresponding to the description, had wasted much money in carousing in the public houses of the town.

Every day Ilya heard something new; the whole town took a keen interest in this crime, so ingeniously carried out, and in all the ale-houses and all the streets nothing else was spoken of. But all the talk had little attraction for Ilya. Fear had fallen from his heart, like the scab from a wound, and instead he only felt now a sense of awkwardness. He listened attentively to all that was said, but thought only—how would his life shape itself now, what had the future in store for him? And the conviction that the murderer would not be discovered, strengthened every day.

He felt like a recruit before the conscription summons, or like a man who is proceeding towards some unknown far-off goal. More than ever he felt the need to live for himself and take thought for himself, but life hissed and boiled round him like water in a kettle, and almost every day came something to distract his mind from its preoccupation. He grew pale and thin.

Of late Jakov had been more drawn to him again. Tousled and carelessly dressed, he wandered aimlessly about the tap room and the courtyard, looking vaguely at everything with wandering eyes and had the appearance of a man brought face to face with strange ideas. When he met Ilya he would ask him mysteriously, half aloud, or whispering, "Have you no time to talk?"

"Wait a bit; I can't now."

"It's something very important."

"What is it?"

"It's a book. I tell you, brother, the things in it——Oh! oh!" said Jakov, with a terrified air.

"Bother your books! I'd rather know why your father always scowls at me now."

But Jakov had no mind for realities.

At Ilya's question he looked astonished, as though he hardly understood, and said:

"Eh? I don't know. That is, once I heard him speaking to your uncle about it; something about your passing false money; but he only said it chaffing."

"How do you know he was only chaffing?"

"Why, what a thing to say—false money," he interrupted Ilya with a gesture as though to wave the subject away. "But won't you talk to me? No time?"

"About your book?"

"Yes, there's a bit in it I've just read. Oh! well!"

And the philosopher made a face as though something had scalded him. Ilya looked at his friend as at a person half idiotic. Sometimes Jakov seemed to him absolutely blind. He took him for an unlucky man, unfit to cope with life.

The gossip ran in the house, and it was all over the street already, that Petrusha was going to marry his mistress, who kept a public house in the town. But Jakov paid absolutely no attention. When Ilya asked him when the wedding was to be, he said:

"Whose wedding?"

"Why, your father's."

"Oh! who's to know? disgusting! A pretty witch he's chosen!"

"Do you know she has a son—a big boy, who goes to the High School?"

"No, I didn't know. Why?"

"He'll come in for your father's property."

"Oh!" said Jakov, indifferently, then with a sudden interest, "A son, you say?"

"Yes."

"A son—that'll just do, father can stick him behind the bar, and I can do what I like. That'll suit me."

And he smacked his lips as with a foretaste of his longed-for freedom. Ilya looked at him with pity, then said, mockingly:

"The proverb is right, 'Give the stupid child a piece of bread if he wants a carrot.' You! I can't imagine how you're going to live."

Jakov pricked up his ears, looked at Ilya with big eyes starting out of his head, then said in a hurried whisper:

"I know how I shall live! I've thought about it! Before everything, one must get one's soul in order; must understand what God wants one to do. Now I see one thing; the ways of men are all confused, like tangled threads, and they are drawn in different directions, and no one knows what to hold to or where to let himself be drawn. Now a man is born—no one knows why—and lives—I don't know why—and death comes and blows out the light. Before anything else I must know what I'm in the world for, mustn't I?"

"You—you've tied yourself up in your cobwebs," said. Ilya with some heat. "I'd like to know what's the sense of that?"

He felt that Jakov's dark sayings gripped his heart more strongly than of old, and waked very strange thoughts in him. He felt as though there were a being in his mind, the same that always opposed his clear, simple conception of a clean, comfortable life, that listened to Jakov with strange curiosity, and moved in his soul like a child in the mother's womb.

This troubled Ilya, confused him, and seemed to him undesirable, and therefore he avoided conversation with Jakov; but it was not easy to get rid of him once he had begun.

"What's the sense? It's very simple. Not to be clear where you're going's like trying to burn without fire, isn't it? You must know where you're going, and why, and if it's the right road."

"You're like an old man, Jakov—you're a bit of a bore. My opinion is, as the proverb says: 'Seeing that even swine long to be happy, how should man do otherwise.' Good-bye!"

After such conversation, he felt as though he had eaten something very salt; he was overcome with thirst, and longed for something out of the common. The thought of the punishment God held over him burned more brightly in him and singed his soul; he sought for loneliness and could not find it. Then he would go to Olympiada, and in her arms seek forgetfulness and peace from torturing thought. Sometimes he would go to see Vyera. The life she led had drawn her deeper and deeper into its deep turbid whirlpool. She used to tell Ilya with excitement, of feasting with rich young tradesmen, with officials and officers, of suppers in restaurants and troika excursions. She showed him new dresses and jackets, the gifts of her admirers. Luxurious, strong, and healthy, she was proud to be entreated and quarrelled over. Ilya rejoiced in her health and good spirits and beauty, but more than once warned her: "Don't lose your head at the game, Vyeratchka."

"What's the odds? It's my way. At least, one lives in style. I take all I can get from life. That's enough!"

"Well, what about Pavel?"

As soon as he named her lover, she lost her gaiety and her brows contracted.

"If only he'd let me go my own way! It troubles him so, and he torments himself so! If only he'd be content with what I can give him. But he wants me altogether, and I can't stop now; I'm like a fly caught in the treacle."

"Don't you love him?"

"I can't help it," she replied, seriously, "he's such a fine fellow."

"Very well, then, you ought to live with him."

"With him? Nice drag I should be on him! He has barely a bit of bread for himself, how's he to keep me too? No, I'm sorry for him."

"Look out that no harm comes of it. He's hot-tempered," Ilya warned her one day; but she laughed.

"He? He's as gentle—I can twist him which way I want."

"You'll break him!"

"Good heavens!" she cried crossly, "what am I to do? Was I born for just one man? Every one wants to enjoy his life, and every one lives for himself, as he pleases, just as you do, and I do."

"N—No! it isn't so exactly," said Ilya gloomily and thoughtfully. "We all live, but not only for ourselves."

"For whom, then?"

"Take yourself, for instance. You live for the young clerks and all sorts of easy-going people."

"I'm easy-going too," said Vyera, and laughed contentedly.

Ilya left her, in a downcast mood. Only twice, and for a moment, had he seen Pavel during this time. Once when he met his friend at Vyera's house, he had sat there dark and troubled, silent, with teeth clenched and a red spot on each cheek. Ilya understood that Pavel was jealous of him, and that flattered his vanity. But he saw too, clearly, that Gratschev was tangled in a net, from which he would hardly free himself without severe injury. He pitied Pavel, and still more Vyera, and gave up visiting her. He was living a new honeymoon with Olympiada. But here too, a cold shadow glided in and took the peace from his heart. Sometimes, in the midst of a conversation, he would sink into a deep moodiness. Olympiada said to him once, in a loving whisper:

"Dear, don't think of it. There are so few men in the world whose hands are clean."

"Listen!" he answered seriously and tonelessly. "Please don't speak of that to me! I'm not thinking of my hands, but of my soul. You are clever, but you can never understand what it is that moves me. Tell me, if you can, how shall a man begin, what shall he do, to live honourably and cleanly, peacefully and rightly to others? That is what I want to know. But say nothing to me of the old man!"

But she could not keep silence, and implored him again and again to forget. He grew angry, and went away. When he returned, she flew out at him, and exclaimed that he only loved her out of fear, or from pity; that she would not endure it, and would rather leave him, rather go away out of the town. She wept, pinched or bit him, then kissed his feet, or tore her clothes like a mad thing, and said:

"Am I not beautiful, desirable? And I love you with every vein, every drop of my blood. Hurt me, tear me, and I'll laugh at it." Her blue eyes would darken, her lips quiver, and her bosom heave. Then he would embrace her and kiss her passionately; but afterwards, as he went home, he would wonder how she, so full of life, so passionate, how could she endure the disgusting caresses of that old man? Then Olympiada appeared so pitiable, so contemptible that he could spit for disgust when he thought of her kisses. One day, after such an outbreak, he said to her, tired of her caresses:

"Do you love me more warmly since I strangled that old devil?"

"Yes, of course. Why?"

"Nothing. It makes me laugh to think there are people who like a stale egg better than a fresh, and would rather eat an apple when its rotten— odd!"

She looked at him wearily, and said in a tired voice:

"'Every beast likes something best,' as the saying goes. One likes the owl, another the nightingale."

And both fell into a heavy moodiness.

One day when Ilya had returned home and was changing his clothes, Terenti came quietly into the room. He shut the door fast behind him, stood a moment, as if listening, then pushed to the bolts.

Ilya noticed this, and looked at him mockingly.

"Ilusha," began Terenti, in a low voice as he sat down on a chair.

"Well."

"There are strange reports going about you; people say evil things of you."

The hunchback sighed, and closed his eyes.

"For instance?" said Ilya, drawing on his boots.

"Some say one thing, some another; some say you were mixed up in that affair when the old merchant was strangled; others say you pass false money."

"They're envious, eh?"

"Different people have been here, secret police it seems—detectives— they questioned Petrusha about you."

"Let them till they're tired," said Ilya, indifferently.

"Certainly, what have they to do with us if we have no sins on our conscience?"

Ilya laughed and stretched himself on the bed.

"They don't come now, but Petrusha is always on about it," said Terenti shyly, in an embarrassed way. "He's always taunting one, Petrusha. You ought to take a little room for yourself somewhere, Ilusha, a room of your own to live in. Yes. 'I can't have these worthy dark gentlemen in my house,' says Petrusha. 'I'm a town councillor,' he says."

Ilya turned, his face red with anger, on his uncle, and said loudly:

"Listen! If he values his ugly face, let him hold his tongue! Tell him that! If I hear one word I don't like, I'll smash his skull for him. Whatever I am, he, at any rate, has no call to judge me, the scoundrel! And I'll go away when I want to. Meantime I shall stay and enjoy this honourable and distinguished company."

The hunchback was terrified at Ilya's wrath; he sat silent a while, rubbing his back, and looking at his nephew with big eyes full of anxious expectation.

Ilya compressed his lips and stared at the ceiling. Terenti looked at him, the curly head, serious handsome face, with the small moustache and strong chin, the broad chest and all the vigorous, well-knit body, and then said slowly, with a sigh:

"What a fine lad you've grown! the girls in the village would crowd after you. We'll go to the village."

Ilya was silent.

"H'm, yes—you'll have a real life there! I'll give you money, and set you up in business, and then you'll marry a rich girl, he! he! And your life will glide along like a sleigh on the snow downhill."

"Perhaps I prefer to go uphill," said Ilya, peevishly.

"Of course, uphill," Terenti caught up his words. "That's what I meant; it's an easy life—that's what I meant; why, uphill, of course, to the very top."

"And when I'm there, what then?"

The hunchback looked at him and chuckled. Then he spoke again, but Ilya did not listen. He was thinking of all his experiences of this later time, and figuring to himself how evenly all life hangs together, like the strings in a net. Circumstances surround men and lead them where they will, as the police do the rogues. He had always had it in his mind to leave this house and live by himself, and now here chance comes to his aid! He was still thinking how he would plan out his life alone, when there came a sudden knock at the door.

"Open it!" cried Ilya crossly to his uncle, who was shaking with fear.

The hunchback drew back the bolts and Jakov appeared, a great, red-brown book in his hand.

"Ilya, come to Mashutka!" he said quickly, and advanced to the bed.

"What's wrong with her?" said Ilya hastily.

"With her? I don't know, she's not at home."

"Where does she always go gadding to in the evenings?" asked the hunchback in a tone of annoyance.

"She always goes out with Matiza," said Ilya.

"She'll get a lot of good there!" answered Terenti, with emphasis.

"It doesn't matter. Come Ilya!"

Jakov caught Ilya by the sleeve and drew him away.

"Hold on!" cried Lunev. "Tell me, have you got your mind clear yet?"

"Think—it's here—the Black Magic's here!" whispered Jakov, radiant.

"Who?" asked Ilya, pulling on his felt slippers.

"Why, you know, the book. Heavens! you'll see. Come. Extraordinary things, I tell you," Jakov went on enthusiastically, as he dragged his friend along the dark passage.

"It's awful to read, it's like falling down a precipice."

Ilya saw his friend's excitement and heard how his voice shook. When they reached the cobbler's room, and had lighted the lamp, he saw that Jakov's face was quite pale, and his eyes dim and happy, like those of a drunken man.

"Have you been drinking?" asked Ilya, suspiciously.

"I? No. Not a drop to-day! I never drink now, anyway, or only when father's at home, to screw up my courage, two or three glasses, no more. I'm afraid of father—always drinks stuff that doesn't smell too strong though—but never mind that, listen!"

He fell into a chair so heavily that it creaked, opened his book, bent double over it, and fingering the old pages, yellow with age, he read in a hollow, trembling voice: "'Third Chapter—On the origin of man.' Now, listen!"

He sighed, took his left hand off the book, and read aloud. The index finger of his right hand preceded his voice, as though writing in the old book. "'It is said, and Diodorus confirms, that the origin of man is conceived according to two ways, by the virtuous men'—d'you hear, virtuous men—'who have written on the nature of things. Some consider that the world is uncreated and imperishable, and that the race of men has existed from eternity, without any beginning.'"

Jakov raised his head, and said in a whisper, gesticulating with his hand in the air:

"D'you hear? Without beginning!"

"Go on!" said Ilya, and looked distrustfully at the old leather-bound book. Jakov's voice continued, softly and solemnly: "'This opinion was held, according to Cicero, by Pythagoras of Samos, Archytas of Tarentum, Plato of Athens, Xenokrates, Aristotle of Stagira, and many others of the peripatetic philosophers, who took the view that all that is, exists from eternity, and has no beginning'—d'you see, again, no beginning—'but that there is a certain cycle of life, those that were born and those that are born, in which cycle is the beginning and the end of every man that is born.'"

Ilya stretched out his hand and struck the book, and said mockingly:

"Throw it away! Devil take it! Some German or other has been showing off his cleverness. There's no sense in it."

"Wait a minute!" cried Jakov, and looked anxiously round, then at his friend, and said gently:

"Perhaps you know your beginning?"

"What beginning?" cried Ilya crossly.

"Don't shout so! Take the soul. Man is born with a soul, isn't he?"

"Well?"

"Then he must know where he comes from, and how? The soul is immortal, they say. It was always there; isn't that true? Wait! It isn't so much to know how you were born as how you lived. When did you live? When did you first know that you were alive? You were born living. Well, then, when did you become living. In the womb? Very well. Why don't you remember more—what happened before your birth, and not only what happened after you were five years old? Eh? And, if you have a soul, how did it get inside you? Eh? Tell me."

Jakov's eyes shone triumphantly, his face broke into a happy smile, and he cried, with a joy that seemed to Ilya very strange: "You see, there you have your soul!"

"Stupid!" said Ilya, and looked at him angrily, "what's that to be glad about?"

"I'm not glad. I'm only saying—I'm only saying——"

"Well, I tell you, throw the book away! You see quite well it's written against God. It doesn't matter a bit how I was born alive, but how I live. How to live so that everything is clean and pleasant, so that no one hurts me, and I hurt nobody. Find me a book that'll make that plain to me."

Jakov sat silent and thoughtful, his head on his breast. His joy vanished when it found no echo. After a time he said: "When I look at you, there's something about you I don't like. I don't understand your thoughts, but I see you've been getting very proud about something or other for some time. You go on as if you were the only righteous man."

Ilya laughed aloud.

"What are you laughing at? It's true. You judge every one so harshly. You don't love anybody."

"There you're right," said Ilya, fiercely. "Whom should I love; and why? What good have men done to me? Every one wants to get his bread by some one else's work, and every one cries out: 'love me, respect me, give me a share of your goods; then perhaps I'll love you!' Every one, every where, thinks of nothing but stuffing himself."

"No. I think men don't think only of stuffing themselves," answered Jakov displeased and hurt.

"I know—every one tries to adorn himself with something, but it's only a mask. I see my uncle try and bargain with God, like the shopman with his master. Your papa gives one or two weathercocks to churches. I conclude from that that he either has swindled some one or is going to; and so they all behave, as far as I can see; there's your penny they say, but give me back five. I read the other day in the paper of Migunov the merchant, who gave three hundred roubles to a hospital, and then petitions the town council to knock off the arrears of his taxes, just a thousand roubles—and so they all do, trying to throw dust in one another's eyes and put themselves in the right. My view is, if you've sinned, willingly or unwillingly, take your punishment!"

"You're right there," said Jakov thoughtfully. "What you said of father and the hunchback, that was right too. Ah! we're both born under an evil star. You have your wickedness at any rate, you comfort yourself by judging everybody, but I have not even that. Oh! if only I could go away somewhere, away from here."

His speech ended with a cry of distress.

"Away from here. Where d'you want to go?" asked Ilya with a faint smile.

"It's all the same. I don't know."

They sat at the table opposite one another, gloomy and silent, and there lay the big red-brown book with the steel clasp.

Suddenly there was a rustling in the passage, a low voice was heard and a hand fumbled at the door for the latch. The friends waited in silence. The door opened slowly, and Perfishka staggered in: he stumbled on the threshold and fell on his knees, holding up his harmonica.

"Prr,"—he said, and laughed drunkenly.

Immediately behind him Matiza crept into the room. She bent over the cobbler, took his arm and tried to lift him up, saying with stammering tongue:

"Ah! How drunk he is! Oh, you soaker!"

"Don't touch me, jade! I'll stand alone, quite alone."

He swayed hither and thither, but got on his legs with difficulty, and came up to the two friends: he stretched out his left hand and cried:

"Welcome to my house!"

Matiza laughed, a deep, silly laugh.

"Where do you come from?" asked Ilya.

Jakov looked at the two with a smile and said nothing.

"Where? From the deep sea! Ha! ha! my dear, good boys. Oh! yes!"

Perfishka stamped his feet on the floor and sang:

"Oh little bones, dear little bones,
I weep for you in piteous tones.
For hardly are you grown at all
Before the shopman cracks you small."

"Sing, you jade, sing too," he screamed, turning to Matiza, "or let's sing the song you taught me, go ahead!"

He leant his back against the stove, where Matiza had already found support, and dug his elbow into her ribs, while his fingers wandered over the harmonica keys.

"Where is Mashutka?" asked Ilya suddenly, in a harsh voice.

"Yes, tell us," cried Jakov, and sprang from his chair. "Where is she? Tell us!"

But the drunken pair paid no heed to the question. Matiza leant her head to one side and sang:

"Ah! neighbour, your brandy is rousing and good."

And Perfishka struck in in a high tenor:

"Drink it, my neighbour, it comforts the blood."

Ilya stepped up to the cobbler, caught him by the shoulder, and shook him, till he fell against the stove.

"Where's your daughter?" he said commandingly.

"And oh! his daughter she vanished away,
In the midnight hour, ere the break of day,"
babbled Perfishka, and held his head with his hand.

Jakov attempted to get the truth from Matiza, but she only said smirking: "I won't tell. I won't. I won't."

"They've sold her, the devils," said Ilya to his friend, gloomily. Jakov looked at him in terror, then asked the cobbler almost weeping:

"Perfishka! listen—Where is Mashutka?"

"Mashutka?" repeated Matiza, scornfully. "Aha! you see. Now you remember."

"Ilya! what shall we do?" cried Jakov full of anxiety.

"We must tell the police," said Ilya, and looked with disgust at the drunkards.

"Aha! jade! d'you hear," shouted Perfishka, beaming, "they want to tell the police! ha! ha! ha!"

"The po—lice?" cried Matiza emphatically, and looked with extraordinary great eyes from Ilya to Jakov and back again. Then stretching out her hands helplessly, she screamed loudly:

"You'll go to your police, will you? Get out of my room! It is my room now, we're just married, we two."

"Ha! ha! ha! laughed the cobbler, holding his sides.

"Come Jakov!" said Ilya. "The devil would be sickened at them! Come."

"Wait!" cried Jakov, in anxious excitement. "Have they really married her? That child? Is it possible? Perfishka, tell me, have you really. Oh, tell me, where is Masha?"

"Matiza, my wife, go for them! Catch them—catch—scream at them, bite them! Ha! ha! where is Masha?"

Perfishka pursed his lips as though to whistle, but could not get out a sound, and instead, put out his tongue at Jakov and laughed again.

Matiza pressed close to Ilya with her huge bosom heaving, and roared:

"Who are you, eh? D'you think we don't know all about you?"

Ilya gave her a push and left the cellar.

In the passage Jakov overtook him, caught him by the shoulder, held him fast in the darkness, and said:

"Is it allowed; can it be done? She's so little, Ilya! Have they really married her!"

"Oh! don't whimper!" said Ilya wrathfully. "That's no good! You ought to have kept your eyes open before; you began it, and now they've finished it."

Jakov was silent for a moment, then at once began again, as he stepped into the courtyard after Ilya.

"It's not my fault. I only knew that she went out to work somewhere."

"What does it matter, if you knew or didn't know?" said Ilya, harshly, and stood still in the middle of the courtyard. "I'll get out of this house anyhow; it ought to be burnt to the ground."

"O God! O God!" sighed Jakov, in a low voice, keeping behind Ilya. Ilya wheeled round. Jakov stood there miserable, his arms hanging helplessly and his head bowed as if to receive a blow.

"Cry away!" said Ilya, mockingly, and went off, leaving his friend in the middle of the dark courtyard. Next day Ilya learnt from Perfishka that Masha was actually married to Ehrenov the grocer, a widower of fifty, who had lost his wife shortly before.

"'I've two children,' he said to me, 'one five years old, one three,'" explained Perfishka, "'and I shall have to get a nurse. But a nurse,' he says, 'is always a stranger. She'll rob me, and that sort of thing. Speak to your daughter, if she'll marry me!' Well, so I spoke to her, and Matiza spoke to her, and since Masha is a reasonable child, she understood it all, and what else was she to do? 'All right,' she says, 'I'll do it!' And so she went to him. It was all settled in three days. We two—I and Matiza—got three roubles, so yesterday we got drunk. Heavens! how Matiza drinks, like a horse!"

Ilya listened in silence. He understood that Masha had done better for herself than would have been generally expected. But all the same, his heart ached for the girl. He had seen little of her of late, and hardly thought of her, but now, without her, the house felt dirtier and more hateful than ever.

The yellow, bloated face of the cobbler grinned down at Ilya from the stove, and his voice creaked like a broken branch in the autumn wind. Lunev looked at him disgustedly.

"Ehrenov made one condition: I'm never to show up at his house! 'You can come to the shop,' he says. 'I'll give you schnapps and odds and ends, but to the house—never! It's shut to you, like Paradise.' Now then, Ilya Jakovlevitch, couldn't you hunt up a five-kopeck piece, to get a drink. Please give me five kopecks."

"You shall have 'em in a minute," said Ilya. "What are you going to do now?"

The cobbler spat on the ground, and replied: "I'll just become an out-and-out drunkard. Till Masha was provided for, I used to worry. I worked sometimes. I had a sort of conscience with her. But now I know she's enough to eat and shoes and clothes, and is shut up in a box, so to speak, I can devote myself, free and unhindered, to the drinking profession."

"Can't you really give up brandy?"

"Never!" answered the cobbler, and shook his shaggy head in a vigorous negative. "Why should I?"

"Is there nothing else in life you want?"

"Give me five kopecks. I don't want anything else."

"I can't understand that," said Ilya, shrugging his shoulders. "I can't understand how a man can live, and want nothing out of life."

"I'm different from the rest," answered Perfishka, with philosophical calm. "I think this way: keep quiet!—Fate gives what it will, and if a man is hollow and empty, so that nothing can be put in him, then, what can Fate do? Once, I admit, I wanted things, while my dead one was alive—I knew of Jeremy's pile. I'd have liked to have a fist in that. 'If I don't rob him,' I thought, 'some one else will.' Well, thank God, two others actually got in before me. I don't complain, but then I understood that one must learn, too, how to wish."

The cobbler laughed, climbed down from the stove, and added:

"Now give me the five kopecks. My inside's on fire. I can't stand it any more."

"There! Have your glass," said Ilya. Then he looked at Perfishka with a smile, and asked:

"Shall I tell you something?"

"Well, what?"

"You're a humbug, and a good-for-nothing, and a miserable drunkard. That's all certain."

"Yes, it's certain," confessed the cobbler, standing before Ilya with the five-kopeck piece in his hand.

"And yet," Ilya went on seriously and thoughtfully, "I don't believe I know a better man than you, by God, I don't."

Perfishka smiled incredulously, and looked at Lunev's serious but friendly face.

"You're joking?"

"Believe it or not, it is so. I don't say it to praise you, but only because, so far as I can see, that's my opinion."

"Wonderful! my head's too stupid I'm afraid; did I understand you to say—.—But let me have a mouthful, perhaps then I'll be cleverer."

"Not so fast!" said Ilya, and caught him by the shirt sleeve. "I want to ask you one thing—do you fear God?"

Perfishka shifted uneasily from one foot to the other, and said in a voice that sounded a little hurt:

"I have no reason to fear God. I do no harm to anyone—never have."

"And now, do you pray?"

"Oh, I pray, of course—not often."

Ilya saw that the cobbler had no desire to talk, and that his whole soul was longing for the tap room.

"There you are, Perfishka—ten more!"

"My word! that's what I call treating!" cried Perfishka and beamed with joy.

"But tell me, how do you pray?" Lunev pressed him again.

"I? Quite simply. I don't know any prayers. I knew 'the Virgin Mother of God' once, but I forgot it long ago. There's a beggar's prayer: 'O Lord Jesus,' and so on, I know that by heart right to the end. Perhaps when I'm old I'll use it. But now I just pray in my own way. 'Lord have mercy,' I say."

Perfishka looked at the ceiling, nodded with conviction, and went on.

"He'll understand up there. Can I go now? I've an awful thirst."

"Go on—go on," said Ilya, and looked at Perfishka thoughtfully. "But see here, when the day comes, when the Lord asks you, How have you lived?"

"Then I'll say, 'when I was born I was small, and when I died I was dead drunk. So I don't know.' Then He'll laugh and forgive me."

The cobbler smiled pleasantly and hurried away.

Lunev remained in the cellar alone. He was strangely moved to think that Masha's pretty little face would never again appear to him in this narrow, dirty cave, and that Perfishka would soon be turned out.

The April sun shone through the window and illuminated the floor, now long uncleaned. Everything there was untidy, hateful, and melancholy, as though a dead body had just been borne away. Ilya sat upright on his chair, looked at the big stove, rubbed away on the one side, and gloomy thoughts passed in succession through his mind.

"Shall I go out and confess?" flashed suddenly up in his heart.

But he thrust the thought away from him angrily.

CHAPTER XVI

On the evening of this day Ilya was compelled to leave Petrusha's house. Events fell out in this way. When he returned, his uncle met him in the courtyard, with downcast countenance, led him aside to a corner behind a pile of wood, and said:

"Now, Ilusha, you must get away from here. The things that have happened here to-day—awful, I tell you." The hunchback closed his eyes, wrung his hands, and broke into a fit of coughing. "Jashka got drunk and called his father to his face, 'You thief' and other bad names—'Shameless beast,' and 'heartless fellow.' He just screamed like a madman, and Petrusha hit him in the mouth, and tore his hair, and kicked him till he bled all over; and now Jashka's lying in his room and groaning and crying.—And then Petrusha began at me. 'It's your fault,' he growled. 'Get your Ilya away.' He thinks you've stirred up Jakov against him. He shouted awfully.—It was terrible!"

Ilya took the straps from his shoulders, handed his box to his uncle, and said, "Wait a minute!"

"Wait! But what? Why? He'll——"

Ilya's hands trembled with wrath against Petrusha and pity for Jakov.

"Hold my box, I say!" he said impatiently, and went into the bar. He clenched his teeth till his jaws ached, and a buzzing noise went through his head. He heard his uncle call after him something about police and damaging himself, and prison, but he did not stop. Petrusha stood behind the counter, smiling and talking to a raggedly-dressed man. The lamp-light fell on his bald head, and it shone as though the whole gleaming cranium smiled.

"Aha! Mr. Merchant!" he cried mockingly, and his brows contracted at the sight of Ilya, "you're just in time."

He stood before the door of his room, his body hiding it. Ilya went close up to him, insolent and overbearing, and said loudly:

"Out of the way!"

"Wh—at?" drawled Petrusha.

"Let me by! I want to see Jakov."

"I'll give you something to remember your Jakov!"

Without another word, Ilya struck out with all his might and hit Petrusha on the cheek. He howled aloud and fell on the floor. The pot-boys ran from all sides, and some one cried: "Hold him! Thrash him!"

The customers sprung up as though boiling water were poured on them, but Ilya sprung over Petrusha's body, went into the room behind, and bolted the door. A tin lamp with a blackened chimney burned flickeringly in the little room, made still smaller by wine-bins and boxes of all kinds.

At first Ilya did not distinguish his friend in the dark, cramped space. Jakov lay on the floor, his head in the shadow, and his face seemed black and dreadful. Ilya took the lamp, and, bending down, examined the maltreated lad. Bluish spots and bruises covered the face like a horrible dark mask; the eyes were swollen; he breathed with difficulty and groaned and evidently could not see, for he asked, as Ilya bent over him:

"Who is it?"

"I," said Lunev softly, and straightened himself.

"Give me something to drink!"

Ilya turned round. There was a loud knocking at the door, and some one called out:

"We'll try it from the stairs at the back!"

"Run for the police!" said another.

Petrusha's whimpering rose above the noise: "You all saw it! I never touched him. O—oh!"

Ilya smiled rejoicingly. He liked to realise that Petrusha was suffering. He stepped to the door and began to parley with the besiegers.

"Hullo, you there! Stop your noise! If I gave him one in the mouth, he won't die of it, and I'll take my punishment from the magistrate. Don't you shove yourselves in! Don't bang on the door! I'll open it."

He opened the door, and stood on the threshold, his fists clenched in case of an attack. The crowd gave back before his strong figure and fighting look. Only Petrusha growled, pushing the others aside:

"Ah, you robber! Wait, I'll— —"

"Take him away—and look here, just look here!" cried Ilya, inviting the crowd to enter, "see how he's handled this fellow!"

Three Men | 173

Several customers came in, with anxious side glances at Ilya, and bent down over Jakov.

One said, astonished and frightened:

"He's smashed him up!"

"He's absolutely cut to ribbons!" added another.

"Bring some water," said Ilya, "and then we must have the police." The crowd was now on his side, he read it in their manner, and said aloud and with emphasis:

"You all know Petrusha Filimonov; you know that he is the biggest rascal in the street, and who has a word to say against his son? Well, here lies the son, wounded, perhaps maimed for life; and the father is to get off scot-free, is he? I have struck him once; I shall be condemned for that, is that right and fair? Is that even justice? And so it is all round. One man may do as he likes, and another must not move an eyelash."

One or two sighed sympathetically, others went silently away. Ilya was going on, but Petrusha burst into the room and turned them all out.

"Get out! Be off! This is my affair. He's my son, I'm his father. Be off! I'm not afraid of the police, and I don't need 'em, either—not a bit of it. I'll settle with you, my lad. Clear out of this!"

Ilya kneeled down, gave Jakov a glass of water and looked with deep compassion at his friend's swollen closed eyes and discoloured face. Jakov drank and whispered:

"He's knocked my teeth out, it hurts me to breathe, get me out of the house, Ilusha, get me away!"

Tears flowed from his swollen eyes down over his cheeks.

"He'll have to be taken to the hospital," said Ilya sternly, turning to Petrusha. Petrusha looked at his son and murmured to himself unintelligibly. Of his eyes, one was wide open, the other swollen up like Jakov's from the blow of Ilya's fist.

"Do you hear?" shouted Ilya.

"Don't shout so!" said Petrusha, suddenly becoming quiet and peaceful. "He can't go to the hospital. There'd be a row! You've made bother enough already here. I'm a town councillor, you know. It's bad for my reputation."

"You old blackguard!" said Ilya, and spat contemptuously. "I tell you, take him to the hospital, or there'll be another sort of row."

"Now, now, don't—keep your temper! you know it's half imagination."

Ilya sprang up at these words, but Filimonov was already at the door and called to a waiter:

"Ivan, call a droshky to go to the hospital! Jakov, pull yourself together, don't make yourself out worse than you are; it's your own father beat you, not a stranger—yes—I usen't to be so tenderly handled, my word, no!"

He moved restlessly about the room, took Jakov's clothes from their pegs, and threw them to Ilya, still dilating freely upon the thrashings he had received in his young days.

"Thanks," said Jakov in a voice hardly audible to Ilya, and the tears flowed on from his swollen eyes over his blood-stained cheeks. Terenti was standing behind the counter; he whispered shyly in Ilya's ear: "What'll you have? three kopecks' worth or five? There—please, five—caviar?—the caviar's all gone. I'm sorry, will you try a sardine?"

After Lunev had left Jakov at the hospital he realised he could not return to Filimonov's house, and he went to Olympiada. He felt as though a cold mist drove through his body, something gnawed at his heart and stole away his strength. Sadness lay heavy on his breast, his thoughts were confused, he walked wearily; one thing only stood out clearly, he could not live much longer in this way. The dream of a little pretty shop, a life apart from the world in cleanliness and comfort, rose up anew and more strongly.

Next day he hired a lodging, a little room next to a kitchen. A young woman in a red blouse let it to him. Her face was rosy, with a little saucy nose and a small, pretty mouth; she had a narrow brow framed in black curly hair that she frequently threw back with a quick movement of her slender, small fingers.

"Five roubles for such a pretty little room, that is not dear!" she said cheerfully, and smiled as she saw that her dark, vivacious eyes threw the broad-shouldered lad into some confusion.

Ilya looked at the walls of his future home, and wondered what sort of young woman this might be.

"You see the paper is quite new, the window looks on the garden, what could be nicer? In the morning I'll put the samovar outside your door, but you must take it in yourself."

"Do you do the waiting here, then?" asked Ilya with curiosity.

The girl ceased to smile, her eyebrows twitched, she drew herself up and said, condescendingly:

"I am not the housemaid, but the owner of this house, and my husband——"

"Why, are you married?" cried Ilya in astonishment, and looked incredulously at her pretty slender figure. She was not angered, but laughed gaily:

"How funny you are! first you take me for a housemaid, then you won't believe I'm married."

"How can I believe it, when you look just like a little girl?" said Ilya, and laughed too.

"And I tell you, that I've been married for three years, and that my man is district inspector—in the police."

Ilya looked in her face and smiled quietly, he did not know why.

"What a silly!" cried the girl, shrugging her shoulders and inspecting Ilya curiously. "Well, anyhow, will you take the room?"

"Agreed! D'you want a deposit?"

"Of course, a rouble, at least."

"I'll bring my things in, in two or three hours."

"As you please. I'm glad to have such a lodger, you're a cheerful one, I fancy."

"Not specially," said Lunev, smiling.

He went out into the street still smiling, with a feeling of pleasure in his breast. He liked both the room, with its blue wall-paper, and the brisk little woman, and he liked specially to think he was going to live in the house of a police inspector.

It seemed to him at once comical, with a certain irony, and rather dangerous.

He was on his way to visit Jakov at the hospital, and took a droshky to get there sooner. On the way he laughed in his heart and considered what to do with the money, and where to hide it. When he reached the hospital, he was told that Jakov had just had a bath, and was now fast asleep. He stood by the corridor window, and did not know whether to go away or wait till Jakov woke up. Patients passed him, shuffling slowly in slippers, in yellow night-gowns, and as they went they looked at him with melancholy eyes. They chattered in low voices with one another, and through their whispers rang a painful, groaning coming from somewhere far off. A dull echo, redoubling every sound, boomed through the long corridor; it was as though some one floated invisible on the heavy air of the hospital, groaning mournfully and lamenting.

Ilya felt he must leave these yellow walls at once, but suddenly one of the patients came up to him with outstretched hand, and said in a muffled voice:

"How are you?"

Lunev looked up, then stepped back in surprise.

"Pavel? Goodness! are you here too?"

"Who else is here?" asked Pavel quickly.

His face was curiously grey, his eyes blinked restlessly and confusedly.

"Jakov is here! his father thrashed him—and now you here too! Been here long?" Then he added compassionately: "Ah, brother, how changed you look!"

Pavel sighed, his lips twitched and his eyes looked strangely dull. He hung his head as though guilty, and repeated hoarsely: "Changed? Oh yes."

"What's the matter?" asked Lunev sympathetically.

"Matter? You can guess, surely."

Pavel glanced at Ilya's face, and then let his head fall again.

"Not Vyera?"

"Who else?" answered Pavel gloomily.

Ilya shook his head, was silent a moment, then said bitterly:

"It's our fate, who knows when my turn'll come?"

Pavel smiled sadly, then came closer and looking confidingly in Ilya's face, he said:

"I thought you'd be disgusted with me. I was walking here and all at once I saw you. I was ashamed and turned my face away as I passed you."

"That was a very clever thing to do," said Ilya, reproachfully.

"How's one to know how people take a thing like that? To tell the truth, it's beastly. Ah, brother! two weeks have I been here. The torture, the dreariness! You go about, and lie in bed and think, think! The nights are awful. Like lying on red-hot coals. The time draws out, like a hair in the milk. It's like being drawn down into a swamp, and you're alone and can't call for help." Pavel spoke almost in a whisper. A shudder passed over his face, as if from cold, and his hands grasped convulsively at the collar of his dressing-gown. He shook his head, and said, still half-aloud: "Once fate starts against you to mock you, it goes like a hammer on your heart."

"Where is Vyera?" asked Ilya, thoughtfully.

"The devil knows!" said Pavel, with a bitter smile.

"Doesn't she come to see you?"

"Once. But I sent her packing. I can't bear the sight of her, the little beast!" cried Pavel angrily.

Ilya looked reproachfully at his altered face, and said: "Nonsense! If you want justice, then be just! Why, is it her fault? Think a minute."

"Then, whose fault is it?" cried Pavel, passionately, but in a low voice. "Whose? Tell me. Often I lie awake all night, and think how it is I have made such a mess of my life. It's just through loving Vyera. She took the place of mother and sister and wife and friends. I loved her. I can't say in words how much, nor even write it on the skies in writing of stars." His eyes grew red, and two big tears rolled down his face. He wiped them away with his sleeve, and went on, in a low voice:

"She lay in my way like a stone that I have stumbled over."

"That is not right," said Lunev, who felt clearly that he pitied Vyera even more than his friend. "What way do you speak of? You had no way. All that's just talk. You have longed for the mead, and praised it, that it was strong; now it has made you drunk, you blame it for getting into your head. And how about her? Isn't she ill too?"

"Yes," said Pavel, then suddenly continued, his voice trembling with emotion, "Do you think I'm not sorry for her?"

"Of course. How can you help it?"

"I'm hard on her. Is it much wonder? I sent her away; and when she went and began to cry, so softly and bitterly, then my heart was wrung. I felt I should weep too, but I had no tears in my soul, only stones. And then I began to think it all over. Ah, Ilya! The life I live's no life at all."

"Yes," said Lunev slowly, with a strange smile. "Things go very oddly in life. There's something takes us all by the throat and strangles — strangles us. There's Jakov, who's good. His father makes his life a burden; they've married Mashutka to an old devil; you're here in hospital — —"

Suddenly he smiled quietly, and said in a lower voice:

"I'm the only lucky one! Fact! As soon as I wish for anything — pat, it comes!"

"How?" asked Pavel, with curiosity and suspicion.

"Trust me. I have luck. It draws me on and on."

"I don't like the way you talk," said Pavel, and looked at Ilya searchingly. "Are you laughing at yourself?"

"No, it's some one else who laughs at me," replied Ilya, and his brows contracted gloomily. "There's some one somewhere, laughs at us all. I could tell you things. Wherever I look, there's no justice anywhere."

"I can see that," cried Pavel softly, but with intensity. "Come, let's go into that corner, there."

They went along the corridor, close together, looking into one another's eyes. Red patches appeared in Pavel's cheeks, and his eyes sparkled brightly, as in the days when he was healthy. "And I can see how we're robbed down to the last stitch," he whispered in Ilya's ear. "Whatever you can see, none of it is for us."

"That's true."

"Everything for the others. See—my little girl. She was as good as my wife. I need her all. Every man wants his wife for himself. But I can't have mine, and she can't live for me, as she wanted. Why? Just because I am poor? Well, but I work, don't I? I've slaved all my life, ever since I was ten years old. Surely I may be allowed to live, at least!"

"Petrusha Filimonov lives without working, so easily and comfortably, and can have everything he wants, do whatever he likes. Why is that?" said Ilya, seconding his friend's speech, with a scornful laugh.

"The doctor shouts at me, as if I were a criminal—why?" went on Gratschev. "He's an educated man. He ought to treat people decently. I'm a man, surely. Eh? And so it comes. I turned Vyerka out, but I know quite well it's not her fault."

"It's not the stick that gives the pain, but the one who uses it."

They stayed in the dark corner close to the corridor window, whose panes were streaked with yellow colour, and here side by side they conversed in passionate words, each catching the other's thought as it flew.

The heavy groaning came again from far away. The monotonous moan was like the muffled tone of a bass string, plucked at regular intervals, which vibrates wearily and hopelessly, as though it knew that no living heart beats fit to understand and appease its melancholy, quivering lament. Pavel was flaming with irritation over the buffets that life's heavy hand had dealt him.

He too, vibrated, like that string, with excitement, and whispered hurriedly, disconnectedly his grievances and complaints, and Ilya felt that Pavel's words fell on his heart like sparks, stirring to life in his own breast something dark and contradictory, that constantly troubled him, now flaming up, now sinking down. It seemed as though, in place of the dull, evil doubt, with which till now he had faced life, something else was suddenly kindled in his soul, brightening its darkness and shaping for it rest and relief for ever.

"Why is a man holy, if he's enough to eat? is he always in the right, if he's educated?" whispered Pavel, standing close to Ilya, and looking round him as though he were aware of the unknown enemy who had spoilt his life. "See," he went on, "if I am hungry, if I'm stupid, still I have a soul! Or hasn't a hungry man a soul? I see that I have no decent, real life, they have ruined my life, they've cut short my wishes and set up barriers on all my ways, and why?"

"No one can say," cried Ilya harshly, "and there's no one we could ask who would understand? We are all strangers."

"That's true, whom can we talk to?" asked Pavel, with a despairing gesture, and was silent.

Lunev looked straight before him down the wide corridor, and sighed deeply.

The dull moaning was heard again, now they were silent, it sounded more clearly; it seemed to come from the breast of a big, strong man, struggling with great pain.

"Are you still with Olympiada?" asked Pavel.

"Yes, still," answered Ilya.

"And think," he added with a strange smile, "Jakov has got on so well with his reading that now he's doubtful about God."

"Really?"

"Yes, he's found such a book! And you, what do you think about that?"

"I, you see," said Pavel, thoughtfully, "I've never thought much about it. I never go to church."

"And I do think about it, I think a lot about it, and I cannot understand how God endures it all!"

And they began to talk again, short, disconnected sentences, and they remained absorbed in their conversation till an attendant came up to them and said severely to Lunev:

"Why are you hiding here? eh?"

"I'm not hiding."

"Don't you see all the visitors are gone?"

"I didn't notice. Good-bye Pavel—give Jakov a look up."

"Now then, get on—get on!"

"Come again soon, for God's sake!" implored Gratschev.

"I tell you, get on!" and the attendant followed Ilya muttering:

"These fellows, loafers, hiding in corners."

Lunev slackened his pace and as the attendant came up to him, he said quietly and maliciously:

"Don't growl, else I'll have to say, 'lie down dog! lie down!'"

The attendant stopped suddenly, but Lunev went quickly on and felt an evil pleasure in having insulted a man.

In the street he fell again into brooding on the fate of his friends. Pavel, since he was a little lad had fended for himself, had been in prison, and tried all sorts of hard work. What hunger and cold, what blows he had endured! And now finally he had come to the hospital.

Masha would hardly see happy days again, and Jakov the same; how should a being like Jakov keep a whole skin in this world?

Lunev saw that, as a matter of fact, of all the four he had the best of it. But this consciousness brought him no comfort, he only smiled, and looked suspiciously about him.

CHAPTER XVII

Ilya settled quietly into his new dwelling-place, and his landlords interested him deeply. The woman's name was Tatiana Vlassyevna. As gay as a little bird, and always ready to chatter, she had given the new lodger a complete description of her life before he had spent many days in the little room.

In the morning, while Ilya drank his tea, she bustled about in the kitchen, with skirts tucked up and sleeves rolled above her elbows, but gave many a smiling glance into his room, and said, cheerfully:

"We're not rich, my husband and I, but we've got education and intelligence. I went to the progymnasium, and he was in the cadet corps, even if he didn't quite finish his time there. But we want to be rich, and we'll manage it too. We've no children; they're the big expense. I do the cooking and go to market, and I keep a maid for the rest, and she lives in the house, and gets a rouble and a half a month. You see what a lot I save!"

She remained in the doorway and, shaking her curls, began to reckon:

"Cook's wages, three roubles, and what she'd cost, seven—makes ten roubles. She'd steal at least three roubles' worth a month—thirteen roubles. Then I let her room to you—eighteen roubles. That's the cost of a cook, you see. Then I buy everything wholesale, butter—half a pood, flour—a whole sack, sugar by the loaf, and so on. I save another twelve roubles that way—that's thirty. If I had a place at the police-station or telegraph office, I should only work as a cook; and now I cost my man nothing, and I'm proud of it. One must understand how to arrange one's life, remember that, young man!" She looked roguishly at Ilya with her laughing eyes, and he smiled with some embarrassment. She pleased him, but yet inspired him with respect. When he waked in the morning she was already working in the kitchen, with a pock-marked, undersized girl, who stared at her mistress and every one else, with colourless, frightened eyes. In the evening, when Ilya came home, Tatiana opened the door to him, smiling and active, with a pleasant perfume surrounding her. When her husband was at home he played the guitar, and she chimed in with her clear voice, or they played cards for kisses. Ilya could hear everything in his room—the tones of the strings, gay or sentimental, the turning of the cards, and the kisses. Their dwelling consisted of two rooms—the bedroom and another adjoining Ilya's apartment, which served the pair for dining and drawing-room, where they spent their evenings. Clear birds' voices resounded from here in the mornings, the titmouse peeped, the siskin and thistle-finch sang for a wager, the bullfinch whistled in between, and, through it all, the linnet sounded his serious, gentle song.

Titiana's husband, Kirik Nikodimovitch Avtonomov, was a man of twenty-six years, tall and big, with a big nose and black teeth. His good-tempered face was thick with pimples, and his watery blue eyes looked at everything with imperturbable calm. His close-cropped light hair stood up like a brush on his head, and in his whole plump figure there was something helpless and comical. His movements were clumsy, and immediately after his first greeting to Ilya, he said, for no particular reason:

"Do you like singing birds?"

"Very much."

"Do you ever catch any?"

"No," answered Ilya, looking wonderingly at the inspector, who wrinkled his nose, thought a moment, then said:

"Used you ever to catch them?"

"No."

"Never?"

"Never."

Kirik Avtonomov smiled in a superior way, and said:

"You can't be said to like them, if you've never caught any. Now, I love them, and have caught them often, and was dismissed from the cadet corps because of that. I'd like to catch 'em now, but I don't want to get into trouble with my superiors, for though the love of singing birds is a noble passion, to catch them is not a proper occupation for an established man. If I were in your shoes I'd catch siskins like anything. The siskin's a jolly bird. That's why he's called God's bird."

Avtonomov looked with the expression of an enthusiast into Ilya's face, and a certain embarrassment came over Ilya as he listened. He felt as though the inspector spoke of bird-catching allegorically, with a hidden reference. His heart palpitated and he pricked up his ears. But the sight of Avtonomov's watery blue eyes quieted him, he saw in a moment that the inspector was quite a harmless individual, without any subtlety; so he smiled politely, and murmured some reply or other. The inspector was evidently taken with Ilya's modest demeanour and serious face, and said, smiling:

Three Men | 183

"Come and have tea with us of an evening, when you feel inclined. We're simple people, without any style. We'll have a game of cards. We don't get many visitors. Visitors are all very well, but you have to treat them, and that's a nuisance and comes expensive." The longer Ilya observed the comfortable life of his landlords, the better it pleased him. Everything they had was so solid and clean, their existence ran so easily and peacefully, and they were evidently much attached to one another. The brisk little woman was like a tomtit, and her husband like a clumsy bullfinch, and their rooms were as tidy and pretty as a bird's nest. When Ilya was home of an evening, he listened to their conversation, and thought: "That's the kind of life!" He sighed enviously, and dreamed more vividly of the time when he would open his shop and have a little bright room of his own. He would keep birds, and live as in a dream, alone and quiet, peacefully and methodically.

The other side of the wall, Tatiana was telling her husband how she bought everything she needed in the market, how much she had spent, and how much saved, and he laughed pleasantly and praised her.

"Ah, the clever little woman! My dear little bird! Come, give me a kiss!"

Then he would begin and relate all that had happened in the town, the processes he had drawn up, what the Chief of Police or any of his superiors had said. They talked of the possibility of a rise of salary for him, and discussed minutely whether, in such an event, they ought to take a bigger house.

Ilya lay and listened till suddenly a melancholy weariness fell on him. The little blue room was too narrow; he looked restlessly round as if to seek the cause of his moodiness, then, unable longer to endure the weight that lay at his breast, he went to Olympiada, or loafed aimlessly in the streets.

Olympiada became more and more full of reproaches. She plagued him with jealousy and more and more frequently they fell into contention. She grew thin, her eyes were sunken and looked darker, her arms were thinner, and all this was not pleasing to Ilya. Still less, however, did he like the fact that of late she had begun to talk of conscience and God, and of going into a nunnery. He did not believe in the genuineness of her words, for he knew she could not live without the society of men.

"You needn't pray for me if you take the veil," he said one day with a mocking smile. "I'll manage my own sins alone."

She looked at him full of fear and sadness.

"Ilya, don't make a jest of it!"

"But I mean it."

"You don't believe that I shall go to a nunnery? You'll see, then you'll believe."

"Not at all—I believe you; lots of people turn monks or nuns out of sheer wickedness."

Olympiada grew angry with him and they quarrelled fiercely.

"You unlucky, proud man!" she cried, with sparkling eyes. "Just wait! However you stiffen your back in your pride, you'll be bent down! What are you so proud of? Your youth and your beauty? It will all go—all, and then you'll creep on the ground like a snake and beg for mercy. 'Have pity!' and no one will care."

She heaped reproaches on him, and her eyes grew so bloodshot that it seemed as though great drops of blood instead of tears would flow over her cheeks. When they quarrelled she never spoke of Poluektov's murder, indeed, in her better moments she would bid him "forget." Lunev wondered at this, and asked her one day after a quarrel:

"Lipa! tell me, when you're angry, why do you never speak of the old man."

She answered readily:

"Because that was really neither my doing nor yours. Since they haven't found you out, it must have been his fate. You were the instrument, not the force; you had no reason to strangle him, as you say yourself. So he only met his due punishment through you."

Ilya laughed incredulously.

"O—Oh! I thought that a man must either be a fool or a rascal—ha! ha! Anything is right for him if only he wants to do it, and in the same way anything can be wrong."

"I don't understand," said Olympiada, and shook her head.

"Where's the difficulty?" asked Ilya, sighing and shrugging his shoulders. "It's quite simple! Show me any one thing in life that holds for every one; find anything that a clever man can't make either right or wrong; anything that stands fast, permanent; you can't. That is what I meant to say. There is nothing fixed in life; it is all changing and confused, like a man's own soul—yes."

"I don't understand," said the woman after a pause.

"And I understand so well," answered Ilya. "That this is just the knot that strangles us all."

At last, after one of the periodical quarrels, when Ilya had not been near Olympiada for four days, he received a letter from her; she wrote:

"Good-bye, my dear Ilyusha, good-bye for ever; we shall never meet again. Don't look for me, you won't find me. I'm leaving this unlucky town by the next steamboat; here I have destroyed my soul for ever. I'm going away, far away, and shall never come back; don't think of me and don't wait for me. With all my heart, I thank you for the good you have brought me, and the bad I will forget. I must tell you the plain truth. I'm not going into a nunnery, I'm going away with young Ananyin, who has been entreating me for a long time. I have agreed at last, what does it matter to me? We go to the sea to a village where Ananyin has fisheries. He is simple, and even means to marry me, good, silly boy! Good-bye! We have met as if in a dream, and when I waked there was nothing. Forgive me too! If you knew how my heart burns with longing. I kiss you—you, the one man in the world for me. Don't be proud before men; we are all unfortunate. I have grown calm, I, your Lipa, and I go as though under the axe,—my heart pains me so.— —

"OLYMPIADA SCHLYKOVA."

"I am sending you a token by the post, a ring. Please wear it.—O.S."

Ilya read the letter and bit his lips till they smarted. He read it again and again, and the more often he read, the better it pleased him; it was at once a pain and a pleasure to read the big irregularly written characters.

Previously, Ilya had given little thought to determine what the nature might be of Olympiada's feelings for himself; now, however, he felt that she had loved him dearly and warmly, and as he read her letter he felt a deep peace sink into his heart. But the peace gave way gradually to a sense of loss, and the consciousness that there was no one now to whom he could reveal the bitterness of his soul depressed him.

The image of this woman stood vividly before his eyes, he remembered her passionate caresses, her sensible talk, her jests, and more and more clearly he felt in his breast a harsh feeling of wretchedness. He stood moodily by the window, looking into the garden, and there in the darkness the elder-bushes rustled softly, and the thin, thready twigs of the birch-trees waved to and fro. From behind the wall the strings of the guitar resounded mournfully, and Tatiana sang in her high voice:

"Let him who will search through the seas
       To find the amber golden——"

Ilya held the letter in his hand and thought: "She always said she was persistent, and that I brought her good fortune, and yet she has left me, so the fortune can not have been so very good after all."

He felt himself in the wrong before Olympiada, and sorrow and compassion weighed heavy on his soul.

"But bring me back my little ring from out the deep blue sea," sounded behind the wall. Then the inspector laughed aloud and the singer chimed in merrily from the kitchen. Then, however, she was silent. Ilya felt her nearness, but dared not turn round to look, though he knew his room door was open. He gave the rein to his thoughts, and stood motionless, feeling himself deserted.

The tree-tops in the garden shivered, and Lunev felt as though he had left the ground, and were floating out there in the cold twilight.

"Ilya Jakovlevitch, will you have your tea?"

"No," answered Ilya.

The solemn note of a bell resounded through the air. The deep tone made the window panes quiver. Ilya crossed himself, remembered that it was long since he had been to church, and seized the occasion to get away from the house.

"I'm going to evening service," he called as he went out.

Tatiana stood in the doorway, her hands against the door-posts, and looked curiously at him. Her inquiring glance confused Ilya, and as if excusing himself, he said:

"I haven't been to church for ever so long."

"Very well. I'll get the samovar ready by nine o'clock," she replied.

As he went, Lunev thought of young Ananyin. He knew the man; he was a rich young merchant, partner in fish business—Ananyin Brothers—a thin, fair young man, with a pale face and blue eyes. He had but recently come to the town and lived there at a great pace.

"That is really living," thought Ilya bitterly, "like a rich young man does—hardly out of the nest before he gets a mate for himself."

He entered the church in a discontented mood, and chose a dark corner, where lay the ladder to light the chandeliers.

"O Lord, have mercy!" came from the left-hand choir. A choir boy sang with a shrill, unpleasing voice, and could not keep in tune with the hoarse, deep bass voice of the precentor. The lack of harmony embittered Ilya's mood still further, and roused a desire in him to seize the boy by the ears. The heating stove made the corner very hot, it smelt of burning rags. An old woman in a fur jacket, came up to him and said, grumbling:

"You're not in your right place, sir."

Ilya looked at the fox tails adorning the collar of her jacket, and went to one side silently, thinking: "Even in the church there's a special place for us."

It was the first time he had been to church since the murder of Poluektov, and when he remembered this, involuntarily he shuddered. He thought of his guilt and forgot everything else, though the idea no longer terrified him, but only filled him with sorrow and heaviness of soul.

"O Lord, have mercy!" he whispered and crossed himself. The choir burst into loud, harmonious song. The soprano voices, giving the words clearly and distinctly, rang under the dome like the clear, pleasant tones of sweet bells. The altos vibrated like a ringing tense string, and against their continued sound, flowing on like a stream, the soprano notes quivered like the reflection of the sun on a transparent pool. The full deep bass notes swept proudly through the church, supporting the children's song; from time to time the beautiful strong tones of the tenors pierced through, then again the children's voices rang out, and rose into the twilight of the dome, whence, serious and thoughtful, clad in white garments, the figure of the Almighty looked down, blessing the faithful with majestic outstretched hands. The waves of sound and the scent of incense rolled up to Him, and flowed round Him, and it seemed as though He floated in the midst, and swept ever higher into the depths of boundless space.

When the music ceased, Ilya sighed deeply. His heart was light, and he felt no fear nor repentance, not even the irritation that had disturbed him when he entered the church. His thoughts flew far away from his own sins. The music had cleansed and lightened his soul. He could not trust his own sensations, feeling so unexpectedly calm and peaceful, and he strove to awaken in himself a sense of remorse, but it was in vain.

Suddenly the thought darted through his mind: "Suppose that woman goes into my room out of curiosity and looks about and finds the money."

He hurried away out of the church, and hailed a droshky to reach home as quickly as he could. All the way the thought tormented him, and set him in a quiver of excitement.

"Suppose they do find the money, what then? They won't lay an information about it, they'll just steal it."

And this thought roused him still more; he became quite positive that if it should happen he would go straight to the police in this same droshky and confess that he had murdered Poluektov. No, he would not any longer be tortured, and live in dirt and turmoil while others enjoy in peace and comfort the money for which he sinned so deeply. The mere idea of it drove him nearly crazy. When the droshky drew up at his door, he darted out and tugged at the bell; his fist clenched and his teeth locked, he waited impatiently for the door to open. Tatiana appeared on the threshold.

"My, what a ring you gave! What's the matter? What's wrong?" she cried, frightened at the sight of him.

Without a word he pushed her aside, went quickly to his room, and assured himself in one glance, that his fears were unnecessary. The money lay behind the upper window-boxing, and he had stuck on a little scrap of down, in such a way that it must be removed if any one tried to get at the packet. He saw the white fleck at once against the brown background.

"Aren't you well?" asked his landlady, appearing at the door of his room.

"I'm all right; I beg your pardon, I pushed you."

"That's nothing; but see here, how much is the droshky?"

"I don't know, ask him please, and pay him."

She hurried away, and Ilya in a moment sprang on a chair, snatched away the packet of money, knew by the feel that it had not been tampered with, and dropped it in his pocket with a sigh of relief. He was ashamed now of his anxiety, and the precaution of the scrap of down seemed foolish and ridiculous.

"Witchcraft!" he thought, and laughed to himself. Tatiana Vlassyevna appeared again.

"I gave him twenty kopecks—but what's the matter? were you faint?"

"Yes. I was standing in the church, and then all at once— —"

"Lie down," she said, and came into the room. "Lie down quietly. Don't worry! I'll sit by you a little. I'm at home alone. My husband's working late and going on to his club."

Ilya sat down on the bed, while she took the only chair.

"I disturbed you I'm afraid," said Ilya, with an embarrassed smile.

"Doesn't matter," she answered, and looked in his face with frank curiosity. There was a pause. Ilya did not know what to talk about. She still looked at him, and suddenly laughed in an odd way.

"What are you laughing at?" said Ilya, and dropped his eyes.

"Shall I tell you?" she asked, mischievously.

"Yes, tell me!"

"You can't pretend well, d'you know?"

Ilya started and looked at her uneasily.

"No, you can't. You are not ill; only you've had a letter that troubles you. I saw—I saw——"

"Yes, I've had a letter," said Ilya slowly.

Something rustled in the branches outside. Tatiana looked quickly out at the window, then again at Ilya.

"It was only the wind, or a bird," she said. "Now, young man, will you listen to my advice? I'm only a young woman, but I'm not a fool!"

"If you'll be so good—please," said Lunev, and looked at her with curiosity.

"Tear up the letter and throw it away," she said in a decided tone. "If she has written you your dismissal, she's acted well, and like a sensible girl. It's too soon for you to marry. You've no settled standing, and you ought not to marry without. You're a strong young man and you work, and you're good-looking. You're bound to get on. Only take care you don't fall in love. Earn a lot of money, and save, and try to get on to something bigger. Open a shop, and then, when you've got firm ground under your feet, you can marry. You're bound to get on. You don't drink, you're unassuming, you've no ties."

Ilya listened, with bowed head and smiled quietly. He longed to laugh out loud.

"There's nothing more silly than to hang your head down," continued Tatiana, in the tone of an experienced man of the world. "It will pass. Love is a disease that is easily cured. Before I was married I fell in love three times, fit to drown myself, but it passed. And when I saw that it was time for me to marry, I married without all that love."

"Ilya raised his head and looked at the woman as she said this:

"What's the matter?" she asked. "Afterwards I learnt to love my husband. It happens often that a woman falls in love with her husband."

"What does that mean?" asked Ilya, opening his eyes. Tatiana laughed gaily. "I was only joking—but quite seriously, you can really marry a man without love, and come to care for him afterwards."

And she chattered away and made play with her eyes. Ilya listened attentively, and looked with great interest at the little, trim figure, and was full of wonder. She was so small and slender and yet she had such foresight and strength of will, and good sense.

"With a wife like that," he thought, "a man couldn't come to grief." He found it pleasant to sit there with an intelligent woman, a real, trim, neat housewife, who was not too proud to chat with him, a simple working lad. A feeling of gratitude towards her arose in him, and when she got up to go, he sprang up at once, bowed, and said:

"Thank you very much for the honour you have done me; your talk has done me a lot of good."

"Really, think of that!" she said, smiling quietly, while her cheeks reddened and she looked for a second or two steadily in Ilya's face. "Well then, good-bye for the present," she added with a strange intonation and slipped out with the easy gait of a young girl.

CHAPTER XVIII

Ilya came to like the Avtonomovs better every day, and he envied them their peaceful, sheltered life. In a general way he had no love for police officials, for he saw many evil qualities among them. But Kirik seemed like a simple working-man, good-tempered, if limited. He was the body, and his wife the soul. He was seldom at home, and not of much importance there. Tatiana Vlassyevna became more and more at home with Ilya. She got him to chop wood, fetch water, empty away slops. He obeyed dutifully, and these little services gradually became his daily duty. Then his landlady dismissed the pock-marked girl who helped her, and only had her on Sundays. Occasionally visitors came to the Avtonomovs. Korsakov, the assistant town inspector, often came, a thin man with a long moustache. He wore dark glasses, smoked thick cigarettes, and could not endure droshky drivers, speaking of them always with great irritation. "No one breaks rules and orders so often as these drivers," he used to say. "Insolent brutes! Foot passengers in the streets you can deal with easily; it only means a police notice in the papers. Those going down the street keep to the right, those going up to the left, and at once you get excellent discipline. But these drivers, you can't get at them with any notice. A driver, well, the devil only knows what he's like!"

He could talk of droshky drivers a whole evening, and Lunev never heard him speak of anything else.

Also the inspector of the Orphan Asylum, Gryslov, came occasionally, a silent man, with a black beard. He loved to sing, in his bass voice, the song: "Over the sea, the deep blue sea," and his wife, a stately, stout woman with big teeth, always ate up the whole provision of sweetmeats, a feat which occasioned remarks after her departure.

"Felizata Segarovna does that on purpose. Whatever sweets come on the table, she always swallows the lot."

Alexandra Fedorovna Travkina used to come with her husband. She was tall and thin, with a large nose and short red hair. She had big eyes and a piping voice, and blew her nose frequently with a sound like the tearing of calico. Her husband suffered from a disease of the throat, and spoke in consequence in a whisper. But he would talk incessantly by the hour, and the sounds that came from his mouth were like the rustling of dry straw. He was very well-to-do, had served in the Excise Department, and was a director of a flourishing benevolent society. Both he and his wife spoke of little else but charitable institutions.

"Just think what has just happened in our society!"

"Ah, yes, yes. Just imagine!" cried his wife.

"An appeal has been presented for assistance."

"I tell you, these charitable institutions ruin the people——"

"A woman writes, her husband is dead. She has three children. They are starving and she is always ill."

"The old story, you know——"

"They were to get three roubles——"

"But, for my part, I don't believe in this widow," cried Alexandra Fedorovna, triumphantly.

"My wife says to me, 'Wait,' she says: 'I'll see first what kind of a person it is.'"

"And what do you think? The husband had been dead five years."

"She's two children, not three."

"The things they say!"

"And she's as healthy as can be."

"Then I said to her: 'See now, my friend, how would you like to be tried for fraud?' Of course, she fell at my feet."

"Ha! ha! ha!" laughed Kirik Avtonomov. And every one praised Fedorovna for her acuteness, and blamed the poor, because of their lying and greed, and want of respect towards their benefactors.

Lunev sat in his room, and listened attentively to the conversations that went on close by. He wanted to understand what these people thought and said of life. But what he heard was incomprehensible to him. It seemed as though these people had made up their minds about life, had settled all questions, and knew everything; and they condemned in the strongest terms every one who lived differently from themselves. Most frequently, they talked of all kinds of family scandals, of different services in the cathedral, or of the evil behaviour of their acquaintances. It wearied Ilya to listen.

Sometimes his landlord invited him to tea in the evening. Tatiana Vlassyevna was merry, and her husband waxed enthusiastic over the possibility of becoming rich, when he would retire from the service and buy himself a house.

"Then I'd keep fowls," he said, and screwed up his eyes. "All sorts of fowls—Brahmahpootras, Cochin Chinas, Guinea-fowl, and turkeys— and a peacock—yes. Think of sitting at the window in a dressing-gown, smoking a scented cigarette, and seeing the peacock, my own peacock, in the courtyard, spreading his tail. That would be something like a life. He'd stalk round like a police officer, and say: 'Brr—Brrll—Brrll!'"

Tatiana smiled, and, looking at Ilya, went on in her turn:

"And every summer I'd go away somewhere, to the Crimea or the Caucasus, and in winter I'd be on some charitable committee. Then I'd have a black cloth dress, quite simple with no ornament, and I wouldn't wear any jewels except a ruby brooch and pearl ear-rings. I read a poem in the 'Niva,' where it said, 'that the blood and tears of the poor are turned to rubies and pearls,'" then with a soft sigh, she added, "Rubies look so nice on dark women."

Ilya smiled and said nothing. It was warm and clean in the room, an odour of tea and of some pleasant scent mingled in the air. The birds, little feather balls, were asleep in the cages. A few gaudy pictures hung on the walls. A little étagère between the two windows was covered with all kinds of pretty little boxes, china birds, and gay Easter eggs of sugar or glass. The whole place pleased Ilya and filled him with a kind of soft, comfortable melancholy. Sometimes however, especially when he had earned little or nothing, this melancholy changed into a restless fretfulness. Then the china fowls and the eggs and the boxes annoyed him; he wanted to throw them on the ground and smash them.

This mood disturbed and frightened him; he could not understand it and it seemed strange and unlike himself. As soon as it came upon him, he maintained an obstinate silence, kept his eyes fixed on one spot, and was afraid to speak lest he should somehow hurt the feelings of these good people.

Once, however, as he was playing cards with them, he could not contain himself, and asked Kirik drily, looking him straight in the face:

"I say, Kirik Nikodimovitch, you've never caught him—the murderer of the merchant in Dvoryanskaya Street?"

As he spoke he felt a pleasant tingling in his breast.

"Poluektov, the money-changer?" said the inspector, thoughtfully, as he examined his cards. "Poluektov? Ah! ah! No! I have not caught

Poluektov—ah! I haven't caught him, my friend; that's to say, of course, not Poluektov, but the man who——I haven't even looked for him. I don't want him, anyhow—I only want to know who has the queen of spades? You, Tanya, played three cards—queen of clubs, queen of diamonds and—what was the other?"

"Seven of diamonds—hurry up!"

"He's quite lost!" said Ilya, and laughed scornfully.

But the inspector paid no attention to him, he was absorbed in the game.

"Quite lost," he repeated mechanically, "and he twisted poor Poluektov's neck—ah! ah!"

"Kirya, do stop that, ah! ah!" said his wife. "Be quick!"

"Patience, patience."

"He must be a smart fellow who murdered him," remarked Ilya.

The indifference with which his words were received roused in him a desire to speak of the murder.

"Smart?" said the inspector slowly. "No! I am the smart fellow! There!" and he played a five, slapping the card down on the table. Ilya could not follow suit, and lost the round.

The husband and wife laughed at him, and he grew more restive. As he was dealing, he said defiantly:

"To kill a man in broad daylight, in the main street of the town, that takes some courage."

"Luck, not courage," Tatiana corrected.

Ilya looked first at her, then at her husband, laughed softly and asked:

"You call it luck to kill some one?"

"Why, yes; to kill some one and not get caught."

"You've given me ace of diamonds again," cried the inspector.

"I could do with an ace," said Ilya seriously.

"Kill a rich man, that's the best ace!" said Tatiana jokingly.

"Hold on a bit with your killing, here's an ace of cards to go on with," cried Kirik, with a loud laugh and played two nines and an ace.

Ilya glanced again at their pleasant, happy faces, and the desire to speak further of the murder left him.

Living side by side with these people, separated only by a thin wall from their sheltered, peaceful life, Ilya was seized more and more frequently with fits of painful dissatisfaction. The feeling poured over him like a dense, cold flood, and he could not understand whence it came. At the same time thoughts of life's contradictions rose up in him, of God who knows everything, yet does not punish but waits patiently. Why does He wait?

Out of sheer boredom he began to read again. His landlady had a couple of volumes of the "Niva," and the "Illustrated Review," and a few other odd volumes. Just as in his childhood, so now, he cared only for tales and romances, in which a strange unknown life was depicted, and not at all for representations of the real, the wrong and misery filling the life that surrounded him. Whenever he read tales of actual life, dealing with simple folk, he found them wearisome and full of false descriptions. Sometimes it is true they amused him, when it seemed as though these tales were written by clever people, anxious to paint this miserable, dull, grey life in fair colours and gloss over its wretchedness. He knew this life and daily learned to know it better. As he passed through the streets he never failed to see something that appealed to his critical faculties. In this way once he witnessed a scene on his way to visit his friend at the hospital which he related to Pavel:

"This is what they call law and order. I saw some people like carpenters and plasterers going along the pavement. Up comes a policeman. 'Now then, you rascals!' he shouts, and turns them off into the road. That's to say, walk with the horses, else your dirty clothes may soil the fine gentry; build me a house, oh, yes, but I'll chuck you out of it, ah!"

Pavel's wrath was aroused too, by the incident, and added fuel to Ilya's flame. He endured tortures in the hospital, little better to him than a prison; his thoughts would not let him rest, and his eyes glowed with despair and grim defiance. To think where Vyera might then be, consumed him, and he grew thin and wasted. Jakov he did not like, and avoided his society in spite of the wearisomeness that plagued him.

"He's half silly," he answered when Ilya asked after Jakov.

But Jakov, two of whose ribs it appeared were broken, lived very happily in the hospital. He had made friends with the patient next him, a servant in a church, whose leg had been amputated a little while before for sarcoma. He was a short, thick-set man, with a big bald head and a black beard that covered his breast. His eyebrows were thick and bushy, and he moved them constantly up and down; his voice sounded hollow as though it came from his stomach. Every time Lunev visited the hospital he found Jakov by the bedside of this man, who lay and moved his eyebrows without speaking, while Jakov read half-aloud out of a Bible, that was as short and thick as its owner.

"'Because in the night Ar of Moab is laid waste and brought to silence,'" read Jakov. "'Because in the night Kin of Moab is laid waste and brought to silence.'"

Jakov's voice sounded weak and creaking, like the noise of a saw cutting wood. As he read, he held up his left hand, as if to summon all the patients in the ward to hear the calamitous prophecies of Isaiah. The blue bruises were not yet quite gone from his face, and the big, thoughtful eyes in the midst of them gave him a very strange expression. As soon as he saw Ilya, he threw down the book, and always asked the same anxious question:

"Haven't you seen Mashutka?"

Ilya had not seen her.

"O God!" said Jakov sadly. "How strange it is! Like a fairy tale! She was there, and suddenly a magician snatches her away, and she's disappeared."

"Has your father been to see you?"

"Yes—he came again."

A shiver passed over Jakov's face, and he looked anxiously here and there.

"He brought a pound of cakes, and tea and sugar. 'You've loafed round here enough,' he said, 'let them send you out!' But I begged the doctors not to send me away yet. It's so jolly here, quiet and comfortable. This is Nikita Jegarowitch. We read together. He has a Bible. He's read it for seven years. He knows it all by heart and can explain the prophecies. When I'm well, I'm going to leave my father and live with Nikita. I'll help him in the church and sing in the choir."

The church servant lifted his eyebrows, underneath which a pair of big dark eyes moved slowly in deep sockets. Quiet and lustreless, they looked at Ilya's face with a fixed, dull look, and Ilya tried involuntarily to avoid them.

"What a lovely book the Bible is!" said Jakov, quite enraptured, Mashka, his father, and all his dreams forgotten. "What things it says, brother! What words!"

His widely-opened eyes glanced from the book to Ilya's face and back again, and he shook with excitement.

"And that saying is in it—do you remember?—that the old preacher said to your uncle in the bar—'The tabernacles of robbers prosper!'—It's there, I found it, and things worse than that!"

Jakov shut his eyes and said solemnly, with uplifted hand:

"'How oft is the candle of the wicked put out, and how oft cometh destruction upon them! God distributed sorrows in his anger'—Do you hear?—'God layeth up his iniquity for his children: He rewardeth him and he shall know it.'"

"Does it really say that?" said Ilya, incredulously.

"Word for word."

"Then I think that is—not right—wicked," said Ilya.

The church servant drew down his bushy brows till they shaded his eyes, his beard moved up and down, and he spoke clearly in a dull, strange voice:

"The boldness of the man who seeks the Truth is not sinful, for it springs from divine prompting."

Ilya shuddered. The speaker sighed deeply, and went on, slowly and distinctly:

"'The Truth itself bids a man seek Me! For Truth is God, and it is written: It is a great glory to follow the Lord.'"

The man's face, covered with thick hair, inspired Ilya with shyness and respect. There was in it something strong, sublime. His brows went up again, he looked at the ceiling, and his big beard moved again:

"Read him, Jakov, from the Book of Job, the beginning of the tenth chapter."

Jakov turned over the leaves quickly, and read, in a low, trembling voice:

"'My soul is weary of my life; I will leave my complaint upon myself; I will speak in the bitterness of my soul. I will say unto God, do not condemn me: Show me wherefore thou contendest with me. Is it good unto Thee that Thou shouldest oppress; that Thou shouldest despise the work of Thine hands?'"

Ilya stretched out his neck and looked at the book with blinking eyes.

"You don't believe it?" cried Jakov. "How silly you are!"

"Not silly, only cowardly," said the church servant, quietly, "because he cannot look God in the face."

He turned his dull eyes from the ceiling to Ilya's face, and went on sternly as though he would shatter him with words.

"There are parts that are more difficult than that one. The third verse of the twenty-second chapter says plainly: 'Is it any pleasure to the

Almighty that thou art righteous? or is it gain to Him that thou makest thy ways perfect?' You need to think very diligently, so as not to go astray in these matters and to understand them."

"And you, do you understand?" asked Lunev softly.

"He?" cried Jakov. "Nikita Jegarowitch understands everything."

But the church servant said, sinking his voice lower:

"For me, it's too late already. It is time for me to understand death; they've taken off my leg, but it's swelling higher up, and the other leg is swelling, and my breast, and I shall soon die of it."

His eyes stared steadily at Ilya and he continued slowly and quietly:

"And I do not want to die yet, for I have lived wretchedly in sickness and bitterness, with no joy in my life. I've worked ever since I was a little boy, and like Jakov, under the scourge of a father. He was a drunkard and a brute. Three times he damaged my skull, once he scalded my leg with boiling water. I had no mother, she died when I was born. I married; I was compelled to take a wife who did not love me; three days after the wedding she hanged herself. Yes. I had a brother-in-law who robbed me, and my own sister said to my face that I drove my wife to her death. And they all said it, although they knew I had not touched her, that she died a maid. Then I lived nine years, alone and solitary. It is terrible to live alone. I've always waited for happiness to come at last, and now I'm dying. That is my whole life."

He closed his eyes, paused a moment, then asked:

"Why was life given to me? Guess that riddle."

Ilya listened, pale, with fear in his heart.

A dark shadow lay on Jakov's face and tears glimmered in his eyes; both were silent.

"Why was I born? I ask. The Lord has done me wrong. I do not pray that He will lengthen my life. I find no words to pray with. I lie here and think and think: Why has life been given to me?"

His voice choked. He broke off all at once, like a muddy brook that flows along and suddenly vanishes under ground.

"For to him that is joined to all the living there is hope, for a living dog is better than a dead lion," said the church servant after a while in the words of the Scripture; then again his eyebrows went up, his eyes opened and his beard moved.

"Also in Ecclesiastes it says: 'In the day of prosperity be joyful, but in the day of adversity, consider. God also hath set the one over against the other to the end that man should find nothing after him.' Well?"

Ilya could hear no more. He got up quietly, gave Jakov a hand, bowed low to the sick man, as though he were taking leave of the dead; and this he did involuntarily.

This time he left the hospital with a new, strangely oppressive feeling. The talk with the church servant had left no clear impression on his brain, but the mournful spectacle the sick man presented was stamped deep on his memory.

Another was added to the men, he knew, whose lives had proved a delusion. He held the words of this man clear in his memory, and turned them over and over to get at their secret meaning. They confused him and disturbed something in the depths of his soul, where he hid his faith in the justice of God, and these words which he could not fathom, awaked in him a bitter gnawing brain-activity that drove him on to examine and analyse all that he saw or experienced. It appeared to him now that somehow, in a way unknown to himself, his faith in the justice of God had sustained a shock and was no longer so firm as of old. Something had gnawed at it, like the rust gnaws the iron. He felt clearly that this had happened; the fierce commotion into which the lament of the church servant had thrown him, convinced him. There were sensations and ideas in his breast as irreconcilable as fire and water, continually at strife. His bitterness against his own past, against all men and all the laws of life, broke out with new strength. In his anger he came finally to the question:

"Thoughts grow in the soul like roots in the ground, but where is the fruit?"

He would gladly have torn all these troubles from his heart, that he might begin the realisation of his dream of a solitary, peaceful, sheltered life.

"I will mix with men no more. It's no good to me or any one. I can't live like this."

He took to wandering the streets for hours, and came back home tired and moody.

Every day the Avtonomovs became more friendly and obliging to Ilya. Kirik clapped him on the shoulder, jested with him, and said, in a tone of conviction:

"You busy yourself with useless things, my friend. So modest and serious a lad must take a wider view. It isn't good to remain district inspector if you're fit to look after the whole town."

Tatiana, too, began to ask Ilya definitely and in detail, how his peddling trade did, and how much he put by every month. He talked freely to her, and his respect for this woman, who could make so tidy and comfortable a life out of small possibilities, grew every day.

One evening, as he sat by the open window of his room, in a dark mood, looking at the garden and thinking of the faithless Olympiada, Tatiana Vlassyevna came out of her dining-room to the kitchen and called Ilya to tea. He accepted the invitation against his will. He could not break free from his moodiness, and had no inclination to talk. He sat at the table, sulky and silent, and, looking at his hostess, noticed that her face wore an unusually solemn and troubled expression. Neither spoke; the samovar bubbled cheerily, a bird fluttered in a cage, the air was full of the scent of fried onions and eau-de-Cologne. Kirik twisted about on his chair, drummed with his fingers on the edge of the tea-tray, and sang under his breath.

"Ilya Jakovlevitch," began his wife, with an important air, "we— my husband and I—have arranged a little matter, and would like to talk seriously with you."

"Ho! ho! ho!" laughed the inspector suddenly, and rubbed his big red hands. Ilya started and looked at him in surprise.

"Wait, Kirik! There's nothing to laugh at," said Tatiana.

"*We've* arranged it," cried Kirik, with a big laugh, then looked at Ilya and winked towards his wife. "Clever little girl!"

"We've saved some money——"

"*We! We've* saved money! Ho! ho! ho! My clever, dear little wife!"

"Kirya, be quiet!" said Tatiana, severely. Her face seemed thinner and more pointed than ever.

"We have saved close on a thousand roubles," she went on half aloud, and bent over towards Ilya and looked him full in the face with her sharp little eyes. He sat quiet, but in his breast something seemed to jump for joy.

"The money's in the bank, and brings us four per cent," went on Tatiana.

"And that's too little, devil take it!" cried Kirik, and struck the table with his hand. "We want——"

His wife silenced him with a reproving look.

"Naturally, we are quite satisfied with this return, but we should like to help you in case you care to start on a bigger scale. You are so steady——" She paid Ilya a compliment or two, and then proceeded:

"They say that a fancy ware shop can bring in twenty per cent., or even more if you go about it the right way. Now, we are ready to find you the money for a bill of exchange, at sight, of course, on condition that you open a shop. You will manage it under my supervision, and we'll halve the profits. You will insure the goods in my name, and you'll give me besides a document of some sort, nothing of importance. And now, think over the matter, and tell us simply—yes or no."

Ilya listened to the thin, clear voice, and rubbed his forehead hard. While she spoke he looked many times at the corner where the golden frame of the eikon shone between the two wedding candles. He felt a kind of helplessness and fear as he listened to his hostess's words. Her proposal all at once assured his dream of years. It astonished him and filled him with joy. Smiling in confusion, he looked at the little woman and thought:

"That's it, it's Fate."

She spoke now in a motherly tone:

"Consider it well, look at it from all sides! whether you have confidence in yourself, if you have enough strength—enough experience for it? And then tell us, what could you put to it besides your work,—our money won't go so very far, will it?"

"I can," said Ilya slowly, "put in five hundred roubles. My uncle will give them to me—I have an uncle—I told you. He'll give me the money, perhaps more."

"Hurrah!" cried Kirik.

"Then is it a bargain?" asked Tatiana.

"Yes. I agree," said Lunev.

"Well, I should think so!" cried the inspector. Then he put his hand in his pocket and called out: "Now, let's have some champagne. Ilya, my boy, run to the wine merchant, and bring some champagne. Let's crack a bottle,—here's the money, you're our guest, of course. Ask for Don Champagne at ninety kopecks, and say it's for me, for Avtonomov, then they'll give it you for sixty-five,—hurry up, my lad!"

Ilya looked smilingly at the beaming faces of the couple and went.

So Fate had pushed him and buffeted him, led him to grievous sin, troubled his soul, and now suddenly she seemed to ask his forgiveness, to smile on him and offer her favours. Now before him the way lay open to a sheltered corner in life, where he could live quietly and find peace for his soul. He had taken a man's life, and for that he would help many and so make amends before the Lord. No, the Lord would not punish him severely, for He knows all. Olympiada was right; in the murder he was only the instrument, not the will, and evidently the Lord Himself was helping him to straighten his course, since he had made easy the attainment of his life's desire. Thoughts whirled through Ilya's head as in a happy dance, and inspired his heart with joys of life unknown till now. He brought from the wine shop a bottle of real champagne for which he paid seven roubles.

"Oho!" cried Avtonomov, "that's what I call proper, my boy; that's an idea! Ha! yes."

Tatiana thought differently; she shook her head disparagingly and said in a tone of reproach, looking at the bottle:

"Seven roubles! Ei—ei! Ilya Jakovlevitch, how unpractical, how foolish!"

Lunev stood before her, happy, deeply stirred; he smiled and said joyfully:

"It's real champagne,—for the first time in my life I'll drink something real. What's my life been up to now? All spoilt, dirt and coarseness, and stuffiness, injuries and insults, and all kinds of torment. Is that a real life do you suppose? Can any one go on living like that?"

He touched the sore place in his heart; his words rang bitterly, his eyes grew gloomy; he sighed deeply, and went on firmly and decidedly:

"Ever since I was small I've looked for the real thing and have lived all the time like a wood-shaving in a brook. I was swept about, now here, now there, and all round me everything was dull and dirty and restless. I didn't know where to catch hold; only misery and injustice and knavishness all round me, and all that disgusts me: and now fate brings me to you, for the first time in my life I see how people can live in peace and comfort and love."

He looked at them with a bright smile and bowed to them.

"I thank you. With you I've found relief for my soul, by God! You've helped me for my whole life, now I can step out boldly, now I know how a man should live! It will go well with me and no other shall suffer for me. How many unlucky ones there are in the world! how many go under. I've seen it all, I know it all."

Tatiana Vlassyevna regarded him with the look of the cat who lies in wait for the bird, ravished by his own song. A greenish fire gleamed in her eyes and her lips twitched; Kirik was busy with the bottle, he had it between his knees and bent over it. The veins of his neck swelled and his ears moved.

"My friends," continued Ilya, "for I have two friends——"

The cork popped, hit the ceiling and fell on the table; a glass that it fell against rang, quivering.

Kirik smacked his lips, filled the glasses and commanded:

"Ready."

Then when his wife and Lunev had taken their glasses, he held his high over his head and cried:

"To the firm of Tatiana Avtonomov and Lunev; may it bloom and flourish! Hurrah!"

CHAPTER XIX

The following days were spent by Lunev and Tatiana Vlassyevna in arranging together the details of the new undertaking. She knew everything and spoke of everything with as much certainty as if she had dealt in fancy wares all her life. Ilya listened with amazement, smiled and was silent. He wanted to find a suitable place to make a beginning as soon as possible, and he agreed to all Tatiana's proposals, without considering their significance at all.

At last everything was settled, and it appeared that Tatiana had a suitable shop ready chosen. It was arranged exactly as Ilya had imagined to himself, in a clean street, small and neat, with a room at the back. Ilya knew the shop; there had formerly been a milk shop there, and he had often visited it with his wares. Everything went splendidly, down to the least detail, and Ilya was triumphant, energetic, and happy. He visited his friends in the hospital. Pavel met him, cheerful for once. "To-morrow I'm to be discharged!" he explained with joyful excitement, even before he answered Ilya's greeting. "I've had a letter from Vyerka. She grumbles, says I insulted her, little devil!"

His eyes shone and his cheeks reddened. He could not keep still a moment, but shuffled with his slippers on the ground and flourished with his hands.

"Take care of yourself," said Ilya. "Be careful."

"Of course. I shall simply say: 'Mam'selle Vyera Kapitanovna, will you marry me? Please! No?—then there's a knife in your heart!'" A convulsive shudder passed over his face.

"Come, come!" said Ilya, laughing. "What, threaten her with a knife straight away?"

"No—believe me, I've had enough of it. I can't live without her. And she too; she's no good without me; she's had enough of her beastly life. She must be sick of it. To-morrow it shall be settled between us, this way or that."

Lunev looked at his friend's face and thought: "In a mood like this he might kill her." Suddenly a clear, simple idea came into his head. He blushed, then smiled. "Pashutka, think, I've made my fortune," he began after a pause, and told his friend shortly what had happened to him. Pavel listened, sighed with bent head, and said:

"Ye—es, you are lucky!"

"Envious?"

"Rather! Devil take it!"

"Really, I'm ashamed of my luck with you, speaking quite honestly."

"Thank you!" said Pavel, with a dull laugh.

"Do you know?" said Ilya slowly, "I'm not boasting. I mean it. I am ashamed, by God!"

Pavel glanced at him without speaking, and hung his head lower.

"And I'll say something to you. We've hung together in bad times. Let us share the good times."

"H—m—m!" growled Pavel. "I've heard that happiness can't be shared, any more than a woman's love."

"Oh, yes, it can! Just you find out all that is wanted to set up as a well-sinker—instruments and so on—and how much it costs, and I'll find the money."

"Wha—at!" cried Pavel, looking at his friend incredulously.

Lunev seized his hand with a lively gesture, and pressed it.

"Really, you silly! I'll find it for you."

But it needed a long conversation to assure Pavel of the seriousness of his intentions. Pavel kept shaking his head, growling, and saying: "No, it'll come to nothing."

Finally Lunev succeeded in convincing him. Then Pashka embraced him, and said, in a voice full of emotion:

"Thank you, brother! You'll pull me out of the pit. Now, listen to me. A workshop of my own—that's not for me. Give me some money, and I'll take Vyerka and go away from here. It will be easier for you, and you won't need to give me so much, and it'll suit me better. I'll go off somewhere and get an assistant's job in a workshop."

"That's ridiculous," said Ilya. "It's much better to be your own master."

"What sort of a master should I be?" cried Pavel. "I don't know how to deal with workmen like a master. No, a business of my own, and all that goes with it, is not to my taste. I know the sort of fellow a man must be for that, it isn't in my line. You can't turn a goat into a pig."

Ilya did not understand clearly Pashka's conception of a master, but it pleased him and drew him still nearer to his comrade. He looked at him full of joy and love, and said jestingly:

"True! You are very like a goat. Just about as thin. Do you know whom you remind me of? Perfishka, the cobbler. Well, then, we'll meet to-morrow, and then I'll give you the money to make a start, till you get a job. And now I'll have a look at Jakov."

"Agreed, and thank you, brother!"

"How do you get on now with Jakov?"

"Same as before; we can't hit it off," said Gratschev laughing.

"He's an unlucky fellow. It's not easy to deal with him," said Ilya thoughtfully.

"Ah, we've most of us something to put up with," answered Pavel, and shrugged his shoulders. "He always seems to me not quite all there, half silly. Well, I'm off."

"Good-bye, then."

And when Ilya had already left him, he called after him once more from the passage:

"Thank you, brother!"

Ilya nodded to him with a smile. He found Jakov quite sorrowful and cast down. He lay on his bed, his face upturned to the ceiling, looking up with wide-open eyes, and did not notice Ilya's approach.

"Nikita Jegarovitch's gone to another ward," he said gloomily.

"That's a mercy," answered Lunev. "He really looked too terrible, and then he said such odd things! God be with him!" Jakov looked at him reproachfully, but said nothing.

"Getting on?" asked Ilya.

"Ye—es," answered Jakov with a sigh. "I mayn't even be ill as long as I want. Yesterday father was here again. He's bought another house. He says he's going to open another inn, and all that'll be on my head."

Ilya wanted to speak of his own success, but something restrained him.

The spring sun shone gaily through the windows and the yellow walls of the hospital seemed still more yellow. In the bright light, the paint showed many spots and gaps. Two patients were sitting on their beds, silently playing cards, quite absorbed in their game. A tall thin man, with his bandaged head bent down, walked noiselessly up and down the ward.

All was quiet, save for an occasional smothered cough, and the shuffling of the patients' slippers as they walked in the corridor.

Jakov's yellow face seemed lifeless and his dull eyes had a troubled expression.

"Oh, I wish I were dead!" he said in his dry, creaking voice. "When I lie here I say to myself, 'it must be interesting to die.' Up there things are very different—so different, that no one has ever seen, no noise, everything is easy to understand and bright and clear." His voice sank lower, became more muffled. "There are kind angels there; they can explain everything to you, and answer all your questions—the angels——"

He was silent and began to blink his eyes, watching the pale reflection of the sun rays play on the ceiling.

"Do you know——?" began Lunev.

Jakov interrupted him at once.

"Haven't you seen Mashutka?"

"N—No."

"Ah! you—you ought to have gone to see her long ago."

"I forgot. I can't remember everything."

"You must remember with your heart."

Lunev was embarrassed and said nothing. A little man on crutches wearing a moustache with pointed ends, hobbled in out of the corridor, and said in a hoarse, hissing voice to the tall man with the bandaged head:

"Schurka has not come again, the rascal."

Jakov looked at him, sighed and threw his head backwards and forwards on the pillow restlessly.

"Nikita Jegarovitch will die, and he doesn't want to,—the surgeon told me, he must die, and I want to die, and I can't. I shall get well again and go behind the counter, and drink brandy and so I go down."

His lips lengthened into a melancholy smile.

"To endure this life, a man needs an iron body and an iron heart, and he must live like all the rest, without thinking, without conscience."

Ilya detected in Jakov's words something hostile and cold, and his brow wrinkled.

"And I'm a glass between stones," Jakov continued, "if I turn, there's a smash."

"You grumble far too much," said Lunev carelessly.

"And what about you?" asked Jakov.

Ilya turned away and did not speak. Then observing that Jakov showed no signs of going on, he said thoughtfully:

"It's hard for us all. Look at Pavel, for instance."

"I don't like him," said Jakov, and made a grimace.

"Why not?"

"Oh! Just I don't like him."

"Well, I do."

"I don't care."

"H'm—yes—well, I must be off."

Jakov held out his hand in silence, and then implored, in a tearful, entreating voice:

"Do find out about Mashutka, will you? for Christ's sake!"

"Yes. I will," said Ilya.

It disturbed and worried him to listen to Jakov's eternal complaints, and he felt relieved when he got away from him. But the entreaty to find out about Masha roused a certain feeling of shame in him for his conduct towards Perfishka's daughter, and he determined to look up Matiza, as she was certain to know how Mashutka was taking to her new life. Like all the people in Petrusha's house, he knew that Matiza used to wash the floors every Saturday at the house of Ehrenov, receiving a quarter-rouble for the task, and also for granting more personal favours. Ilya took the road towards Filimonov's tavern, and his soul was full of thoughts of his future. It seemed to smile sweetly on him, and lost in his fancies, he passed the tavern without noticing, and when he discovered his mistake felt no inclination to turn back. He went on right out of the town; the fields stretched away in front of him, bounded far off by the dark wall of the forest. The sun was setting; its rosy reflection gleamed on the tender green of the turf. Ilya strode forward with head high and looked up to the sky, where purple clouds stood almost motionless, flaming in the sun's rays. He felt at ease, wandering thus aimlessly; every step forward, every breath awakened a new thought. He imagined himself rich and mighty and with the power to ruin Petrusha Filimonov, in his dream he had brought him to beggary, and Petrusha stood before him weeping, but he addressed the suppliant:

"Have compassion, should I? And you, have you ever had compassion on a soul? Have you not maltreated your son, and led my uncle into sin?

Have you not looked down on me and despised me? In your accursed house no one has ever been happy, no one has ever known joy. Your house is rotten through and through, a trap for men, a prison for those that live in it."

Petrusha stood there, shivering and groaning with fear, lamenting like a beggar and Ilya thundered on at him:

"I will burn your house, for it brings misery to all who dwell in it, and do you go out in the world and beg forgiveness from all that you have wronged; go, wander till the day of your death, and then die of hunger, like a dog!"

The evening twilight had fallen on the fields, the forest rose in the distance like a thick dark wall, like a mountain range. A little bat flitted noiselessly through the air like a dark speck, seeming to sow the darkness. Far off on the river was heard the beating noise of a steamboat's paddles; it was as though somewhere in the distance a monstrous bird were wheeling, making the air tremble with mighty strokes of its wings. Lunev remembered all the people who had opposed him on his way through life, and haled them all without mercy before his judgment seat. A pleasant sense of relief came to him, and as he strode alone through the fields, wrapped now in darkness, he began to sing softly. Suddenly the odour of rubbish and decay filled the air. He stopped singing; but the odour had only pleasant associations for him. He had reached the town rubbish-heap, in the narrow valley where he had so often searched with Jeremy.

The stench seemed to him more penetrating and suffocating than in his childhood.

The vision of the old rag-picker rose in his memory, and he glanced round to find in the twilight the spot where the old man used to rest with him. But he could not find it; evidently it was buried under new mountains of refuse and rubbish. He sighed, and felt that there was a part of his soul smothered beneath the refuse of life.

"If only I hadn't killed that man; then I should want nothing." The thought flashed through his brain; but immediately from his heart came another, answering: "What has that man to do with my life? He is only my misfortune, not my sin."

Suddenly there was a slight rustling, a little dog slipped past Ilya's feet, and fled, whimpering softly. Ilya shuddered; he felt as though a part of this darkness of night had taken life and then vanished again, groaning.

"It's all the same," he thought. "Even without that, there'd be no peace in my heart. How many injuries I have endured; how many more I have seen others bear! Once the heart is wounded, it never ceases to feel pain."

He paced slowly along the edge of the valley. His feet sank in the dust. He could hear the wood-shavings and pieces of paper rustle and crackle as he walked. An open part of the ground, not yet encumbered with rubbish, led away into the valley like a narrow tongue of land. He went to the end of it, and there sat down. Here the air was fresher, and as his eyes travelled along the gully, they rested far off on the steely ribbon of the river. The lights of invisible vessels glimmered on the water, which seemed as still as ice, and one light swayed, like a red speck, in the air. Another glowed steadily, green and foreboding, without rays; and at his feet, full of mist, the wide throat of the valley seemed itself like the bed of a stream, wherein black air-waves rolled noiselessly. Deep melancholy fell on Ilya's heart. He looked down and thought, "A moment ago I felt full of courage, light, and happy, and now it's all gone again. Why does life drive a man on and on against his will, where he has no desire to go? Everything in life is so oppressive and heavy, full of injustice, full of perplexity! Perhaps Jakov is right—men must first of all understand themselves, how they live and by what laws?"

He remembered how strange, almost hostile, Jakov had been towards him to-day, and he grew more sorrowful as he remembered. Suddenly there was a noise in the valley, a mass of earth had loosened and rolled down. The damp night wind breathed on Ilya's face; he looked up to the sky. The stars burned shyly, and over the wood the great red ball of the moon heaved slowly up, like a huge, pitiless eye. And like the bat through the twilight, dark images and memories fluttered through Ilya's soul. They came and went without solving the riddles that oppressed him, and denser and heavier grew the darkness over his heart.

"Men rob and torment and strangle one another, and no one dreams of making life easier for his fellows, but each watches only for a chance to fight his way out and rest in a peaceful corner. I, too, am seeking for such a corner, and where is the Truth and Reality and Steadfastness in this life?"

He sat a long time there, thinking, looking now at the sky, now at the valley. All was still in the fields. The moonlight looking into the dark gully, showed its clefts and the bushes on its slopes, that threw vague shadows on the ground. The sky was pure and clear, nothing showed but the moon and stars. A cold shiver ran through Ilya, he got up and went slowly to the town, whose lights gleamed in the distance. He had no further wish to think at all. His breast was now filled with cold indifference.

He reached home late, and stood thoughtfully before the door, hesitating to ring. The windows were dark already. Evidently his landlord had gone early to rest. He disliked to disturb Tatiana Vlassyevna so late, for she always saw to the door herself; but he had to get in. He pulled the bell gently. The door opened almost immediately, and the slender form of Tatiana appeared, dressed in white.

"Shut the door quickly," she said, in a strange voice. "It is cold; I've hardly anything on. My husband's not at home."

"I'm so sorry to be late," murmured Ilya.

"Yes, you are late. Where have you been?"

Ilya closed the door and turned round to answer, and suddenly felt her close to him; she did not move, but nestled closer; he could not give way, the door was at his back. Then suddenly she laughed—a soft, trembling laugh. Lunev put his hands tenderly on her shoulders; he shook with excitement and longing to embrace her. Then all at once she straightened herself, laid her slender warm arms round his neck, and said in a ringing voice:

"Why do you wander abroad in the night? Why? You can be happy nearer home—for a long time you might have been—my dearest, my beautiful, strong boy!"

As if in a dream, Ilya felt for her lips and swayed beneath the convulsive embrace of the slender body; she clung to his breast like a cat, and kissed him again and again. He caught her in his strong arms and bore her away, carrying his burden as easily as though he trod on air.

In the morning Ilya woke with trouble in his heart.

"How can I look Kirik in the face?" he thought, and shame was added to the anxiety that the thought of the inspector aroused in him.

"If only I had quarrelled with him, or didn't like him. But to injure him, and so deeply, without any cause——" he thought with fear in his heart, and a feeling of disgust arose in him for Tatiana. He felt that Kirik was certain to find out his wife's unfaithfulness, and he could not imagine what would happen.

"How she fell on me, as if she were starving!" he thought, in restless, painful doubt; and yet felt, too, a pleasing sense of gratified vanity. This was no "tradesman's darling," as he used to call Olympiada in his thoughts, but a woman, respected by all the world—an educated, pretty married woman.

"There must be something special about me," his vanity whispered to him. "It's too bad—too bad! But I'm not made of stone, and I couldn't turn her away."

He was young in fact, and his fancy was full of the woman's caresses. Besides his practical mind saw involuntarily several advantages that might arise from this new relationship. But close on the heels of these ideas, like a dark cloud, came other gloomy thoughts.

"Now I'm in a corner again. Did I want it? I respected her! I never had an evil thought about her; and now it's happened like this."

Then again, all the disturbance and contradiction in his soul was covered by the joyful thought that soon now his sheltered, clean life would begin. But to the end the painful, stabbing thought persisted:

"It would have been better without this."

He stayed in bed, pondering, till Avtonomov went to his duties. He heard the inspector say to his wife, smacking his lips:

"Let me have meat pasties for dinner, Tanya. Take a little more pork, and then just brown them a little, till they look like tiny little sucking pigs on the plate—you know; and just a little pepper with them, my dear, the way I like it. Then I'll bring you some marmalade, shall I?"

"Now, go along! go along! As if I didn't know what you like!" said his wife tenderly.

"And now, my darling, my little Tanya, give me one more kiss!"

Lunev shuddered. It all seemed to him horrible and ridiculous.

"Tchik! tchik!" cried Avtonomov as he kissed his wife, and she laughed. As soon as she had shut the door behind him, she danced into Ilya's room, and cried:

"Kiss me quick—I've no time."

"You've just kissed your husband," said Ilya moodily.

"Wha—at? Eh? Aha! He's jealous!" she cried, delighted, then sprang up and drew the window curtain.

"Jealous!" she said. "That's so nice! Jealous men are always passionate lovers."

"I didn't say it out of jealousy."

"Don't talk!" she commanded, and put her hand on his lips. Then, when she had been kissed enough, she looked at Ilya, with a smile, and could not keep from saying:

"Well, you're a bold fellow—a downright daredevil—to carry on like this under the husband's nose."

Her greenish eyes sparkled impudently, and she cried:

"Oh, it's quite a common thing, not in the least unusual! Do you suppose there are many women true to their husbands? Only the ugly ones and the sick ones—a pretty woman always wants to enjoy herself and have a little romance."

During the whole morning she instructed Ilya on this point, told him all sorts of stories of wives who were untrue to their husbands. In her red blouse, with her skirts tucked up, and her sleeves rolled above her elbows, supple and light, she danced about the kitchen, preparing the pasties for her husband, and chattering all the time in her clear, ringing voice:

"A husband!—d'you think a wife must be always content with him? The husband can sometimes be very disagreeable, even if you love him; and then he never thinks twice if he has a chance to be false to his wife. So it's dull for a wife, too, to think of nothing all her life but—my husband, my husband, my husband."

Ilya listened, as he drank his tea, which seemed to have a bitter taste. In this woman's speech there was something defiant, unpleasantly provocative, that was new to him. Involuntarily he remembered Olympiada, the deep voice, the quiet movements, and the glowing words that had power to grip his heart. For the rest Olympiada was a woman of no great education, who might have been the wife of a small tradesman, but even because of that she was simpler in her shamelessness. Ilya answered Tatiana's pleasantries with a slight laugh, and had to force himself even to laugh. His heart was sick, and he only laughed because he did not know what to speak of. Her words aroused a painful melancholy in him, and yet he listened with deep interest, and finally said thoughtfully:

"I did not believe that such things happened in your set?"

"Things, my dear, are the same everywhere."

"You don't mind much, do you? Why do you look so cross?"

Ilya stood in the doorway and looked fixedly at her, wrinkling his brow. She went up to him, put her hands on his shoulders, and looked into his face curiously.

"I'm not cross," said Ilya seriously.

"Really? Oh! thank you—ha! ha! ha! how good you are!" She laughed brightly.

"I was only thinking," said Ilya, speaking slowly—"It's all quite right, what you say—but there's something bad in it too."

"Oho! What a touchy person you are! Something bad, eh? What then—explain to me!"

But he could not. He himself did not understand what it was in her words that displeased him. Olympiada had often spoken, more simply, more plainly; but her words had never given him the pain of soul that he felt from the chatter of this pretty little bird. He pondered all day obstinately on the strange feeling of discomfort that had arisen in his heart through this new intimacy, so flattering to his vanity, and he could not arrive at the source of the sensation.

When he came home that night, Kirik met him in the kitchen, and said in a friendly way:

"I say, Ilya, Tanyusha did some cooking to-day—meat pasties—I tell you, it seemed almost a pity to eat them! Almost as bad as eating living nightingales. I've left a plateful for you, brother. Hang up your box, sit down, and see what you will see."

Ilya looked at him conscience-stricken, and said with a forced laugh:

"Thank you, Kirik Nikodimovitch." Then he added, with a sigh: "You're a good fellow, by Jove!"

"What," answered Kirik, "a plate of pasty—that's nothing! No, brother, if I were chief of police—then you might perhaps thank me, but I'm not. I shall give up the police altogether, and start as agent or manager in a big business. A manager, that's something like a good position; if I get it I'll soon get a little capital together."

Tatiana was busy at the stove and singing softly. Ilya looked at her, and again felt a painful discomfort; but almost immediately the sensation vanished under the influence of new impressions and cares. During these days he had no time to give to brooding; the arrangement of the shop and the purchase of goods occupied him entirely, and from day to day amidst his work he grew accustomed to this woman, almost without knowing, like a drunkard to the taste of brandy. She pleased him more and more as a mistress, although her caresses often caused him shame, even anxiety; her caresses and her talk together slowly destroyed his respect for her as a woman. Every morning after she had seen her husband off to work, or in the evenings when he was on duty, she called Ilya to her or came into his room, and told him all sorts of stories "of real life;" and all her stories were curiously vicious, as though they related to a country inhabited only by liars and scoundrels of both sexes, whose greatest pleasure lay in adultery.

"Is that all true?" asked Ilya gloomily. He didn't want to believe, but felt helpless and unable to contradict.

He listened, and life seemed to him like a swill-tub, and men moving in it like worms.

"Ugh!" he said wearily, "is there nothing clean or true anywhere?"

"What d'you call true? What d'you mean?" asked Tatiana in surprise.

"Why, something honourable!" cried Lunev angrily.

"Why, it's honourable people I'm speaking of—how funny you are! I don't make it all up."

"That's not what I mean. Is there anywhere anything honourable—pure, or not?"

She did not understand and laughed at him. Sometimes her conversation took a different tone; looking at him with greenish eyes, darting an uncanny fire, she asked him:

"Tell me, what was your first experience of women?"

Ilya was ashamed of the memory, it was hateful to him. He turned away from the glance of his mistress, and said in a low reproachful voice:

"What horrid things you ask! I think you ought to be ashamed—men don't even speak like that with one another."

But she laughed happily, and went on talking till Lunev often felt defiled with her words as with pitch. But if she read in his face any hostile feeling, or perceived in his eyes any weariness, or distress, or sorrow, she knew how to kindle his desire afresh and banish by her caresses all feelings hostile to her influence.

One day when Ilya returned from the shop, where already the joiners were putting in the shelves, he saw to his astonishment, Matiza in the kitchen. She was sitting at the table, her big hands folded in her lap, and conversing with the mistress of the house, who was standing by the hearth.

"Here," said Tatiana, and nodded at Matiza, "this lady has been waiting for you, for ever so long."

"Good evening!" said Matiza, and got up clumsily.

"Why," cried Ilya, "are you still living?"

"Even pigs don't eat dirty bits of wood," answered Matiza in her deep voice.

Ilya had not seen her for a long time, and looked at her now with mingled feelings of compassion and pleasure. She was dressed in ragged fustian, an old faded kerchief covered her head, her feet were bare. She moved with difficulty, but supporting herself with her hands on the wall, she crept slowly into Ilya's room, sat heavily in a chair, and spoke in a hoarse toneless voice:

"I shall soon die. You see, I can hardly move my feet, and when I can't walk, I can't find food, and then I must die."

Her face was horribly bloated and covered with dark flecks. The big eyes were hardly visible between the swollen lids.

"What are you looking at?" she said to Ilya. "You think some one has struck me? No, it is a disease, devouring me."

"What are you doing?"

"I sit by the church door and beg for coppers," said Matiza, indifferently, in her deep, resonant voice. "I'm come on business. I heard from Perfishka that you were living here, and so I came."

"May I give you some tea?" asked Lunev. It hurt him to hear Matiza's voice and see her big, slack body perishing visibly.

"The devil wash his tail in your tea! Give me five kopecks, do! I came to you—well, you can ask me why."

Speech was difficult. She breathed short, and an overpowering odour came from her.

"Well, why?" asked Ilya, turning away and remembering how he had insulted her once.

"Do you remember Mashutka? What? You've a poor memory! You've grown rich!"

"I remember, of course I remember," said Ilya quickly.

"What's the good of your remembering?" she interrupted. "Has that made her life any easier?"

"What's the matter with her? How is she getting on?"

Matiza's head swayed, and she said briefly:

"She hasn't hanged herself yet."

"Oh, speak out!" cried Ilya roughly. "What do you begin at me for? You sold her yourself for three roubles."

"I don't reproach you, only myself," she answered quietly and emphatically, then began to tell of Masha, choking with the exertion.

"Her old husband is jealous and torments her, he lets her go nowhere, not even into the shop. She sits in one room, and mayn't go into the courtyard without leave. He's got rid of his children somehow, and lives alone with Masha. He pinches her and ties her hands, he treats her so badly because his first wife was untrue, and the two children are not his. Masha has run away twice, but both times the police have brought her back, and the old man pinches her and starves her for it. See, what a life!"

"Yes, you and Perfishka did a good deed," said Ilya gloomily.

"I thought it was better," said the woman, in her toneless voice. Her face motionless as though carved in stone, and her dead voice, weighed on Ilya.

"I thought—it was cleaner so. But the worse would have been better. She might have been sold to a rich man, he would have given her a home and clothes, and everything, and afterwards she would have sent him off and lived like all the others. Ever so many live like that."

"Well, why have you come to me?" asked Ilya.

"You live here, in a policeman's house. You see, they always catch her. Tell him to let her go, let her run away. She'll manage somehow. Is one not allowed to run away?"

"You really came for that?"

"Yes, why not? They ought not to stop her, tell them!"

"Ah, you people!" cried Ilya, trying to think what he could do for Masha.

Matiza rose from her chair, and shuffled carefully over the floor. She sighed and groaned, and she was not like a human being walking, but like an old, decayed tree falling slowly down.

"Good-bye! We shan't meet again! I shall soon die," she murmured. "Thank you, thank you, my fine, trim fellow! Thank you!"

As soon as she was gone, Tatiana hurried into Ilya's room, embraced him, and asked smiling:

"That's the one—your first love, eh?"

"Who?" asked Ilya slowly, absorbed in memories of Masha.

"That horror— —"

Ilya unclasped her hands from his neck, and said moodily:

"She can hardly drag one foot after the other, but she cares for those she loves."

"Whom does she love?" asked the woman, and looked with wonder and curiosity at Ilya's anxious face.

"Wait, Tatiana, wait! Don't make fun of her."

He told her briefly of Masha, and asked: "What is to be done?"

"Here, nothing," answered Tatiana, shrugging her shoulders. "By the law, the wife belongs to her husband, and no one has any right to take her from him." And, with the important air of one who knows the law well and is convinced of its stability, she explained at length that Masha must obey her husband.

"She must just hang on for the present. Let her wait—he's old; he'll soon die. Then she'll be free, and all his money will go to her. And then you'll marry the rich young widow, eh?"

She laughed and continued to instruct Ilya seriously.

"It would be best for you to give up your old acquaintances. They're no use to you now, and they might get in your way. They're all so coarse and dirty—that one, for instance, you lent money to—such a skinny fellow, with wicked eyes."

"Gratschev?"

"Yes. What funny names common people have—Gratschev, Lunev, Petuchev, Skvarzov.—In our set the names are much better, prettier— Avtonomov, Korsakov—my father's name was Florianov. When I was a young girl I was courted by a lawyer, Gloriantov. Once at the skating, he stole my garter, and threatened to make a scandal if I did not go to his house to get it back——"

Ilya listened, remembering his own past. He felt his soul bound by invisible threads fast to the house of Petrusha Filimonov, and it seemed this house would always hold him back from the peaceful life he longed for.

CHAPTER XX

At last Ilya Lunev's dream was realised. Full of calm joy, he stood from morning to night behind the counter of his own business, and swelled with pride over all he saw round him. Boxes of wood and cardboard were ranged carefully on the shelves; in the window was a display of waist-buckles, purses, soap, buttons, with gay-coloured ribbons and laces. It was all bright and clean, and shone in the sunshine in rainbow colours. Handsome and steady-looking, he received his customers with a polite bow and displayed his goods on the counter before them. He heard pleasant music in the rustling of his laces and ribbons, and all the girls—tailoresses, who bought a few kopecks' worth—seemed to him pretty and lovable. All at once life became pleasant and easy, a clear, simple meaning seemed to have entered into it, and the past was veiled in a cloud. No thoughts came to him save of business, and goods and customers. He had taken on an errand boy, dressed him in a well-fitting grey jacket, and took great care that the lad washed himself well, and kept as clean as possible.

"You and I, Gavrik," he said, "deal in fine goods, and we must be clean."

Gavrik was a lad of twelve years, rather fat, snub-nosed and slightly pock-marked, with little grey eyes and a lively face. He had passed through the town school, and considered himself a full-grown, serious man. He took a great interest in his work in the clean little shop; it delighted him to handle the boxes, and he was at great pains to be as polite to the customers as his master. But this he found difficult—his talents for mimicry were too strongly developed, and he was apt to reproduce on his coarse face any expression that he observed in a customer. Above all he was the sworn foe of all little girls, and could seldom resist the temptation to pinch them or push them, or pull their hair, and generally make their lives a burden. Ilya watched him, and remembered how he had served in the fish shop, and as he had a liking for the boy, he joked with him and spoke to him in a friendly way when there were no customers in the shop.

"If you're dull, Gavrik, read books when there's no work to be done," he advised. "Time passes easily with a book, and reading's pleasant."

From this time Lunev began to regard mankind cheerfully and attentively, and he smiled as much as to say:

"I'm a lucky one, you see; but patience! Your turn will come soon."

He opened his shop at seven and closed at ten. There were few customers; he sat on a chair near the door basking in the rays of the spring sun, and resting, almost without a thought, without a wish. Gavrik sat in the doorway, observed the passers-by, imitated their ways, enticed the dogs to him, and threw stones at the pigeons and sparrows, or else read a book, and breathed heavily through his nose. Sometimes his master would make him read aloud, but the actual reading did not interest Ilya, he listened rather to the stillness and peace in his heart. This inner peace filled him with delight, it was new to him and unspeakably pleasant. Now and then, however, the sweetness was disturbed, there was a strange, incomprehensible sensation, a premonition of unrest; it could not shatter the peace in his soul, but rested lightly on it like a shadow. Then Ilya began to talk to the boy.

"Gavrik! What is your father?"

"He's a postman."

"Are you a big family?"

"Big? There's a crowd of us. Some grown-up, but some are still little."

"How many little ones?"

"Five, and three grown-up. We three have all got places. I'm with you, Vassili is in Siberia in a telegraph office, Sonyka gives lessons. She earns a lot, twelve roubles a month. Then there's Mishka—he is older than I am, but he's still at school."

"Then there are four grown-up, not three?"

"No, how?" cried Gavrik, and added sententiously: "Mishka is still learning, but a grown-up is one who works."

"Do you have a hard time at home?"

"Rather," answered Gavrik indifferently, and sniffed loudly. Then he began to explain his schemes for the future.

"When I'm big, I shall be a soldier. Then there'll be a war, and I'll go to the war. I'm brave, and so I'll rush at the enemy before all the others and capture the standard—that's what my uncle did—and General Gourko gave Kim a medal and five roubles."

Ilya listened, smiling, and looked at the pock-marked face, and the wide, twitching nostrils. In the evening when the shop was shut, Ilya went into the little room at the back. The samovar made ready by the lad was on the table, and bread and sausage. Gavrik had his tea and bread and went into the shop to sleep, but Ilya sat long by the samovar, often as much as two hours. Two chairs, a table, a bed, and a cupboard for household utensils made up all the furniture of Ilya's new home. The room was small and low, with a square window from which could be seen the feet of the passers-by, the roofs of the houses over the way, and the sky above the roofs. He hung a white muslin curtain before the window. An iron railing cut the window off from the street, and this displeased Ilya very much. Over his bed was a picture—"The Steps of Man's Life." This picture was a great favourite with Ilya, and he had long wished to buy it, but for one reason and another he had never possessed it till he opened his shop, though it cost but ten kopecks.

The steps of man's life were arranged in the form of an arch, under which was represented Paradise; here the Almighty, surrounded with rays of light and flowers, talked with Adam and Eve. There were seventeen steps in all. On the first stood a child supported by his mother, and underneath, in red letters: "The first step." On the second the child was beating a drum, and the inscription ran: "Five years old—he plays." At seven years of age he began "to learn;" at ten, "goes to school;" at twenty-one he stood on the step with a rifle in his hand, and a smiling face, and underneath was written: "Serves his time as a soldier." On the next step he is twenty-five, he is in evening dress, with an opera hat in one hand and a bouquet in the other—"he is a bridegroom." Then his beard is grown, he has a long coat and a red tie, and is standing near a stout lady in yellow, and pressing her hand. Next he is thirty-five; he stands with rolled-up shirt-sleeves by an anvil and hammers the iron. At the top of the arch he is sitting in a red chair reading the paper, his wife and four children are listening to him. He himself and all his family are well dressed, respectable, with healthy, happy faces. At this time he is fifty years old. But note how the steps begin to go down; the man's beard is already grey, he is clad in a long yellow coat, and in his hands he holds a bag of fish and a jar of some sort. This step is labelled: "Household duties." On the following step the man is rocking the cradle of his grandson; lower down "he is led," being now eighty years old; and in the last—he is ninety-five—he is in a chair with his feet in a coffin, and behind the chair stands Death, with the scythe in his hand.

When Ilya sat by the samovar he looked at the picture, and it pleased him to see the life of man so accurately and simply depicted. The picture radiated peace, the bright colours seemed to smile at him, and he was persuaded that the series represented honourable life wisely and intelligibly, as an example to men—life exactly as it should be led. As he gazed at this representation of life, he thought that now that he had attained his desire, his career must henceforth follow the picture exactly. He would mount upwards, and right at the summit, when he had saved enough money, he would marry a modest girl who had learned to read and to write.

The samovar hummed and whistled in a melancholy way. The sky looked dull through the glass of the window and the muslin curtain, and the stars were hardly visible. There is always something disturbing in the glance of the stars.

"Perhaps it would be better to marry at forty," thought Ilya. "Life is so disturbed with women; they bring such useless hurrying and so many petty things: and it is better to marry a girl who is close on thirty. But then, if you marry late, you die and never have time to start your children for themselves."

The samovar whistles more gently but more shrilly. The fine sound pierces the ears unbearably; it is like the buzzing of a fly, and distracts and confuses thought. But Ilya does not put the lid on the chimney, for if the samovar ceases to whistle, the room becomes so still. In his new house, new feelings, hitherto unknown, come to visit him. Formerly he had lived constantly close to people, separated from them only by thin partitions; now he was shut off by stone walls and felt no man at his back. "Why must we die?" Lunev asks himself suddenly, looking at the man declining from the height of his fortune towards the grave. Then he remembers Jakov, who was always pondering on death, and Jakov's saying: "It is interesting to die."

Angrily Ilya thrusts the memory away, and tries to think of something quite different.

"How are Pavel and Vyera getting on?" he wonders suddenly. A droshky drives by; the window-panes shake with the noise of the wheels on the stony street, the lamp trembles on the wall. Then strange sounds arise in the shop—it is Gavrik talking in his sleep. The dense darkness in the corner of the room seems to move. Ilya sits propped up at the table, presses his temples with the palms of his hands, and looks at the picture. Next to the Almighty is a fine big lion, on the ground crawls a tortoise, and there is a badger and a frog jumping, and the Tree of the Knowledge of Good and Evil is adorned with great blood-red flowers. The old man with his feet in the coffin is like Poluektov, he is bald-headed and lean, and his neck is of just the same thin kind. A dull noise of footsteps sounds from the street. Some one goes slowly past the shop. The samovar has gone out, and now the room is so still that the air in it seems thickened and as solid as the walls.

The memory of Poluektov did not trouble Ilya and, generally speaking, his thoughts were not disturbing—they lay soft and easily on his soul, enwrapping it as a cloud the moon. The colours of the picture were made a little pale by them, and a vague dark spot appeared on it, while the stillness round about grew denser. Frequently he thought with calmness, as he had done after the murder of Poluektov, that there must be justice in life, and that, sooner or later, men must be punished for their sins. After such thoughts, he would look sharply into the dark corner of the room, where it was so mysteriously still, and where the darkness would take on a definite form. Then he undressed, lay down, and extinguished the lamp. He did not put it out at once, but turned the wick first up, then down. The light would all but go out, then again flare up, and the darkness danced round the bed, now threw itself on the bed from all sides, now again sprung back into the corner of the room. Ilya watched how the pitiless black waves tried to overwhelm him, and he played in this way for a long time, whilst trying to pierce the darkness with wide-open eyes, as though he expected to catch sight of something. At last the light flickered for the last time, and went out in a moment. The blackness flooded the room, and seemed to waver as though still disturbed by its struggle with the light. Then the dull bluish patch of the window became visible. When the moon shone, black streaks of shadow from the railings in front of the window fell across the table and the floor. There was so tense a stillness in the room that it seemed as if his whole frame must quiver if he sighed. He wrapped the bed-clothes round him, drawing them up to his chin, but with his face uncovered, and lay and looked at the twilight of the window till sleep overpowered him. In the morning he woke fresh and rested, almost ashamed of his follies of the night before. He had tea with Gavrik at the counter and looked at his shop as at a new thing. Sometimes Pavel came in from his work, covered with dirt and grease, in a scorched blouse and with smoke-blackened face. He was working again with a well-sinker, and carried with him a little kettle, with lead piping and soldering-iron. He was always in a hurry to get home, and if Ilya asked him to stay, he would say, with a shame-faced smile:

"I can't. I feel, brother, as though I had a wonderful bird at home, but as if the cage were too weak. She sits there alone all day, and who knows what she thinks about? It's a dull kind of life for her. I know that very well—if only we had a child!"

And Gratschev sighed heavily. Once when Ilya asked him if he still wrote poems, he replied smiling:

"On the sky, with my finger! Oh, the devil! How can you make cabbage soup of bast shoes. I'm on the sand-bank, brother, altogether. Not a spark in my head, not one little one! I think of her all the time. I work, begin to solder or something, and at once dreams of my little girl fly through my head. You see that's my poetry nowadays—ha! ha! Surely, honour to him who devotes himself body and soul!—You see, though I think this, she thinks differently—yes, it's hard for her."

"And you?" asked Ilya.

"Oh, yes; it's hard for me because of her. If she could have a happier life! She's used to being happy, that's it. She dreams of money all the time. If we had money, anyhow, she says everything would be different. I'm stupid she says; I ought to rob a rich man; she's always talking nonsense. She does it all out of compassion for me—I know. It is hard for her."

Presently Pavel became restless and departed.

Often the ragged half-naked cobbler came to Ilya with his inseparable companion, his harmonica, under his arm. He told what had happened at Filimonov's and of Jakov. Thin and dirty and dishevelled, he pushed into the door of the shop; smiling all over his face, and scattering his jests.

"Petrusha is married, his wife is like—like a beetroot, and the stepson like a carrot. Quite a vegetable garden, by God! The wife is thick and short and red, and her face is built in three storeys; three chins she has, but only one mouth; eyes like a beautiful pig, they are little and can't look up. Her son is yellow and long, with spectacles—an aristocrat. He's called Savva—speaks through his nose. When his lady-mother's there he's an absolute sheep, but if she's away, chatterbox isn't the word! Such a crew—with all due respect! Jashutka looks now as if he'd like to crawl into a crack like a terrified black beetle. He drinks on the quiet, poor lad, and coughs away like anything. Evidently his dear papa has damaged his liver for him; they're always at him. He's a feeble fellow; they'll soon swallow him down. Your uncle has written from Kiev; I think he is worrying himself for nothing. Hunchbacks don't get in to Paradise, I'm thinking. Matiza's feet are no good at all now. She goes about in a little cart. She's got a blind man for partner, harnesses him to the cart, and guides him like a horse—it's really funny. They get enough to eat out of it though. She's a good sort, I say. That's to say if I hadn't had such a wonderful wife I'd marry this Matiza right away. I say boldly, there are two real women in the world—on my word I mean it—my wife and Matiza. Of course she drinks, but why not? A good man always drinks."

"But what about Mashutka?" Ilya reminded him. At the mention of his daughter all the cobbler's jests and laughter came to a sudden end, like the leaves torn from the trees by the winds of autumn. His lips quivered, his yellow face lengthened, and he said in a confused low voice:

"I don't know. Ehrenov said to me plainly I won't have you about my house, else I'll thrash you.—Give me something, Ilya Jakovlevitch, for a little drink of brandy."

"You'll come to grief, Perfily," said Ilya compassionately.

"I'm on the way," admitted the cobbler. "Lots of people will be sorry when I'm dead," he went on with conviction. "For I'm a good fellow, and I like to make people laugh. Every one cries—ah! and alas! and laments and talks of God and sin; but I sing little songs and laugh. Whether you sin a pennyworth or a pound's-worth, you've got to die all the same. You go under, and the Devil will torment you anyhow; and besides the world needs good fellows."

Finally he went off, laughing and jesting, like a tousled old greenfinch. But Ilya, when he had seen him out, shook his head; while he pitied Perfishka, he saw the uselessness of his compassion. His own past seemed far behind him, and all that reminded him of it made him uncomfortable. Now he resembled a weary man who rests and sleeps quietly, but the autumn flies buzz persistently in his ear and will not let him have his sleep out. When he talked to Pavel or listened to Perfishka's tales, he smiled in sympathy, but when they were gone, he shook his head. Especially he found Pavel's conversation melancholy and troubling. At such times he hurriedly and obstinately offered him money, gesticulated, and said: "What else can I do to help you? I should advise you—break with Vyera!"

"I can't," said Pavel, softly. "You only throw away things you don't want. But I need her—ah, yes, and others want her too, and would like to take her from me, that's the trouble. And perhaps I don't love her with my soul, but out of wickedness and desperation. She's the best that life has offered me. All my good fortune. Why should I let her go? What shall I have left? No, I won't sell her. It's a lie.—I'll kill her, but I won't let her go."

Gratschev's drawn face was covered with red patches, and he clenched his fists convulsively.

"Do you find, then, that people hang about after her?"

"No, no!"

"How do you mean, then—they'd like to take her away?"

"There's a power that will snatch her from my hands. Ah! the devil! My father came to grief through a woman, and seems to have left me the same fortune."

"It's impossible to help you, I'm afraid," said Lunev, and felt a certain relief as he said it. Pavel distressed him more than Perfishka, and when his friend spoke with hate and anger, a similar feeling surged up in Ilya's breast against some undefined person. But the enemy that caused the suffering, that ruined Pavel's life, was not there, but invisible, and Lunev felt anew that his enmity or his compassion availed nothing, like nearly all his sympathetic feelings towards other men. It seemed these feelings were all superfluous, useless. Pavel went on, more gloomily:

"I know—it's impossible to help me.—How could I be helped? Who is there? We're alone in life, brother; our lot is settled—work, suffer, be silent—and then go out. Devil take you!"

He looked searchingly into his friend's face, and added in a decided, sinister tone:

"Look! You've crawled into a corner and sit quiet there. But I tell you, there's some one, who watches by night, thinking how to drag you out."

"No, no!" said Lunev smiling. "I'll make a fight for it. It's not so easy."

"Ah, don't be so sure! You think you'll run this business all your life, eh?"

"Why not?"

"They'll have you out, or else you yourself will give it up."

"But how? You'll have to wait to see that!" said Ilya, smiling.

But Gratschev maintained his statement. He looked hard at his friend, and said obstinately:

"I tell you, you'll leave it. You are not the kind to sit quiet and warm all your life, and it's certain either you'll take to drink or you'll go bankrupt. Something's bound to happen to you."

"Yes, but why?" cried Lunev, in surprise.

"For this—You can't stand a quiet life. You're a good fellow, you've a good heart, there are a few like that—they live healthy lives, are never ill, and all of a sudden—bang!"

"What d'you mean?"

"They fall down dead."

Ilya laughed, straightened himself, stretched his strong muscles, and breathed out a deep breath.

"That's all rubbish," he said. But at night, as he sat by the samovar, Gratschev's words returned involuntarily, and he considered his business relations with the Avtonomovs. In his delight at their proposal to open a shop, he had agreed to everything that was suggested. Now, suddenly he perceived that, although he had put into the business about four hundred roubles of Poluektov's money, he was rather a manager, engaged by Tatiana Vlassyevna, than her partner. This discovery surprised and annoyed him.

"Aha! that's why she kisses me, so as to pick my pocket more easily," he thought. He determined to use the rest of his money to get the business away from his mistress and then separate from her. Even earlier, Tatiana Vlassyevna had seemed to him unnecessary, and of late she had become a burden. He could not reconcile himself to her caresses, and once said to her face:

"You're absolutely shameless, Tanyka!"

She only laughed. As before, she constantly told him tales of the people of her circle, and once he remarked, doubtfully:

"If that's all true, Tatiana, your respectable life isn't good for much."

"Why, pray? It's very jolly!" she replied, and shrugged her pretty shoulders.

"Jolly? In the day, a fight for crumbs, and at night—beastliness. No! There's something wrong about that."

"How simple you are! Now listen," and she began to praise the orderly, respectable middle-class life, and as she praised, strove to hide its hideousness and foulness.

"Is that what you call good, then?" asked Ilya.

"How odd you are! I don't call it good; but if it weren't it would be very dull."

Sometimes she would advise him:

"It's time you gave up wearing cotton shirts—a respectable man must wear linen. And listen to the way I pronounce words, and learn. You're not a peasant any longer, and you must drop your peasant ways, and get a little polish."

More often she would point out the difference between him, the peasant, and herself, the educated woman, and by the comparison frequently hurt his feelings. When he lived with Olympiada, he felt constantly that she was near him, like a good comrade. Tatiana aroused no feeling of comradeship; he saw that she was more interesting than Olympiada, and studied her with curiosity, but completely lost his respect for her. When he lived with the Avtonomovs, he used sometimes to hear Tatiana praying before she went to sleep:

"Our Father, Who art in heaven"—her loud rapid whisper sounded behind the partition. "Give us this day our daily bread, and forgive us our trespasses—Kirya, get up and shut the kitchen door—there's a draught at my feet."

"Why do you kneel on the bare floor?" answered Kirik lazily.

"Be quiet, don't interrupt me!" and again Ilya would hear the rapidly murmured prayer. The haste displeased him; he saw well she prayed from custom, not from inner need.

"Do you believe in God, Tatiana?" he asked her once.

"What a question," she cried. "Of course I do. Why do you ask?"

"Oh, then when you pray, you hurry up so as to get away from Him, I suppose," said Ilya laughing.

"First of all, don't say hurry up, but make haste; in the second place, I'm so tired with my day's work that God must forgive my haste."

And she closed her eyes, and added in a tone of deep conviction:

"He will forgive everything. He is merciful."

Olympiada used to pray silently and for a long time. She knelt before the eikon, hung her head, and remained motionless as if turned to stone. At such times her face was downcast, serious; and she did not answer if addressed. Now that Ilya grasped that Tatiana had cleverly over-reached him over the business, he felt a kind of disgust towards her.

"If she were a stranger—well and good," he thought. "All men try to cheat one another, but she is almost like my wife." He began to behave coldly and suspiciously towards her, and to avoid meeting her on all sorts of pretexts.

Just at this time he became acquainted with another woman. This was Gavrik's sister, who came now and then to see her brother. Tall, thin, and lanky, she was not pretty, and though Gavrik had said she was nineteen she seemed to Ilya much older. Her face was long and thin and yellow; fine wrinkles furrowed the brow. She had a flat nose, and the wide nostrils seemed distended with anger, while the thin lips were usually pressed together. She spoke distinctly, but as it were through her teeth, and unwillingly. She walked quickly with her head high, as though she were proud to display her ugly face, though possibly it was her long, thick black hair that drew her head backwards. Her big dark eyes looked serious and earnest, and the whole effect of her features was to give her tall figure an air of definite uprightness and inflexibility. Lunev felt afraid of her. She seemed to him proud and inspired him with respect. Whenever she appeared in the shop, he offered her a chair politely and said:

"Please take a seat."

"Thank you," she said shortly—bowed slightly and sat down. Lunev looked secretly at her face, absolutely different from the women's faces he had seen hitherto, her dark-brown well-worn dress, her patched shoes and yellow straw hat. She sat there, and talked to her brother, while the long fingers of her right hand drummed rapidly but noiselessly on her knee; in her left hand she swung some books, strapped together. It struck Ilya as strange to see a girl so badly dressed, so proud. After sitting two or three minutes she would say to her brother:

"Well—good-bye. Behave yourself!" Then she would bow silently to the owner of the shop and go out into the street with the stride of a brave soldier going to the attack.

"What a serious sister you've got," said Lunev once to Gavrik.

Gavrik distended his nostrils, rolled his eyes wildly, and drew out his lips into a straight line, and so gave his face a carefully caricatured resemblance to his sister's. Then he explained with a smile:

"Yes—but she only puts it on."

"But why should she?"

"It looks well. She likes it.—I can imitate any face you like."

The girl interested Ilya very much; he thought about her as he used to think of Tatiana Vlassyevna.

"There, that's the kind of girl to marry—she's got a heart, for certain."

Once she brought a thick book with her and said to her brother:

"There—read it! It's very interesting."

"What is it, may I see?" asked Ilya politely.

She took the book from her brother and passed it to Ilya saying:

"Don Quixote—the story of a worthy knight."

"Ah! I've read a lot about knights," said Ilya with a friendly smile, and looked her in the face. Her eyebrows twitched, and she said quickly in a dry way:

"You've read fairy tales, but this is a fine clever book. The man in it devotes himself to help the unfortunate and unjustly oppressed—this man was always ready to give his life for others. You see? The book is written amusingly—but that's because of the conditions under which it was written. It must be read seriously and attentively."

"Then that's how we'll read it," said Ilya. This was the first time she had spoken to him; he felt curiously pleased, and smiled. But she looked in his face, said drily:

"I fancy you won't like it."

Then she went away. Ilya felt that she had spoken with intention and was annoyed. He spoke sharply to Gavrik who was looking at the pictures in the book.

"Now then—it's no time for reading now."

"But there are no customers," answered Gavrik without closing the book.

Ilya looked at him and said nothing; the girl's words rang in his ears, but he thought of her with a feeling of discomfort in his heart.

"My word; doesn't she think a lot of herself!"

CHAPTER XXI

Time passed on. Ilya stood behind the counter, twisted his moustache, and conducted his business, but it began to seem to him that the days went more slowly. Sometimes he felt a desire to close the shop and go for a walk, but he knew that such a proceeding would be bad for his business and he did not go. To walk in the evenings was inconvenient; Gavrik was afraid to be alone in the shop and there was a certain risk in leaving him, he might set the place on fire by accident or let in some rascal or other. Business went fairly well. Ilya thought it might be necessary to take an assistant. His intimacy with Tatiana had insensibly grown less, and she seemed willing that it should come to an end. She laughed cheerfully when she came, and looked very carefully through the book that recorded the day's business. While she sat and made calculations in Ilya's room, he felt that this woman with the bird's face was repugnant to him; but still from time to time she would be pert and gay, jesting and making eyes at him, and calling him her partner. Then he would rouse himself and re-enter what in his heart he called a horrible web. Sometimes Kirik came too, stretched himself out in a chair by the counter and cracked jokes with the tailoresses who came in to make purchases while he was there. He had discarded his police uniform, and boasted of his success in his new commercial employment.

"Sixty roubles salary and then in different ways I make as much again extra—not so bad, eh? I work very carefully for the extras, keep within the law—ho! ho! We've moved, did you hear? We've a jolly house now. We've taken on a cook—cooks splendidly, the wretch! When the autumn comes we'll ask lots of our friends and play cards; it's very pleasant, by Jove! To have a good time and make money at it; we play into one another's hands, I and my wife, one of us must always win, and the winnings pay the cost of entertainment, ho! ho! my boy! There, that's living cheaply and pleasantly!"

He settled himself in a chair, puffed out the smoke of his cigarette and went on, lowering his voice:

"A little while ago, brother, I was in a village—have you heard? I tell you, the girls there—d'you know, such children of Nature, so solid you know, you can't pinch them, the rascals,—and so cheap, too; a bottle of Schnapps, a pound of honey cakes, and she is yours!"

Lunev listened, but said nothing. For some reason or other he was sorry for Kirik, and pitied him without realising why this fat and stupid fellow should rouse such a feeling. At the same time he almost always wanted to laugh at the sight of him. Ilya did not believe Kirik's tales of his adventures in the village, but thought he was only boasting, talking as he had heard others talk. But when he was in a gloomy mood, then he listened to Kirik and thought: "Fighting for crumbs!"

"Yes, brother, it's splendid to make love in the bosom of Nature, in the shade of the leaves as they say in books."

"But if Tatiana Vlassyevna knew?"

"She won't know, brother," answered Kirik, and winked cheerfully.

But when Avtonomov departed Ilya thought of his words, and felt hurt. It was evident that Kirik, good-tempered and ridiculous though he were, yet held himself to be a man out of the common, whom Ilya could not hope to equal, higher in station and more important. Yet he profited by the business Ilya carried on with his wife. Perfishka had told them that Petrusha laughed at his shop and called him a rascal. Jakov had said to the cobbler that formerly Ilya was better and more friendly than now and did not think so much of himself, and Gavrik's sister constantly demonstrated that she thought herself superior to him. The daughter of a postman, who went about almost in rags, behaved as though it were too much for her to live on the same world as he did. Ilya's ambition had grown since he had opened his shop, and he was more sensitive than before. His interest deepened in this girl who was so ugly, but had so strong a personality; he sought to understand whence came this pride in a poor ragged girl, a pride which grew to annoy him more and more. At first she would not talk to him, and that pained him. Her brother was his servant, and therefore she ought to be more friendly with him, the employer. He said to her once:

"I'm reading the book of 'Don Quixote.'"

"Well, do you like it?" she asked, without looking at him.

"Rather, most amusing,—he was a funny old owl that fellow!"

She looked at him, and Ilya felt as though her proud dark eyes pierced his face angrily.

"I knew you would say something like that," she said, slowly and with meaning.

Ilya was conscious of something reproachful, contemptuous and hostile in her words.

"I'm an uneducated man," he said, and shrugged his shoulders.

She said nothing as though she had not heard him.

Once again the mood that long ago had possessed Ilya, began to invade his soul again; once more he was angered at mankind, pondered long and deeply upon justice, and his sins, and what might be in store for him in the future. The last question troubled him persistently. He liked his shop, he liked almost all his life at this time; in comparison with the life of his younger days it was cleaner, more peaceful, freer. But would it always be like this; to squat in his shop from morning to night, then sit awhile with his thoughts by the samovar, and then go to sleep, only to wake and begin again in the shop? He knew that many tradesmen, perhaps all, lived just such a life. But then they were married, and had children, they drank brandy, played cards, and among them all there was hardly one like himself.

He had many reasons, outward as well as inward, to consider himself an unusual man, unlike the rest.

He did not care for tradesmen; some of them were like Kirik, boasted of everything and spoke of nothing but their business, others swindled openly. Once, as he meditated on all these things, he remembered Jakov's words: "God guard you from good fortune—you are greedy," and the words appeared to him a deep insult. No, he was not covetous; he wanted to live simply, cleanly, and quietly, to have men respect him and to have no one say: "I stand higher than you, Ilya Lunev, I am better than you."

Again he began to wonder what the future held in store for him. Would the murder be avenged on him or not? Up and down, he thought, whether it would be unjust for the sin to be avenged on him. He had had no desire to strangle the man, it happened of itself, he said to himself a hundred times. In the town there live many murderers, libertines, robbers, all know they are murderers and robbers and libertines of their own choice, yet all live, and enjoy the good things of life, and no punishment is swift to fall upon them. In justice, every injury done to man must be avenged on the evildoer, and in the Bible it is written: "He rewardeth him and he shall know it." These thoughts set all his old wounds throbbing and a raging thirst burned in his heart to revenge his blighted life. Sometimes the idea came to him to do some daring deed; to go and set fire to Petrusha's house, and when it began to burn, and people began to run from it, to cry out: "I have done it, and I have murdered Poluektov, the merchant." Then men would seize him and judge him, and send him to Siberia as they had sent his father. This thought roused him and narrowed his thirst for revenge to the desire to tell Kirik of his intimacy with Tatiana, or to visit old Ehrenov and thrash him for torturing Masha.

Often he lay on his bed in the darkness listening to the deep stillness, and felt as though all round him life quivered, and twisted in a wild whirlpool with noise and outcry. The whirlpool would suck him in, and sweep him away like a feather or a fallen leaf, and destroy him, and he shuddered with the premonition of something uncanny.

One evening, as he was about to close the shop, Pavel appeared, and said quietly, without greeting him: "Vyera has run away."

He sat down on a chair, rested his elbows on the counter, and whistled softly as he gazed out into the street. His face was as though turned to stone, but his fair moustache twitched like a cat's whiskers.

"Alone?" asked Ilya.

"I don't know; it's three days ago."

Ilya looked at him without speaking. The quiet face and voice made it impossible to tell how Gratschev felt the flight of his companion, but in the stillness Ilya was aware of an unalterable resolution.

"What are you going to do?" he asked at length, when he saw that Pavel would not speak. Pavel stopped whistling, and said sharply, without turning round: "I'll cut her throat!"

"Ah! talking like that again!" cried Ilya, and with a gesture of annoyance.

"She's trod my heart under foot," said Pavel half-aloud. "There's the knife!" He drew from his bosom a little bread-knife and shook it.

"I'll stick it in her throat."

Ilya caught his hand, tore the knife away, and threw it on the counter, and said angrily:

"An ox once raged against a fly——"

Pavel sprang from his chair and turned his face on Ilya. His eyes were blazing, his face convulsed, and he trembled in all his limbs; then he sank back again on his chair and said, contemptuously:

"You're a fool!"

"You're so very clever, aren't you?"

"The strength is in the hand, not in the knife."

"Talk!"

"And if my hands fall off, I'd tear her windpipe with my teeth."

"Don't talk so horribly!"

"Don't talk to me Ilya," said Pavel, once more quietly. "Believe or don't believe, but don't torment me. Fate is bad enough."

Three Men | 235

"Think, think, you silly fellow——" began Ilya, speaking in a friendly tone.

"I've thought for two years. Everything's settled long ago. Anyhow, I'll go—how can a fellow talk to you? You're well fed; you're no comrade for me."

"Get rid of your crazy thoughts!" cried Ilya reproachfully.

"But I'm hungry, body and soul."

"It surprises me, the way men judge," said Ilya mockingly and shrugged his shoulders. "A woman is to be a man's property, like a cow or a horse! Will you do what I want? All right, you shan't be beaten,—won't you? then crack! there's one on the head for you, devil! A woman is like a man, and has a character of her own."

Pavel looked at him and laughed hoarsely.

"Then who am I, am I no man?"

"Well, ought you to be just or not?"

"Oh, go to the devil with your old justice!" shouted Gratschev furiously, and sprang up again. "Be just, that's easy for the well fed, d'you hear? Now, good-bye."

He went quickly from the shop and in the doorway, for some reason, took off his cap. Ilya sprang from behind the counter after him, but already Gratschev was away down the street, holding his cap in his hand, and shaking it excitedly.

"Pavel!" cried Ilya. "Stop!"

He did not stop, nor turn round once, but turned into a side street, and disappeared.

Ilya turned slowly back and felt his face burn with the words of his friend as though he had looked into a hot oven.

"How angry he was!" said Gavrik.

Ilya smiled.

"Whose throat did he want to cut?" asked the boy, and came up to the counter. He held his hands behind his back, his head thrown up, and his coarse face was red with excitement.

"His wife," said Ilya.

Gavrik was silent for a moment, then he wrinkled his forehead and said softly and thoughtfully to his master:

"There was a woman near us poisoned her husband last Christmas with arsenic, because he was always drinking."

"It does happen," said Lunev slowly, thinking of Pavel.

"But this man, will he really kill her?"

"Go away now, Gavrik."

The boy turned round and went to the door murmuring: "Marry! O Lord!"

The dusk of twilight filled the streets and lights appeared in the windows opposite.

"It's time to shut up," said Gavrik quietly.

Ilya looked at the lighted windows. Below they were decked with flowers and above with white curtains. Between the flowers, golden frames could be seen on the walls within. When the windows were opened, sounds of song and guitar and loud laughter poured into the street. There was singing and music and laughter in this house almost every evening. Lunev knew that a man, Gromov, lived there, of the district court of justice, a fat, red-cheeked man, with a big, black moustache. His wife was stout, too, fair-haired, with little friendly blue eyes; she went proudly along the street like the queen in a fairy tale, but if she was talking to any one, she smiled all the time. Gromov had an unmarried sister, a tall, brown-skinned and black-haired girl, a crowd of young officials courted her; they all assembled at Gromov's almost every evening and laughed and sang.

Gromov's cook bought thread of Ilya, complained of her employers, and said that they fed their servants badly and were always behindhand with their wages, and Lunev thought:

"There—there are people who live well."

"Really it is time to shut up," persisted Gavrik.

"Shut up then."

The boy closed the door and the shop grew dark; there was a noise as the key turned in the lock.

"Like a prison," thought Ilya.

The insulting words of his friend about his well fed condition stabbed his heart like splinters. As he sat by the samovar he thought angrily of Pavel, but did not believe he could murder Vyera.

"It was no good trying to help them, hang them; they don't know how to live, they spoil one another," he thought crossly.

Gavrik drank noisily out of his saucer and shuffled his feet under the table.

"Has he killed her or not?" he asked his master, suddenly.

Lunev looked at him moodily and said:

"Drink your tea, and go to bed."

The samovar boiled and bubbled as though it would jump off the table. From the courtyard of a neighbouring house an angry cry resounded. "Nifont! Ni—if—ont."

Suddenly a dark figure appeared at the window, and a trembling, timid voice asked:

"Does Ilya Jakovlevitch live here?"

"Yes, he does," cried Gavrik, sprang up and flew to the door of the courtyard so quickly that Ilya had no time to say anything.

"It's sure to be she," he said in a loud whisper, holding the latch of the door.

"Who?" asked Ilya, involuntarily lowering his voice.

"Why—she—he wanted to kill."

He pushed open the door and the thin small figure of a woman appeared, wearing a cotton dress and a small kerchief on her head. She supported herself by the doorpost with one hand and with the other pulled at the ends of her kerchief. She stood sideways, as though ready to go away again at once.

"Come in," said Lunev roughly; he looked at her and did not recognise her. She started at the sound of his voice, then lifted her head with a smile on the pale small face.

"Masha!" cried Ilya, and sprang up. She laughed softly, shut the door fast behind her and came towards him.

"You didn't know me—you didn't know me a bit," she said and stood in the middle of the room.

"God! Yes. I can recognise you now. But—how—you've changed!"

Ilya took her hand with exaggerated politeness, and led her to the table, bowed, looked at her face and did not know how to say in what way she had changed. She was incredibly thin and walked as though her feet gave under her.

"Where have you come from? Are you tired? Ah—you—how you look!"—he murmured, settled her carefully in a chair and looked steadily at her.

"See how he treats me," she said, and looked at Ilya with a smile. His heart contracted painfully. Now that the lamplight fell on her, he saw her face plainly. She leant back in the chair, with her thin hands in her lap, bent her head sideways, and her flat chest heaved in shallow rapid breathing. She looked as though made of skin and bone; through the cotton stuff of her dress showed the bony shoulders, elbows and knees, and her face was terrible in its thinness. Over the temples, and the cheek-bones and chin, the bluish skin was tight drawn, the mouth was half open, the thin lips did not cover the teeth, and the expression of pain and fear stared from the long narrow face. The eyes looked dull and dead.

"Have you been ill?" asked Ilya.

"N—no," she answered slowly. "I'm quite well—he has made me like this."

"Your husband?"

"Yes—my husband."

Her slow, drawling speech came like groans, the uncovered teeth gave her a fish-like, dead look—it seemed as though the dead might smile as she smiled now and then.

Gavrik stood beside her and looked at her with lips compressed and fear in his eyes.

"Go to bed!" said Lunev to him.

The lad went into the shop, moved about a little there—then his head appeared again in the doorway. Masha sat motionless, only her eyes moved and wandered from one thing to another. Lunev poured her out some tea, looked at her, but asked her no questions.

"Ye—es—he torments me so," she said. Her lips trembled and her eyes closed for a moment; when she opened them again two big, heavy tears rolled down from under the lashes.

"Don't cry," said Ilya, turning away.

"Drink your tea—and tell me all about it—then it will be easier."

"I'm afraid—he'll come," she said, and shook her head.

"We'll turn him out."

"He's strong," Masha warned him.

"Have you run away?"

"Yes—it's the fourth time—when I can't bear it any more, I run away—before I meant to drown myself—but he caught me—and beat me and hurt me so." Her eyes grew unnaturally big from the fear her memories roused, and her lower jaw trembled. She hung her head and said in a whisper:

"He always hurts my feet."

"Ah," cried Ilya. "What's the matter with you? Haven't you a tongue? Tell the police—say—he tortures me! He can be punished for that; put in prison."

"But—he's one of the judges," said Masha, hopelessly.

"Ehrenov?—a judge? What do you mean?"

"I know. A little while ago, he was on the bench for two weeks—judging. He came back angry and hungry. He pinched my breast with the tongs and twisted it and turned it like a rag—look!"

She unbuttoned her dress with trembling fingers and showed the small withered breast, all covered with dark patches, as though it had been gnawed.

"Don't!" said Ilya gloomily. It made him sick to see the tortured, lacerated body—he could not believe that it was Masha, the friend of his childhood, once so gay, who sat before him. She bared her shoulder and said in a toneless voice:

"See how my shoulder is knocked about! Everything he can, all my body is pinched and hair torn out."

"But why?"

"He's a beast. He says, 'You don't love me,' and he pinches me."

"Perhaps—before he married you, there was some one else?"

"How could there be? I saw only you and Jakov—no one ever touched me. Yes, and now I hate all that. It hurts me. I hate it. I'm always sick."

"Don't—don't—Masha," said Ilya gently. She was silent, sat once more as though turned to stone, her breast still bare. Ilya looked from behind the samovar again at her thin bruised body and said: "Do up your dress!"

"I don't mind you," she answered mechanically, and began to button her blouse with shaking fingers. All was still. Then the sound of loud sobbing came from the shop. Ilya got up and went to the door and closed it, saying crossly:

"Be quiet—Gavrushka—go to sleep!"

"Is that the boy?" asked Masha.

"Yes."

"Crying?"

"Yes."

"Is he frightened?"

"No. I think—he's sorry."

"For what?"

"For you."

"Ah—the boy!" said Masha, indifferently; but her lifeless face did not move. Then she began to drink her tea, but her hands shook so that the saucer rattled against her teeth. Ilya looked on and wondered—was he sorry for Masha—or not? But his heart was heavy, and he thought of her husband with hatred.

"What will you do?" he asked after a long pause.

"I don't know," she answered with a sigh. "What can I do? I'll rest—till they catch me again."

"You ought to complain to the police," said Lunev, firmly. "Why should he torment you? Who has any right to torment any one like that?"

"He did the same to his first wife," said Masha. "He tied her to the bed by her hair—and pinched her—just the same—and once I was asleep and suddenly I felt a pain and woke and screamed—he'd burnt me with a lighted match."

Lunev sprang up and said fiercely and loudly that the very next morning she should go to the police and show her bruises and demand to have her husband condemned. She listened to him, shifting unceasingly to and fro, looked at him in terror, and said:

"Don't shout—don't shout, please! They'll hear you."

His words only distressed her. He soon perceived this little girl, once so cheerful and gay, had been beaten and crushed till all human spirit was tortured out of her.

"Very well," he said, and sat down again. "I'll see to it. I'll find a way. You'll stay here, Mashutka—d'you hear?"

"Yes. I hear," she answered softly, and looked round the room.

"You can have my bed, and I'll go into the shop—but to-morrow."

"I'll lie down at once, I think. I'm tired." He folded back the coverlet from the bed. She fell on it and tried to cover herself with the bedclothes, but could not manage it, and said with a dull smile:

"How silly I am. I might be drunk."

Ilya drew the coverlet over her, arranged the pillows, and was going away, when she said anxiously:

"Don't go. Stay a little. I'm so frightened alone—there's something haunts me." He sat down by the bed, looked once at her pale face, framed in its curls, and turned away. All at once he was full of shame that she should lie there, hardly alive. He remembered Jakov's entreaties, and Matiza's account of Masha's life, and he hung his head.

"And his father beats Jasha, they say. Matiza says, 'What a life!'" she said.

"Such fathers," said Lunev between his teeth, interrupting her soft, lifeless speech. "Such fathers—ought to go to penal servitude—your father and Petrusha Filimonov."

"No, my father is weak—he isn't wicked."

"If you can't look after your children you've no business to have any."

From the house opposite came the music of two voices singing together, and the words of the song drifted through the open window into Ilya's room. A strong, deep bass sang fiercely:

"My heart is disenchanted."

"There. I shall go to sleep," murmured Masha. "How nice it is—so peaceful—and the singing—they sing well."

"Oh, yes—they sing,", said Lunev smiling, grimly. "Though the skin is torn off one, the others can shout."

"It will not trust again," sang the tenor voice, the clear, round tones ringing through the quiet night lightly and freely up into the sky. Lunev got up and shut the window crossly; the song was unendurable, it tormented him. The noise of the window-frame made Masha start. She opened her eyes, raised her head in terror and asked: "Who's there?"

"I. I was shutting the window."

"For Heaven's sake—are you going?"

"No, no—don't be afraid."

She turned on her pillow and went to sleep again. Ilya's least movement, or the noise of footsteps in the street, disturbed her. She opened her eyes at once and cried in her sleep.

"Coming—oh—I'm coming."

Or she stretched out her hand to Ilya and asked: "Is that a knock at the door?" While he tried to sit still, and looked out of the window which he had opened again, Ilya pondered how he could help Masha, and determined grimly not to let her go till the matter was in the hands of the police.

"I must work it through Kirik."

"Please, please—go on!" through the windows came the sound of lively appeals and applause from Gromov's house. Masha groaned in her sleep, but the music began again.

"A pair of bay horses, and early away."

Lunev shook his head despairingly. The singing and outcry and laughter disturbed him. He propped his elbows on the window-ledge and stared at the lighted windows opposite, with wrath and fierce resentment, and thought how good it would be to cross the street and hurl a paving stone through into the room; or to have a gun and send a charge of shot among these cheerful people. The shot would come whizzing in—he imagined the terrified bleeding faces, the confusion and outcry, and smiled with an evil joy in his heart. But the words of the song crept involuntarily into his ears, he repeated them to himself, and suddenly grasped with amazement, that these happy people were singing of the burial of a mistress. This surprised him; he began to listen more attentively and thought:

"Why do they sing that? What sort of pleasure can there be in such a song? See, what a thing to think of—the fools! A funeral—such a funeral! And here—ten steps away lies a living, suffering human being."

"Bravo! Bravo!" came from over the street.

Lunev smiled, looked first at Masha, and then at the street; it seemed to him ridiculous that men should find amusement in singing of the burial of a light-o'-love.

"Vassily—Vassilitch," murmured Masha. "I won't. O God!"

She threw herself about in bed as if she were burning, threw the coverlet on the floor, stretched her arms out, and stared in front of her. Her mouth was half open, she rattled in her throat. Lunev bent quickly over her, he was afraid she was dying. Then, relieved by hearing her breathe, he covered her up again, crawled back to the window, leaned his face against the bars and looked over at Gromov's house. There they were still singing, now one voice, now two, now several in chorus. Music was followed by laughter. Past the windows flitted ladies dressed in white or pink or blue. He listened to the music and marvelled how these men could sing long-drawn, melancholy songs of the Volga and of funerals and of desert lands, and laugh at the end of every song as though it were all nothing, as if they had sung of indifferent things. Is it possible that they find sorrow amusing? But every time that Masha attracted his attention, he looked at her stupidly and wondered what was to become of her. Suppose Tatiana came in and saw her—what was he to do with Masha? He felt as though caught in a mist; his heart was weighed down with the songs and Masha's groans, and his own heavy, disconnected thoughts. When he felt sleepy he crawled from under the window-ledge, lay down on the floor by the bed and put his overcoat under his head. He dreamed that Masha was dead and lying on the ground in a big shed, and round about were standing ladies, dressed in white and pink and blue, and singing songs over her; and when they sang mournful songs they all laughed, and when the songs were cheerful they wept bitterly, and nodded their heads sadly and wiped away their tears with white pocket-handkerchiefs. In the shed it was dark and damp, and in the corner stood Savel the smith, hammering at an iron railing and striking noisy blows on the red-hot bars. On the roof of the shed someone went round about and cried, "Ilya. Il—ya."

But he lay in the shed, bound somehow fast, he could hardly turn, he could not speak.

CHAPTER XXII

"Ilya, get up please."

He opened his eyes and recognised Pavel Gratschev. Pavel was sitting on a chair, kicking Ilya's legs gently. The bright sunlight streamed into the room and shone on the samovar boiling on the table; Lunev blinked, dazzled.

"Listen, Ilya."

Pavel's voice was hoarse, as though after heavy drinking, his face was yellow, his hair disordered. Lunev looked at him, then sprung up from the floor and cried half aloud:

"What?"

"She's caught," said Pavel, and shook his head.

"What? Where is she?" asked Ilya, bending over him and catching him by the shoulder. Gratschev swayed and said miserably:

"They've put her in prison, yesterday morning, they say; they brought her to the prison."

"What for?" asked Ilya in a loud whisper. Masha waked up, shuddered at the sight of Pavel, and stared at him terrified. From the door into the shop Gavrik looked in, his lips compressed in disapproval.

"They say she's stolen six hundred roubles from a merchant, a pocket book, bills, and so on."

Ilya laid a hand on his friend's shoulder, and then moved silently away.

"When they searched they found the money at her house," said Gratschev, in a dull way. "The police inspector, she struck him in the face."

"Oh, of course," said Ilya with a harsh laugh. "If you've got to go to prison, why not go in style!"

When Masha understood that all this did not concern her she smiled and said softly: "If they'd take me to prison."

Pavel looked at her, then at Ilya.

"Don't you know her?" asked Ilya. "Masha, Perfishka's daughter, you remember."

"Oh, yes," said Pavel slowly and indifferently, and turned away, although Masha, who had recognised him, greeted him with a smile.

"Ilya," said Gratschev gloomily. "If she's done that for me? She spoke of it."

"Oh, I don't know for whom, for you or for herself, it's all the same! Her song is finished."

Lunev could not collect his thoughts. Weary for want of sleep, unwashed, and dishevelled, he sat down at Masha's feet, and looked first at her, then at Pavel, and felt overwhelmed.

"I knew," he said slowly, "the whole business could come to no good end."

"She wouldn't listen to me," said Pavel, in a lifeless tone.

"That's it, of course!" cried Lunev ironically. "That's the whole trouble, that she wouldn't listen to you! What could you say to her?"

"I loved her."

"What's the good of your love? in the devil's name! What can you get with that? Apart from anything else you never got her enough to eat by your work."

"That's true," said Pavel, sighing. Lunev was irritated, he felt that all these lives, Pavel's, Masha's, stirred him to wrath, excited him, and not knowing where to direct his feelings, he vented them on his friend.

"Every one wants to be decent and happy, you too, but you say to her, I love you, therefore live with me, and suffer want; do you think that's the way to take it?"

"How should I then?" asked Pavel gently.

The question calmed Ilya a little, involuntarily he fell to thinking of it. "It would be easier for me to kill her with my own hands," said Pavel.

Gavrik looked in. "Ilya Jakovlevitch! shall I open the shop!"

"Oh, go to the devil!" shouted Lunev in anger. "Don't worry me with the shop."

"Am I in the way," asked Pavel.

He sat in the chair leaning forward with his elbows on his knees, and looked at the floor. A vein, full of blood, swelled on his temple.

"You," cried Lunev, and looked at him. "You don't disturb me, nor Masha; it's a very different thing! I've told you before, that there's something gets in the way of us all, you and me, and Masha. It's our folly or something. I don't know what; but it's not possible to live like human beings!"

Lunev looked round his little room at Masha sitting on the bed, motionless with downcast expression, into the shop where Gavrik was having his tea, into the street, through the railed-in window, and continued with despair in his soul, excitedly, angrily, and hoarsely:

"It's impossible to live. It's cramped and stupid, and absurd; you find a quiet corner, and there's no peace there! Everything is impure, heavy, painful; you can't understand; everything goes wrong, you hear people singing and you think you're happy. But it hurts you to hear their songs if your soul's in pain."

"What are you talking of?" asked Pavel, without looking at him.

"Of every one," cried Lunev. "I feel now that nothing's any use, damn it! I don't understand, perhaps, well then I don't! But I do understand what I want. I want to live like a man, cleanly, and honourably, and happily! I don't want to see trouble and horrors and sin, and all sorts of beastliness. I don't want it! But— —"

He stopped and grew pale.

"Well?" said Pavel.

"No, that's not it. I only meant— —" began Lunev, and his voice dropped.

"You always speak of yourself," observed Pavel.

"And whom do you speak of? Of her? But who is it she troubles, me or you? Every man cares for his own wounds, and groans with his own voice. I don't speak of myself only, I speak of every one, for every one troubles me."

"I'll go," said Gratschev, and got up heavily.

"Ah," cried Ilya. "Don't be hurt, try to understand. I'm hurt too, and sufferers should understand one another, then it will be clear who it is who torments us."

"Brother, it's as though you hit me on the head with a stone. I don't understand. I'm sorry for Vyera—there, I am, really. What can I do? I don't know."

"You can't do anything," said Ilya firmly. "I tell you she's done for! They'll condemn her, she's caught in the act."

Gratschev sat down again.

"But if I declare she did it for me?"

"Are you a prince? Say it, and they'll put you in prison too. Anyhow, we must pull things together. You had better have a wash, and you, too, Masha. We're going into the shop, but you get up and tidy yourself, have some tea, make yourself at home."

Masha shuddered, raised her head from the pillow and asked:

"What, am I to go home?"

"No. You're home is where, at any rate, you're not tortured. Come Pasha!"

When they were in the shop, Pavel asked gloomily:

"Why is she here? She's like a corpse."

Lunev told him briefly how matters stood. To his astonishment, Gratschev seemed cheered.

"My word, the old devil!" he said, and smiled.

Ilya stood by him, looking round his shop, and said:

"Theft and lying, and robbery, and drunkenness—all kinds of filth and disorder—that is life. You don't want it, but it's all the same, you go down the same stream as the rest and the same water soaks you; live as you have to! You can't get out of it anyhow. Run away to the forest? or a monastery? You told me a little while ago that I should find no peace here."

He indicated the shop with a sweeping gesture, nodded and smiled unpleasantly. "Right, there is no peace. What's the good to me to stand on one spot and do business? Plenty of worry, but no freedom. I can't go out. Before, I went where I liked, in the streets, if I found a nice comfortable place I sat down and enjoyed myself, but now here I squat, day in day out, and that's all."

"See, you might have taken Vyera as an assistant," said Pavel.

Ilya looked at him, but said nothing.

"Come in," cried Masha.

At tea, hardly a word was spoken.

The sun shone on the street, the bare feet of the children shuffled along the pavement, the hawkers of vegetables went by the window.

"Fresh leeks, onions!" a woman cried.

"Fresh cucumbers!"

Everything spoke of spring, of fine warm, clear days, but in the little room it smelt damp and close. From time to time a melancholy, sorrowful word was uttered, the samovar hummed and glittered in the sunshine.

"We sit here as if we were at a funeral," said Ilya.

"Yes, Vyera's," added Gratschev. He sat there like a beaten hound. His hands moved slackly, his face was despairing, and he spoke slowly in a dull voice.

"Pull yourself together," said Ilya to him coldly. "It's no good giving way."

"It's my conscience," said Gratschev, shaking his head. "I sit here and think that I drove her to prison."

"That's quite possible," said Ilya remorselessly.

Gratschev raised his head and looked at his friend reproachfully.

"Why do you look at me?"

"You're a bad-hearted man."

"Well, why should I be good? What joy have I to make me cheerful?" cried Ilya. "Who has ever done any good thing for me? Who has cared for me? One soul perhaps in all the world, and she was a ne'er-do-well, a vicious woman, ah! Every one may strike me, and I'm to keep quiet? No thank you!"

His face flushed as anger welled up in him, his eyes grew bloodshot; he sprang up in a paroxysm of rage, longing to scream, to insult them, to strike the walls or the table with his fists. Masha, terrified, cried aloud like a child:

"I want to go home, let me go," she said in a trembling tearful voice, and moved her head as though trying to hide it.

Lunev was silent; he saw Pavel look at him with enmity.

"Well, what are you crying at?" he said ill-temperedly. "I didn't shout at you, and you needn't go. I'll go, I must. Pavel will stay with you."

"Gavrilo! If Tatiana Vlassyevna——"

"Who's that?"

There was a knock at the door of the courtyard. Gavrik looked inquiringly at his master.

"Open," said Ilya.

Gavrik's sister appeared on the threshold. She stood without moving for a few seconds, as straight as a dart, her head drawn back, and looked at them all with screwed-up eyes. Then on her cold, ugly face appeared a grimace of disgust, and without noticing Ilya's bow, she said to her brother:

"Gavrik, come here a moment."

Ilya flared out. The blood rushed to his face at the insult with such force that his eyes burned.

"If you're saluted, madam, you might acknowledge it," he said emphatically, restraining himself as well as he could. But she held her head higher and her brows contracted. With lips close-pressed, she measured Ilya with her eyes, and said nothing. Gavrik also looked with anger at his master.

"You are not visiting drunkards or rascals," Ilya went on, quivering with his emotion. "You receive a respectful greeting, and as a well-mannered lady, you are bound to acknowledge it."

"Don't be stuck up, Sonyka," said Gavrik suddenly, in a peaceful tone, and took her hand. A painful silence followed. Ilya and the girl faced one another and waited. Masha shrunk silently into a corner. Pavel blinked stupidly.

"Speak up! Sonyka," said Gavrik impatiently. "Do you suppose they'll hurt you?" and he added with an unexpected smile, "You are funny, you people."

His sister snatched away her hand and said to Lunev coldly and sharply:

"What do you want?"

"Nothing, only——"

But here a fine idea came into his head. He advanced and said as politely as he could:

"Allow me; you see we are three uneducated people, quite obscure. You are an educated lady."

He was eager to speak out his thought but could not. The stern, open glance of the dark eyes confused him; it never wavered and seemed to drive his senses from him. Her nostrils twitched, and her fingers pressed her brother's hand nervously. Ilya lowered his eyes and murmured confusedly and angrily:

"I don't know how to say it right off; if you've time, come in, sit down," and he made way for her.

"Stay here, Gavrik!" said the girl, left her brother by the door and went into the room. Ilya pushed a stool towards her. She sat down; Pavel went into the shop, Masha shrank into the corner by the stove, but Lunev stood motionless two paces from the girl and sought for words to speak.

"Well," she said.

"See, this is the business," said Ilya, with a deep sigh. "You see, this girl, that is, she's not a girl, she's married to an old man, who bullies her;

she is all bruised and tortured and she ran away, she came to me. Perhaps you think that means something sinful. It doesn't at all." He confused his words and spoke vaguely between his desire to tell Masha's story and give the girl his own thoughts about it. He wanted especially to make his hearer share his own thoughts. She looked at him, and her face was more yielding, though her eyes flashed strangely.

"I understand," she interrupted. "You don't know what to do. First of all you must get a doctor; he must examine her. I know a good doctor, if you like, shall I take her to him? Gavrik, what's the time? Close on eleven. Good, that's his consultation hour. Gavrik, call a droshky, and you introduce me to her."

But Ilya did not move. He had not imagined that this stern, serious girl could speak in such a soft voice. Her face, too, amazed him; still proud, but now wholly anxious, and in it something good, kind, capable, that Ilya had never seen before. He looked at her and smiled in silent amazement. She, however, had turned away already, and going over to Masha, spoke to her gently.

"Don't cry, dear; don't be frightened, the doctor is a good man, he'll examine you and make out a certificate, and that's all. I'll bring you back here; now my dear, don't cry like that." She put her hands on Masha's shoulders, and tried to draw her closer.

"A—ah! that hurts," groaned Masha softly.

"How? What is it?"

Lunev heard and smiled.

"How? Good heavens, how awful!" cried the girl, falling back; her face was pale, and fear and anger glittered in her eyes.

"How she's bruised! Ah!"

"You see how we live!" cried Lunev, flaring up again. "Do you see? I can show you another, there! Allow me, my comrade, Pavel Savelitch Gratschev." Pavel came slowly out of the shop, and held out his hand without looking at the girl.

"Medvedeva, Sofia Nikonovna," she said, as she looked at Pavel's despairing face. "And you are Ilya Jakovlevitch?" and she turned again to Lunev.

"Yes," said Ilya, pressed her hand, and went on, still holding it— —

"You see, since you're so good—that's to say—as you've helped in one business, you won't despise the other. There's a trouble here too."

She looked attentively and seriously in his handsome excited face and tried quietly to withdraw her hand; but he told her of Vyera and Pavel, speaking warmly, passionately, feeling that a load was falling from his heart. He shook her hand hard and said:

"He makes verses and all sorts of things. But he's quite knocked over by this. And she too, you think, that it's all right because she's—that kind of woman? No, don't think that! No one is all good or all bad!"

"How d'you mean?"

"I mean, even if any one is bad, still there's something good there, and if he's good, there's sure to be something bad. All our souls are two-coloured—all."

"That's well said," she agreed, and nodded seriously. "That's thought like a man! but please let go my hand, you hurt me."

Ilya began to apologise, but she did not attend to him, saying to Pavel in a tone of conviction;

"You ought to be ashamed of yourself, Gratschev; you mustn't be like that; you must do something. One must always try to do something, either defend or attack. We must get her a lawyer, an advocate, d'you see? I'll find you one, and nothing will happen to her because he'll get her off. I promise you, he'll get her off."

Her face was flushed, the hair on her temples disordered, and her eyes burned with a strange joy. Masha stood by her and looked at her with the trustful curiosity of a child. But Lunev looked at Pavel and Masha triumphantly, and felt mingled pride and joy at the presence of this girl in his room.

"If you can really help," said Pavel, with a trembling voice, "help us. I'll never forget it as long as I live; although I don't believe it can come to a good end, yet I *will* believe it!"

"Come to me at seven o'clock, will you? Gavrik will tell you where."

"I'll come. I don't know how to thank you."

"Why—thank me?"

"But I feel— —"

"Don't say anything! we ought to help one another."

"Yes, men think that, don't they?" cried Ilya, ironically.

The girl turned round on him quickly. But Gavrik, who felt himself in this confusion the only healthy, sensible person, caught her hand and said:

"There, get on, you chatterbox!"

"Yes, Masha, get your things on!"

"I haven't anything to put on," said Masha shyly.

"Ah! well, anyhow, let's go. You'll come then, Gratschev, eh? Good-bye Ilya Jakovlevitch."

The men pressed her hand respectfully and silently, then she went out leading Masha. In the door, however, she turned round, threw her head up, and said to Ilya:

"I forgot, but it's important! I didn't acknowledge your greeting when I came in. That was abominable. I beg your pardon."

Her face flamed red, and her eyes were lowered; Ilya looked at her and his heart rejoiced.

"I'm sorry, very sorry! I thought you had a drinking party; it was very stupid, but——"

She broke off as though the words choked her.

"When you blamed me for not speaking, I thought he's speaking as the employer, and I was wrong. I'm very glad it was a real human feeling that spoke."

She broke into a bright happy smile and said sincerely, and as though it gave her pleasure to say it:

"Oh! it is so good to recognise human feeling in any one. I'm very glad, very; everything has come right, so splendidly—splendidly."

She disappeared like a little grey cloud, lighted with the rays of the morning sun. The friends looked after her; both faces were solemn and withal a little comic. Lunev looked round the room and said:

"Quite jolly here? eh?" Pavel laughed softly.

"Well, she's a good sort!" Lunev continued with a little sigh. "How she——ah!"

"She just swept everything clean like the wind!"

"There, did you see?" cried Ilya in triumph, pulling at his curly hair, "How she apologised, eh? You see what it's like to be really cultivated; you can respect a person, but you're never the first to make advances, see?"

"She's good," Gratschev confirmed him. "How long was she here? Close on an hour; it seems like a minute or two."

"Like a star."

"Yes, and put everything straight in no time; told us how and where and when."

Lunev laughed excitedly; he was delighted that this proud girl should have shown herself so capable and cheerful, and he was pleased with himself for knowing how to conduct himself worthily.

"Ah, yes," he cried regretfully. "I forgot; she took me by surprise with her apology."

"What did you forget?"

"I ought to have kissed her hand; that's what they do, educated people; it shows special respect."

Gavrik came in apparently loafing aimlessly.

"Ah, Gavrik!" said Ilya, and clapped him on the shoulder. "Your sister's a brick."

"Yes, she's a good sort," the boy agreed condescendingly. "Are we going to work to-day, or have a holiday? for I'd like to go into the country."

"No work to-day. Pavel, come, let's go for a walk."

"I shall go to the police station," said Pavel, and his face clouded over again.

"Perhaps they'll let me see her."

"I shall go for a walk," said Ilya.

Fresh and happy he strolled through the streets thinking of Gavrik's sister, and comparing this strange girl with all the people he had ever known. It was clear to him that she was better than them all, and had treated him better. The words of her apology rang in his ears, and he saw before him her face, with its wide nostrils, and every feature stamped with an expression of striving towards some unknown goal.

"And how she used to look down on me at first," he said to himself smiling, and began to wonder why at first she had treated him so proudly and distantly when she did not know him, and had hardly exchanged a word with him.

Life surged round about him. Students went by laughing, droshkys and carts of goods rolled past, a beggar limped along in front of him, his wooden leg tapping loudly on the stone pavement.

Two prisoners, guarded by a soldier, were carrying a wooden tub on a pole between them. A seller of pears passed along shouting, "Garden pears! Cooking pears!" Behind him ran a little dog with lolling tongue, rattle and crash, shouting and tramping, every sound blended in a lively, exciting hubbub. A warm dust whirled aloft and tickled the nostrils; the sun flamed out of a deep clean sky, and flooded the whole world with radiant splendour. Lunev looked at everything with a joy to which he had long been a stranger; everything in the streets seemed new and interesting; there, almost dancing along, goes a pretty girl with a merry red-cheeked face, and looks Ilya in the eyes, frank and friendly, as though she would say: "How nice you are!" Lunev smiled back at her. A droshky driver took off his hat, bowing sideways, with a grin, and said to a fat lady standing on the pavement: "It's too little, lady, five kopecks more." Ilya saw by his face that he was lying, the rascal—he had his proper fare. A young man hurries out of a shop with a copper can in his hand, pours out the cold water, sprinkling the passers-by, and the lid of the can rings cheerfully. The street is hot, stifling, noisy, and the thick green of the old lime-trees in the town churchyard is enticing with its peace and cool shade. The churchyard is surrounded with a white stone wall, and the thick foliage of the old trees sweeps up in a mighty wave to heaven, crowned with a spray of pointed green leaves. Against the blue every leaf stands out, and slowly quivering seems to melt away, and high over the foam of leaves shines the golden crosses of the church, a net-work of glancing, trembling rays.

Lunev entered the churchyard and went slowly along the broad alley, drawing deep breaths of perfume from the blossoming limes. Between the trees, under the branches' shade, stood monuments of marble and granite, stout and heavy, overgrown with moss and lichen. Here and there in the mysterious twilight crosses or half-erased inscriptions glimmered; golden honeysuckle, acacia, whitethorn and elder grew in the hedges, and their branches hid the graves. Here and there in the dense green a slender grey wooden cross appeared and was lost immediately among the surrounding bushes. White stems of young birch-trees glimmered like velvet through the thick network of leaves; they seemed to choose the shade with calculated modesty in order to be seen more easily. On green mounds, behind railings, shone gay flowers, a bee buzzed by in the stillness, two white butterflies played in the air; all kinds of flies swarmed noiselessly; and everywhere grasses and plants made towards the light, hid the mournful graves, and all the green of the churchyard was full of a tense striving to grow, to develop, to drink in air and light and change the richness of the earth to colour and scent and beauty for the joy of eyes and hearts. Everywhere life prevails and will prevail.

Lunev rejoiced to wander at will in the quiet and breathe in the sweet perfume of the flowers and the lime-trees. In his heart, too, there was rest and peace, he thought of nothing, but tasted the joy of solitude long unknown to him. He turned to the left out of the alley by a narrow path, and went slowly reading the inscriptions on crosses and gravestones. The graves hemmed him in with their railings, ornamental and wrought, or plain cast-iron.

"Beneath this cross rest the ashes of Vonifanty, servant of God."

He read and smiled, the name seemed ridiculous. Over the ashes of Vonifanty was set a huge granite stone. Near by in another enclosure rested "Peter Babushkin, twenty-eight years old."

"A young fellow," thought Ilya.

On a pillar of white marble he read:

"Earth's little flower is plucked and dies,
A new star shines in heaven's skies."

Lunev read the couplet over and felt something touching in it. Suddenly he felt as though he had been struck to the heart, he swayed and shut his eyes; but through his closed lids he still saw clearly the inscription that had terrified him. The shining, golden letters on the big, brown stone seemed to have been cut on his brain:

"Here lies the body of the merchant Gilde Vassily Gavrilovitsch Poluektov, the younger."

After a moment or two, terrified at his own fear, he opened his eyes quickly, and looked suspiciously round about him. No one was there, only far off a burial service was being conducted. Through the stillness rang a thin tenor voice singing:

"Let us pray."

A deep, rather unpleasant voice answered, "Have mercy," and the clinking of the censers was just audible.

Lunev stood with his back against a maple-tree, his head thrown back, staring at the grave of the man he had murdered. He had pushed his cap off his brow, and it was pressed against the tree by the back of his head. His eyebrows were dark, his upper lip twitched, showing his teeth; his hands were deep in his jacket pockets, and his feet braced against the ground.

Poluektov's monument represented a coffin, and carved on it an open book, and a skull and crossbones. Beside it in the same enclosure was another smaller stone with an inscription that beneath it rested Eupraxia Poluektov, twenty-two years old.

"The first wife," thought Lunev. The thought came from only a small part of his brain, that remained free from the straining labour of his memory. He was gripped by the recollections of Poluektov; the first meeting, the murder, the feeling of the old man's saliva on his hands. But while all this stirred to life in his memory, he felt no trouble, no remorse, he looked at the gravestone with hate and bitterness and deep ill-will; and under his breath, with hot anger in his heart, and a real conviction of the truth of his words, he addressed the merchant:

"It's for you, damn you, that I ruined all my life, for you! You devil. What life is it I lead, through you! I have smirched myself for ever through you."

The words "for you" thumped in him like hammer strokes. He longed to cry with all his might these words for every one to hear, and he could hardly restrain the fierce desire. He pressed his teeth together till they ached, and stared before him while the thought of his life took hold of his soul like fire. Before him appeared the little, spiteful face, and near it somehow the wicked, bald head of Strogany with the red eyebrows, the self-satisfied face of Petrusha, the stupid Kirik, the grey head of Ehrenov, snub-nosed and pig-eyed—a whole crowd of familiar faces. There was a roaring in his ears, and it seemed as though all these men surrounded him, pressed on him, crowded him obstinately. He stepped away from the tree; his cap fell down behind him; as he bent to pick it up, he could not help stealing a sidelong glance at the money-changer's gravestone. He felt hot and sick, his face was full of blood, his eyes were strained with the tenseness of their gaze. With great difficulty he tore them away, walked straight up to the enclosure, grasped the railings in his hands and trembling with hate, spat on the grave; as he went away he stamped his feet on the ground as though to free them from a pain.

He could not go home; his soul was heavy and a sense of sick, cold weariness grew suffocatingly upon him. He walked with slow steps without looking at any one, without caring for anything, without thinking. In this way he walked along one street, turned mechanically into a second at the corner, went on a little further, and then found himself close to Petrusha Filimonov's tavern; the thought of Jakov came into his mind. As he passed by the door he felt that he must go in, though he had no wish to do so. As he went up the steps he heard Perfishka's voice.

"Oh! good people, be tender with your hands and spare my sides."

Lunev stood still in the open door; he saw Jakov behind the counter through the clouds of dust and tobacco smoke. His hair plastered down, in a coat with short sleeves, he was hurrying about, putting tea in teapots, counting lumps of sugar, pouring out brandy, and drawing the drawer of the till noisily in and out. The waiters hurried up and called, throwing the counters on the table: "Half a bottle, two beers, roast meat, ten kopecks' worth."

"He's grown handier," thought Lunev with an almost malicious pleasure, as he saw how quickly his friend's red hands moved.

"Ah! I'll remember that half-rouble against him," growled the loud harsh voice of a customer.

"Ah!" cried Jakov in delight, as Ilya came up to the counter, then looked nervously at the door behind him. His forehead was wet with perspiration, his cheeks yellow, with red patches. He grasped Ilya's hand and shook it, coughing at the same time, a harsh, dry cough.

"How are you?" asked Lunev, forcing a smile.

"Pretty well. I help in the business."

"Brought into the yoke at last?"

"What's a fellow to do?"

Jakov's shoulders were bowed, and he looked as if he had grown smaller.

"What ages it is since we met," he said, and looked in Ilya's face with his loving mournful eyes. "I'd like a bit of a talk with you. Father isn't there as it happens. See here, come in, and I'll ask the step-mother to let me away for a little."

He opened the door of his father's room slightly, and called respectfully:

"Mamma, can I speak to you a minute?"

Ilya entered the room that he had shared with his uncle, and looked round with interest. It was hardly altered; the wall-paper was darker, and instead of two beds there was only one, and above it a shelf of books. On the spot where he used to sleep stood a high, stout chest.

"There, I've got off for an hour," said Jakov cheerfully as he came in, and then shut and bolted the door. "But would you like some tea? All right. Ivan, tea," he called loudly, then began to cough and coughed for a long time; he supported himself with a hand against the wall, bowed his head and bent his back as though he would force something from his chest.

"That's a pretty noise to make," said Lunev,

"It's consumption, but I am glad to see you again, and my word, how you look! so swell, quite splendid! Well and how are you getting on?"

"I? What?" answered Lunev hesitatingly.

"Oh! I get along, but you, tell me, that's much more interesting."

Lunev felt absolutely disinclined to give information about himself; he hardly wanted to speak at all. He looked at Jakov and seeing him suffering, pitied him, but it was a cold pity, almost an empty, unmeaning feeling.

"I, brother? I endure my life as well as I can," answered Jakov, half aloud.

"Your father sucks your blood."

"Oh, he's in a tight place himself."

"Serves him right!"

"Step-mother's the chief person in the house now; if she says a thing, that's the law."

"Child, what use is money to you?
Give me a kiss, I'll give you two,"

sang Perfishka in a piping voice in the next room, and played on his harmonica.

"What kind of a chest is that?" asked Ilya.

"That? That's a harmonium. Father bought it for me for four roubles. 'Learn to play it,' he said, 'then I'll buy you a good one at three hundred roubles,' he said, 'and we'll put it in the restaurant, and you can play to the guests and be some use, anyhow.' It was smart of him; they have organs in all the taverns now except ours, and I like playing."

"He's a mean wretch!" cried Lunev.

"Not at all! Why? Let him alone. It's quite true, I'm no use to him."

Ilya looked darkly at his friend, and said bitterly:

"Here's a good idea for him! Tell him when you die to make a show of you in the bar, and charge to see it, five kopecks a head. Then you'll be worth something to him."

Jakov laughed in an embarrassed way, and began to cough again, holding his hand first against his chest, then against his throat.

And Perfishka went on cheerfully:

"He kept the fast days as 'tis fit,
He did not eat or drink a bit,
His empty stomach felt the pain,
But oh! his soul was clean again!"

"So, ho—holiness!" And his harmonica drowned the words with a confused medley of sounds.

"How do you get on with your step-brother?" asked Ilya when Jakov ceased coughing. His friend raised his face, quite blue with the exertion of coughing, and said, struggling to get his breath:

"He doesn't live here. His superiors won't let him—because of—the business. He—is bearable—a little uppish—plays the gentleman. Comes often for money to his mother. He's always wanting money."

Jakov lowered his voice, and went on in a troubled way:

"Do you remember that book? You know? Yes—he took it away from me—it was rare he said—that it was worth a lot—and so he took it away. I begged him—leave it to me—but no!—he would have it." Ilya laughed aloud. Then the two friends began their tea. Through the chinks in the wooden partition all kinds of noises and different odours made their way into the little room. One angry voice, towering above the rest, shouted:

"Mitry Nikolayitch—don't you throw my words back at me!"

"I'm reading a story now, brother," Jakov went on again; "it's called 'Julia, or the Subterranean Vault of the Muzzini Castle'—most interesting. And you? What are you doing that way?"

"Go to the devil with your subterranean vaults. I don't live so very high above ground myself," was Lunev's sulky answer.

Jakov looked at him sympathetically, and asked:

"Is there anything gone wrong with you?"

Lunev did not reply. He was wondering whether to tell Jakov of Masha or not; but Jakov began again gently:

"Ilya, you're so touchy and bitter—about nothing, as far as I can see. Because you see—after all—it isn't anybody's fault. It's all settled. They haven't any hand in it—it was all arranged and ordered long before them."

Lunev drank his tea and said nothing.

"And you know—every man shall be rewarded according to his deeds—that is certain. There's my father—to tell the truth. What is he? Why, a tyrant! And then comes along Thekla Timofeyevna and—crock! She has him under the harrow. He leads a life of it now—ah! ah! He's begun to drink out of worry—and how long is it since they were married? And so for every man there's a Thekla Timofeyevna somewhere for his evil deeds."

Ilya was weary and uninterested; he pushed away his teacup and said suddenly:

"And what are you looking for now?"

"How do you mean? From whom?" replied Jakov in a low voice with eyes wide open.

"Why—in the future—what are you looking for?" Ilya repeated his question sharply.

Jakov hung his head and became thoughtful.

"Well?" said Ilya half aloud, feeling a burning restlessness at his heart and a wish to get away as soon as possible.

"What could I look for?" Jakov began at last softly and without looking at his friend.

"To look for? There's no more of that for me. I shall die—that's all—and soon—that's certain."

He held up his head and went on with a gentle happy smile on his wasted face.

"I always see things blue in my dreams—d'you know? as if everything were sky-blue—not only the sky, but the ground and the trees and the flowers and the grass. Everything! And so quiet—quite, quite peaceful! As if nothing at all existed—everything seems so still—and all bright blue. I feel so light—as though I could go anywhere, without feeling tired—go right on and never stop—and you can't tell whether it's really you or not—so light, so light. Dreams like that—that's a sign of death."

"Good-bye!" said Lunev, and got up.

"Where are you going so soon? Stay a little."

"No. Good-bye!"

Jakov got up also. "Very well then—go!"

Lunev pressed his hot hand and looked at him silently, finding no words to bid his comrade farewell; he wanted to say something, wanted so strongly and so much that his heart pained him.

"Why do you look at me like that?" asked Jakov, smiling.

"Forgive me, brother," said Lunev slowly and heavily, lowering his eyes.

"What then?"

"Just that—forgive."

"Am I a priest then?" said Jakov, smiling gently. "But wait, wait a minute. I forgot what I wanted to say to you. Mashutka—you know?"

"What?"

"She too—have you heard? She has a bad time too."

"Yes. I heard."

"You see, we all have the same fate. You too. I feel sure. Your heart is sad—isn't it?"

He spoke with a dull smile. The tone of his voice, and every word of his conversation, everything about him seemed bloodless, colourless; Lunev let go his hand—and it fell slackly down.

"Well, Jasha—forgive me, anyway."

"God forgives! You'll come again?"

Ilya went out without replying. Once in the street his heart felt lighter and less weary. He saw that Jakov must soon die, and the knowledge irritated him vaguely. He did not exactly pity Jakov, because he could not imagine how this gentle, quiet youth could live in this world. Long ago he had come to regard his friend as one who was ordained to depart from the riot of life. But what irritated him was the thought—Why do people torture this harmless man? Why do they drive him out of the world before his time? And from this thought his hostile feeling against life now became almost the most deeply rooted of his sensations, grew and strengthened. That night he could not sleep. In spite of the open window the room was close.

He went out into the courtyard and lay down on the ground under the elm-tree by the fence. Lying on his back, he looked up into the clear sky, and the more intently he gazed the more stars he could see. The Milky Way stretched across the heavens from one end to the other, like a silver tissue, and to look up at it through the branches of the tree was at once pleasant and saddening. The sky where no one lives glitters with stars, and the earth—What is there to adorn it? Ilya blinked his eyes, the branches seemed to mount up higher and higher; against the blue velvet of the arch of heaven sown with sparkling stars, the black outlines of the leaves looked like hands stretched up in the attempt to scale the heights. Ilya thought involuntarily of his friend's "blue dreams," and before his mind appeared the image of Jakov—blue, light, and transparent, his kind eyes shining like stars. There— that was a man, and he was martyred because he lived peaceably. But the tormentors live on as their hearts desire, and will live long.

CHAPTER XXIII

From henceforth there was a new and rather disturbing feature in Ilya's life. Gavrik's sister began to visit his shop almost every day. She appeared always anxious over one thing or another, greeted Ilya with a hearty handshake, and vanished again after exchanging a few words with him. But always she left something new in Ilya's mind. Once she asked him:

"Do you like a business like this?"

"Not so very much," answered Ilya, shrugging his shoulders; "but a man must earn his living some way or other."

She looked at him attentively with her serious eyes, and her face looked even more tense than usual.

"A man must live!" repeated Ilya with a sigh.

"Have you never tried to make your living by work?"

Ilya did not understand.

"How?"

"Have you ever worked?"

"Always. All my life. I—sell things," answered Ilya doubtfully.

She smiled, and Ilya felt a little hurt at her smile.

"You think—selling things—is work?"

"Yes, surely. It often makes me tired." Looking in her face he felt that she was not joking, but speaking earnestly.

"Oh, no"—the girl went on with a condescending smile. "To work means to make something by the exercise of one's strength—to create something. Thread or ribbons or chairs or chests—d'you see?" Lunev nodded and blushed; he was ashamed to say that he did not understand.

"But trade—what's the good of it? it makes nothing," she said with conviction, and looked challengingly at Ilya.

"Yes," he answered slowly and carefully. "You're right there—it isn't difficult when you're used to it. But still trade must be some use, or else there wouldn't be any, would there?"

She did not reply to this, but turned away and began to speak to her brother. Soon after she took her leave, only nodding to Ilya as she went. Her expression was cold and proud, even as it was before the encounter with Masha. Ilya pondered on this; could he by any chance have hurt her feelings by a careless word? He thought over everything he had said, and could find nothing in it to wound her. Then he began to consider her words, and the more he thought the more they occupied him. What sort of difference could she see between trade and work?

She interested him more and more; but he could not understand why her features looked cross and irritable when she herself was so kind, and could not only sympathise with people, but also help them. Pavel had visited her at home, and was full of enthusiastic praises for her and all the mode of life in her family.

"The minute you come in—at once, they say, 'Welcome.' If they're at table, then—'Sit down with us.' If they're having tea—'Have a cup of tea with us.' It's so simple—and the people, there—my word!—and so happy—they drink tea and talk all at once and quarrel over books; and the books all lie about as if it were a book-shop. It's often crowded, you knock into your neighbour, and he laughs. All educated people—one is an advocate, another will soon be a doctor, and students and that sort. You forget altogether who you are, and laugh as if you were in your own set, and smoke and so on. It's splendid—so jolly, and so sensible."

"Ah—they'll never ask me," said Lunev, gloomily, "that proud young lady."

"Proud?—she?" cried Pavel. "I tell you, she's simplicity itself. Don't wait for an invitation—meet her by accident at the house door—and there you are. All people are equal, there—like in an inn, my boy. You feel so free. I tell you—what am I compared to you? But after two visits—like a child of the house!—and interesting—the noise, the row—the words start up—it's like a game."

"Well, and how's Mashutka?" asked Ilya.

"Pretty well, she's picked up a bit—sits and smiles now and then. They look after her—give her lots of milk—as for Ehrenov, he'll catch it! The advocate said the old devil would get it properly. Masha will be taken to the Judge of Inquiry—and as for my girl, they're taking a lot of trouble to bring the case on soon. Ah—it's good to be near them—the little house—people there like wood in the stove—they glow."

"But she, she herself?" asked Ilya.

Of "her" Pavel began to talk, as once he had talked of the prisoners who taught him to read and write. Every nerve was tense, and he talked emphatically, his speech full of interjections.

"She, brother? Oh—ho! Where did she learn it? She orders them all about, and if any one says anything unfair, or else—she, frrr—like a cat."

"I know that," said Ilya, and smiled involuntarily.

Yet he envied Pavel; he longed to visit the house, but his self-conceit forbade him to take the straight way there.

Standing behind the counter he thought obstinately:

"All the men there are, every one looks out for a chance to get something somehow from the rest. But she, what good does it do her to take up Mashutka and Vyera? She's poor; perhaps everything in the house has to be reckoned. That means she must be very good. And yet she talks to me that way, how am I worse than Pavel?"

These thoughts troubled him so, that he began to feel almost indifferent to everything else. A chink seemed to have opened in the darkness of his life, and through it he felt, rather than saw, something glimmer that he had never perceived before.

"My friend," said Tatiana Vlassyevna to him, coldly but impressively: "The stock of narrow tape wants renewing; the trimming, too, is almost used up, and there's very little black thread number fifty. A firm offers us pearl buttons at—the traveller came to me. I sent him on here. Has he been?"

"No," answered Ilya shortly.

This woman became more repugnant to him daily. He had a suspicion that she had taken Karsakov, recently named District Chief of Police, for a lover. She appointed meetings with Ilya more and more seldom, although she had just the same tender, gay manner with him as before. He did his best to avoid even these rarer meetings on one pretext or another, and finding that she was not at all annoyed, he called her in his heart fickle and shameless.

She was especially irksome to him when she came to the shop to inspect the stock. She turned about like a top, jumped on the counter, hauled out the cardboard boxes from the highest shelves, sneezing in the dust she raised, shook her head, and worried the life out of Gavrik.

"An apprentice in business must be quick and ready, he isn't fed to sit in the door all day and rub his nose; and when he's spoken to he ought to listen attentively, and not stare like a scarecrow."

But Gavrik had a character quite his own. While he listened to her flood of comments he preserved a complete indifference. Especially when she was rummaging about among the upper shelves, and holding up her skirts, Gavrik would look mischievously at his master. When he addressed her it was roughly and without any sign of respect, and when she departed he would remark: "There goes the plover at last."

"You mustn't speak of your mistress like that," said Ilya, trying to hide a smile.

"What sort of a mistress is she?" answered Gavrik. "She comes here and chatters, and hops off again! You—are the master."

"She is, too," said Ilya feebly, for he liked the honourable, high-spirited lad.

"Ah; she's a plover," insisted Gavrik.

"You teach that youngster nothing," said Madame Avtonomov to Ilya on another occasion. "And I must say, frankly, that lately everything seems carried on without enthusiasm, with no love for the work."

Lunev said nothing, but in his soul he hated her so that he thought:

"I wish to goodness, you she-devil, you'd break your leg; coming skipping about here."

One day he received a letter from his uncle, and learnt that Terenti had not only been to Kiev, but also the Sergius Monastery and in Valvam. He had nearly gone to Solovky, on the Dvina, but had abandoned that pilgrimage, and expected soon to reach home again.

"Another joy," thought Ilya bitterly. "He'll come here to live for certain."

He considered eagerly how to arrange that his uncle should live alone. But he had little time for thought; customers came in, and while he was busy with them, Gavrik's sister appeared. She seemed tired and out of breath, greeted him, and asked, nodding at the door of the room behind:

"Is there any water there?"

"I'll get it," said Ilya.

"No, I'll go."

She went into the room and stayed there till Lunev had finished with his customers, and followed her. He found her standing before the "Steps of Man's Life." Turning her head towards him, she said, indicating the picture:

"What awful taste!"

Confused by the remark, Ilya smiled, and felt somewhat guilty.

"Burr! What middle-class sentiment!" she repeated with disgust, and before he could ask for an explanation she was gone. A few days later she brought her brother some new linen, and reproved him for being careless with his clothes, tearing and soiling them.

"Well," said Gavrik, crossly. "That's enough. That woman's always on at me, and now you're beginning."

"What's the matter with him? Is he very rude?" she asked Ilya at this.

"N—no. He doesn't mean to be," answered Ilya kindly.

"I—I always keep quite quiet!" said the boy.

"His tongue goes a little fast!" said Ilya.

"Do you hear?" asked his sister, knitting her brows.

"Oh, yes, I hear!" cried Gavrik crossly.

"It doesn't matter much," said Ilya good-humouredly. "A man who can show his teeth has always an advantage over the rest. A man who bears blows silently gets beaten to his grave by the stupid people."

She listened and a smile of pleasure came over her face. Ilya noticed it.

"I wanted to ask you— —" he began, in some confusion.

"Well?"

The girl came closer and looked right into his eyes. He could not meet her glance, but hung his head and went on:

"As far as I can make out, you don't care for tradesmen?"

"Not much."

"Why?"

"Because they live on the work of others," she explained, speaking very distinctly.

Ilya threw up his head, and his brows contracted. The words did not only astonish him, but pained him; and she said them so simply, so much as if it were a matter of course.

"But—excuse me—that isn't true!" he said loudly, after a pause.

Her face twitched and she blushed.

"How much does this ribbon cost you?" she asked coldly and sternly.

"Ribbon?—this ribbon?—Seventeen kopecks the arshin."

"And how do you sell it?"

"At twenty"

"Very well. The three kopecks that you make don't really belong to you, but to the one who made the ribbon. Do you see?"

"No," confessed Lunev frankly.

A flame shot from her eyes. Ilya saw it, and was afraid, yet angered with himself because of his fear.

"Yes. I thought it wouldn't be easy for you to understand such a simple idea," she said, and turned away towards the door. "But see, now—imagine you are a worker, that you've made all this yourself,"—she swept her hand round with a big gesture, and went on to explain to him how labour enriches all except the labourer. At first she spoke in her ordinary manner, coldly, distinctly, and her ugly face was unmoved; but presently her eyebrows quivered and contracted, her nostrils dilated, and, standing close to Ilya, with head erect, she hurled mighty words at him, nerved by her youthful, unshakeable confidence in their truth.

"The retailer stands between the worker and the purchaser. He does nothing himself, he only increases the cost of the goods. Trading! It's only legal, permissible robbery."

Ilya felt deeply hurt, but he could find no words to answer this bold girl, who told him to his face he was a loafer and a robber. He clenched his teeth and listened silently, but did not believe, he could not believe; and while he ransacked his brain for the word to controvert her argument, to silence her forthwith, while he marvelled at her boldness, the contemptuous phrases, so amazing to his ears, stirred in his mind the question: "Why—what have I done to her?"

"All that is just not true," he interrupted her finally in a loud voice, feeling that he could not listen any longer without contradicting. "No—I can't agree with you."

"Then disprove it!" the young girl replied quietly. She sat down on a stool, drew the long plait of her hair over her shoulder, and began to play with it. Lunev turned away to avoid her challenging glance.

"I'll disprove it!" he cried, no longer able to contain himself. "I'll disprove it by my whole life. I—perhaps I did commit a great sin once before I came to this."

"So much the worse—but this is no argument," answered the girl; and her words fell on Ilya like a cold douche. He supported himself with both hands on the counter, and bent forward as though he were going to spring over, and gazed at her for some seconds in silence, cut to the heart, and astonished at her quietness. Her glance and her unmoved countenance, full of profound conviction, restrained his anger and confused him; he felt something fearless, impregnable in her, and the words he needed to refute her died on his tongue.

"Well? What then?" she asked with a cool challenge, then laughed, and said triumphantly:

"It's impossible to disprove it, because I spoke the truth."

"Impossible?" repeated Ilya in a dull voice.

"Yes, impossible. What can you say against it?"

She laughed again condescendingly.

"Good-bye!" and she went out, her head even higher than usual.

"That's all nonsense! It isn't true, excuse me"—Lunev shouted after her. But she did not turn round. Ilya sat down on the stool. Gavrik stood at the door and looked at him, evidently well pleased with his sister's behaviour; his face had an important triumphant expression.

"What are you staring at?" cried Lunev crossly, feeling annoyed by the boy's expression.

"Nothing."

"Oh! oh!" cried Lunev threateningly; then after a short pause he added: "You can go, take a holiday."

He felt the necessity for solitude, but even when alone he could not collect his thoughts. He could not grasp the sense of the girl's words; they pained him before everything. Leaning his elbows on the counter, he thought in irritation:

"Why did she abuse me? What have I done to her? And she's kind, too. Comes here, condemns me, and goes away—without any justice; without even finding out anything. She is very clever; but wait till you come back here—I'll answer you."

But even while he threatened his mind was searching for the fault wherefore she had so attacked him. He remembered what Pavel had said of her intelligence and simplicity.

"Pashka—no fear—she wouldn't hurt him."

Raising his head he saw his reflection in the mirror, and as he looked he seemed to question his image. The black moustache moved on his lip, the big eyes looked weary, and a red flush burned on his cheek-bones; but yet, in spite of its look of annoyance over his defeat, the face was handsome, with a coarse, peasant's beauty; certainly more handsome than Pavel's yellow, bony countenance.

"Does she really like Pashka better than me?" he thought, and at once answered his thought:

"What good's my face? I'm no man for her. She'll marry some doctor or advocate, or official. Whatever interest could she take in us?"

He smiled bitterly, and began to question again:

"But why has she asked Pashka to go and see her? Why does she despise me? A tradesman—is he a thief? He doesn't work—think. I live on the work of others? And who is it stands here stiff and tired all day long, and never gets away?"

Now he began to oppose her, and found many words to justify his life; but now she was not there, and his fine words did not console him, but only increased the feeling of exasperation that glowed within him. He got up, went into his room, swallowed a mouthful of water, and looked round him. It was close and stuffy in the low room, with the iron railings in front of the window; the picture caught his eye with its bright colours; standing in the doorway, he raised his eyes to the "Steps of Life," so accurately measured out, and thought:

"All a lie! As if life were like that!" He looked long at the picture, comparing in his mind his own life with this sample, set out in such glowing colours.

"Is that life?" he repeated to himself, and suddenly added, hopelessly: "Yes, even if it were really, it's dreary and monotonous—clean enough, but not jolly!"

He stepped slowly up to the wall, tore the picture down, and carried it into the shop. There he laid it on the counter, and began again to observe the development of man as it was here depicted. Now he regarded it with scorn, but while he looked, he thought only of Gavrik's sister.

"As if she knew that I strangled the old man! However little she likes me, why need she say such things?"

His thoughts circled in his brain slowly and heavily, and the picture wavered before his eyes. Then he crumpled it up and threw it under the counter, but it rolled out again under his feet. Still more exasperated, he crushed it into a tighter ball, and flung it out into the street. The street was full of noise. On the other side some one was walking with a stick. The stick did not strike the pavement regularly, so that it sounded as though the man had three feet. The doves cooed; the clank of metal sounded somewhere, probably a chimney-sweep going over a roof. A droshky went by; the driver was drowsy and his head nodded to and fro. Everything seemed to sway round Ilya. Half asleep he took his reckoning frame and counted off twenty kopecks. From them he took seventeen—three were left. He flipped the little balls with his finger-nail, and they slid along the wire with a slight noise, separated out and stopped. Ilya sighed, laid the frame aside, threw himself on the counter, and lay so, listening to the beating of his heart. Next day Gavrik's sister came back. She looked just the same, in the same old dress, with the same expression.

"There!" thought Lunev angrily, looking at her from his room. He bowed ungraciously as she greeted him, but she laughed suddenly and said in a friendly way:

"Why are you so pale? Aren't you well?"

"Quite well!" answered Ilya shortly, and tried to conceal from her the feeling that her friendly observation of him had roused. It was a warm, happy feeling. Her smile and her words touched his heart, but he resolved to show her he felt hurt, hoping she would give him another smile or friendly word. He resolved, and waited therefore sulkily without looking at her.

"I'm afraid—you feel hurt!" her usual firm voice said. The tone was so different from that of her earlier words that Ilya looked at her in surprise. But she was as proud as ever, and in her dark eyes lay something disdainful, angry.

"I'm used to being hurt," said Lunev now, and smiled at her in challenge, but with the coldness of disillusion in his heart.

"Ah, you're playing with me!" was his thought. "First you'll stroke me, and then strike? Well, you shan't!"

"I didn't mean to hurt you!" Her words sounded to Ilya hard, even condescending.

"It would be hard for you to hurt me, really," he began loudly and boldly. "I think I know now the kind of lady you are. You're a bird that doesn't fly very high."

At these words she drew herself up, astonished, with eyes wide open. But Ilya noticed nothing now, the hot desire to pay her back for what she had done to him burned in him like a flame, and he used hard, harsh words, slowly and carefully.

"Your superiority—this pride—they don't cost much. Any one who has the chance of education can get them. If it wasn't for your education, you'd be a tailoress or a housemaid. As poor as you are, you couldn't be anything else!"

"What's that you say?" she exclaimed.

Ilya looked at her and was glad to see how her nostrils quivered and her cheeks reddened.

"I say what I think; and I do think it. All your cheap airs of superiority aren't worth a button."

"I've no airs of superiority!" the girl cried in a ringing voice. Her brother hurried to her, took her hand and said loudly, looking angrily at his master, "Come away, Sonyka."

Lunev glanced at the pair and answered, with aversion, but coldly:

"Please do go! I am nothing to you, nor you to me."

Both gave one strange lightning glance at him, and then disappeared. He laughed as they went. Then he stood alone in the shop for several minutes, motionless, intoxicated with the bitter sweetness of complete revenge. The angry face of the girl, half astonished, half frightened, was stamped on his memory, and he was pleased with himself.

"But that rascal—he——" a sudden thought buzzed in his brain. Gavrik's behaviour annoyed him and disturbed his self-satisfied mood.

"Another of the conceited lot!" he thought. "Now, if only Tanitshka were to come, I'd talk to her too—now's the time."

He experienced the desire to thrust all mankind away from him, harshly and contemptuously, and felt the strength in him now to do it.

But Tanitshka did not come; he was alone all day, and the time hung very heavily on his hands. When he lay down to sleep he felt isolated, and his sense of injury at his isolation was greater even than at the girl's words. He remembered Olympiada, and thought now that she had been kinder to him than any one. Closing his eyes, he listened in the stillness of the night; but at every sound he started, raised his head from the pillow, and stared into the darkness with eyes wide open. All night he could not get to sleep, because of his terrified expectation of something unknown—a feeling as though he were imprisoned in a cellar, gasping in a damp, close air, full of helpless, disconnected thoughts. He got up with an aching head, tried to get the samovar going, but gave it up. He washed, drank some water, and opened the shop.

About midday Pavel appeared, his forehead wrinkled in anger. Without any greeting, he asked:

"What on earth's the matter with you?"

Ilya understood the drift of the question, and shook his head hopelessly. He was silent awhile, thinking: "He's against me, too."

"Why have you insulted Sophie Nikonovna?" said Pavel sternly, standing very straight.

Ilya read his condemnation in Gratschev's angry face and reproachful eyes, but he bore that with indifference. He said slowly, in a tired voice:

"You might say 'good day' when you come in, don't you think? and take off your cap. There's an eikon here."

Pavel simply clutched his cap and drew it on more firmly, while his lips twitched with anger. Then he began, speaking fast and bitterly, with a trembling voice:

"Go on! Got lots of money, haven't you? and plenty to eat? You'd better think how you once said: 'There's no one to care about us,' and then you find one, and you turn her out. Ah, you—you pedlar, you!"

A dull feeling of slackness prevented Lunev from replying. With an unmoved, indifferent look he regarded Pavel's angry contemptuous features, feeling that the reproaches could not bite into his soul. On Pavel's chin and upper lip lay a thin yellow down, and Lunev found himself looking at this as he thought, indifferently:

"Now he's beginning. She must have complained of me to him. Did I really insult her? I might have said far worse things."

"She, who understands everything and can explain everything; and it's to her—you——Ah!" said Pavel, his talk full of interjections as usual: "All of them—there, are good—clever—they know everything you can think of by heart. Yes!—you ought to have held to her—and you——"

"That'll do anyhow, Pashka," said Lunev slowly. "What are you trying to teach me? I do what I like.'

"Yes, but what do you do? It's a shame!"

"Whatever I like I'll do. I've had enough of all of you! Only get away and chatter what you like." Lunev leaned heavily against the boxes of goods, and went on thoughtfully, as though questioning himself:

"And what could you tell me that I don't know?"

"She can do anything," cried Pavel, with deep conviction, holding up his hand as though prepared to take an oath. "They know everything."

"Then go to them!" cried Ilya, with complete unconcern. Pavel's words and his excitement were distasteful to him, but he felt no wish to contradict his friend. A dull, blank weariness hindered him from speaking or thinking or even moving. He wanted to be alone, to hear nothing and see nothing and nobody.

"And I'll leave you, once and for all," said Pavel threateningly. "I'll go because I understand one thing—I can only live near them, near them I can find all I need—I—they know right and truth! Life to me was never before what it is now, worthy of a man! Who ever respected me before?"

"Don't shout so!" said Lunev half aloud.

"You wooden idol you!" screamed Pavel.

At this moment a little girl came into the shop for a dozen shirt-buttons. Ilya served her politely, took her twenty kopeck piece, twirled it a moment in his fingers, and then gave it back, saying:

"I've no change. You can bring it by-and-bye." He had change in his till, but the key was in his room, and he had no inclination to fetch it. When the child had gone Pavel made no show of renewing the quarrel. He stood by the counter, striking his knee with his cap, and looked at his friend as though he expected something from him; but Lunev, who had turned half away, only whistled softly through his teeth. The groaning sound of heavy waggons in the street and the noise of hasty footsteps of passers-by came into the shop, the dust drifted in.

"Well—what?" asked Pavel.

"Nothing!"

"Oh, very well, then—nothing!"

"For God's sake, let me alone!" said Ilya impatiently.

Gratschev threw on his cap and walked quickly out without another word. Ilya followed him slowly with his eyes, but did not move his head.

"Am I ill, I wonder?" he thought.

A big, fox-coloured dog looked in at the door, wagged his tail, and made off again. Then an old beggar-woman, quite grey, with a big nose, she begged in a half-whisper:

"Please, give me something, kind gentleman."

Lunev shook his head. The noise of the busy day swept by outside. It was as though a huge stove were kindled, where wood crackled in the flames, and glowing heat poured out. A cart, loaded with long iron bars, goes by; the ends of the elastic bars reached the ground and struck, clanking, on the pavement. A knife-grinder sharpens a knife; an evil, hissing sound cuts the air.

"Cherries from Vladimir!" shouts a fruit-seller in a sing-song voice. Every moment brings forth something new and unexpected; life amazes our ears with the multiplicity of its noises, the unwearied persistence of its movement, the strength of its restless creative might. But in Lunev's soul everything there was calm and dead. Everything there was still together. There was there no thought, no wish, only a dull weariness. He spent the whole day in this state, and was tortured all night by nightmare and wild dreams—and many days and nights thereafter passed in the same way. People came, bought what they needed, and went again; his only thought was:

"I don't need them, and they don't need me. That's only strange at first; I shall get used to it! I will just live alone. I will live!"

Instead of Gavrik, the former cook of the owner of the house saw to his samovar and brought him his midday meal. She was a lean, sinister woman, with a red face and eyes that were colourless and staring. Sometimes when he looked at her Ilya felt fear deep down in his soul. "Shall I, then, never see anything beautiful in my life?" And darkly, despairingly, he said to himself: "See how life goes." There had been a time when he had grown accustomed to the manifold impressions of life, and although they irritated him and angered him, he yet felt—it is better to live among men. But now men had disappeared from the world, and there were only customers left. His sense of a common humanity and the longing for a better life vanished together in his indifference towards all and everything, and again the days slipped slowly by in a suffocating stupor.

One evening, when he had closed the shop, he went out into the courtyard, lay down under the elm-tree, and listened to the noise on the further side of the fence. Some one clicked with the tongue, and said softly:

"O—Oh! Good dog! Good little dog!"

Through a chink between the planks Ilya saw a fat old woman, with a long face, sitting on a bench; a big yellow dog had laid one of his fore-paws on her knee, and raising his muzzle, tried to lick her face. The woman turned her face away, and stroked the dog, smiling.

"People caress dogs, then, if there's no one else," Ilya mused. With deep pain in his heart, he thought of Gavrik and his stern sister; then of Pashka, Masha. "If they wanted me they'd come. They can go to the devil. To-morrow I'll go and see Jakov."

"My good dog!" murmured the woman beyond the fence.

"If even Tanyka would come!" thought Ilya, sadly. But Tatiana Vlassyevna was living in a country house a good way from the town, and never appeared in the shop.

CHAPTER XXIV

Ilya did not succeed in visiting Jakov next day, because his uncle Terenti arrived in the town. It was early morning.

Ilya was just awoke, and sat on his bed saying to himself that another day was here that must be lived through somehow.

"It's a life—like travelling through a swamp in autumn, cold and muddy—and you get more and more tired, and hardly get on at all."

There came a knocking at the door of the yard, repeated, single knocks. Ilya got up, thinking the cook had come for the samovar, opened the door, and found himself face to face with the hunchback.

"Ha! ha!" laughed Terenti, shaking his head playfully: "Close on nine, Mr. Shopman, and your shop still shut up!"

Ilya stood, blocking the entrance, and smiled at his uncle. Terenti's face was sunburnt and looked younger; his eyes were cheerful and happy; his bags and bundles lay at his feet, and amid them he himself looked almost like another bundle.

"How goes it, my dear nephew? Will you let me into your house?"

Ilya stood aside, and began to collect the bundles without speaking. Terenti's eyes sought the eikon, he crossed himself, and said, bending reverently: "Thanks be to thee, oh Lord! I am home again. Well, Ilya!"

As Ilya embraced his uncle he felt that the body of the hunchback had grown stronger and stouter.

"If I could have a wash," said Terenti, standing and looking round the room. He stood less bent than of old. Wandering with a knapsack on his back seemed to have drawn down his hump. He held himself straighter, and his head higher.

"And how are you?" he asked his nephew, as he washed his face.

Ilya was glad to see his uncle looking so much younger. He made him sit down at the table, and prepared tea, and answered questions pleasantly, though a little hesitatingly.

"And you?"

"I? Splendid!" Terenti closed his eyes and moved his head with a happy smile. "I have made a good pilgrimage; couldn't have done better. I've drunk of the Water of Life, in one word."

He settled himself at the table, twisted a finger in his beard, put his head on one side, and began to relate his experiences.

"I went to St. Athanasius and the other holy miracle workers, to Mithrophanes at Voronesh, and the holy Tichon on the Don. And I went to the island of Valaam too. I've travelled a great way round. I've prayed to many Saints and Holy ones, and I've now come from the last—St. Peter and the holy Febroma in Murom."

Evidently it delighted him to tell of all the Saints and places; his face was mild, his eyes moist and confident. He spoke in the half singing way that experienced storytellers adopt in their tales and legends of Saints.

Outside it began to rain; at first the rain drops struck the window as it were carefully and without hurry, then by degrees harder and faster till the glass rang under the shower.

"In the depths of the sacred monasteries there's an unbroken stillness; the darkness is over everything; but through it the lamps before the shrines shine like the eyes of children, and there's a perfume of holy oil of unction." The rain increased; a sound as of weeping and sighing came from outside the window; the galvanised iron on the roof rattled and groaned, the water pouring off it splashed, sobbing, and a network of strong steel threads seemed to quiver in the air.

"This oil of unction, the Chrism, comes from the heads of the Saints."

"O—oh!" said Ilya, slowly. "Well, did you find peace for your soul?"

Terenti was silent for a moment, then straightened himself in his chair, bent forward to Ilya and said, lowering his voice:

"See, it's like this, my unwilling sin crushed my heart like a wooden boot. I say unwilling because if I had not obeyed Petrusha—bang! he would have kicked me out! He would have thrown me on the streets, wouldn't he?"

"Yes," Ilya agreed.

"Well, then, as soon as I began my pilgrimage, my heart was lighter at once, and as I went I prayed. 'Oh, Lord, see, I am going to Thy holy Saints. I know I am a sinner.'"

"That's to say, you bargained with Him?" asked Ilya, with a smile.

"His will be done! How He received my prayer I do not know," said the hunchback, looking upwards.

Three Men | 277

"But your conscience?"

"How do you mean?"

"Is it at peace?"

Terenti considered for a moment, as if he were listening, then said:

"It is silent."

Lunev smiled.

"Prayer, if it comes from a clean heart, always brings relief," said the hunchback, softly but emphatically.

Ilya got up and went to the window. Wide streams of dirty water flowed down the gutters; little pools were formed between the stones of the pavement; they trembled under the descending shower, so that it looked as though all the pavement quivered. The house over the way was quite wet and gloomy, its window-panes were dim and the flowers behind them invisible. The streets were deserted and quiet; only the rain hissed and all the little gutters splashed along. A solitary pigeon was sheltering under the eaves by the gable-window, and a damp, heavy dreariness invaded the town from all sides.

"Autumn is here!" The thought shot through Lunev's brain.

"How else can a man set himself right with God except through prayer?" asked Terenti, as he began to open one of his bags.

"It's very simple," remarked Ilya gloomily, without turning round. "You sin as you please; then you pray hard, and it's all right! All settled, begin again, sin some more!"

"But why? On the contrary, live honestly!"

"Why?"

"How d'you mean?"

"What I say. Why should you?"

"To have a clear conscience."

"What's the good of that?"

"Oh—oh!" said Terenti, slowly and reproachfully, "How can you say that?"

"I do say it, though," said Ilya obstinately and firmly, turning his back.

"That is wicked!"

"Tcha! Wicked!"

"Punishment will follow."

"No!"

At this he turned away from the window and looked Terenti in the face. The hunchback, in his turn looked searchingly at his nephew's strong face, moving his lips, he tried to find a word in reply, and at last he said, emphatically:

"'No' you say; but it does come! There—I fell into sin, and have been punished for it."

"How?" asked Ilya, darkly.

"Is anxiety nothing? I lived in fear and trembling. Any moment it might be found out, and I should— —"

"Well. I fell into sin, and I'm not afraid at all," said Ilya, with an insolent laugh.

"Don't jest!" said Terenti warningly.

"It's a fact! I'm not afraid! Life is hard for me, but— —"

"Aha!" cried Terenti, and stood up in triumph. "Hard, you say?"

"Yes! Every one keeps away from me as if I were a mangey dog."

"That's your punishment! D'you see?"

"But why?" screamed Ilya, almost in fury; his jaw quivered, and he tore at the wall behind his back with his fingers. Terenti looked at him in terror, and flourished in the air with a piece of string.

"Don't shout—don't shout so!" he said, half aloud.

But Ilya went on unheeding. It was so long since he had spoken to any one, and now he hurled from his soul all that had accumulated there in these last days of loneliness; he spoke passionately and furiously.

"You've been on a pilgrimage for nothing—nothing—nothing! It's all the same. Nothing would have happened to you. It's not only stealing; you can kill if you like. Nothing will come of it. There's no one to punish you! The stupid get punished; but the clever man—he can do anything, everything!"

"Ilya," answered Terenti, approaching him anxiously, "Wait, wait. Don't get so excited! Sit down. We can talk of it quite quietly."

Suddenly from the other side of the door came the noise of something breaking; there was a rolling and a cracking, and finally whatever it was came to a stop close to the door. The two men startled and were silent for a moment. All was still again; only the rain poured down.

"What was that?" asked the hunchback, softly and timidly.

Ilya went silently to the door, opened it, and looked through.

"Some card-board boxes have fallen down," he said, closed the door and returned to his old place by the window. Terenti still stood up arranging his belongings. After a short silence he began again.

"No—no, think a moment! You say such things! Such Godlessness does not anger God, but it destroys you yourself. Try to understand that; they are wise words. I heard them on my pilgrimage. Ah! how many wise sayings I heard!"

He began again to tell of his travels, looking sideways at Ilya from time to time. But his nephew listened, as he listened to the patter of the rain, and wondered all the time how he should live with his uncle.

Things adjusted themselves fairly well.

Terenti knocked a bed together out of some old boxes, placed it in the corner between the stove and the door, where the darkness was thickest at night. He observed the course of Ilya's life and took upon himself the duties Gavrik had formerly fulfilled; he set out the samovar, swept the shop and the room, went to the tavern to fetch the mid-day meal, humming all the time his pious hymns. In the evening he related to his nephew how the wife of Alliluevov had saved Christ from his enemies by throwing her own infant into the glowing fire and taking the child Jesus in her arms. Or he told of the monk who had listened to the bird's song for three hundred years; or of Kirik and Ulit and of many others. Lunev listened and followed the course of his own thoughts. At this time he made a point of taking a walk every evening, and was always overjoyed to leave the town behind him. There in the open fields, at night, it was still and dark and desolate, as in his own soul.

A week after his return Terenti went to the house of Petrusha Filimonov, and came away sad and grieved. But when Ilya asked him what was wrong, he answered: "Nothing—nothing at all. I went. I mean I saw them all, and we had a talk—h'm—yes!"

"What's Jakov doing?" asked Ilya.

"Jakov? Jakov is dying; he spoke of you; so yellow, and coughs."

Terenti was silent and looked at one corner of the room, sad and melancholy, gnawing his lips.

Life went on uniformly and monotonously every day as like the rest as copper pennies of the same year. Dark misery hid in the depths of Ilya's soul like a huge snake, that swallowed the sensations of the days. None of his old acquaintances visited him; Pavel and Masha seemed to have found for themselves another road in life; Matiza was run over by a horse and died in hospital; Perfishka had disappeared as if the earth had swallowed him. Lunev determined from time to time to go and see Jakov, and could not carry out his determination; he felt only too well that he had nothing to say to his dying comrade.

In the morning he read the newspaper, all day he sat in the shop and watched the yellow withered leaves whirl down the street before the autumn wind. Sometimes a leaf would drift into the shop.

"Holy Father Tichon intercede for us in Heaven," murmured Terenti in a voice that seemed to resemble the dry leaves, while he busied himself about the room.

One Sunday, when Ilya opened the newspaper, he saw a poem on the first page: "Then and Now," and the signature at the end was P. Gratschev.

> "Once my heart like a strife-weary warrior
> Torn by black thoughts as by fierce birds of prey,
> All hope seemed dead and for evermore buried,
> Torment and pain were my portion each day."

So Pavel wrote. Lunev read the verse and before his eyes he seemed to see the lively face of his comrade; now restless, with bright bold eyes, now sad and darkened, concentrated on one thought. In his verses Pavel told again how he wandered poor and alone in a foreign town, receiving no greeting or friendly word. But when he was at the point of death from longing and want, then he found kind people, who bade him welcome to their hearth, where he drank new life: "Drank from their words that were radiant with love," words that fell upon his heart like sparks of fire:

> "Hope flamed again in the heart of the hopeless,
> Songs of rejoicing resound through his soul."

Lunev read to the end, and then pushed the paper impatiently aside.

"Always rhyming, always with some crank in your head! Wait a little! these kind people of yours will handle you presently! kind people!" A scornful smile drew his mouth awry. Then suddenly he thought as though with a new soul. "Suppose I went there? Just went and said: 'Here I am, forgive me?'"

"Why?" he asked himself the next moment, and he ended with the gloomy words: "They'll turn me out."

He read the verses again with sorrow and envy, and fell into a new meditation on the girl. "She's proud. She'll just look at me, and well; I should go away the way I'd come."

In the same newspaper among the official information, he found that the case against Vyera Kapitanovna for robbery would be tried in court on September 23rd.

A malicious feeling flared up in him, and in his thought he addressed Pavel: "Make verses do you? and she—she's in prison!"

"Lord be merciful to me a sinner," murmured Terenti with a sigh, and shook his head sadly. Then he looked at his nephew who was turning over his paper and called to him: "Ilya!"

"Well?"

"Petrusha——" the hunchback smiled sadly and stopped.

"Well—what?"

"He has robbed me!" Terenti explained in a slow, conscience-stricken voice, and smiled again in a melancholy way.

"Serves you right!"

"He's done me fairly!"

"How much did you steal altogether?" asked Ilya quietly. His uncle pushed his chair back from the table, and with his hands on his knees began to twist his fingers.

"Say, ten thousand?" asked Lunev again.

The hunchback turned his head quickly, and said in a long-drawn tone of astonishment.

"T—e—n?"

Then he waved his hand and added:

"Whatever's got into your head? good Lord! Altogether it was three thousand seven hundred and a little over, and you think ten thousand—ten; you've fine ideas!"

"Jeremy had more than ten thousand," said Ilya, laughing mockingly.

"That's a lie!"

"Not a bit; he told me himself."

"Why, could he reckon money?"

"As well as you and Petrusha."

Terenti fell into deep thought, and his head sank again on his breast.

"How much has Petrusha to pay you still?"

"About seven hundred," answered Terenti, with a sigh. "Well, well, more than ten."

Lunev was silent; he hated the sight of his uncle's troubled, disappointed face.

"Where on earth did he hide it all?" asked the hunchback thoughtfully and wonderingly. "I thought we had taken the lot; but perhaps Petrusha had been there already, eh?"

"I wish you'd stop talking of it!" said Lunev harshly.

"Yes, it's no good now; what's the good of talking?" agreed Terenti with another deep sigh.

Lunev could not keep his mind off the greed of mankind, and the evil and miserable meanness practised for money. Then he began to think; if he possessed all this money, ten thousand, a hundred thousand then he'd show the world! How they should creep on all fours before him! Carried away with revengeful feelings, he smashed on the table with his fist; at the blow he started, glanced at his uncle, and saw that he was staring with terrified eyes and mouth half open.

"I was thinking of something," he said moodily, and stood up.

"Yes, of course," said his uncle suspiciously, as Ilya passed into the shop he looked searchingly at Terenti, and saw his lips moving silently; he felt the suspicious look behind his back, though he could not see; he had noticed for some time that his uncle followed his every movement and seemed anxious to find out something, or to ask something. But this only made Lunev anxious to avoid all conversation; every day he felt more plainly that his hunchbacked guest troubled the course of his life, and more and more often he asked himself:

"Will it go on much longer?"

It was as though a cancer were gnawing at his soul; life became daily more wearisome, and worst of all was the sense that he had no longer any desire to do anything. Days passed aimlessly, and often his feeling was that he sank slowly, but every hour deeper, into a bottomless abyss. Convinced that mankind had deeply injured him, he concentrated all the strength of his soul on one point—the bitter sense of injury; he stirred the flames by constant brooding and found therein the exculpation for every fault he had himself committed.

Shortly after Terenti's arrival, Tatiana Vlassyevna appeared, after a holiday spent some distance from the town. When she saw the hunchbacked peasant in brown fustian, she pinched her lips together in disgust and asked Ilya:

"Is that your uncle?"

Three Men| 283

"Yes"

"Is he going to live with you?"

"Naturally."

Tatiana perceived dislike and challenge in her partner's answers and ceased to take any notice of Terenti. But he, who had Gavrik's old place by the door, twisted his yellow beard and followed the small, slender woman in grey clothes with eager curious eyes.

Lunev noticed how she hopped about the shop like a sparrow, and waited silently for further questions, fully prepared to hurl at her rough ill-tempered words. But she spoke no more, after stealing a glance at his grim, cold face, standing at the desk, turning over the leaves of the book of daily sales. She remarked how pleasant it was to spend a couple of weeks in the country, and live in a village; how cheap it was, and how good for the health.

"There was a little stream, so quiet and still, and pleasant company, a telegraph official, for instance, who played the violin beautifully. I learned to row, but the peasant children! a perfect plague! like flies, they worry, and beg and whine—give—give! they learn it from their parents; it's disgusting!"

"No one teaches them anything!" replied Ilya coldly. "Their parents work, and the children live as they can—it's not true what you say."

Tatiana looked at him in astonishment and opened her mouth to speak; but at that moment Terenti smiled propitiatingly and remarked:

"When ladies come to the villages nowadays, that's quite a wonder to the people. Formerly the owner used to live there all his life, and now they only come for a holiday."

Madame Avtonomov looked at him, then at Ilya, and without saying anything fixed her eyes on the book. Terenti was confused, and began to pull at his shirt. For a minute no one spoke in the shop, only the rustling leaves of the book and a kind of purring as Terenti rubbed his hump against the door posts.

"But you," said Ilya's calm, cold voice suddenly, "before you address a lady, say, 'Excuse me, or allow me, and bow.'"

The book fell from Tatiana's hand and slipped over the desk; but she caught it, slapped her hand on it and began to laugh. Terenti went out, hanging his head. Tatiana looked up smiling into Ilya's gloomy face, and asked softly: "You're cross, is it with me? Why?"

Her face was roguish, tender; her eyes shone teasingly. Lunev stretched out his arm and caught her by the shoulder.

All at once his hate against her flared up, a wild tigerish desire to embrace her, to hug her till he heard her bones crack. He drew her towards him, showing his teeth; she caught his hand, tried to loosen his grasp, and whispered:

"Let go, you hurt me, are you mad? you can't kiss me here. And listen: I don't like your uncle being here, he's a hunchback, and people will be afraid of him; let go, I say. We must get rid of him somehow, d'you hear?"

But he held her in his arms and bent his head down to her, with wide-open eyes.

"What are you doing, it's impossible here. Let go!"

Suddenly she let herself sink to the ground and slipped out of his hands like a fish. Through a hot mist he saw her standing in the street door, straightening her jacket with trembling hands: she said:

"Oh, you're brutal! can't you wait, then?"

In his head was a noise of running waters; standing motionless, with fingers intertwined, he looked at her from behind the counter as if in her alone he saw all the evil and sorrow of his life.

"I like you to be passionate, but, my dear, you must be able to control yourself."

"Go!" said Ilya.

"I'm going. I can't see you to-day, but the day after to-morrow, the twenty-third, it's my birthday, will you come?"

As she spoke she fingered her brooch without looking at Ilya.

"Go away!" he repeated, trembling with desire to clutch and torture her.

She went. Almost immediately, Terenti reappeared and asked politely:

"Is that your partner?"

Ilya sighed with relief and nodded.

"A fine lady! isn't she? Small but— —"

"She's a beast!" said Ilya.

"H'm—h'm," growled Terenti suspiciously. Ilya felt the searching look on his face, and asked angrily, "Well what are you looking at?"

"I? good Lord! nothing."

"I know what I'm saying. I said a beast, and that's all about it. And if I said worse things it'd be just as true!"

"A—ha! Is that it? O—Oh!" said the hunchback slowly, with an air of condolence.

"What? cried Ilya roughly.

"Only that."

"Only what?"

Terenti stood shifting from one foot to the other, frightened and hurt at being shouted at; his face was sorrowful and he blinked his eyes rapidly.

"Only, you know best, of course," he said at last.

"And that's enough," cried Ilya. "I know them; these people that are so clean and tidy outside!"

"I talked with the boot boy once," said the hunchback gently, as he sat down, "about his brother, the magistrate sentenced him to seven days, think! The lad said he was such a peaceable fellow, never drunk, and yet all at once he broke out as if he were mad. He got drunk and smashed up everything; hit his master on the nose, and the shopman, and before, think! his master had often struck him and he kept quite quiet, never did anything."

Lunev listened and thought.

"I'll have to drop all this and get away. This beautiful life can go to the devil! There's no life left for me! I'll give it all up and go. I'll get away—here, I'm just going to pieces."

"He bore it, bore everything and then at last bang, like a bombshell!" Terenti went on.

"Who?"

"Why, the boy's brother. He got seven days for assault."

"Ah!"

"Seven days! I say, the fellow had borne it, stood everything, but it had all piled up in his soul like the soot in the chimney, and then all of a sudden it catches fire, and the flames flare up."

"Uncle, look after the shop for a bit! I'm going out," answered Lunev.

His uncle's monotonous, well-meant words rang in his ears as mournfully as the sound of bells in Lent, and it was cold in the shop and there seemed no room to move, but it was hardly more cheerful in the street. It had been raining now for several days steadily. The clean, grey pavement stones stared unwinkingly back at the grey sky, and seemed weary like the faces of men. The dirt in the spaces between the stones, showed up clearly against the cold, clean surface. The air was heavy with damp, and the houses seemed oppressed with it. The yellow leaves still left on the trees seemed to shudder with the knowledge of approaching death.

At the end of the street behind the roofs clouds, bluish-grey or white, rose up to the height of the sky. They shouldered over one another higher and higher, constantly changing their shapes, now like the reek of a bonfire, now like mountains, or waves of a turbid river. They seemed to mount to the summit only to fall the heavier on houses and trees and ground. Lunev grew weary of the moving wall and turned back to the shop, shivering from dreariness and cold.

"I must give it up, the shop and all, uncle can see to it with Tanyka, but I, I'll go away."

In his mind he had a vision of a wet, boundless plain, arched by grey clouds; there was a broad road set with birch-trees; he himself walked forward, his knapsack on his back; his feet stuck fast in the mud, a cold rain drove in his face, and on the plain and on the road no living soul, not even crows on the branches.

"I'll hang myself," he thought, without emotion, when he saw that he had no place to go to, nowhere in all the world.

CHAPTER XXV

When he awoke on the morning of the next day but one, he saw on his calendar the black figure 23, and remembered that this was the day that Vyera would appear for trial. He rejoiced at the excuse to get away from the shop, and felt keen curiosity over the girl's fate. He dressed hastily, drank his tea, almost ran to the court, and reached it too early. No one was admitted yet—a little crowd of people pressed about the steps, waiting for the doors to open; Lunev took his place with the rest and leant his back against the wall. There was an open space before the court-house, with a big church in the middle of it. Shadows swept over the ground. The sun's disc, dim and pale, now appeared, now vanished behind the clouds. Almost every moment a shadow fell widely over the square, gliding over the stones, climbing the trees, so that the branches seemed to bend under its weight; then it wrapped the church from base to cross, covered it entirely, then noiselessly moved further to the court of justice and the waiting crowd.

The people all looked strangely grey, with hungry faces; they looked at one another with tired eyes and spoke slowly. One—a long-haired man in a light overcoat buttoned to his chin and a crushed hat, twisted his pointed red beard with cold red fingers, and stamped the ground impatiently with his worn out shoes. Another in a patched waistcoat, and cap pulled down over his brows, stood with bent head, one hand in his bosom, the other in his pocket. He seemed asleep. A little swarthy man in an overcoat and high boots looking like a cockchafer, moved about restlessly. He looked up to the sky showing a pale pointed little nose, whistled, wrinkled his brows, ran his tongue over the edge of his moustache and spoke more than all the others.

"Are they opening?" he called, listening with his head on one side.

"No—h'm. Time is cheap! Been to the library yet, my boy?"

"No—too early," answered the long-haired man briefly.

"The Devil! it *is* cold!"

The other growled agreement and said thoughtfully:

"Where should we warm ourselves if it weren't for the law courts and the libraries?"

The dark man shrugged his shoulders. Ilya looked at them more carefully and listened. He saw they were loafers—people who passed their lives in various "shady" businesses either cheating the peasants, for whom they drew up petitions or papers of different kinds, or going from house to house with begging letters. Once he had feared them, now they roused his curiosity.

"What's the good of these people? Yet, they live."

A pair of pigeons settled on the pavement near the steps. The man with the bent head swayed from one foot to the other and began to circle round the birds, making a loud cooing noise.

"Pfui!" whistled the dark little man sharply. The man in the waistcoat started and looked up; his face was blue and swollen, and his eyes glassy.

"I can't stand pigeons," cried the little man watching them as they flew away. "Fat—as rich tradesmen—and their beastly cooing! Are you summoned?" he asked Ilya, unexpectedly.

"No."

"You're not called?"

"No."

The dark man looked Ilya up and down and growled: "That's strange."

"What is strange?" asked Ilya, laughing.

"You have the kind of face," answered the little man speaking quickly. "Ah, they're opening."

He was one of the first to enter the building. Struck by his remark Ilya followed him and in the doorway pushed the long-haired man with his shoulder.

"Don't shove so, you clown!" said the man half aloud, and giving Ilya a push in his turn passed in first. The push did not anger Ilya, but only astonished him.

"Odd!" he thought. "He pushes in as if he were a great lord and must go in first, and he's only just a poor wretch."

In the court of justice it was dark and quiet. The long table covered with a green cloth, the high-backed chairs, the gold frames round the big full-length portraits, the mulberry coloured chairs for the jury, the big wooden bench behind the railing—all this inspired respect and a sense of gravity. The windows were set deep in gray walls; curtains of canvas hung in heavy folds in front of them, and the window panes looked dim. The heavy doors opened without noise, and people in uniform walked here and there with rapid silent steps. Everything in the big room seemed to bid the spectators to remain quiet and still. Lunev looked round him, and a painful sensation caught at his heart; when an official announced—"The Court," he started and sprang up before any one else, though he did not know that he was expected to rise. One of the four men who entered was Gromov, who lived in the house opposite Ilya's shop. He took the middle chair, ran both his hands over his hair, rumpling it a little and settled the gold-trimmed collar of his uniform. The sight of his face had a calming effect on Ilya; it was just as jolly and red-cheeked as ever, only the ends of the moustache were turned up. On his right sat a good-natured looking old man with a little, grey beard, a blunt nose, and spectacles—on the left a bald-headed man with a divided foxy beard, and a yellow, expressionless face. Besides these a young judge stood at a desk, with a round head, smoothly plastered hair, and black prominent eyes. They were all silent for a few moments, looking through the papers on the table. Lunev looked at them full of respect and waited for one of them to rise and say something loudly and importantly. But suddenly, turning his head to the left Ilya saw the well-known fat face of Petrusha Filimonov shining as if it were lacquered. Petrusha sat in the front row of the jury, with his head against the back of the chair looking placidly at the public. Twice his glance passed over Ilya, and both times Ilya felt a wish to stand up and say something to Petrusha or to Gromov or to all the people.

"Thief, who killed his son!" flamed through his brain, and there was a feeling in his throat like heartburn.

"You are therefore accused," said Gromov in a friendly voice, but Ilya did not see who was addressed; he looked at Petrusha's face, oppressed with doubt and could not reconcile himself to the thought that Filimonov should be a dispenser of justice.

"Now, tell us," asked the president, rubbing his forehead. "You said to the tradesman Anissimov, you wait! I'll pay you for this!"

A ventilator squeaked somewhere, "ee—oo, ee—oo."

Among the jury Ilya saw two other faces he knew. Behind Petrusha and above him sat a worker in stucco—Silatschev, a big peasant's figure with long arms and little ill-tempered face, a friend of Filimonov and his constant companion at cards. It was told of Silatschev, that once in a quarrel he had pushed his master from a scaffolding, with fatal result. And in the front row, two places from Petrusha sat Dodonov, the proprietor of a big fancy-ware shop. Ilya bought from him and knew him for hard and grasping and a man who had been twice bankrupt, and paid his creditors only ten per cent.

"Witness! when did you see that Anissimov's house was on fire?"

The ventilator lamented steadily, seeming to echo the sadness in Lunev's breast.

"Fool!" said the man next him in a whisper. Ilya looked round, it was the little dark man who now sat with his lips contemptuously drawn.

"A fool," he repeated, nodding to Ilya.

"Who?" whispered Ilya stupidly.

"The accused—he had a fine chance to upset the witness and lets it go. If I—ah."

Ilya looked at the prisoner. He was a tall, bony peasant with an angular head. His face was terrified and gloomy; he showed his teeth like a tired, beaten dog, crowded into a corner by its foes and without strength to defend itself. Stupid, animal fear was impressed on every feature; and Petrusha, Silatschev and Dodonov looked at him quietly with the eyes of the well fed. To Lunev it seemed as though they thought: "He's been caught— that is, he is guilty."

"Dull!" whispered his neighbour. "Nothing interesting. The accused—a fool, the Public Prosecutor a gaping idiot, the witnesses blockheads as usual. If I were Prosecutor I'd settle his job in ten minutes."

"Guilty?" asked Lunev in a whisper, shivering as if with cold.

"Probably not. But easy to condemn him. He doesn't know how to defend himself. These peasants never do. A poor lot! Bones and muscles— but intelligence, quickness—not a glimmer!"

"That is true. Ye—es."

"Have you by any chance twenty kopecks about you?" asked the little man suddenly.

"Oh, yes."

"Give it to me."

Ilya had taken out his purse and handed over the piece of money, before he could make up his mind whether to give it or no. When he had parted with it he thought with an involuntary respect as he looked sideways at his neighbour:

"He's quick, but that's the way to live; just take——"

"A stupid ass, that's all," whispered the dark man again, and indicated the accused with his eyes.

"Sh!—sh!" said the usher.

"Gentlemen of the jury," began the Prosecutor with a low but emphatic voice, "look at the face of this man—it is more eloquent than any testimony of the witnesses who have given their evidence without contradiction—er—er—it must be so—it must convince you that a typical criminal stands before you, an enemy of law and order, an enemy of society—stands before you."

The enemy of society was sitting down; but as it evidently troubled him to sit while he was being spoken of, he stood up slowly with bent head. His arms hung feebly by his sides, and the long gray figure bowed as though before the vengeance of justice.

Lunev let his head fall also. His heart was sick, almost to death; helpless thoughts circled slowly and heavily in his head—he could find no words for them, and they fought him and strangled him. Petrusha's red, uneasy face drifted through his thoughts, as the moon through clouds.

When Gromov announced the adjournment of the sitting Ilya went out into the corridor with the little man who took a damaged cigarette from his coat pocket, pressed it into shape and began:

"The silly fellow stands there and swears he has not kindled the fire. Oaths are no good here. It's a serious business—some shopkeeper's been injured—you have done it or another—that doesn't matter. What does matter is to have it punished—you walk into the net. Very well, you shall be punished."

"Do you think he's guilty, that fellow?" asked Ilya thoughtfully.

"Of course he's guilty, because he's stupid; clever people don't get condemned," said the little man calmly and quickly, and smoked his cigarette vigorously. He had little black eyes like a mouse, and his teeth were also small-pointed and mouse-like.

"In that jury," began Ilya slowly and with emphasis, "there are men."

"Not men, tradesmen," the dark-headed man improved the phrase. Ilya looked at him and repeated:

"Tradesmen. I know some of them."

"Aha!"

"A fine sort—not to put it too finely."

"Thieves—eh?" his companion helped him out. He spoke loudly, but in an ordinary way, then threw away his cigarette end, pinched up his lips in a loud whistle and looked at Ilya with eyes bold almost to insolence; all these movements followed one another in eager restlessness.

"Of course; anyway, justice so-called is mostly a pretty good farce," he said shrugging. "The fat people improve the criminal tendencies of the hungry people. I often come to the courts, but I never saw a hungry man sit in judgment on the well fed—if the well fed do it among themselves—it happens generally from extra greed and means—don't take everything, leave me some!"

"It also means—the well fed can't understand the hungry," said Ilya.

"Oh, nonsense!" answered his companion. "They understand all right—that's what makes them so severe."

"Well—well fed and honourable—that might pass!" Ilya went on half aloud. "But well fed scoundrels, how can they judge other men?"

"The scoundrels are the severest judges," the black-haired man announced quietly.

"Now, sir, we'll hear a case of robbery."

"It's some one I know," said Lunev softly.

"Ah!" cried the little man and shot a glance at him. "Let us have a look at your acquaintance!"

In Ilya's head all was confusion. He wanted to question this clever little man about many things, but the words rattled in his brain like peas in a basket. There was in the man something unpleasant, dangerous, that frightened Ilya, but at once the persistent thought of Petrusha in the seat of justice, swamped every other idea. The thought forged an iron ring round his heart and kept out every other.

As he drew near to the door of the hall he saw in the crowd in front of him the thick neck and small ears of Pavel Gratschev. Overjoyed, he twitched Pavel by the sleeve and smiled in his face; Pavel smiled too, but feebly, with evident effort.

"How are you?"

"How are you?"

They stood for a few moments in silence, and the thought of each was expressed almost simultaneously.

"Come to see?" asked Pavel with a wry smile.

"She—is she here?" asked Ilya.

"Who?"

"Why—your Sophie Nik——"

"She isn't mine," answered Pavel, interrupting coldly.

Both went into the hall without further speech. "Sit near me!" asked Lunev.

Pavel stammered. "You see—I—I'm with some people."

"Oh, very well."

"I say—d'you know," added Pavel quickly. "Listen to what her advocate says."

"I'll listen," said Ilya quietly, and added in a lower voice: "So—good-bye—brother."

"Good-bye—we'll meet presently."

Gratschev turned away and walked quickly to one side. Ilya looked at him with the sensation that Pavel had rubbed an open wound. Burning sorrow possessed him, and an envious, evil feeling to see his friend in a good new overcoat, looking, too, healthier, clearer in the face. Gavrik's sister sat on the same bench with Pavel; he said something to her, and she turned her head quickly to Lunev. When he saw her expressive, eager face, he turned away and his soul was wrapped more firmly and densely in dark feelings of injury, enmity and inability to understand. His thoughts stormed giddily in his head like a whirlwind, one tangled in another; suddenly they stopped—vanished; he felt a void in his brain, and everything outside seemed to move against him malevolently—and he ceased to follow the course of events.

Vyera had already been brought in. She stood behind the railing in a grey dress, reaching to her heels like a night-gown, with a white kerchief. A strand of yellow hair lay against her left temple, her cheeks were pale, her lips compressed, and her eyes, widely opened, rested earnestly and immovably on Gromov.

"Yes—yes—no—yes," her voice rang in Ilya's ears, as though muffled.

Gromov looked at her kindly, and spoke in a subdued low voice like a cat purring.

"And do you plead guilty, Kapitanovna, that on that night——" his insinuating voice glided on.

Lunev looked at Pavel; he sat bent forward, his head down, twisting his fur cap in his hands. His neighbour, however, sat straight and upright, and looked as though she were sitting in judgment on every one there, Vyera and the judges and the public. Her head turned often from side to side, her lips were compressed scornfully, and her proud eyes glanced coldly and sternly from under her wrinkled brows.

"I plead guilty," said Vyera. Her voice broke and the sound was like the ring of a cup that is cracked.

Two of the jury, Dodonov and his neighbour, a red-haired, clean-shaven man, bent their heads together, moved their lips silently, and their eyes, that rested on the girl, smiled. Petrusha, holding with both hands to his chair, bent his whole body forward; his face was even redder than usual and the ends of his moustache twitched; others of the jury looked at Vyera, all with the same definite attentiveness, which Lunev understood but hated furiously.

"They sit in judgment, and every one of them looks at her lustfully!" he thought, and clenched his teeth; he longed to call out to Petrusha:

"You rascal! what are you thinking? Where are you? What is your duty?"

Something stuck in his throat, like a heavy ball, and hampered his breath.

"Tell me, Kapitanovna," said Gromov lazily, while his eyes stood out like those of a lustful he-goat, "have you-ah—practised prostitution long?"

Vyera passed her hand over her face as though the question stuck fast to her fiery red cheeks.

"A long time."

She answered firmly. A whisper ran among the people like a snake. Gratschev bowed lower as though he would hide, and twisted his cap ceaselessly.

"About how long?"

Vyera said nothing, but looked earnestly, seriously at Gromov out of her wide-open eyes:

"One year? Two? Five?" persisted the president.

She was still silent; her grey figure stood as though hewn from stone, only the ends of her kerchief quivered on her breast.

"You have the right not to reply, if you wish," said Gromov, stroking his beard.

Now an advocate sprang up, a thin man with a small pointed beard and long eyes. His nose was long and thin, and the nape of his neck wide so that his face looked like a hatchet.

"Say, what compelled you to adopt this, this profession!" he said loudly and clearly.

"Nothing compelled me," answered Vyera, her eyes fixed on the judge's.

"H'm, that's not altogether correct; you see, I know, you told me."

"You know nothing!" answered Vyera.

She turned her head towards him, and looking at him sternly, went on angrily:

"I told you nothing, you yourself have made it all up!"

Her eyes glanced quickly over the audience, then she turned back to the judges and asked with a movement of her head towards her defender:

"Need I answer him?"

A new hissing whisper crawled through the room, but louder and plainer. Ilya shivered with the tension and looked at Gratschev. He expected something from him, awaited it with confidence. But Pavel, looking out from behind the shoulders of the people in front of him, sat silent and motionless. Gromov smiled and said, his words were smooth and oily; then Vyera began not loudly but quite firmly:

"It's quite simple. I wanted to be rich, so I took it, that is all, there's nothing else, and I was always like that."

The jury began to whisper together; their faces grew dark and displeasure appeared on the features of the judges. The room was still; from the street came the dull regular sound of footsteps on the pavement; soldiers were marching by outside.

"In view of the prisoner's confession," said the Prosecutor.

Ilya felt he could sit still no longer. He got up, and took a step forward.

"Sh—silence!" said the usher loudly. He sat down again and hung his head like Pavel. He could not see Petrusha's red face, now puffed out importantly, and apparently annoyed at something; but for all the unaltered friendliness of Gromov's face, he saw a cold heart behind the kind demeanour of the judge, and he understood that this cheerful man was accustomed to condemn men and women as a joiner is to plane boards. And an angry, oppressive thought rose in Ilya's mind:

"If I confessed, it would be the same with me. Petrusha would judge; to the prison with me, while he stays here."

At this he stopped and sat there, to listen, seeing nobody.

"I will not have you speak of it," came in a trembling, sorrowful cry from Vyera; she screamed, cried, caught at her breast, and tore the kerchief from her head.

"I will not. I will not."

A confused noise filled the room.

The girl's cry set all in movement, but she threw herself down behind the railing as though burnt, and sobbed heart-brokenly.

"Don't torture me, let me go, for Christ's sake!"

Ilya sprang up and tried to force his way forward, but the people opposed him and before he could realize it he found himself in the corridor.

"They've stripped her soul," said the voice of the black-haired man.

Pavel, pale, and with dishevelled hair, stood against the wall, his jaw quivering. Ilya went up to him and scowled at him in anger; people stood or moved round them talking eagerly. There was a smell of tobacco smoke in the air.

"It's imprisonment! She can scream till she's tired, it's all the same."

"She confessed, little fool!"

"But they found the money."

"Why didn't she say he gave it to her."

The words buzzed about the corridor like autumn flies, and penetrated into Ilya's ears.

"What?" he asked Pavel gloomily and angrily, going quite close to him.

Pavel looked at him and opened his mouth but said nothing.

"You've ruined a human being," said Lunev. Pavel started as though he had been lashed with a whip; he raised his hand, laid it on Ilya's shoulder, and asked in a sorrowful voice:

"Is it my fault?"

Ilya shook off the hand from his shoulder; he wanted to say: "you—oh! don't be afraid, no one called out that it was for you she stole," but he said instead, "and Petrusha Filimonov to condemn her, that's as it should be, isn't it?" and laughed.

Then with scorn in his face he went out into the street, and went slowly along with a sense as though he were fast bound by invisible cords. Anxiety lay like a heavy stone on his heart; it sent a coldness through him confusing his thoughts, and until the evening he wandered about aimlessly, from street to street, like a stray dog, tired and hungry. No wish, no desire moved within him, and he saw nothing of all that passed round about him, till at last a sick feeling of hunger roused him from his brooding.

CHAPTER XXVI

It was already dark; lights shone in the houses, broad yellow streaks fell across the road, and against them stood out the shadows of the flowers in the windows. Lunev stood still, and the sight of these shadows reminded him of Gromov's house, of the lady who was like the queen in a fairy tale, and the sorrowful songs that did not disturb the laughter—a cat came cautiously across the street, shaking its paws.

He went on till he reached a place of four cross roads, then stood still again. One of the houses at the corner was brilliantly lighted up, and from it came the sound of music.

"I'll go into the Restaurant," Ilya decided, and began to cross the road.

"Look out!" cried a voice. The black head of a horse sprang up close to his face—he felt its warm breath. He jumped to one side, while the droshky driver swore at him; he went on away from the tavern.

"There's no fun in being run over," he thought quietly. "I must get something to eat!—and now Vyera is done for."

His mind ran still on the girl, his thoughts revolved about her almost mechanically. All the time he felt with one small part of his brain, that he ought to be thinking of himself, and not of Vyera, but he had no strength of will to change the course of his reflections.

"She's proud too—she wouldn't say a word of Pashka—saw that it was no good, there—she's the best of the lot—Olympiada would have. No! Olympiada was a good sort too—but Tanyka."

Suddenly he remembered that to-day Tatiana Vlassyevna had a birthday festivity, and that he was invited. At first he felt quite disinclined to go, but almost at once came an ill-tempered desire to compel himself against his wish, and then a sharp burning sensation shot through his heart. He called a droshky, and, a few minutes later, stood at the dining-room door, blinking his eyes in the strong light. He looked at the company sitting packed round the table in the big room, with a stupid smile.

"Ah! there he is at last!" cried Kirik.

"How pale he is!" said Tatiana.

"Have you brought any sweetmeats? a birthday present, eh? What's the matter, my friend?"

"Where have you come from?" asked his hostess.

Kirik caught him by the sleeve, and led him round the table presenting him to the guests. Lunev pressed several warm hands, but the faces swam before his eyes, and blended into one long cold face, smiling politely and showing big teeth. The reek of cooking tickled his nose; the chattering of the women sounded in his ears like rushing rain; his eyes were hot, a dull pain prevented him from moving them, and a coloured mist seemed to widen out before them. When he sat down he felt that his knees were aching with weariness, while hunger gnawed his entrails. He took a piece of bread and began to eat. One of the guests blew his nose loudly, while Tatiana said:

"Won't you congratulate me? You're a nice person! You come here, and say nothing, and sit down and begin to eat."

Beneath the table she pressed her foot hard on his, and bent over the teapot as she poured him out his tea. Ilya heard her whisper through the noise of pouring,

"Behave yourself properly!"

He put his bread back on the table, rubbed his hands, and said loudly. "I've been at the law courts all day."

His voice dominated the noise of conversation, and there was a silence among the guests. Lunev was confused as he felt their glances on his face, and looked back at them stupidly from under his brows. They looked at him a little suspiciously, as though doubting if this broad-shouldered, curly-haired youth could have anything interesting to relate. An embarrassed silence continued in the room. Isolated thoughts circled in Ilya's brain— disconnected and gray, they seemed to sink and suddenly disappear in the darkness of his soul.

"Sometimes it's very interesting in the courts," remarked Madame Felizata Yegarovna Grislova, nibbling a piece of marmalade cake. Red patches appeared on Tatiana's cheeks, Kirik blew his nose loudly and said:

"Well, brother, you begin, but you don't go on. You were at the court— —?"

"I'll let them have it!" thought Ilya, and smiled slowly. The conversation began again here and there.

"I once heard a murder trial," said a young telegraph official, a pale dark-eyed man with a small moustache.

"I love to read or hear about murders," cried Madame Travkina; her husband looked round the table and said, "Public trials are an excellent institution."

"It was a friend of mine, Yevgeniyev—you see he was on duty in the strong room, got playing with a young fellow and shot him by accident."

"Ah—how horrible!" cried Tatiana.

"Dead as a door nail!" added the telegraph official, with distinct enjoyment.

"I was called as a witness once," began Travkin now in a dry, creaking voice, "and I heard a man condemned who had carried out twenty-three robberies—not so bad, eh?"

Kirik laughed loudly. The company fell into two groups, one listening to the tale of the boy who was shot, the other to the drawling remarks of Travkin on the man who had carried out twenty-three robberies. Ilya looked at his hostess, and felt a little flame begin to flicker within him— it illuminated nothing but caused a persistent burning at his heart. From the moment he realised that the Avtonomovs were anxious lest he should commit some solecism before their guests, his thoughts became clearer as though he had found a clue to their course.

Tatiana Vlassyevna was busy in the next room at a table covered with bottles. Her bright red silk blouse flamed against the white walls; in her tightly-laced corset she flitted about like a butterfly, all the pride of the skilful housewife shining in her face. Twice Ilya saw her beckon him to her with quick, hardly noticeable gestures, but he did not go and felt glad to think that his refusal would disturb her.

"Why, brother, you're sitting there like an owl!" said Kirik, suddenly. "Say something—don't be afraid—these are educated people who won't be offended with you!"

"There was a girl being tried," Ilya began loudly all at once, "a girl I know, she is a prostitute, but she's a good girl for all that."

Again he attracted the attention of the company, and all eyes were once more fixed on him. Felizata Yegarovna showed her big teeth in a broad, mocking smile; the telegraph official twisted his moustache, covering his mouth with his hand; almost all tried hard to seem serious and attentive. Tatiana suddenly dropped a handful of knives and forks, and the clash rang in Ilya's heart like loud martial music. He looked quietly round the company with widely opened eyes and went on:

"Why do you smile? There are good girls among— —"

"Quite possible," Kirik interrupted, "but you needn't be quite so frank about it."

"These are cultivated people," said Ilya, "if I say anything that is unusual, they won't be offended."

A whole sheaf of bright sparks shot up suddenly in his breast; a sneering smile appeared on his face, and he felt almost choked with the flood of words that poured from his brain.

"This girl had stolen some money from a merchant."

"Better and better," cried Kirik, and shook his head with a comical grimace.

"You can readily imagine under what circumstances she stole it, but perhaps she did not steal it, perhaps he gave it to her."

"Tanitshka!" cried Kirik, "come here a minute! Ilya's telling such anecdotes."

But Tatiana was already close to Ilya, and said with a forced smile and a shrug of her shoulders: "What's the fuss about? It's a very ordinary story; you, Kirik, know hundreds of cases like that, there are no young girls here. But let us leave that till later, shan't we?—and now we'll have something to eat."

"Yes, of course," cried Kirik, "I'm ready, he! he! Clever conversation is all very well, but— —"

"Anyhow, it gives an appetite," said Travkin, and stroked his throat.

All turned away from Ilya. He understood that the guests did not want to hear, that his hosts were anxious he should not continue, and the thought spurred him on. He rose from his chair and said, addressing the company:

"And men sat in judgment on this girl, who perhaps had themselves more than once made use of her. I know some of them, and to call them rascals is to put it mildly."

"Excuse me," said Travkin, firmly, holding up a finger, "you must not speak like that! They're a sworn jury, and I myself— —"

"Quite right, they're sworn in," cried Ilya. "But can men like that judge fairly if— —"

"Excuse me, the jury system is one of the great reforms instituted by the Czar Alexander the Second. How can you make such aspersions on a state institution?"

He hurled his words in Ilya's face, and his fat, smooth-shaved cheeks shook, and his eyes rolled right and left. The company crowded round in the hope of a rousing scandal. Felizata Yegarovna looked at her hostess condescendingly, and Tatiana, pale and excited, plucked her guests by the sleeve and called hurriedly:

"Oh, do let that alone! it is so uninteresting. Kirik, ask the ladies and gentlemen— —"

Kirik looked distractedly here and there and cried: "Please, for my sake, these reforms, and all this philosophy— —"

"This is not philosophy, it's politics," croaked Travkin, "and people who express opinions like this gentleman are called untrustworthy politicians."

A hot whirlwind swept round Ilya. He rejoiced to oppose this fat, smooth-shaved, wet-lipped man, and see him grow angry. The consciousness that the Avtonomovs felt embarrassed before their guests filled him with malicious pleasure.

He grew calmer, and the impulse to have matters out with these people, to say insolent things to them and drive them to fury, swelled up in his breast, and raised him to a mental height that was at once pleasant and terrifying. Every moment he felt calmer, and his voice sounded more and more assured.

"Call me what you like," he said to Travkin. "You are an educated man. I hold to my opinion, and I say, 'can the well fed understand the hungry?' The hungry man may be a thief, but the well fed was a thief before him."

"Kirik Nikodimovitch!" shouted Travkin in fury. "What does this mean? I—I cannot— —"

At this moment Tatiana Vlassyevna slipped her arm through his and drew him away, saying loudly:

"Come along, the little rolls you like are here, with herrings and hard-boiled eggs, and grated onions with melted butter."

"Ha! I ought not to let this pass," said Travkin, still excited, and smacked his lips. His wife looked contemptuously at Ilya, and took her husband's other arm, saying: "Don't excite yourself, Anton, over such foolishness!"

Tatiana continued to quiet her most honoured guest. "Pickled sturgeon with tomato——"

"That was not right, young man," said Travkin suddenly, in a tone both reproachful and magnanimous, standing firm and turning round towards Ilya. "That was not right! you should know how to value things—you need to understand them."

"But I don't understand," cried Ilya, "that's just what I'm talking about. How does it come about that Petrusha Filimonov is the lord of life and death?"

The guests went past Ilya without looking at him, and carefully avoided even touching his clothes. Kirik, however, came close up to him, and said in a harsh, insulting voice, "Go to the devil, you clown, that's what you are!"

Ilya started, a mist came over his eyes as though he had received a blow on the head, and he moved threateningly against Avtonomov with his fist clenched. But Kirik had already turned away without heeding his movements, and entered the other room. Ilya groaned aloud. He stood in the doorway, regarding the backs of the people round the table, and heard them eating noisily. The bright blouse of the hostess seemed to colour everything red, and make a cloud before his eyes.

"Ah," said Travkin. "This is good, quite excellent."

"Have some pepper with it?" asked the hostess tenderly.

"I'll add the pepper," thought Lunev scornfully. He was strung to the highest tension, and in two strides was standing by the table with head erect. He grasped the first glass of wine he saw, held it out towards Tatiana Vlassyevna, and said clearly and sharply, as though he would stab her with the words:

"To your health, Tanyka!"

His words had an effect on the company as though the lights had gone out with a deafening crash, and every one stood frozen to the floor in dense darkness. The half-open mouths, with their unswallowed morsels, looked like wounds on their terror-stricken faces.

"Come! let us drink! Kirik Nikodimovitch, tell my mistress to drink with me! Don't be disturbed—what do these others matter? Why should we sin always in secret? Let us deal openly. I have resolved, you see, from henceforth everything shall be done openly."

"You beast!" screamed the piercing voice of Tatiana.

Ilya saw her hand shoot out, and struck aside the plate she hurled at him. The crash of the flying pieces added to the confusion of the guests. They crept aside slowly and noiselessly, leaving Ilya alone face to face with the Avtonomovs. Kirik was holding a small fish by the tail, and blinked, looking pale and miserable and almost idiotic. Tatiana Vlassyevna shook in every limb, and threatened Ilya with her fists; her face was the colour of her dress, and her tongue could hardly form a word.

"You liar—you liar!" she hissed, stretching out her head towards Ilya.

"Shall I mention some of your birthmarks?" said Ilya quietly, "and your husband shall say if I speak the truth or no."

There was a murmur in the room and suppressed laughter. Tatiana stretched up her arms, caught at her throat and sank on a chair without a sound.

"Police!" cried the telegraph official. Kirik turned round at the cry, then suddenly ran at Ilya headlong. Ilya stretched out his arms and pushed him away as he came, shouting roughly,

"Where are you coming?—you're too impatient. I can send you flying with one blow. Listen—all of you—listen, you'll hear the truth for once."

Kirik paid no attention, but bent his head forward and attacked again. The guests looked on silently; no one moved except Travkin, who went quietly on tiptoe into a corner, sat down on the seat by the stove and put his clasped hands between his knees.

"Look out. I'll hit you!" Ilya warned the furious Kirik. "I've no wish to hurt you—you're a stupid ass, but you never did me any harm—get away."

He pushed Kirik off again, this time more forcibly, and got his own back against the wall. Here he stood and began to speak, his eyes travelling over the company.

"Your wife threw herself into my arms. Oh, she's clever—but vicious! In the whole world there's no one worse. But all of you—all are vicious and degraded. I was in the court to-day—there I learnt to judge."

He had so much to say, that he was in no condition to arrange his thoughts, and hurled them like fragments of rock.

"But I will not condemn Tanya—it just happened so—just of itself—as long as I've lived, everything seems to happen of itself—as if by accident. I strangled a man by accident. I didn't mean to, but I strangled him—and think, Tanyka—the money I stole from him is the money that helps to carry on our business!"

"He's mad," cried Kirik in sudden joy, and sprang round the room from one to the other, crying with joy and excitement.

"D'you hear? d'you see? he's out of his mind! Ah, Ilya—oh you—how you hurt me!"

Ilya laughed aloud; his heart was easier and lighter now that he had spoken of the murder. He hardly felt the floor under his feet, and seemed to rise higher and higher. Broad-shouldered and sturdy, he stood there before them all with head erect, and chest thrown out. His black curls framed his high pale brow and temples, and his eyes were full of scorn and malice.

Tatiana got up, tottered to Felizata Yegarovna, and said in a trembling voice:

"I've seen it coming on—a long time—his eyes have looked so wild and terrible for ever so long."

"If he's mad, we must call the police," said Felizata, looking in Ilya's face.

"Mad? of course he's mad!" cried Kirik.

"He may attack us all," whispered Gryslov, and looked anxiously round the room.

All were afraid to move.

Lunev stood close to the door, and whoever wanted to go out had to pass him. He laughed again; he loved to see how these people feared him, and when he looked at their faces, he saw that they had no compassion for their hosts, and would have listened all night, while he held them up to scorn, had they not themselves been afraid of him.

"I am not mad," he said, and his brows contracted, "I only want you to stay here and listen. I won't let you out, and if you come near I'll strike you—and if I kill you—I am strong."

He held up a long arm and powerful fist, shook it, and let it drop again.

"Tell me," he went on, "what sort of men are you? What do you live for? Such stingy wretches—such a rabble!"

"Here, listen—you—you shut up!" cried Kirik.

"Shut up yourself! I will speak now. I look at you—stuffing and swilling, and lying to one another—and loving no one. What do you want in this world? I have striven for a clean honourable life—there's no such thing. Nowhere is there such a thing. I have only soiled and destroyed myself. A good man cannot live among you—he must go under—you kill good men—and I—I am bad, but among you I'm like a feeble cat in a dark cellar among a thousand rats—you—are everywhere! You judge, you rule—you make the laws—you wretches—you have devoured me—destroyed me."

Suddenly a deep sorrow overcame him.

"And now—what am I to do now?" he asked, and his head sank and he fell into a dull brooding. In a moment the telegraph official sprang by him and slipped out of the room.

"Ah! I've let one get away!" said Ilya, and held his head up again.

"I'll fetch the police!" came a cry from the next room.

"I don't care—fetch them!" said Ilya.

Tatiana went by him, tottering, walking as if asleep, without looking at him.

"She's had enough," said Lunev with a scornful nod at her, "but she deserves it, the snake."

"Shut up!" cried Avtonomov from his corner; he was on his knees fumbling in a box.

"Don't shout, good stupid fellow," answered Ilya, sitting down and crossing his arms, "Why do you shout? I've lived with you, I know you—I killed a man too—Poluektov the merchant. I've spoken of it with you ever so many times, do you remember? I did it because it was I who strangled him—and his money is in our business—by God!"

Ilya looked round the room. Terrified and trembling the guests stood round the walls in silence. He felt that he had said his say, that a yawning, melancholy emptiness was growing in his breast, from which echoed the cold inquiry:

"What now?" and he said, listening to the ring of his own words:

"Perhaps you think I'm sorry, that I'm making amends here before you all? Ha! ha! you can wait for that. I rejoice over you—do you understand?"

Kirik sprang from his corner, dishevelled and red; he brandished a revolver, and rolled his eyes and shouted:

"Now you shan't escape! Aha! you have murdered, too, have you?"

The women screamed, Travkin sprang from the bench where he had been sitting and running aimlessly to and fro croaked: "Let me go—I can't bear it—Let me go!—this is a family affair."

But Avtonomov paid no attention; he ran backwards and forwards before Ilya aiming at him and screaming:

"Penal servitude! wait—that's what we'll give you."

"Listen—your pistol is not even loaded, is it?" asked Ilya indifferently, looking at him wearily, "why do you make such a fuss? I shan't run away. I don't know where to go. Penal servitude, eh? Well, as for that, it's all one to me now."

"Anton! Anton!" shrieked Madame Travkin. "Come at once!"

"I can't, my dear, I can't."

She took his arm, and both slipped by Ilya, huddled together, with bowed heads. Tatiana sat in the next room, whimpering and sobbing, and in Lunev's breast the dark cold feeling of emptiness grew and grew.

"All my life is ruined," he said slowly and thoughtfully, "and there's nothing to be pitied about—who has destroyed it?"

Avtonomov stood in front of him and cried triumphantly:

"Aha! how you want to work on our feelings! but you won't."

"I don't want that, go to the devil all of you! I shall not make you sorry, the only thing that can do that is the money that doesn't reach your pocket, nor am I sorry for you. I'd far sooner pity a dog. I'd rather live with dogs than with men. Ah! why don't the police come. I am tired; get out, Kirik, I can't bear the sight of you."

It really troubled him to sit opposite Avtonomov. The guests left the room, slipped out softly with anxious glances at Ilya. He saw nothing but grey flecks floating before him, that roused in him neither thought nor feeling. The emptiness in his soul grew and enfolded everything. He was silent for a space, listening to Avtonomov's cries, then suddenly proposed jestingly:

"Come Kirik, come and wrestle."

"I'll put a bullet in you," growled Kirik.

"You haven't a bullet there," answered Ilya mockingly, and added, "I'll throw you in a minute!"

After that he said nothing, but sat there without moving, without thinking. At last two policemen came with the district inspector. Lunev shuddered at the sight of them, and stood up; close behind them came Tatiana Vlassyevna, she pointed to Ilya, and said in breathless haste:

"He has confessed that he murdered Poluektov the money-changer, you remember?"

"Do you admit that?" asked the inspector harshly.

"Oh yes! I admit it," answered Ilya, quietly and wearily. "Good-bye Tanyka, don't trouble, don't be afraid, and for the rest of you, go to the devil!"

The inspector sat down at the table, and began to write; the two policemen stood right and left of Lunev; he looked at them, sighed and let his head fall. The room was still, save for the scratching of the pen; outside in the street, the night built up its black impenetrable walls. Kirik stood by the window, and looked out into the darkness; suddenly he threw the revolver into a corner of the room, and said:

"Savelyev! give him a kick and let him go, he's quite mad."

The official looked at Kirik, thought a moment, and answered: "Can't now, information's been laid before me, my assistant knows."

"A—ah! sighed Avtonomov.

"You're a good fellow, Kirik Nikodimovitch," said Ilya and nodded. "There are dogs like that, you beat them and they fawn on you, but perhaps you're afraid I shall speak of your wife in court? Don't be afraid, that won't happen! I'm ashamed to think of her, much less speak of her."

Avtonomov went quickly into the next room, and sat down noisily on a chair.

"Now," began the inspector, turning to Ilya, "can you sign this?"

"Yes, I will."

He took the pen and signed without reading, in big letters, Ilya Lunev. When he raised his head, he noticed that the inspector was gazing at him with astonishment. They looked at one another silently for a moment or two, one with curiosity and a certain pleasure, the other indifferently and quietly.

"Your conscience would not be still?" asked the inspector half aloud.

"There's no such thing," answered Ilya firmly.

Both were silent, then Kirik's voice was heard in the next room. "He's out of his mind."

"We'll go," said the inspector, shrugging. "I won't tie your hands, but don't try to escape! The police are close by at the foot of the hill."

"Where should I go to?" answered Ilya briefly.

"Oh! I don't know that. Swear you won't try, say, by God!"

Ilya looked at the inspector's face, wrinkled and now moved with an expression of sympathy, and said moodily, "I don't believe in God."

The inspector waved his hand. "Forward!" he said to the policemen.

When the damp darkness of the night wrapped him round, Lunev sighed deeply, stood still and looked up at the sky, which hung black and low over the earth like the smoky ceiling of a small, stuffy room.

"Come along, come along!" said one of the policemen. He moved on, the houses rose like huge rocks on each side of the road, the wet filth of the street slopped under foot, and the way led on and on, where the darkness was thickest; Ilya stumbled over a stone and nearly fell. Always the obstinate question rang in the despairing emptiness of his soul, "What now!" Suddenly a vision of the court came before him; the good-natured Gromov, the red face of Petrusha. He had bruised his toes on the stone and they hurt him; he went more slowly. In his ears sounded the words of the little impudent, dark man. "The well fed understands the hungry well enough—that's why he's so severe." Then he heard Gromov's friendly voice, "Do you plead guilty?" and the Prosecutor said slowly, "Tell us."

Petrusha's red face was overcast, and his swollen lips twitched.

Lunev began to limp, and dropped back a pace or two. "Get on—get on!" the policeman said harshly. An unspeakable grief as hot as glowing iron and as sharp as a dagger darted through Ilya's heart. He made a spring forward, and ran with all his might down hill. The wind whistled in his ears, his breath gave out, but he hurled his body forward into the darkness, urging himself on with his arms. Behind him the policeman ran heavily, a sharp shrill whistle pierced the air, and a deep bass voice roared, "Stop him!" Everything round him, houses, pavement, sky—quivered and danced, and moved on him like a heavy black mass. He rushed forward, feeling no weariness, lashed by the hot desire to avoid Petrusha. Something grey and regular rose up before him out of the darkness, breathing despair into his heart. Memory flashed sharply into his brain; he knew that this street turned almost at a right angle away to the main street of the town— men would be there, he would be caught!

"Ah—fly away, my soul!" he screamed with all his might, and bending his head down began to run faster than ever. The cold grey stone wall rose before him. A dull crash, like waves meeting, sounded through the night and died away at once.

Two dark figures rushed up to the wall. They threw themselves on another dark form that lay in a heap, and at once stood up again. People hurried down from the hill, with noise of footsteps and cries, and a piercing whistling.

"Smashed?" asked one of the policemen breathlessly. The other struck a match, and bent down. At his feet lay a quivering hand, and the clenched fingers straightened slowly out.

"The skull's smashed to pieces."

"Ah—yes—see—the brains."

Black figures started up out of the darkness round about.

"Ah—the madman!" said one policeman. His comrade straightened himself up, crossed himself, and still breathless, said in a dull voice:

"Let him—rest in peace—O Lord!"